London-born Catherine Andersen has lived and worked in several countries throughout the world, including Canada, Norway, Denmark, Holland, Sudan, Saudi Arabia, in the Eastern Province on the Arabian Gulf, and Jeddah in the Western Province on the Red Sea.

She has travelled with her husband, a Danish engineer, and wrote this book whilst accompanying him in a two-year work assignment in America. They actually lived in a two hundred-year-old converted Presbyterian church in the small New Jersey town of Asbury, which having changed very little from when it was settled, provided the inspiration for this novel.

The Hetherington Women

Part 1

For Pat ...
 A very dear friend.

I hope you enjoy reading this novel, as much as I enjoyed writing it.

   With my love,
      Paddy xxx

Catherine Andersen

Catherine Andersen

The Hetherington Women

Part 1

Olympia Publishers
London

www.olympiapublishers.com
OLYMPIA PAPERBACK EDITION

A CIP catalogue record for this title is
available from the British Library.

ISBN: 978-1-84897-449-4

(Olympia Publishers is part of Ashwell Publishing Ltd)

This is a work of fiction.
Names, characters, places and incidents originate from the writer's imagination.
Any resemblance to actual persons, living or dead,
is purely coincidental.

First Published in 2014

Olympia Publishers
60 Cannon Street
London
EC4N 6NP

Printed in Great Britain

To Kjeld, my husband, my heartfelt gratitude for the unswerving love and support he has given me. Many thanks, also, to my good friend Josephine, without whose enthusiasm and encouragement this book would never have been published.

Celia 1845

One

Michael O'Malley and his family stood on the dock amidst all the other starving emigrants who had set their sights on the distant shores of the New World, in the year of our Lord 1845, for in August a mysterious blight had wiped out the entire crop of potatoes, just as it was ready to be harvested. This brought about a famine the like of which the Irish had never known, and before it was over it was to take the lives of almost two million of them. They died of starvation, typhus and cholera in this their island home, and it wreaked such misery and despair upon the already criminally under-privileged families of the poor, that they had flocked in their thousands to the docksides of Cork and Galway in an effort to flee their unmerciful conditions.

Nothing but the most dire of circumstances could have forced them to undertake such a journey, for the Atlantic Ocean at the beginning of winter was formidable in the extreme. Its awe-inspiring qualities could instil the most dreadful apprehension in the stoutest of men, particularly when they heard tell of the many poor souls who perished at its mercy whilst being transported across its wide expanse. Of all the migrations across this vast ocean, that from this tiny isle was the most dramatic, for Ireland was isolated and the peasants were left without food, and what was worse, without hope of ever obtaining any. So they were forced to flee the land of their birth, after having watched their loved ones dying of hunger and disease. Those who were strong enough, or whose very instinct to survive had not yet diminished, made their way to the seaports, while the oldest and weakest simply sat in their meagre one-roomed cottages and waited for death. As the numbers of the dead grew, these same cottages were turned into charnel houses, places in which to lay out the corpses. Row upon row of emaciated bodies were laid in the very houses in which they had once lived, laughed and loved, and for those who survived, the sheer horror of it was never to be forgotten.

"Oh, Michael... Michael, do you think we are doing the right thing?" cried Philomena, as she gazed around at all the gaunt-looking faces that surrounded them.

Her husband looked at her and at his two daughters, Mary and Celia, and nodded his head. "We'll put our trust in the good Lord Philly. He has seen fit to bring us this far me darlin' and I believe that he'll see us safely to the other side of the world, sure he will." He placed an arm around his wife's sagging shoulders and drew her close, resting his cheek gently on her head. He knew that she was thinking of her dying mother, who just a few days before had pleaded with them to leave, before they too perished. It was clear that she herself was very near to death, and having already watched her husband die from starvation, she could not bear the thought of her daughter and grandchildren suffering the same fate. In her final hours she had beckoned her daughter to come near, and in whispered tones had divulged to her the secret place where decades before she had hidden a small leather pouch containing three gold coins. Philomena had known nothing of the treasure that had lain for all of her life in the recesses of the kitchen wall, and her eyes had almost fallen from their sockets as she removed the tightly wedged stone to the side of the hearth and discovered what was concealed there. "Why Mother, where on earth did this come from?" she had asked incredulously. Her mother's face was wet with tears as she told of how, when she was a young woman, in the first months of her marriage, she had been waylaid in the woods one day by the son of the landowner. She had been collecting kindling for the fire when he had come upon her, and there was no one nearby to heed her cries for help, as she had tried to run from him. She was not the first, and by no means the last, to be set upon by this arrogant youth, and when he was done with her he had flung the leather pouch on to the ground where she lay sobbing. Thus he had bought her silence and salved his conscience, and as he fastened his breeches, he had hissed at her, "Not a word of this mind, or, twill be the worse for you." Then he had ridden away. Philomena leant forward and took the skeletal form of her mother into her arms. "There, there… don't cry my poor darlin', don't cry, 'tis all over now."

Her mother gave a shuddering sigh, then went on, "I have carried this shameful secret in my heart all these years, the secret of how you came to be born… but I'll not take it with me to my grave."

Philomena drew back in shocked disbelief. She sat silently for several moments, her mother's words going around and around in her head. She could not believe what she had been told. "Do you mean that Da was not my true father? But how can you know…? He never showed it, never once. God rest his dear soul."

Her mother sobbed. "Because he never knew. I couldn't bring myself to tell him. How could I? Twas my shame and mine 'alone to bear. I could never tell him the truth and burden him with it. Sure, twas enough that I had been so cursed, and I knew that you were not his child. I couldn't lie with him after what had happened, but he never ever guessed that you were not his own. He loved you more than life itself, so how could I break his dear heart? May God forgive me." She tried to cross herself, but her arm fell limply on to her chest. "Please child, take the money, for 'tis yours by right, and perhaps some good will come from it after all. I hope so… I hope so."

Now Philomena stood looking up at the ship, all four hundred tons of her. The last of the cargo of pig iron had been taken aboard, and now came the turn of the pitiful human cargo, starving, ragged and depressed. Suddenly, this seething crowd surged towards the gangplank, pushing and pulling at one another in their frantic efforts to flee their living hell once and for all. Their eager anticipation was soon dispelled, however, as they came below and saw the small spaces allotted to them, for then they realised that they had simply exchanged one kind of purgatory for another. The O'Malleys looked at their four eighteen inch wide berths, fitted into an area of no more than six feet square, and their hearts sank; they could not believe that they were expected to exist in such confined conditions for the whole of the perilous journey, which could take anything from six to ten weeks if they ran into bad weather.

"Sure you'd think it was cattle they were shipping to America," exclaimed Michael O'Malley, when he saw how closely the emigrants' quarters resembled horses' stalls, or

14

cattle pens. "How on earth do they expect us to manage, when we've to sit, eat and sleep, day after day?"

"And what of our belongings. Where will we put our clothing and provisions?" asked his wife.

The berths were no more than wooden shelves, crudely knocked together, of fir or pine; they were then fastened to the wall with a narrow strip of wood nailed to the outer edge; to prevent the occupants from falling out when the ship rolled. There were no mattresses, so most passengers slept on the bare wood. There was not enough light or ventilation nor adequate toilet facilities, so that the atmosphere was unbearable. Despite this privation, there were many completely destitute who sought to stow away by hiding in barrels and chests, or beneath lifeboats and sails. The crew were coming around to search out these penniless vagrants, before the ship left the dock and slipped silently out to the open sea. Once on the move, Michael O'Malley urged his wife and daughters up on to the deck, so that they could bid their last farewell to their native land. They breathed in the fresh sea air and marvelled as they looked aloft at the sails unfurling. It was good to fill their lungs from clean salt breezes, after suffering the stench of the rotting vegetation that had permeated the whole of Ireland since the blight. It was the sulphurous sewer-like odour that had first alerted them to the pestilence, and it had never abated.

It seemed that the entire number of their fellow passengers had been of the same mind, because now the small area in the waist of the ship was completely packed with people. This lay just above and forward of their living quarters, and as it was the one and only place that they were allowed to use, it was obvious that they would never have enough space in which to walk. The Captain and cabin passengers stayed aft; they were the only ones privileged to use the rear section of the ship and this was cordoned off to ensure their privacy at all times. Nor were the steerage passengers allowed on the quarter deck, which was the only completely open space on the ship, so their world was suddenly to become frustratingly confined and cramped.

Philomena was filled with dread; already she felt the urge to jump from the overcrowded deck. A feeling of claustrophobia enveloped her. All she wanted to do was escape, but people were closing in on her, their bodies pressing closer and closer as more of them pushed up on to the deck. Her legs felt weak, her head was swimming. She opened her mouth to cry out, but no sound came. Then she was sliding, sliding… down into a black void… down into merciful oblivion.

When she opened her eyes again, she was lying on her back, the faces of Mary and Michael floating above her in the semi-darkness. She felt the soothing effects of a cool damp cloth about her face.

"Philly… Philly… are you all right me darlin'?"

The sound of her husband's voice brought her back to reality. "You fainted up there on the deck, so we brought you below to rest a while. Are you feeling better now?" Michael was holding her small limp hand between his own two strong ones, gently caressing it back to life, while her daughter bathed her forehead with cool water.

His concerned face gradually became clearer to her. "Oh Michael, I'm all right I' m all right now. I don't know what came over me… now don't worry, I'll be fine in a minute or two. Don't worry now." She placed her other hand on top of her daughter's, as it gently rested on her forehead. "Thank you Mary… that feels lovely, sure it does. I'll be better in no time at all." She lied convincingly, to put their minds at rest, but deep within her heart she knew that she would never have the strength to withstand the rigours of this fateful journey.

*

The long arduous days crept into interminable weeks, and Michael O'Malley prayed as he had never prayed before, but eventually he began to realise that there was a will much greater than his own that had determined his wife's fate. He lifted her head gently and held the cup to her lips; so that she might sip the cool water he had saved for her. He looked at her white translucent face and wondered how much longer she could survive in these fetid inhuman conditions. She had hardly eaten since they set sail, which was little wonder when most of their food was rotten. What provisions they had brought for themselves had long since been eaten, and the meagre rations that were intermittently distributed by the captain, were not fit to feed to swine. He realised, too late, that they had been badly cheated by the agent who had arranged their passage. Gone were two of Philomena's gold coins, and he knew full well that he had not received anywhere near the true value of what they were worth. Although he had purchased only the cheapest tickets, so that they would have a little money with which to start their new life in America, he could never have imagined the deprivation to which they had been subjected on this horrendous voyage. Even the fresh drinking water had run out long since, but mercifully they had encountered a heavy storm several days before, and when the parched passengers had seen the crew up on deck holding out sails to catch the precious raindrops, they too had rushed to fetch pots and pans, or any other kind of vessel that would hold water. Philomena opened her eyes and looked at her husband. "I love you Michael," she whispered. "You're a lovely man, that you are." Her voice caught in her throat as she retched one last time.

Michael pulled her to him and held her close, his face buried against her neck. He sobbed softly, "Philly, don't leave me... don't leave me, not now. I need you me darlin'... I need you."

His daughter Mary took him by the shoulders and whispered in his ear, "'Tis no good Da, she's gone. She's at peace now, sure she is, so you come away. I'll do what has to be done, don't worry."

"No... no... I'll take care of her Mary. You go up and find Seeley... Tell her, will you? I'll need to see about the burial. Oh, dear God, why... why did it have to happen, why here?" He hung his head and his tears fell softly on to his wife's face, as he laid her on to the bunk. He used them to bathe her, because there was not enough of the precious drinking water to spare. Then he went in search of some strong rope, to bind around her frail body after he had wrapped it in a cloth.

Mary found her sister looking out to sea, over the ship's rail. "Seeley... Da sent me to find you."

"I know Mary, I know. Please don't say anything."

The younger girl had been dreading to hear the news of her mother's passing, but she knew that it would come. Now she turned to her sister. "When will all the dying stop Mary? 'Tis so terrible I thought we'd be escaping it when we left Ireland, but sure it'll go on and on·'til there are none of us left." Mary wrapped her arms around her sister and the two girls clung together for comfort, wondering what would become of them now that they had lost their beloved mother. Their sobs were muffled by the sound of the harsh turbulent sea, as it pounded relentlessly against the ship's hulk, and the tears that they shed were borne away by the wind, to merge into its fine salt spray.

A well-dressed young man was standing by the rope that segregated the steerage passengers from those in the first-class section of the ship. He was hoping to catch sight of the beautiful young girl whom he had seen day after day up on the deck with her family. Yes, there she was; he could see her clinging to her sister by the ship's rail. He presumed that the two young girls were sisters, because they bore such a strong resemblance to one another, but the younger one, with whom he had become so deeply enamoured, was more strikingly beautiful than her sister. She reminded him exactly of a porcelain doll; her features were delicate and her deep blue eyes, which always seemed so mournful, had completely captivated him. Who was she, he wondered? Despite the obvious fact that the family was poor, she had a look of quality about her. She usually wore a woven shawl around her head and shoulders, to ward off the chill of the raw sea breeze, but beneath it he had occasionally caught a glimpse of her raven black hair, which hung in a thick long braid down her back. How beautiful she was, and how he longed to speak to her, if only for a few moments. In all the hours he had spent observing her during this long and arduous sea voyage, she had never once become aware of him, or looked his way, but yet she fascinated him. There must be something amiss... he had noticed that her parents had not been up on deck to take the air for the past several days; he supposed that possibly their mother was finding it difficult to withstand the rigours of the voyage, because she had always appeared to him to be extremely unwell.

He felt concern for them, but it was common knowledge that these poor emigrants, in their inadequate, inferior accommodation, suffered abysmally. He had heard that conditions were appalling in their cramped, vermin-ridden quarters below deck, so it was to be expected that many of them would perish on the relentless journey. As he watched, there was a sudden subdued disturbance and an uneasy silence fell over the crowded deck. The people drew back respectfully in an awkward shuffle, to clear a narrow passageway. The men removed their hats in deference and bowed their heads; the women crossed themselves and moved their lips silently in prayer. Then he saw the girls' father, deeply distressed, being helped to carry what was obviously a corpse securely wrapped in a heavy cloth and tightly bound with rope. He realised with horror that this must be the mother, who had met her sad demise... yes, he could see the girls pushing to their father's side to comfort him. The young man was very much moved at their sad plight and the distress that they were so obviously suffering, and wished that there was something he could do to help them. Why, he wondered, should this family in particular cause him such concern, for he had witnessed all manner of similar heart-breaking events on previous voyages? In his heart he knew that it was because of the young girl that his interest had been aroused on this occasion, and he was to find it impossible to forget her. He remained still as the brief burial service was carried out by the captain, who was always called upon to perform this unhappy task, then as the body descended into the fathomless depths of the ocean, he turned away slowly and made his way back to his cabin.

Two

As the voyage neared its end, the restlessness and tension aboard ship was growing into open hostility, and when at long last a cry was heard that land had been sighted in the distance, the excitement among the passengers reached fever pitch. There was loud shouting, joyful singing and much hugging and kissing; even the rowdies among them, who a few hours earlier had been threatening to murder one another when their frayed tempers raged out of control, grabbed one another by the shoulders and danced the Irish jig, old grievances forgotten now that they were about to plant their feet in the 'promised land'. There was frenzied activity and much hustling and bustling, as belongings were gathered together, accompanied by loud exchanges when certain missing items were traced to those who could not give a satisfactory explanation of how they came to be in possession of them, but finally the ship drew alongside the dock at the Battery, on the southern tip of Manhattan, and there discharged its boisterous, foul-smelling, ragged, unkempt human cargo. Once again the naïve and ignorant peasants were forced to run the gauntlet of the rogues and scoundrels who lay in wait for them as they stepped from the gangplank on to the dock. Here they found cheerful sharp-eyed natives from the 'old country', sporting shamrock in their hats or buttonholes, anxious to assist them with their baggage and guide them to the cheap boarding houses that waited with open doors to receive them. The exploitation of these 'greenhorns', as they were known, was notorious, and there was no shortage of villains only too ready to relieve them of what little they had in the way of possessions.

"Now you stay close by me girls," warned Michael O'Malley. "And keep hold of your bundles, for in this unruly mob you're likely to lose them before you know where y'are." They were swept forward, at times their feet barely touching the ground, then gradually the crowd dispersed, spreading out slowly at first, a little apprehensively, unaccustomed as they were to the freedom of movement, after their long term of incarceration on the ship; then gradually thinning and drifting away into the wide open space for which they had all been craving throughout the voyage. It felt mightily strange, but it felt so good, to stand once again upon solid ground that was not pitching and rolling beneath their feet; to be able to extend their arms to either side, without touching anything. The young children were ecstatic, spinning around like tops and jumping up and down, shouting and screaming hysterically, unable to believe that they had at last arrived at the fairytale place, that until now had been but a mere figment of their imaginations.

A small foxy-looking man appeared from nowhere and grasped the largest bundle that Mary was struggling to carry. "Here, let me help you mavourneen," he said, eyeing her from head to toe. "Do you have anywheres to go, or would you like me to take you to a good respectable house just here nearby?" Mary tightened her grasp around her belongings and pressed closer to her father for protection, but before he had time to open his mouth and blurt out a warning to this oily little character, a highly polished walking stick was thrust against the chest of their aggressor. "These people are well taken care of Patrick. Now you be on your way, there's a smart fellow." The little chap had already released his grasp upon Mary's bundle, and realising that there were to be no easy pickings for him from the 'greenhorns', he diverted his attention elsewhere, but not before aiming a tirade of colourful invectives at the gentleman who had 'queered his pitch'. "All right… all right Mr Forbes, I'm going. Sure there's no need for you to be getting on your high horse. I was only trying to give a helping hand, that I was."

"Well, you're out of luck this time Patrick, and they can well do without the kind of help that you're likely to give them, so be off with you."

"All right, all right. I've said I'll be on me way, and may the curse of the devil be upon you, an, all, an, all. 'Tis a sorry day, that it is, when a man can't be giving a little help where it is needed." He was still muttering as he disappeared into the crowd and was gone.

"Please allow me to introduce myself. Ian Forbes." The well-dressed gentleman raised his hat and inclined his head. Michael O'Malley was struck dumb, not knowing what to say or do.

"I thank you for your kindness," broke in Mary.

"Oh, I know Patrick Casey too well to have left you at his mercy. He's a first-class rogue. There are many of them in New York, as you'll soon learn. They work for the boarding house keepers who charge exorbitant rates to any unsuspecting newcomers, such as yourselves, and once you fall into the trap, or accept any help from those thieves, you'll never break free again. They'll take every penny you could ever earn… and you'll still be in debt. Something should be done about their criminal exploitation of the innocent. In fact, I believe there are moves afoot right now to set up some kind of Commission, to take care of all new immigrants and help them to establish themselves when they first arrive. That will put pay to all this racketeering. Something has to be done to stop it."

Michael O'Malley found his tongue at last. "'Twas good of you to help us sir, indeed it was… and I thank you kindly. I'm Michael O'Malley and these are my daughters Mary and Celia." The girls bobbed a curtsy. "Now, could you be after telling me where I'm likely to find somewheres decent for the girls and meself to stay, just until I can find a job? I have some money to start us off, sure I do, but I've no notion of how to go about getting us lodgings, or the like."

Ian Forbes looked from one to the other of them sympathetically. Their bedraggled appearance would have evoked the sympathy of even the most hard-hearted of men. For the past few weeks on the ship, he had been constantly trying to formulate ideas of how he might help these poor unfortunates, and now he was to put his ideas to the test. "Well, I hope you'll forgive me Mr O'Malley, but I could not help noticing your sad bereavement during the voyage, and I was most touched by the distress it caused you, all three of you. It set me to thinking that there might be something I could do to assist you when the ship docked, for in your vulnerable state you would be an easy prey for the likes of Patrick Casey; maybe even more than most, I daresay. Now I do have a suggestion to make, that I think may be acceptable to you, here is what it is. I rent a small storehouse not far from here, where I keep my goods. I'm a merchant, you see, and I frequently travel back and forth between New York and Europe, trading whatever there is to trade. It occurred to me that I ought to find a store-keeper to take care of my stock now that New York is growing so rapidly. I shan't be able to leave my property unattended, as I used to, now that the city is becoming so over-crowded... I know that, for there are so many villains afoot these days, and if they see that there's no one about, then it is bound to attract the attention of the worst sort eventually. Now what would you say to becoming my storekeeper? I'll explain to you exactly what I'd want you to do. There are three rooms above the ground floor storage area, they're only small, and have never been used, but I think that maybe the young ladies could make quite nice living quarters of them. What do you say?"

Michael O'Malley's mouth dropped open.

"At least let me take you there, so that you can see what the place looks like. I have a carriage waiting, would you like to accompany me?"

Mary and Celia looked at their father and saw the look of amazement on his face. He simply could not believe that he was to be the recipient of all this bounty, particularly after all the bad luck that had befallen him of late.

"Say something Da. What do you think?" queried Mary, tugging at his sleeve. She had taken over her mother's role since her death, for he seemed so lost without her.

"Er... um... why yes, of course, of course. Thank you, sir, 'tis most kind of you," was all he could stammer.

"Right then, come this way. My carriage is just over here... it won't take long to get to the storehouse. At least you'll have somewhere to stay for a day or two, until you find your way around. Then if you decide not to take my offer, you can move on."

The grateful trio followed close on his heels as he made his way to the waiting carriage, and they felt exactly like royalty itself as they stepped up into the fine vehicle and drove off through the hotchpotch of narrow streets that led from the docks. Their eyes stared in wonderment at all that they saw as they drove the short distance to the storehouse. New York was teeming with life. There was continual hubbub. They could hear languages and accents that were completely unknown to them, coming from strangely dressed people who crowded its unmade roads and spilled out of its shabby ramshackle buildings. They bore no resemblance to anyone they had ever before seen in their lives. It was obvious that this New World into which they had come, was a place very far removed from their own small green island home, and they were filled with apprehension as all three realised that they were now to become part of this strange, foreign community.

In less than fifteen minutes, they pulled up in front of a small wooden building, which seemed sturdily built and very well-kept. It stood along a short narrow street in a row of similar buildings, most of which showed distinct signs of dilapidation and neglect. However, Mary and Celia nudged one another hopefully as their benefactor unlocked the strong wooden door that secured the property, and ushered them into its darkened interior. He quickly made his way to the bottom of an open wooden staircase in the middle of the room and lit a large oil lamp that was suspended from an oak beam across the ceiling. They found themselves in what appeared to them to be an Aladdin's cave. There was a numerous variety of boxes and crates, all shapes and sizes, stacked along the walls; barrels and casks one on top of the other, bearing strange markings, and bundles of skins and furs lying in haphazard piles everywhere. They had never before seen such an array of merchandise, and there was a strange aroma pervading the atmosphere, unknown to them, but not entirely unpleasant. "Come this way, will you?" said Mr Forbes, leading them into the centre of the storehouse. He ascended the stairs and they followed him to the upper level. The girls gasped with delight as they saw what was soon to be their new home. There was one large room, with two smaller rooms leading from it; these were directly above the storage area, and had several windows overlooking the front and rear of the building. It was far superior to the poor one-roomed mud and wattle cottage that had been their home in Ireland. "Well, what do you think?" asked Mr Forbes.

"Oh, I think, 'tis grand... just grand. Sure I can't believe it at all, at all," replied Michael O'Malley. "What of you Mary... Seeley? What would you say to living here then?"

"Oh yes... 'tis lovely Da," whispered Celia shyly. Ian Forbes noticed that she very rarely spoke, and he found her shyness most appealing.

"Yes, we could fix it up in no time at all," said Mary, turning around and taking it all in, her eyes wide in admiration. "It'll be just fine. Thank you... thank you Mr Forbes."

"Right then, that's settled. Now I should imagine that you are all ready for something to eat. You must be starving, after the way you were deprived of food on the ship. I'll show you where you can get a good meal at very little cost, so just follow me."

Michael O'Malley immediately began to rummage around in the inside pocket of his jacket. "I have a gold coin here Mr Forbes. I'm not without money to start us off."

Ian Forbes laid a hand on the older man's arm and said kindly, "You keep that safely hidden Mr O'Malley. There may come a time when you'll be needing it far more than you do now. I'll give you some coinage to buy the things that you'll be needing, and you can pay me back gradually from your wages. That's fair enough, isn't it? Mind you, not many coins change hands here. The usual way to trade is by barter, but you'll soon become familiar with all that."

Michael O'Malley grasped the hand of this benevolent young man between his own and pumped it up and down. "Oh, thank you, sir, thank you... that's more than fair, sure it is. God bless you, sir."

The daylight was fast fading as they stepped out into the street again, but the glow from the lighted windows that they passed, threw welcoming beams to guide their feet between the shadowy buildings. "The place is just here along the street. You'll be able to get a good meal." Ian Forbes escorted them a short way, pointing out the establishment in question. "Don't worry about your baggage, the driver can take it into the store for you. Just go and get something to eat now." He turned to walk away. "Oh, I almost forgot... here, you'd better take this key, so that you may let yourselves into the place, when you go back. I'll call to see you in the morning and we can discuss everything then... and until you're able to get some furniture, you can make use of anything you might find among the stock. The skins and furs will make warm beds to lie on, until you find something better. I'll wish you good-bye now, and I hope that you have a comfortable night." He raised his hat and walked away.

"Good night to you, sir… and may the good Lord shower you with his blessings," said Michael O'Malley. Then, jingling his newly acquired coins lightly in his hand, he proudly escorted his daughters into the delightful establishment that stood beckoning them with its warm welcoming atmosphere, and there they sat, each one of them savouring the luxury of the first wholesome, nutritious meal they had eaten for what seemed to be an eternity.

Three

Life for the O'Malleys seemed suddenly to have taken a turn for the better. They soon settled into their new surroundings, and true to her word Mary, with the help of her sister, had managed to transform the bare rooms above the storehouse into a charming and comfortable home. There was no inside sanitation or water supply, so they had to make use of the crude amenities outside, as did all the other tenants who lived in the ramshackle buildings around them; and every drop of water had to be carted from an outside pump. However, they had never known any other kind of sanitation in their homeland, so this was of no consequence to them. The local people took very kindly to the sweet Irish colleens who had come into their midst, as did their benefactor, Ian Forbes. He called on them from time to time, to bring in new goods for storage, or to despatch consignments to the docks. Sometimes he came with strange-looking men, clad in skins and furs and carrying shotguns; they were Indian agents and he was pleased to introduce them to his new storekeeper. At the same time he told them that in future they would be able to fetch their goods for trading at any time, and not have to wait for his occasional visits to their shores, as Mr O'Malley was to remain at the storehouse permanently. He was more than happy with this arrangement, because it would enable him to conduct his business far more efficiently and conveniently in the future. He was also deeply impressed at the way in which the two young girls had managed to make such a cosy home in their meagre accommodation. They touched him in a way that he couldn't truly understand, and he often brought them small gifts that he thought they would find useful. To Mary and Celia they were unknown luxuries and they were overwhelmed by his generosity.

Early the following Spring he announced that he would soon be departing once again. He had acquired a large selection of goods throughout the winter months, to ship with him; goods that were very much in demand in the cities of Europe. In particular, the skins and furs that the Indian agents had procured for him: sable, mink and ermine; beaver and marten; buffalo and bear skins, wolf, fox and raccoon. He had also traded the goods that he had shipped over from Europe, for the delicious Jamaican rum that was always in great demand on the other side of the Atlantic.

He bade farewell to Michael and the girls with a heavy heart; he knew that he would miss them sorely.

He shook Michael's hand warmly, then took Mary's hand and lifted it gently to his lips, but when he came to Seeley he hesitated, and stood for several seconds looking into her deep blue eyes as they gazed up at him lovingly, and filled with tears.

He placed his hands on either side of her beautiful face and kissed her tenderly on the forehead. "I shall miss you very much Seeley," he whispered hoarsely.

"I shall miss you too, Mr Forbes. I wish you didn't have to go. What will we do without you?"

"I shall come back again as soon as I can," he promised. "It won't be many months before I return to America again."

They stood at the door·and watched until his carriage was out of sight. They were very sorry to see him go, because they had grown extremely fond of him in the months since he had first befriended them. They had never before known such kindness from any stranger, and their days would be the sadder for his leaving.

*

The days lengthened into Summer, and New York sweltered in the heat. As more and more immigrants poured in, so the slums grew, and they brought with them their virulent diseases that spread alarmingly in the unsanitary over-crowded tenements. Those who were weakest succumbed soonest to the pestilence, and the death toll amongst the poor was devastating. Mary herself began to complain of feeling unwell, then one morning she was completely overcome by the headache and nausea from which she had been suffering for the past few days. She knew how concerned her father and Celia would be, so she tried bravely to reassure her young sister. "'Tis this heat Seeley," she moaned feebly, as they struggled up the wooden stairs with their heavy water cans. "I think I'll just lie down for a bit. Now don't you worry, I'll be feeling better in no time at all." She sank thankfully on to her bed, completely oblivious to all that was going on around her.

For the next four days Celia watched over her very carefully, sponging her down as she burned with fever, and soothing her forehead with cool damp cloths when she constantly complained of the pains in her head. Her condition did not improve at all, and the young girl's fears for her sister grew. When Mary developed a cough and her stomach became swollen, she clung to her father and wept. "What is it, Da, what is it… why doesn't she get better?"

Michael O'Malley had seen too many die of the disease in Ireland, not to know what it was. "Our Mary has the typhoid fever me darlin', that's what is ailing her, the dear girl. 'Tis little wonder with all that stinkin' filth that's oozing everywhere into the streets. In this heat we'll all be taken off with the disease. Dear God, will we never know any peace? Just as I was beginning to think that our lives had taken a blessed turn for the better."

They both did everything they could think of to ease Mary's suffering, and when she became delirious, they sat by her bedside throughout the night, praying and willing her to recover, and occasionally drifting into disturbed sleep from the sheer exhaustion of their nightly vigils. Then one morning, in the early hours, as they unwittingly nodded off to sleep in their chairs, she slipped quietly away to find merciful release from her pain and suffering. To find the long awaited peace that could come only with her death.

Michael O'Malley bolted upright in his chair as Seeley's piercing cry rent the air. "No, no… Mary… don't die, I won't let you." The young girl lay across her sister's lifeless form sobbing. "Oh Mary… my Mary."

Her father lifted her gently and wrapped her in his arms, not able to find one word with which to comfort her. His own heart was too full. They stood together, trying to understand why this lovely girl had been taken from them, and not knowing how they could go on living without her. Their loss was all the more devastating, coming so soon after the death of her dear mother. It was too much for either of them to withstand.

*

Somehow they managed to attend to the necessities of her burial, which was due to the kindly assistance of their many desperately poor but generous neighbours, but in the aftermath Michael O'Malley plumbed the depths of despair. He could no longer accept what fate had so cruelly destined for him. He could no longer struggle against the overwhelming adversity that had befallen him. He had reached the final limits of his endurance, and his God had abandoned him. He wandered about aimlessly, not caring what became of him. Every ounce of fight had gone out of him. So, in his despair, he turned to drink. It numbed his brain and eased away the pain. He drank... and drank... and drank, like so many more of his countrymen, and drowned his memories in the easiest way he knew how.

Celia too was heartbroken. She stayed in day after day, not really caring what became of her. She knew that her father was spending his every waking hour in the taverns and dram shops, for she hardly ever saw him, and she was witness to his unseemly behaviour on the few occasions that he did come home to his bed. There was nothing she could do to stop him. It seemed to her that it would be only a matter of time before each of them would die of some dreadful malady, so what was the use? Then one night, as she lay in her bed, she heard her father returning from one of his nocturnal trips; he was stumbling noisily as usual, in his drunken stupor...what was that she heard? Was it someone else? She raised herself up on to her elbow and craned her neck, listening intently. Then she could make out another voice… yes, a man's voice that she didn't recognize, talking to her father. She felt worried. Why would he bring a man into the store at this time of night? She hurriedly wrapped a shawl around herself and crept stealthily down the stairs. There was a stranger looking around the store, and she could see her father slumped on one of the large boxes, drunk as usual. She felt very afraid, but to feign bravery she leant over the bannister and called loudly, "Da… is that you Da?" The stranger spun around and looked towards her. She couldn't see his face clearly, it was too dark, but she could determine that he was very tall and his hair looked pale in colour, from what little she could see of him in the dimness.

Suddenly he spoke, and his voice was cultured. "Oh, I was not aware that there was anyone here. I take it that this must be your father. He was not in any fit state to find his way home alone, so I brought him in my carriage. I'll leave now. Are you able to take care of him?"

"Yes I am. Thank you, sir," said Celia sharply. She mistrusted this tall stranger, but she did not know why. Maybe she was frightened because she had not expected anyone to come in with her father at this hour of the night, or maybe it was that she objected to him surreptitiously rummaging around when he thought that he was unobserved. As soon as the door had closed behind the stranger, Celia ran to her father calling urgently, "Da, oh Da, wake up, come on now." She gripped the sleeve of his jacket and shook him hard. "Da, will you wake up. Come on now. Please Da… please." Tears began to course down her cheeks. It was no good, her father was in a stupor from which she could not arouse him. She tried to lift him up, but his dead weight was too much for her, so she gradually rolled him off the box, resting his solid weight against her own slight frame, and guiding his body as gently as possible down on to the floor. Then she fetched a few of the largest furs that were lying around and manoeuvred him between them on the floor where he lay, hoping that he would sleep off the paralysing effects of the alcohol by morning.

He was still snoring loudly when Celia came down to check on him early the next day, and she was desperately trying to awaken him when there was a sudden loud hammering on the door of the storehouse.

"Who is it?" she called.

"Gilbert Hetherington," came back the reply. "I brought your father home last night in my carriage and I was concerned to know how he is."

Celia stood rooted to the spot, wondering what to do. She felt most reluctant to open the door to this stranger. After an embarrassingly long silence, there was another loud knocking on the door. It was not the sound made with a hand. Gilbert Hetherington was hammering on the heavy door with his walking stick. "Hello... hello. Are you there; may I come in?"

Celia glanced back over her shoulder. The noise had awoken her father and he was beginning to stir. "What's that? What on earth is that?" he asked. "Oh, me head... me poor aching head; 'tis pounding like the very devil. I feel like I'm dyin' sure I do."

Seeing that her father was awakened, Celia's apprehension eased a little. She started to undo the bolts, just as the stranger hammered loudly again on the door. "All right, all right," she said, as she pulled open the door and came face to face with a very tall fair-haired man.

The frown on his face dissolved into a wide smile when he saw how beautiful she was. He was quite taken aback, and made no effort to hide his admiration. He raised his hat politely. "Forgive me Miss... er..."

"O'Malley sir. Celia O'Malley."

"Well, forgive me, Miss O'Malley, but I was concerned about your father, in view of the poor condition he was in last night. I hope he has recovered a little."

"Who is it Seeley? Who is it?" called her father impatiently.

"Perhaps you'd better step inside for a moment, sir, then you can see for yourself how he is."

Again Celia noticed how keenly interested he seemed to be in the contents of the storehouse; far more interested, in fact, than he appeared to be in the condition of her father. She was very puzzled and wondered what his interest was.

"Oh, 'tis you, sir... ooh... me head," groaned Michael O'Malley, as he tried to raise himself from the floor. He stood up unsteadily and Celia hurried to his side to support him.

"I think you'd better come upstairs now, Da. I'll get you some breakfast... it'll make you feel better."

"Would you like me to help your father up the stairs? He seems a little unsteady, he might fall."

"No, no, we'll not bother you. I'll manage fine thank you," said Celia tartly. She wished he would go, so that she could tend to her father. His presence made her feel extremely uneasy.

"As you wish. Perhaps I should call upon your father when he is feeling a little better. Good day to you Miss O'Malley, Mr O'Malley."

He placed his hat on his head and left, closing the door firmly behind him.

"Who is that man, Da? Where did you meet him?" asked Celia, as she struggled to help her father up the stairs.

"Oh, I don't know, I've seen him in the taverns around here. He's a gentleman you know."

"But what would a gentleman be doing taking a drink in an area like this? There's something not quite right about him, to be sure. You be careful of him Da."

"He's all right, sure he is, there's no need for you to go fretting yourself Seeley. He's no different from our Mr Forbes, and look what a good friend he turned out to be. You like him well enough, don't you?"

Celia knew instinctively that this man was not at all like Ian Forbes, and she was deeply concerned that her father was so trusting of him. If only Mr Forbes were here now. She wondered how long it would be before they would see him again. He would know what to do about this suspicious stranger who had come into their lives. She knew that they would be perfectly safe if only Mr Forbes were there to deal with him.

Four

It took Michael O'Malley several days to recover from the effects of his latest drinking spree, and he was filled with remorse for the trouble he had caused his daughter Celia. She fed him and bathed him and fetched and carried for him uncomplainingly, so that he reproached himself bitterly for not being a better father to her. He looked at her lovingly, as she sat by the window working on a piece of sewing; she loved her needlework and would spend hour after hour with it. He walked over to her and gently stroked the top of her head, saying softly, "You're a fine girl Seeley. the best daughter anyone could ever have, and you deserve better than this, sure you do."

Celia looked up at her father. "Oh, Da... don't say that. Just as long as we have one another, then we'll be all right, you'll see. Mr Forbes will be back soon, I'm sure he will, then things will be better. I know you miss Mam and Mary... 'tis terrible trying to live without them, but we mustn't give up. They wouldn't want that. I've been thinking a lot about them these past weeks, and it's as though they're looking down on us Da, and wanting us to make a good life here after all the heartache we've had. Try not to give up Da... please."

Her father stood looking out of the window for a long time, then he said softly, "If only I could make your life better Seeley, then it wouldn't matter so much. At least then

I'd feel that something good had come of all this, that we had something to be thankful for."

As he spoke, there was a loud banging on the door down in the storehouse. "Who can that be at this time of day?" he said, hurrying from the room. Celia's heart lurched; somehow she knew that it was the tall fair stranger calling upon them again. Why couldn't he leave them alone, she thought.

Her father called up to her that he was just going out for a while. "I'll not be too long me darlin'," he said.

"What about your coat Da? Don't you want your coat?" Celia wanted him to come upstairs again before he went out, so that she could warn him not to be too trusting of this new friend he thought he had made.

"Oh, no Seeley, I'll not be needing me coat, for 'tis a lovely evening. I'll be fine, sure I will."

Celia heard the door slam as her father left and her spirits sank. She wondered how long he would be gone this time, and what kind of state he would be in when he returned.

*

So it went on for the next few weeks. Her father spent most of his time with Gilbert Hetherington who, unknown to Celia, had introduced him to the evils of the gambling saloons. At first it seemed an innocent enough pastime to Michael O'Malley, it was exciting and kept him from remembering all the heartache he had recently endured. His wagers were not too high and he had several spates of good luck; just enough to encourage him to become more reckless.

But it was not long before his luck changed and he began to lose steadily. Then he foolishly fell into the trap that had been so insidiously laid for him by his companion.

He upped his stakes, as he desperately tried to recover his losses, but this inevitably plunged him further and further into debt. Day after day, night after night, Gilbert Hetherington watched and waited, and encouraged Michael O'Malley in his foolhardiness, knowing that eventually he could turn his unsuspecting victim's misfortune to his own advantage. He knew full well that this witless Irishman would be no match for his cunning, and in his troubled state would become more and more easy to manipulate.

Late one night, Celia again heard her father return with his new companion, and she was puzzled by the muffled sounds coming from below. She made her way quietly down the stairs to see her father, ably assisted by Gilbert Hetherington, dragging and pulling at the casks and barrels that lined the walls, and carrying several of them outside. She was horrified; what was her father thinking of? She almost fell down the remaining few stairs and grabbed her father's arm, pleading with him, "Stop this Da... what are you doing?" She must stop him. He struggled past her with a heavy cask, as though he hadn't heard her. She shrieked, "Da stop... stop. What will Mr Forbes say?"

The troubled man dropped the heavy cask to the floor and turned to his daughter, his guilt evident as he spoke confidentially to her, "'Twill be all right Seeley, sure I'm only borrowing, not stealing. I'll soon be able to replace what I'm takin'. Now don't worry me darlin', you know I'd never cheat Mr Forbes, God bless him."

"But why are you doing this Da? I don't understand."

"I'm in a bit of a bother Seeley. I'll explain it all to you later. Now you just go upstairs to your bed, there's a good girl... and I'll see you in the mornin'."

"But they're not yours to take Da... I'm begging you... please, don't do it."

All this time Gilbert Hetherington hovered outside, listening carefully to what was going on between father and daughter. He wanted to avoid a confrontation with the distraught girl; let her father deal with it.

As Michael O'Malley slammed the door behind him, the whimpering girl slumped at the foot of the stairs, her arms clutched tightly around her. She rocked to and fro, moaning softly, "Oh, dear Mary, Mother of God, please help us. ...please let Mr Forbes come back before 'tis too late... please, please." There was no one else to whom she could turn for help, so she prayed as though her very life depended upon it.

Celia could not sleep that night. She tossed and turned in her bed, worried sick about what her father was doing. He had always been a decent living man, even though they were poor and she knew, without doubt, that if he was in any kind of trouble, then his newfound friend must be at the root of it. She realised how dangerous he was and she could not understand why her father was so enamoured with him. Look at how easily he had been led astray, when she knew him to be an honest man. Normally, he would never contemplate stealing another's belongings, for stealing it was, no matter what he had called it. To take something that belonged to another was stealing in Celia's eyes, and she could never condone it, no matter what the circumstances.

Now she sat glued to the window, hoping against hope that he would soon return. She was determined to find out the reason for her father's criminal activity, and try to put a stop to it. She watched for hour after hour, but finally she saw him coming along the road, staggering from side to side, waving his arm in the air and loudly greeting everyone that he met, whether he knew the person or not. Celia heaved a dejected sigh; she loved her father dearly, but his behaviour of late was the cause of extreme embarrassment to her. She leapt to her feet as he came into the room. "At last you're home… at long last. I've been worrying about you all night Da… where have you been… what have you been doing?"

"I've been trying to make us a fortune, is what I've been doing, me darlin' daughter."

"What on earth are you talking about, and what were you up to, taking Mr Forbes' goods? It's that man leading you into bad ways, isn't it Da? Why don't you get rid of him, can't you see that he's up to no good?"

"Now that's where you're wrong Seeley." Her father fell heavily on to a chair and waved his forefinger at her. "He's showing me how to become rich, like himself, sure he is. He's been telling me what to do at the gaming tables… all right, all right I'll admit I've had a run of bad luck just lately, but it won't last. That's why I needed to borrow some of those casks of rum from downstairs. I've had to trade them in the saloons, to help pay for me wagers, but as soon as I come into a winning streak again, then I'll sure enough be able to buy some more to replace them. Mr Forbes wouldn't mind, I know he wouldn't, for 'tis only until I make a big win. Why, by the time he comes back to see us again, I'll have everything back in order… you'll see me darlin' you'll see."

Celia could not believe what she was hearing. Gaming tables... her father? She could not take it in. She stood before him and bent forward, pushing her face close to his. "Do you know what you're saying Da? When have you ever been a gambling man? Have you gone mad? What would me mam say if she were here? Look at you sitting there... drunk... and talking like a fool."

She fell to her knees sobbing, and laid her head in his lap. "Oh, Da... Da... what is happening to you? I feel so afraid."

Her father laid his hand on her head. "Oh Seeley don't upset yourself like this. I've told you that Mr Hetherington is a gentleman. He'll see us all right, just like Mr Forbes did. You'll see... you'll see."

"No Da... he won't, because he's not like Mr Forbes, and he never will be. Can't you see that? Look at the trouble he's brought upon you already. You'll never win back money you've already lost. Can't you see that? It's impossible."

She stayed quiet for a while, trying desperately to think of a way in which to convince her father that he must get away from Gilbert Hetherington, for she fully realised that his debts would go on mounting if he continued to gamble. Suddenly she thought of the gold coin that he had. "Da... now listen to me," she said urgently. "What about the gold coin you have... the last of those that Granny gave us? Sure it was meant for an emergency such as this... why don't you trade that, pay off your debts, and then replace the stock you took from Mr Forbes? Oh, please Da... for I couldn't face him if he came back and found out that you had been stealing from him." Her father was already beginning to fall into a stupor, but he was alert enough to hear what she had just suggested to him.

"No Seeley... no, no child. That gold coin is for you, and I'll not touch it; and don't say I've been stealing... sure, 'tis only borrowing, like I told you."

Celia could see that it was no use trying to argue with him now; better to let him sleep it off first. She helped him into bed, and her tears fell softly as she pulled off his shoes. He was already fast asleep and snoring loudly before she had crept from the room and closed the door.

*

She was ready and waiting the next time Gilbert Hetherington came calling. She ran quickly down the stairs when she espied his carriage coming along the street, and had pulled open the outer door before he could hammer on it and awaken her father. "Good day to you, Miss O'Malley," he said politely. "I trust I find you well."

"I am perfectly well, thank you sir,' she replied. "But I cannot say the same for my father. He has been very poorly these past two days. I don't know if you are aware of it Mr Hetherington, but he has never been a drinking man, so it has a terrible effect upon him when he takes too much." She noticed that he was scrutinizing her closely, which she found rather disconcerting, but she would not be deterred now that she had the opportunity to tell him how she felt about his association with her father. "Therefore, I would very much appreciate it if you did not come here again. My father has been entrusted to take care of this storehouse for Mr Ian Forbes, and he will be in serious trouble if that gentleman ever finds out that his stock has been stolen." She nodded her head as an indication that she had said her piece. Gilbert Hetherington noticed the colour rising in her cheeks as she spoke; was it his nearness causing her to blush in shyness; maybe it was her anger, or perhaps a combination of both? Her eyes too had darkened to an impenetrable depth, as she became more irate. She really is a most delightful girl, he thought.

"I'm afraid your father is in far more serious trouble than you could possibly imagine Miss O'Malley. The stock that he borrowed from Mr Forbes is the least of his worries. I happen to know Mr Forbes very well."

Celia interrupted him, "You know Mr Forbes?" She was obviously taken aback.

"Yes. We are well acquainted with one another. I am also a merchant, you see, so naturally our business dealings bring us into contact with one another quite frequently."

Celia became thoughtful. Perhaps her father was right after all... perhaps she had misjudged this tall fair-haired man; or, at least, judged him too harshly. "Would you just step inside for a moment, sir?" she asked meekly. She left the door wide open to throw more light into the dim interior of the storehouse. "I can't offer you a seat, Mr Hetherington, but I must know what you meant when you said that my father is in more serious trouble. Would you kindly tell me what that trouble might be?"

"He has incurred tremendous debts because of his gambling, and now those debts have to be honoured. That is why I suggested to your father that he borrow some of Mr Forbes' stock just as a temporary measure, to satisfy those who are out for his blood."

"Out for his blood... what on earth do you mean? You make it sound so serious."

"It is indeed serious. The people to whom he owes money will stop at nothing if they are not paid. If their clients don't pay with money, then very often they pay with their lives."

Celia's hands flew to her face as she gasped, "Oh no, how could such a thing have happened; how could he get into such debt?"

"Your father is a very unhappy man Miss O'Malley. His personal problems have weighed very heavily upon him of late, and when men are burdened down with grief, they sometimes tend to do stupid things; things that they would normally never dream of doing. So it was with your father, and now I'm afraid that his life is in danger."

Celia felt as though her legs had turned to water. She groped behind her and her hand touched a low wooden crate. She collapsed on to it, whispering softly to herself, "Oh Da... Da, what have you done?" She held her hand to her forehead, her eyes cast down, so she did not see the sly smirk that played on Gilbert Hetherington's face for a mere second.

"Why don't you allow me to help you Miss O'Malley? This is no life for a beautiful young lady like you. I could take you away from this place, give you a life of luxury; a life you have never dreamed of."

Celia looked up at him, aghast at his suggestion. "I am quite happy here, sir... or at least I was until you came into our lives. My father would not be in this trouble if he hadn't met you... if you hadn't led him astray with the gambling."

"Come, come now Miss O'Malley. I have protected him these past weeks. Who knows what would have happened to him in his drunken state, if I had not brought him home when I did."

Celia could not argue with that. It was true; so many times over the past few weeks she had not known the whereabouts of her father. She was confused; she did not know what to think. "Please would you go now Mr Hetherington. I'm feeling a little unwell," she said. She shook her head sadly. "This has all come as a shock to me, sure it has, and I don't know quite what to do at the moment."

"Very well… I'll leave you now, but remember what I said. I could take you away from all this trouble, to a place of safety. Please give it some thought, will you? I'll call again later, for I must speak to your father urgently. Good day to you."

Celia heard the door close behind him and she sat for a long time in the darkened storehouse, trying to gather her thoughts. She heard her father's footsteps on the stairs, then he called concernedly, "Seeley… Seeley, are you there?"

She stood up and turned towards him; all the anger in her melted away when she saw how dishevelled he looked. He was a broken man, there was no doubt of that, so how could she blame him for the foolish things he had done in his moments of weakness?

"I'm here Da," she called wearily. "'Tis all right, I'm coming now."

"What are you doing down here Seeley… all by yourself in the dark?"

"Mr Hetherington has been here Da. He wanted to speak to you urgently, but I told him you were poorly, so he went away again. Don't worry. He'll be back later on."

"What was he wanting me darlin'?"

She helped her father back up the stairs. "I want to talk to you Da... come and sit down now; we must talk."

They sat facing one another across the small wooden table where they usually sat to eat; it was covered with a pretty cloth, one of the many presents that Mr Forbes had given them. Celia plucked nervously at the border of it as she struggled to find the words to say to her father.

He was looking intently at her. "What is it Seeley... why do you look so worried me darlin'? Sure you look ill, that you do. Are you not feeling well?"

"Da... Mr Hetherington told me that you are in serious trouble because of your gambling. He said that your life was in danger. Do you know about that?"

Michael O'Malley sighed deeply. He could not look his daughter in the eye. "I just wanted to give you a better life, that I did. Sure it seemed harmless enough. I never thought there would be all this trouble." He became animated. "You should have seen me when I first started the gambling Seeley, me luck was unbelievable, but this past few weeks everything has been against me. If I had half a chance, sure I could win back what I've lost, and more... I know I could... but the divils are after me. They won't give me the chance to win me money back."

Celia broke in, "Stop it Da... stop it. 'Tis a fool's game, you know it is. How do you think those kind of people make their money? 'Tis from men like you... men they know they can trick and cheat. Now just you forget about ever winning back what you've lost, for 'tis impossible... and if you're honest with yourself, you know that what I'm saying is right. Isn't it Da... isn't it?" She thrust her hands across the table and he took hold of them.

He looked up at her sorrowfully. "I'm sorry. I'm sorry me darlin'. Do you think we should try to get away? Maybe we could... to somewhere safe. Somewhere they'll never find us. What do you think Seeley?"

"I don't know... dear God, I don't know. Where would we go... supposing they come looking for us? We should be forever wondering if we were safe."

She thought of Gilbert Hetherington, of what he had said about taking her away. Would he take her father too? "Oh, dear Mary, mother of God, what am I thinking of?" she whispered under her breath. But at least the idea began to take shape in her mind.

Suddenly there was the most dreadful loud banging downstairs on the storehouse door. They almost jumped out of their skins. Michael O'Malley leapt to his feet, pressing his forefinger to his lips. "Sshh... don't make a sound Seeley," he whispered. He slowly made his way out of the door and down the stairs on tiptoe.

"What is it Da... do you think it's them after you?" asked Celia, as she followed closely behind her father, her heart thumping loudly. She pressed her hands over her chest, as if to still it.

Bang bang. Bang again. The door rattled as though it was about to burst open. She was terrified. Again her father pressed his forefinger to his lips. "Sshh... sshh," he breathed. They stood perfectly still, waiting, afraid to move, then came loud shouting... raucous voices intermingled with the banging. "Are you in there O'Malley? Come out here, or we'll break this door down O' Malley... do you hear us? Come out, we know you're in there."

Celia clung to her father for support, burying her face in his chest. For the second time that day, she felt as though her legs would not hold her. "Oh, Da... Da," she whispered almost inaudibly. "They've come to murder you." She glanced up at her father, as she felt his breath coming in short, frightened gasps. His eyes were wide with terror. She crossed herself and gazed upwards to the ceiling, silently praying to the Blessed Virgin for any help that she could give them.

Miraculously it seemed, her prayers were answered almost immediately, for the loud banging stopped abruptly. There was a brief silence, then a cultured voice that could not be mistaken rang out loudly. Celia and her father stood with mouths agape, as they heard Gilbert Hetherington disperse the ruffians who were trying to break in. There were gruff retorts, but they could not hear what was being said; then noisy scuffling, followed by the sound of heavy footsteps gradually dying away.

"Mr O' Malley... are you all right? Let me in. The coast is clear now... there is no danger." There was further knocking on the door, but this time it was much more subdued. Michael O'Malley hurried to open it. He drew it back very slowly, a mere inch or two, and peered through the small crack with one eye, to make absolutely sure that it was safe, then he pulled it open a little wider, beckoning his saviour inside, and slammed it shut after him, as quickly as he could.

"I came to warn you Mr O'Malley, but it seems that you already know how much danger you are in. I'm afraid that they won't be driven away so easily next time."

"Oh, Mr Hetherington, sir... what am I to do?"

"Without the means to settle your debts, you're a dead man, Mr O' Malley."

Celia intervened, "Oh, Da. what about the gold coin? You'll have to pay them with it... you must, please... please."

Her father was glad of the gloom in the storehouse, so that his daughter could not see his face reddening in shame. "My father has a gold coin that was given to us by my grandmother, Mr Hetherington. Do you think it would help to clear what he owes?"

There was an uneasy silence, then Michael O' Malley cleared his throat noisily; it felt dry and parched. He could hardly force his words from his mouth. He croaked, "I don't have the gold coin Seeley. I don't have it... not any more."

There was another deadly silence as Seeley tried to absorb what her father had just confessed. She was too shocked to speak. Her father could sense her despair... could sense how she must be feeling. "I'm sorry Seeley... believe me, I'm sorry... may God forgive me for what I've done to you."

Gilbert Hetherington added to her dismay.

"Your father lost his gold coin quite a while ago, I'm afraid, Miss O'Malley. He has been playing for very high stakes, and that was only possible because he was thought to be of good means. I can assure you that the possessor of gold coinage is greatly welcomed in any gambling saloon."

Celia could find no words to say, and her father knew that in their desperate situation, words were no longer of any use. He must take action. Again he implored Gilbert Hetherington, "What am I to do?"

His gentleman friend knew that his hour had come. "I might have a solution for you, Mr O'Malley," he said. "Could we not sit down somewhere and talk about it."

"Certainly sir... certainly... come on upstairs; I'd be glad of anything you might suggest that would get me out of all this trouble, sure I would. Just wait a moment while I light the lamp, so you can see where you're going."

Celia led the way upstairs, and Gilbert Hetherington followed behind her, barely able to conceal the look of satisfaction that he felt at having so easily accomplished his purpose.

Celia sat motionless and dejected whilst the two men talked earnestly with one another. She felt numbed by the fact that their fortune had once again taken such an ominous turn for the worse. Suddenly she became aware of Gilbert Hetherington's voice; of the words he was speaking. "My sister and her husband own a cotton plantation down in North Carolina, we could go there for a while; I'm sure your daughter would love it. Then eventually, I would like to return to New Jersey, for I have my eye on a property along the river Muscanetcong, and I intend to buy it. I need a wife Mr O'Malley and your daughter would not want for anything, of that I can assure you."

"Seeley... what do you say me darlin'? 'Twoud be a grand life you'd be living... better than any I could ever provide for you. Now what do you think?"

Celia's numbness disappeared in an instant; her face began to burn with embarrassment. She looked at her father. "Oh, Da... how could I marry a gentleman like Mr Hetherington? 'Tis peasants we are, and for sure gentlemen never wed the likes of us."

Gilbert Hetherington threw back his head and laughed loudly. "Why Miss O'Malley, have you not realised yet that you're in a brave, New World, where many of the old traditions are falling by the wayside? In any case, I do believe that there is far more than the blood of peasants coursing through your veins, and it shows in you young lady. I saw it from the first moment we met. There is a definite look of quality about you, which will become even more apparent when you are attired as befits a lady. Now don't put forth unnecessary argument; think of your father and of his safety, as well as your own. It is obvious that you cannot remain here, and if you will agree to become my wife, then I shall settle your father's debts, and you shall both have the opportunity to start a new life. Now what do you see so wrong in that?"

Michael O'Malley looked at Celia, his eyes shining with eagerness. "Oh, please Seeley... please say yes to Mr Hetherington's proposal. Sure he can give you the kind of life that you deserve. 'Tis true, you've never been a poor Irish peasant, not deep down you haven't. Sure you've always taken after your darlin' mother, God rest her soul. She had a quality about her somehow, that I could never really fathom, not until your grandmother told her who her real father was. It has come out in you Seeley... your sister, Mary, was more like me, but you're different and I want something better for you... can't you see?"

He broke down and covered his face with his hands.

Celia could not bear to see her father in such distress; she was beside him immediately, bending over him and trying to soothe him with her words. "All right Da... 'tis all right." She stroked his head gently. "We can't go on like this, I know we can't." She swallowed hard and closed her eyes. "Sure if it will make us safe, then I'll agree to marry Mr Hetherington... there, 'tis done."

She could not believe the words that she had just uttered. It was as though she was asleep and dreaming; it all seemed so unreal.

Her father gazed up at her. "Oh, Seeley will you do that... will you really do that for me? It was as though he too could not believe that she had acceded to his request. "You're a wonderful daughter, that you are. Sure you're too good for the likes of me, but now you'll have the kind of life that you deserve, thanks to Mr Hetherington."

That gentleman stood up and stepped towards Celia. He took her hand and raised it to his lips. "Right then Miss O'Malley, it is all settled, so I shall leave you now, but please be ready tomorrow at noon; I'll call for you in my carriage and we shall drive into town to buy you the finest wedding dress that money can buy."

After he had left, Celia and her father sat and mulled over all that had happened. Michael O'Malley was overjoyed at the turn of events that had seemingly brought such a wonderful opportunity to his beautiful daughter. "Why Seeley, sure it seems that all that has taken place these past few weeks, all me troubles, were meant for a purpose. How else would you ever have finished up marrying such a fine gentleman? I don't care now what happens to me, just as long as I can see you happily settled and well provided for. That's as much as any man could ask for his daughter, and 'tis all I've been wanting since we came here to this strange land. Now, tell me are you happy about it me darlin'?"

Celia bit her lip thoughtfully. Everything had happened so quickly and unexpectedly, that she could hardly believe it was true, but she fully realised that it was the only immediate solution to their problems. She was aware that the burden of responsibility for their safety now rested upon her shoulders. She could see that her father had been so devastated by the deaths of his wife and eldest daughter, that he was in no fit state to fend for himself. Of course she was not happy at the prospect of marrying a comparative stranger, but what other alternative was there?

"Well Da, 'tis our only choice if we want to get away from here, and you know I'd do anything for you... anything at all. I am worried about Mr Forbes though. I'm sorry that we won't be here when he comes back, for he'll wonder what has happened to us, and where we are. Maybe I could ask Mr Hetherington to explain to him why we had to leave. I hope that he'll understand, and realise that you would never have let him down if your life hadn't been in danger. Do you think he'll understand Da?"

"Sure he will darlin', sure he will... for a kinder man never lived. God willing, we might even meet up with him again ourselves one day, seeing as he and Mr Hetherington are friends, so don't you go giving it another thought now, there's a good girl."

Five

Celia was nervously awaiting the arrival of the carriage the following day, as it pulled up outside the storehouse. She kissed her father good-bye, as she slipped quickly out of the door, warning him not to put a foot outside while she was gone. She had put on her prettiest dress, one that she had made herself from some fine silken material that Mr Forbes had given her. Another of his generous gifts. She had washed and brushed her hair until it glistened, and had pinned it on top of her head in a most becoming style, that was complimented by the small flowered bonnet she wore, and even though her outfit was of a simple home-made design, its neatness of line made her appear far more mature than her seventeen years. In fact, when Gilbert Hetherington stepped down and took her hand to help her up into the carriage, he felt his heart miss a beat. He decided that his choice had been the right one, and he gloated over his successful conquest. He sat opposite her in the carriage, as they drove towards the centre of New York, so that he could more easily admire the beauty of his young future bride. She gazed out of the window, fascinated by all the new and interesting sights that she beheld, and he found her obvious naiveté extremely alluring. She suited his purpose admirably, for she was nothing like the bawdy saloon women whose company he normally sought, but of course, they were not the marrying kind. No more would he have been, were it not for the fact that it suited his purpose at this particular time. The role of the respectable married man had never appealed to him in the least, this was simply to impress his father in order to obtain the monies he had promised, when once he had proven that he was married and settled down at last to a decent respectable life. He silently cursed that gentleman for the severe stipulations he had imposed upon both himself and his brother Douglas, when he had expedited them from their home in England, but now he had devised a method of satisfying those stipulations in a way that might not be too unpleasant, after all.

He could well remember the day that his father had summoned him and his brother into his study, and told them that he had arranged a passage for them on the next available ship to America. All that had concerned him was maintaining the family's untarnished reputation, at all costs. He had then contacted their older sister Lilybee in North Carolina, and charged her with the responsibility of ensuring that the two boys each received a substantial sum of money upon their arrival in the 'New World', to start them off handsomely in their new life, with the provision that upon their marriage to decent respectable women, they should each receive an additional sum, with which to set up a home and provide for their families. Now he meant to ensure that he received that additional sum, for he desperately needed it, and to that end he had procured this innocent, unsuspecting female, who had not the slightest notion of what lay before her. She was perfect in every respect; she would be of little or no trouble, he had easily detected that, and once he had introduced her to his sister, then his father's settlement would be his for the taking. He smiled inwardly; his plan was evolving far more satisfactorily than he could ever have hoped.

The next few hours sped by as Celia was guided through every conceivable fashion emporium in New York. Her wedding gown was the first and most important item of purchase: a sumptuously extravagant creation in palest ivory silk, delicately worked with embroidery and beads, but what delighted her even more were the accompanying accessories and under-garments of the daintiest design. She was entranced; she had never before seen, or indeed imagined, such luxurious apparel. The sales assistants too were in a flurry as they proudly paraded all the most expensive of merchandise, in their endeavour to please her generous benefactor. They exclaimed loudly in genuine admiration at the transformation they accomplished as they helped this charming young girl to choose her new wardrobe, for seldom did they have the opportunity of dressing someone of her rare beauty.

And transformation it was, for Gilbert Hetherington himself could scarcely believe what a difference all the finery had made to his simple young peasant girl. Now he could not wait to escort her around the town, and introduce his beautiful bride to his sister and her husband when he took her to North Carolina. Yes indeed, his masterful plan had worked magnificently.

*

When their shopping was done, and he felt that Celia's attire now adequately befitted her new role as his wife, he took her out to dine before returning her home safely to her father.

On the morrow they were to be wed, but there was still one other matter of extreme urgency which needed his attention. Something vitally important that he had already carefully planned and which had now to be executed with infinite cunning.

Michael O'Malley's cup was full to overflowing as his daughter related all that had happened on her trip to New York, and he was astounded at the generosity of Gilbert Hetherington when Celia opened up all the boxes and packages to reveal the many gifts he had bought for her.

"Oh, Seeley… I've never seen the like in all me life. 'Tis wonderful, and no one deserves it more than you me darlin'. Sure you'll be living like a lady from now on." He hugged her with joy at the thought that in two more days all their troubles would be over, when they set off for North Carolina with Gilbert Hetherington.

Celia had resolved to make the very best of the situation for her father's sake, and now she was anxious for the wedding to be over, so that they could make a fresh start. She carefully packed all her belongings to take with her the following day, as she would not be returning to the storehouse after the wedding. Instead, Gilbert Hetherington had arranged to take her back to his hotel, where she would wait while he drove her father home to the storehouse. Then, after their wedding night, he would bring her in his carriage to pick up her father, and they would all travel down to North Carolina together.

She was not at all happy at the thought of her father being left alone overnight, but as Mr Hetherington had promised to take care of his debts, then he would probably be quite safe until they came to fetch him the following day.

Despite the fact that her father seemed happier than he had been for many long months, Celia's apprehension would not ease, and she knew without a shadow of doubt that it was because she still mistrusted the man who was soon to become her husband.

*

As she stood beside her groom in the small wooden church, the young bride felt no joy, just a cold emptiness deep inside. She had never looked more beautiful than she did in her ivory silk gown, and yet she had no sense of it. It was as though she were a character in a charade, playing a part. The extravagance of her dress made it seem more so. This was not real; she felt that once the ceremony was over, and her performance finished, then she could return to normal once again. Oh how she wished that that were possible. She continually thought of Mr Forbes; she could not get him out of her mind. Every time she glanced at her bridegroom during the simple ceremony, she saw his dear face. Again and again over the past few days, she had prayed that he might return and put an end to all this madness, but now it was too late. Her fate had been sealed.

*

Now they were driving to the hotel where she was to spend her wedding night. She could not believe that she was married. This was not how she had imagined it would be. She was completely overawed at the grandeur of the hotel, and she clung to her father when he kissed her goodbye, not wanting him to leave her there. She had never before felt so lonely and afraid; this was the first time in her life that she and her father had been apart, but she reassured herself with the thought that she would see him again the very next day.

"Sleep well Da," she whispered, as he walked away. "You'll have no more worries after tonight."

It seemed perfectly natural to Michael O'Malley that he and his newfound relative should stop for a drink on their way back to the storehouse, for this was too grand an occasion not to celebrate. Indeed it was... and celebrate they did, so it was not long before the devious younger man had rendered his Irish companion completely helpless. Then, just as soon as the light had faded from the sky, he gathered his victim unceremoniously in his arms and heaved him out to his carriage. In a very few minutes they were in front of the storehouse, and Gilbert Hetherington took no time in locating the key in the drunken man's pocket. He unlocked the door and roughly shoved Michael O'Malley into the gloomy building, where he collapsed in a stupor on to the floor. His initial work completed, he stepped outside again, making sure that the door remained open. He raised his hand in a pre-arranged signal, beckoning his accomplices, who lurked menacingly in the shadows. Within seconds, four burly-looking men appeared from nowhere: those same ruffians who, but a few days before, had hammered on the door of the storehouse and terrified Michael O'Malley and his daughter with their coarse threats. This time though, they had no need to hammer on the door, for it stood slightly ajar, inviting their illicit entry.

"Where are the wagons? We have no time to lose," hissed Gilbert Hetherington, to the tallest, most gruesome-looking of the group. A giant of a man, with an evil countenance.

"Here, just along the side street... I'll fetch 'em right away," came back the reply.

He motioned to the others, who immediately set about the task of removing every last piece of merchandise from the storehouse, and their activity caused not the slightest shred of suspicion to the few uninterested passers-by, for it was quite usual to see wagons come and go, loading and unloading goods, at all times of the day and night. Michael O'Malley stirred uneasily and tried to raise his head, but he slumped to the floor again with a groan. "Don't forget to take care of him before you leave, and then fire the place with the lantern. Make sure that nothing remains... nothing, is that understood?" growled Gilbert Hetherington.

"Aye sir... we'll make sure that everything is done exactly as you ordered. There'll not be anything left here when we've finished... you need have no fear. Then before morning, we'll be well on our way to New Jersey with the wagons just as arranged."

"Good Dutch... I know I can trust you," said Gilbert Hetherington. "Then you take the stuff straight to the store along the Muscanetcong, the usual place, and I'll see you there in a week or so. I'll be off now... you do the job well. Good night to you."

When the wagons were loaded and secured, Dutch cautioned his men to wait outside and keep watch while he went back into the storehouse to carry out his final and most heinous task. He could see the prostrate form of Michael O'Malley in the dim glow of the oil lamp, and his lips drew back in an ugly grimace as he raised his foot and delivered a vicious kick to the small of his back. Then he grabbed his coat collar and yanked him upright, as though he were a rag doll, spun him around to face him and smashed his enormous fist full force under his jaw. The stupefied man moaned in agony as he staggered backwards and crashed against the wall. Just as his legs crumpled beneath him, his powerful assailant leapt in front of him again and grabbed him by the throat, before his violently aching body could reach the ground. Michael O'Malley sank into oblivion as the bones in his neck crunched and the last breath was choked out of him by the vice-like grip of those gigantic hands, so he could not feel the ferocious heat of the flames, as they writhed unhindered around his lifeless body, and swept in a relentless fury through the dry wood building. When the raging fire finally subsided into glowing embers, his charred remains were all that could be seen amongst the smoking rubble.

*

After having removed himself from the immediate scene of his crime, Gilbert Hetherington had stepped from his carriage at a place that was not too far distant from it, in order that he might enjoy, to the full, the macabre spectacle. He was the most evil of men, and his blood raced as he savoured the thought of the destruction he had wrought. He was determined not to miss one single detail; he must witness everything that was happening, feel the excitement as the storehouse exploded into flames, its brilliance lighting up the darkened sky as a myriad of sparks flew in intermittent bursts, leaping and cracking high into the air. The sensation was thrilling; he too was on fire. Then, at long last, he decided to return to his unsuspecting bride, who was awaiting him back at the hotel. He licked his lips lasciviously at the thought of his innocent young victim, for she was yet to provide a pleasurable end to this truly momentous day.

*

Celia yawned sleepily and snuggled down under the coverlet. As the hour was so late, she had finally decided to go to bed, but she was too troubled to sleep; her mind was in a turmoil. She lay worrying and wondering where her bridegroom could be, especially as he was supposedly just to have escorted her father back home. She suspected that possibly they might have visited an alehouse together, but he should surely have returned by now. Eventually, her eyes closed from sheer exhaustion and she drifted off into a disturbed slumber.

The assault upon her father, of which she knew nothing, was inconceivably violent and unwarranted, but mercifully it had come to an abrupt end with his death. Not so the assault that she too was forced to endure that very same night. Her suffering was the more unspeakable, for with it came the realisation that this was but the first of a continuing succession of violation that she would be forced to endure for the rest of her life.

Six

As the carriage pulled up in front of the gaping void, where once the storehouse had stood, Celia's misery welled up inside her and overflowed, to be emitted in a long mournful wail that she simply could not withhold. She covered her face with her hands and bent forward, sobbing pitifully. She knew without any shadow of doubt that somehow or other this vile man, who sat beside her, was responsible. "You monster... you monster," she cried shrilly. "What have you done to my father, what have you done?"

Gilbert Hetherington took her by the shoulders and shook her vigorously. "Stop this, stop it at once. I have done nothing to him."

She intervened, "Where is he then?" Her voice rose to a shout. She banged her clenched fists against the windows of the carriage. "Da... oh Da," she moaned. "Not you too... please God... no... no."

Again she felt herself being shaken vigorously. "Will you stop... try to get a hold of yourself, while I go to see what has happened here. Now if you can control yourself for a few moments, I shall go and investigate. Wait here."

Celia watched him as he stood looking at the ruins; he seemed oddly fascinated by what he saw, almost transfixed. She opened the carriage door and climbed down. She too wanted to see the blackened mess, although she was afraid of what it might reveal. Perhaps it would tell her something of what had happened. She still could not believe her eyes. Her movement attracted Gilbert Hetherington's attention; he spun around and stood before her to block her view.

"Get back into the carriage at once," he commanded. "There is nothing here, everything has been destroyed... everything. Now get away."

"But my father... what of my father?"

He took hold of her firmly and propelled her away. "I have seen him... he is there... there is nothing we can do. Come now, get into the carriage, we must be on our way, or we'll miss the stage."

Celia's legs buckled beneath her and she swayed unsteadily. He held her fast against him and led her back, lifting her bodily into the carriage.

As they drove off, she became strangely quieted and calm. Suddenly, it was as though she were not there; no longer a part of all that was going on around her. She sat staring in front of her, her eyes unseeing, her brain numbed. So she remained for the whole of the journey down to North Carolina. She was oblivious to all that was happening. Even in the stifling heat of the stagecoach, she showed no sign of distress. She appeared to be in a dreamlike state, completely cut-off from reality. She had been cruelly duped by the man to whom she was bound in marriage, and the enormity of her plight had completely over-powered her sense of reason.

*

After days and days of travel, with innumerable stops for food, rest and fresh teams of horses, they finally came to 'White Lakes'. It was unlike any place that Celia had ever seen. It was imposing, magnificently grandiose in design, and stood resplendent within the acres and acres of land that surrounded it. Elizabeth Mansfield-Brown too was unlike any woman that Celia had ever known. She was a lady in every sense of the word, genteel, kind and generous of spirit. Her personality permeated the atmosphere of her home and captivated all who were fortunate enough to enter it. She and her husband Percy could not have welcomed her brother and his new bride more warmly when they arrived, and their generous hospitality and loving care were exactly what Celia needed to bring her back to life again.

In those crucial first weeks, she came to experience a peace and tranquillity that she had never known existed; a sublime happiness that she could never have imagined, and her genuine affection and respect for Lilybee and Percy developed into a love that would endure for the rest of her life. The older woman took immediately to this beautiful young Irish girl, and it soon became apparent to her why her brother Gilbert had so cunningly chosen her to be his wife; a fact that had at first mystified her. She was deeply shocked and saddened to learn of all the tragedy that had befallen Celia since coming from her native land, and this explained the poor girl's trauma when they had first met. Now Lilybee decided to do everything in her power to equip this naive young girl for the kind of life that she knew she was destined to live with her ruthless spouse. She felt enormous sympathy for her, and would stop at nothing in order to give her the support that she so desperately needed.

*

It was not many weeks before Gilbert announced that he must be on his way back to New Jersey; he had not intended to spend any time at all at 'White Lakes', for he wanted to dispose of the property he had stolen from Ian Forbes, as quickly as possible. He needed to ensure that there was no evidence to connect him with the dastardly crime he had committed. If there was one thing that he prided himself upon, it was that he could always extricate himself from trouble, whenever necessary; or deflect it towards another. He was a past master in the art of deceit. He had been delayed whilst waiting for his father to arrange the despatch of the promised fortune, but now he was anxious to be on his way.

As he had yet to complete the purchase of a home for his new young bride, he gladly agreed to leave her in the care of his sister, who was not in the least sorry to see him leave. She had never been particularly fond of him, and his latest ruse to extract an additional fortune from their father in England, did nothing to enhance her opinion of him. However, the joy she found in her new young charge truly delighted her. She taught her all the social graces; how to behave in any given situation; how to speak; how to dress; how to eat properly, and how to entertain in style, and Celia blossomed. She became even more radiant in her peaceful, luxurious surroundings. She thoroughly enjoyed learning everything her warm hearted sister-in-law could teach her about her new lifestyle, and in so doing she slowly recovered from the horror of all that had befallen her since she had first met Gilbert Hetherington. Free from his menacing presence, she now became relaxed and contented, and within a very few weeks, Lilybee was overjoyed to notice that Celia's sickly, lethargic condition was not due to the damp oppressive climate, but had been brought about by the fact that she was with child. Never was there more celebration at 'White Lakes', for Lilybee and Percy had never been so blessed, even though they would both have loved to rear a family. In fact, they both fussed and coddled Celia to such an extent, that she forgot her initial shock and horror at learning that she was carrying Gilbert Hetherington's child. She despised him so deeply, that the very thought of him was abhorrent to her, but he was now very far removed, so her life with his sister and her husband could not have been more idyllic.

*

Every afternoon, the two women would sit out on the wide verandah in their comfortable chairs, contentedly sipping cool drinks, and idly chatting about anything and everything, and it was during these perfect, still afternoons that Celia gradually came to learn of her husband and his family history. Lilybee loved to tell the story of her life; to reminisce about her childhood, and with an appreciative listener, like Celia, she related every last detail. She told how when she was a young girl, just four years old, her mother had died of cholera in India. Her father had been working for the East India Company in Calcutta for a number of years, but upon his wife's tragic death he had decided to return to England, because he was fearful that the disease might also rob him of his only child. He was devastated by his sad loss, and for several months had spent most of his time at his club in London, leaving Lilybee in the care of her nanny. However, as he began to recover from his grief and pick up the threads of his life once again, he had met a most attractive, vivacious young woman, who completely swept him off his feet. She was in no way similar to his former wife, but nevertheless he married her. Lilybee could vividly remember her first encounter with her step-mother Evelyn, but she had no wish to dwell upon the elements of their relationship with one another. Unfortunately, it had not been too pleasant, so she chose to forget it.

During the first two years of their marriage, his new wife proudly presented her father with two strapping sons, Gilbert and Douglas, but being the social butterfly that she was, she now considered that her wifely duties had been satisfactorily fulfilled, with the consequence that no more children were forthcoming. She soon resumed her former mode of life and spent her time in pleasurable pursuits, very much as she had done before her marriage to Lawrence Hetherington. By mutual consent, they each began to lead their own separate lives, although on occasion it suited Evelyn to retreat for a while into the solace and comfort of the family home. On the rare occasions that she did put in an appearance, during her son's formative years, she proved to be a most disruptive influence upon them. She strongly opposed any form of discipline that they received and permitted them to run wild whenever they were in her company. It was her method of compensating them for her prolonged absences, and in that way she tried to buy their affection. In actual fact, all she ever succeeded in doing was to thoroughly spoil them, to such an extent that it became impossible for their father to keep them under control. Then, when she decided that she had had enough of them and of the domestic scene, she would disappear once again, leaving their father to restore them to an orderly routine. This see-saw existence thoroughly ruined the boys' lives, and destroyed their relationship with their father, so it was of little wonder that they developed serious behavioural problems.

At times their father was at his wits' end, trying to prevent their various nannies and tutors from deserting their posts, with the result that he finally packed them both off to a boarding school that was renowned for its harsh discipline. In this establishment, with its Spartan regime, it was believed that the rebelliousness of the two boys would be satisfactorily curbed, but in effect it simply exacerbated the problem, so that when they reached adulthood, their behaviour was a constant source of embarrassment and torment to their distraught father. They had become completely inseparable, never out of each other's company, and when they came upon the London scene, tales of their wild escapades were upon everyone's lips. The more their father entreated them to behave in a proper manner, as befitted gentlemen, the more wilfully would they disobey him, with the result that their reputations became notorious. They gambled and drank to excess; frequented houses of ill-repute, and kept company with the most disreputable of women. Time and time again, they accrued exorbitant gambling debts, which their father settled begrudgingly, but when the murder of a young street girl rocked the foundations of London's society, and it was intimated that one of the Hetherington boys was thought to be involved, Lawrence Hetherington could tolerate no more. Drastic steps were needed to extricate Gilbert, for it was he who had come under suspicion, so the two were despatched post-haste to America. Lilybee shook her head and tut-tutted disapprovingly, then quite happily continued with her colourful account of the family's history. It was evident that she thoroughly enjoyed re-living old memories in its telling.

She and Percy had been in America for seven years when Gilbert and Douglas were sent to join them in 1838; they had come to 'White Lakes' Plantation as newly-weds, but that was another story. Her father had entrusted her with a substantial sum of money that she was to divide equally between her two brothers upon their arrival in New York. If used wisely, it was sufficient to give each of them an indulgent lifestyle, one to which they were well accustomed. Gilbert was almost twenty years old at that time, and Douglas approaching nineteen, so Lilybee suggested that they join her and dear Percy at 'White Lakes' until they decided what they wanted to do with their lives. Douglas readily accepted his sister's invitation to travel down to North Carolina with her and her husband, where he could establish himself in a decent respectable manner, but Gilbert was not so easily persuaded. With an ample fortune at his disposal, he envisaged a life filled with excitement, and much more to his satisfaction. From what he had seen upon his arrival in rapidly developing New York, the opportunities were unlimited for men such as himself. He wasted no time in bidding his younger brother farewell, and they parted company for the first time in their lives, much to the distress of poor Douglas. However, it pleased Lilybee that he had taken to life on the plantation immediately, and it soon became apparent that now he had been freed from his brother's evil influence, he was making a determined effort to settle down.

From what Celia had experienced over the past few weeks in her sister-in-law's magnificent home, she could well imagine why it had not been difficult for Douglas to do so, for the luxury and opulence of the place was quite beyond her comprehension. In fact, it was still difficult for her to believe that she had entered into such a world, one that had hitherto been completely unknown to her. It was not just the grandeur of the house and its contents that so overwhelmed Celia, but the very lifestyle itself. She was mesmerized by the vast number of black slaves and servants everywhere, ready to wait upon their masters and mistresses at the slightest command. Could she ever become accustomed to their obeisance, she wondered? When she voiced her doubts to Lilybee, the older woman chuckled kindly and assured her that she would have no problems whatsoever, for the house servants became almost like family members, particularly the personal ladies' maids and the gentlemen's menservants. Celia soon learned exactly what her sister-in-law meant, for she had noticed the affection between Lilybee and Grace, her personal maid. They were more like sisterly companions than mistress and slave.

It was obvious too that Percy's manservant Mose held his master in affectionate regard. Lilybee promised Celia that when the day came for her to leave 'White Lakes' and take up residence in her own home, she could take with her as many of the slaves as she would need, for there was an abundance of them on this vast plantation.

Seven

Christmas came and went with much joyful celebration, and Celia was thankful that her husband had not joined them for the festivities. He had sent word that he was far too busy with business matters, and in supervising the building of their new home. Apparently, he had found a really superb property in an ideal location overlooking the Muscanetcong river, in a little town called Asbury, in New Jersey, some sixty miles west of New York. The building of it had been started several years previously, but for some unknown reason the owner had suddenly decided to leave New Jersey and travel to the West. Gilbert Hetherington had seen the impressive half-finished structure on one of his trading expeditions, and had determined to acquire it and have the building of it completed. He promised to travel down to North Carolina at the end of the winter, when the weather was more favourable. Celia wondered what his reaction would be when he learned that he was to become a father. According to Lilybee's calculations, the birth should take place the following June, and she had said that she hoped Gilbert would agree to Celia remaining at 'White Lakes' for the happy event.

When Gilbert put in an appearance at the end of March, however, he made it abundantly clear to his sister that his child was to be born in his own home. Furthermore, he insisted that he could not remain for longer than two weeks at 'White Lakes', due to his business commitments. No matter how much Lilybee pleaded on Celia's behalf, and warned of the dangers of undertaking such a journey in her condition; no matter how much she tried to deter him from his foolhardiness, he was adamant that his wife should travel back to New Jersey with him. So it was with great reluctance that the two women were forced to say a tearful farewell to one another, but not before Lilybee had very carefully hand-picked ten trustworthy, reliable slaves to accompany Celia on her journey north, for she knew how dependent upon them this innocent young girl would become. It gave her great comfort to know that with these five men and five women in her household, Celia would be well cared for, even though she would never ever receive any kindness or protection from the man who had taken her for his wife.

*

Lillybee's fears were well grounded, and Gilbert Hetherington's wish was granted, for within twenty-four hours of arriving in her new home, Celia collapsed in violent pain. The rigours of the long tiring journey, added to her husband's brutal inconsideration of her delicate state, had brought about the premature birth of a beautiful son. Celia was terrified when the pains first started, and she clung in desperation to Beulah and Jasmine as they skilfully and patiently brought her firstborn into the world. They gently soothed her forehead with cool, wet cloths, as the sweat poured from her; they coaxed and cajoled as she struggled to free her body of its excruciatingly painful burden; they confidently reassured her and gave her the courage to fight on bravely, when she felt that she must surely die from the overwhelming agony that her immature young body was being forced to endure, but finally, in one enormous, gigantic, paralyzing burst of effort, her battle was won, and her young trusting heart was lost to these two beautiful black-skinned women, who had so lovingly carried her through her hours of anguish, and then proudly presented her with God's greatest gift, her new born child.

As they laid the tiny squawking infant in her arms, Celia's deep blue eyes gazed up in wonder at the two pairs of deep brown ones that were transfixed upon her face, and she was overcome with gratitude. There was no need for her to utter a word, for her look told them all they wanted to know, and in that moment a bond was forged, that the years would never erode. Celia did not know, she had no way of knowing, that this was to be the pattern of her life from now on. Her husband had gone off and left her in the house shortly after their arrival, intent upon some business or other, and had not bothered to return. In her loneliness, she had clung to the only source of comfort that there was: the slaves who Lilybee, in her wisdom, had so carefully chosen for her, and they had not failed her. So it would be from that day forward, for she had no one else. They became her family, her strength and comfort; her closest friends, to encourage and sustain, and sensing how great was her need of them, they would foster and protect her until their dying day.

*

As soon as she had recovered from her confinement, Celia set about making a life for herself and her child. Her husband had come on a short visit a week after his birth, had given him a cursory glance, then announced that the boy was to be named Edmund. There his involvement with his son had ended; but the child would never want for affection, for his mother adored him, as did each and every one of the servants. Celia could never bring herself to refer to them as slaves. She came to know them all individually, and they respected her deeply for her kindly appreciation of all that they did for her. The men ranged in age from fifteen years to forty; the youngest, Clarence, had come with his mother and father, his twin sister and an older brother, Harvest, who was seventeen. Their father Joshua was forty, then there was Amos twenty-five, and Kingston thirty-two; each one of them sturdy and reliable. The women too were capable and experienced in all household duties. Clarence's twin, Clarissa, fifteen years old; her thirty-five year old mother Jasmine, called Jassy; Beulah, thirty-four, and Maybelle twenty-three, who had specially asked that her best friend be allowed to come with her, Delilah, aged nineteen. They soon settled most happily into their new home, and the only time they found cause for grievance, was when their master came home on one of his brief visits. Fortunately for the whole household, these visits were few and far between, for the atmosphere changed to one of gloom and despondency whenever he set foot inside the house.

*

With the arrival of the warm spring weather, Celia set off on a thorough exploration of the grounds around the house. It was a truly impressive property, that her husband had named 'Fortune's Hand'. It stood on high ground overlooking the Muscanetcong River, that flowed and wended its way out into the Delaware River, which marked the boundary between New Jersey and Pennsylvania. The tall elegant windows to the front of the house overlooked a sweeping driveway, that led into a short leafy lane, and out to Main Street, which ran across the bridge and on through the town. The land to the rear of the house was thickly wooded and sloped down to the shallows of the river, where it altered course and curved sharply as it flowed beneath the bridge. Celia spent hour after hour wading in the cool clear water, with Edmund gurgling happily in her arms, although she missed the fresh gentle climate of her beloved Emerald Isle. She would not allow herself to think too often of all that she had loved and lost, for she knew that it was gone forever, no matter how her poor heart yearned.

As the months passed, Celia grew to love the small New Jersey town, and gradually came to know its people on the many occasions that she drove down to the shops along Main Street in her buggy.

Kingston took care of the stables and the livestock, and he also made it his responsibility to drive his mistress around, whenever she wanted to take an outing. He kept the livery and the vehicles immaculately, cleaning the harness and polishing the bodywork and upholstery, so that the fine appearance of Celia and her baby, being driven proudly around by her handsome manservant, became a familiar sight to the people of Asbury.

She involved herself with all that happened in the town, and was fascinated to learn its history and origins. This endeared her to the local inhabitants, who welcomed her into their thriving community and viewed her presence amongst them as a great asset.

She learned that the town had been settled in the early 1700s, prior to the Revolutionary War, and had originally been known as Hall's Mills, because a man named Hall had owned the grist mill there, but in 1796 it was re-named Asbury, in honour of Bishop Francis Asbury, who laid the cornerstone of the Methodist church which was built at that time. He had been a 'circuit rider', and appointed as a lay-preacher by Wesley, to carry message and ministry to out of the way places. Celia renounced her Catholic faith and became a member of the Methodist Society, so that she would be more readily accepted into the social life of the town. As a Catholic, her life would have been an extremely lonely one, for her husband was not a Catholic and consequently, their marriage had not taken place in a Catholic church. With her family now dead and gone, Celia decided to take the easiest, least troublesome course; she did not have the fortitude, or moral courage to withstand the prejudice and the hostility that was so often directed at members of her particular faith. As it was, she became involved with many fund-raising events for the gradual improvement of the town. She was one of the first members to join a group called 'The Village Improvement Society' who put on all manner of entertainments at the Academy, to raise funds. She particularly enjoyed the Women's Sewing Circle, and regularly attended the sessions which were held in the members' homes. She took great delight in welcoming her friends to 'Fortune's Hand' whenever it was her turn to do so.

Time passed very quickly for Celia, and she could hardly believe that a full year had gone by when her first wedding anniversary came around in the September. Edmund was only five months old, and she was expecting another child the following April.

Beulah and Jassy were most concerned for their young mistress, whom they thought should have had a little more time to nurse her firstborn, but Celia brushed aside their fears and told them that it would be good for Edmund to have a playmate near his own age. However, as the months went on, Celia began to feel unwell. At first she dismissed it as just a temporary condition, probably a slight chill, due to the harsh winter weather, but finally she took to her bed and Joshua was sent to fetch the doctor. He advised Celia to rest as much as possible, or he feared she might suffer a miscarriage, particularly as her first child had been born prematurely. He was not at all happy that she was bearing another child so soon after her first one, but Celia could not bring herself to discuss her husband's violent and inconsiderate demands upon her, with this comparative stranger, despite the fact that he was a qualified medical practitioner.

Then in February, quite unexpectedly, Beulah and Jassy were once again called upon in the middle of the night to take care of Celia when her second baby decided to enter the world two months before it should. This time it was a beautiful little girl, and Jassy was just placing her in her mother's arms as the doctor hurried into the bedroom. It was 2 o'clock in the morning, and he had been out on another emergency call when Joshua had gone to fetch him just before midnight, but he praised Beulah and Jassy for their capable handling of the birth. Their faces were wreathed in smiles as they looked lovingly at mother and baby, peacefully resting after their exhausting ordeal.

Eight

From the day she had left North Carolina, Celia had regularly corresponded with Lilybee and her husband Percy, keeping them informed of everything that happened at 'Fortune's Hand'. They constantly expressed their desire to see their nephew Edmund, and now that he had a new little sister, who had been named Rosalind by her father, they entreated Celia to pay them a visit. When Celia mentioned to Gilbert that she would love to take the children down to North Carolina for a holiday, much to her surprise, he agreed to go. They waited until the end of September, when the weather was more suitable for them to travel, and then they set forth.

As was to be expected, there was much rejoicing upon their arrival at 'White Lakes' and Lilybee was in her element with the two infants to spoil and fuss over. Their month's holiday passed all too quickly, and it was soon time for the visitors to depart. As they were preparing to leave, Percy very generously offered Celia a gift for the two infants, a new nursemaid to help care for them. He suggested that they choose one of the younger slaves, who would also be a playmate, for it was obvious to both Lilybee and Percy that Celia would be adding yet another brother or sister to her family in the early part of the coming year. Gilbert insisted that he should go and make the selection, and before they all set off, he had found a small wistful looking child of between eight and nine years old, whose name was Minnie. Celia felt desperately sorry for the tiny child as she was bundled roughly into the coach. She cowered in the corner, behind all the luggage and Celia wondered how her poor mother must have felt at having to part with her small daughter so suddenly. At least she would have a good home at 'Fortune's Hand', she intended to make sure of that, and the work would not be so arduous as that which she might have been forced to do in the cotton fields.

The servants were all sitting around the huge kitchen table having their meal when young Minnie was introduced to them. Celia had taken her by the hand and led her in to meet them. Clarissa jumped up immediately she saw the young girl and sidled around the table, looking at her with curiosity. "We knows you... you's Minnie from down 'White Lakes' plantation, ain't you?" she said, smiling broadly. Minnie nodded shyly.

"Sho, she is... she Grace's girl," said Jasmine. "Well ain't that somethin', I knowed your mama well... so you's come to live up here in the North too."

"Will you take care of her Maybelle? Give her something to eat and then she'll probably want to get·to bed. It's been a long tiring journey for a little one. She'll need a good long sleep, then we'll settle her in tomorrow," said Celia.

"Sho Ma' am... you jus' leave it to me."

"She's going to be nursemaid and playmate for Rosalind. Maybe she'll be able to keep her happy and quiet, to give us all some peace," laughed Celia, as she left the room.

This was to be the start of an unbelievably close relationship between the young black child and the fractious red-headed baby, whom no one had been able to pacify for very long from the moment she was born, but it seemed that immediately Rosalind set eyes on Minnie, her heart was captivated.

She thrust out her chubby little arms for Minnie to take hold of her, and she clung to her, clasping the young girl tightly around the neck and burying her face against her shoulder. When she was awake she gurgled happily the whole time that Minnie was within her sight, and when she grew tired, Minnie crooned softly in her beautiful melodious voice, until she dropped off into a contented sleep. Minnie too found a comfort with this tiny baby that she could not find with anyone else, since the unbearable heartache of being snatched from her mother. Rosalind, with her copper-gold hair, fascinated her and their innocent joy in one another was contagious. Everybody watched as the bond between the two developed, and their happiness spread through the household, weaving its magic spell and brightening the atmosphere for every one of them.

Had it not been for the periodic visits of the master of the house, life at 'Fortune's Hand', would have been idyllic, for as Lilybee had once told Celia, the servants would become like family members, and that is exactly what they were as far as Celia was concerned. They had all settled in and undertaken the different tasks to which they were accustomed. Joshua, with the help of his older son Harvest, had cleared the land immediately around the house, and planted different sections of it with flowering shrubs, fruit and vegetables. The women had undertaken all the work of running the household. Delilah did the cooking; Jassy and Maybelle the laundry and housework; Beulah took care of Celia and waited at table, and young Clarissa helped with the children and gave a hand wherever else she was needed;

whilst Amos and Clarence between them carried out the heavy duties that the women couldn't manage, and kept the house in perfect running order.

It was only when the master put in an appearance that the orderly routine would violently disrupt. Everyone was in fear of his foul moods, which were usually brought on by his heavy bouts of drinking, and Celia was no exception. She was now carrying her third child, as Lilybee and Percy had suspected, and it was due in the early part of May. She had been feeling extremely unwell from the moment she had first learned that she was carrying it. Fortunately, once again, her husband had spent Christmas away from home, so it had been a time of peace and happiness, when she was able to take the rest that she needed, but he arrived home again, unexpectedly, a few days before the end of December, announcing that he wanted to give a party to celebrate the coming New Year. The house was thrown into a turmoil with the preparations, and despite the fact that Celia could hardly face the prospect of entertaining the thirty or so guests that her husband proposed to invite, she set about the arrangements with the servants, and together they managed to complete everything just in time for the arrival of the guests on New Year's Eve.

As always, Celia was deeply embarrassed by the volume of alcohol that her husband consumed, and she was much relieved when midnight came and the New Year had been appropriately welcomed in. Then, as soon as the last of the guests had left, she hurried upstairs to check on her daughter. Earlier in the evening, when she had looked in on the children as they were going to bed, Rosalind had been rather fretful and appeared to be a little feverish. She had told

Minnie to call her if the baby became any worse. Jassy reassured her by promising that the child was just teething, and would be fine after drinking down one of her home-made balms. Sure enough, Celia found both Rosalind and Minnie sound asleep when she crept into the nursery, and it was not long before she too had climbed thankfully into bed and dozed off.

Gilbert Hetherington greedily drank several more brandies before he decided to go to bed, and he was not too pleased to find that his wife had retired before him. Until that night, Celia had suffered his callous assaults uncomplainingly, always too terrified to breathe a word, but now she felt so wretched, that when he awoke her in his usual brutal way, she moaned softly, pleading with him, "Please... no. I am not feeling well. I beg you, please let me sleep."

Suddenly the bedclothes were flung back and she felt him tightly clasp her arm and almost wrench it from its socket. She cried out in pain as a resounding slap knocked her head back on to the pillow, and she realised in that instant what a foolish mistake she had made in daring to voice her rejection of him.

He pressed his face close to her own, his breath reeking, and snarled at her, "How dare you... you'll sleep when I say so, and not before. Do I make myself clear madam? You lost your independence on the day we were wed; now you dance to my tune."

When his frenzied attack was over, and she was alone once again, Celia somehow managed to make her way slowly and painfully to her closet, where she bathed her bruised and swollen face with cool water, and rinsed the blood from her mouth. Her body was shaking violently, and she sobbed uncontrollably as she crawled back to her bedside and pulled the bell cord to summon her maid. As she did so, another far more dire pain racked her body; she gasped for breath as she fell to her knees and doubled over, clutching at her stomach. Beulah was horrified when she saw the condition of her mistress. She lifted her gently on to the bed, then rushed off to tell Joshua to fetch the doctor.

She was still trying to pacify Celia when the doctor arrived, and despite the lateness of the hour, he praised Beulah's alacrity, for she had ensured that he was there to give her mistress the medical attention that she so urgently needed when she lost her unborn child just an hour later.

She languished for weeks after her husband's inhuman attack upon her, and the kindly doctor called time and time again, insisting that she rest in order to make a full recovery before attempting to leave her bed. He knew that her report of accidentally falling down the stairs was untrue, for he had witnessed the evidence of such beatings many times before. He treated his patient with gentleness and concern, and tried to give her advice, but she refused to acknowledge that her husband was in any way responsible. He could never understand, and it saddened him to see, the way in which women would always take the guilt and shame upon themselves in such cases, as though they were somehow responsible.

Nine

When the warm spring sunshine once again kissed the earth with its soft golden rays, and coaxed the dormant plants and trees into vibrant new life; when the birds began to busy themselves with building their nests; when every living creature slowly stirred and ventured forth in search of its mate, Celia found it in her heart to take up her correspondence with Lilybee once more. As she sat on the shaded terrace that had been fashioned for her by Joshua, gazing into the distance at the gently undulating form of the Appalachian mountains that adorned the horizon, softly tinged with green as the fresh young buds slowly formed upon the stark woods, she too felt a renewed surge of energy awakening within; a need to pick up the threads of her life and fill her days with interest. She had received several letters from her sister-in-law over the past few months, which had lain unanswered, but now she took up her pen and poured out her innermost thoughts and feelings, something she had never had the inclination to do before. It gave her an unbelievable sense of relief to be able to confide in this kind and caring human being; to share with her all the sadness and despair that she had for so long kept hidden inside herself, and because of the distance between them, she somehow found it easier to tell of her mortification. There seemed not the deep sense of guilt or impropriety in the written word, that she knew she would experience if she sat down with Lilybee and tried to express herself aloud. She knew that she could never speak the words she had written, for it would seem that she lacked discretion; nor could she talk of the humiliation that she suffered at the hands of her violent husband. But even so, she had an overwhelming desire to purge herself; she needed to be rid of the pain he inflicted. She felt defiled by him, as though she were contaminated by his very association with her. Of all people, she knew that her kindly sister-in-law would understand and sympathize with her distressing plight, for had she not been the one to reveal to Celia what a truly despicable character her brother was.

As much as she loved dear Jassy and Beulah, as close as they had grown to one another, Celia could not confide in them; she could not divulge to them the depths of her misery, for she knew it would cause them far too much anguish. She could not bring herself to voice to them her disapproval of her husband's abominable behaviour, for she knew they were perfectly well aware of everything she suffered at his hands. She thought longingly of Lilybee and Percy, of their deep love for one another; of Percy's kindly concern for his wife; of their happy relationship. Her thoughts drifted back to Ian Forbes, as they had done so many times since she had left the storehouse in New York. He too was a kind considerate man. She thought sadly of the innate cruelty of her husband, and wondered why he derived so much pleasure from the evil things that he did. She would never understand him and she knew that he would never change. All these things she poured out in her letter to Lilybee, knowing that the older woman would understand her need to free herself from the misery and pain that was destroying her life.

Lilybee was deeply moved when she learned of Celia's sad plight. She found it difficult to imagine how the poor girl could live in such agony of mind. She knew, when she handed the touching letter to Percy, exactly what his reaction would be. He was in full agreement that she should go to Celia immediately, to give her the love and comfort that she so desperately needed. She did not wait to send a reply by letter; instead she set off at once, to deliver her words of comfort and reassurance in person. Her heart felt heavy as she bid farewell to her husband; it was the first time that they had been apart since their marriage eighteen years ago. To add to her sorrow, she could not take her maid Grace, whom she adored, for she had been married to Mose, Percy's manservant, in the autumn, and was now happily awaiting the birth of their first child. Grace had begged to be allowed to accompany her mistress to New Jersey, but Lilybee insisted that she stay at 'White Lakes' lest any harm should come to her unborn baby. So it was settled, and another of the housemaids very happily undertook the long tiring journey with her mistress.

*

Celia collapsed in a flood of tears as Lilybee gathered her into her arms. She could not remember ever being so glad to see someone in her life. As usual, Gilbert Hetherington was away on business, or whatever else he found to occupy his time, so the two women were able to spend endless delightful hours talking and laughing and exchanging news with one another.

Lilybee took a great interest in Celia's new home, and complimented her on its charm and elegance. She played with the children and enjoyed coming to know them once again.

After a week or so, when Lilybee had had time to recover from her long journey north, and she felt that Celia was in a very much happier frame of mind, she suggested to her that it would be rather nice if they could take a trip to New York together, to do some sightseeing, do some shopping, maybe visit the theatre, and generally enjoy themselves for several days. At first Celia seemed hesitant, not wanting to leave her children, but Lilybee soon talked her into accompanying her, especially when she pointed out how well looked after the children were by the servants. "You need to get away for a while," said Lilybee. "And in any case, who do you think has taken care of your son and daughter while you have been so ill? Now stop worrying about them and think of yourself for once in your life. I want to spoil you for a change."

Once she had made up her mind to go, Celia's excitement mounted. It was to be Lilybee's treat, and as she had not been to New York since she and Percy had met her two young brothers from their ship in 1838, she was determined to make this trip a truly memorable one. She wanted to see and do everything, for she knew that it would probably be another eleven years before she had the opportunity again.

*

Upon their arrival, they booked into the Irving Hotel, one of the very best, which had had private baths installed since Lilybee's last visit. Then they set off on a tour of the fast-growing city.

They dined in the most select restaurants; went shopping along Fifth Avenue in all the fancy shops, and were delighted to find that the top fashion houses employed mannequins to model their latest creations. Lilybee enquired for how long these beautiful girls had been employed for the delight and pleasure of the customers, and was told that the first mannequin had been introduced in 1844, five years before. Lilybee shook her head in disbelief at all the sophisticated changes that had taken place in such a very few years.

The two women were having a marvellous time, in fact Celia had never had so much fun in her life before. Lilybee bought her the most beautiful things imaginable; she seemed to derive the greatest pleasure from adorning her attractive sister-in-law in the latest fashions from Europe. She bought her lavish dresses of the loveliest materials; extravagant hats; fine shoes, and then the most exquisite jewellery to add the finishing touch. When Celia protested loudly, she told her that it was no more than she deserved, after the abominable way she had been treated by her despicable husband.

"You are a Hetherington, after all," said Lilybee sternly. "And as such, you are deserving of the very best that money can buy, so let's not hear any more of your complaining." She glanced mischievously at Celia, and then collapsed into a fit of laughter. The sales assistants looked wide-eyed in amazement at their two fashionable customers, who always seemed in such high spirits. "For sure they must think we have been drinking, from our unseemly behaviour," said Celia and the two hugged one another as they laughed again.

They went to the Broadway Theatre, which had had air conditioning installed the previous year, for the comfort of their patrons, and again Lilybee exclaimed aloud in appreciation of all the wonderful changes that had taken place since she and her dear Percy had enjoyed this vibrant city so many years before. She was just as enthralled by it all, as was her delightful young companion.

*

On the third night of their visit, they decided that they would stay in and eat dinner in their hotel, as they were exhausted from their rounds of shopping and sightseeing that day. They made themselves ready, and at seven o'clock they entered the elegant dining room together, attired in their newest, most flattering gowns. They had each had their hair dressed up in the very latest style, and had donned their finest gems, that sparkled magnificently as they moved towards their table. Every head in the room turned in their direction as they were led in by their waiter; their presence lit up the whole room. "Stop blushing Celia," whispered Lilybee, as they were assisted on to their chairs. "You look adorable enough, without that captivating glow highlighting your complexion."

The two women laughed softly; in fact, it seemed to Celia that they had not stopped laughing since the first day they had arrived in New York. She could have sworn that she was dreaming, for she had never been so happy in her life. How she loved Lilybee; she really was the kindest woman she had ever met, and she considered herself fortunate indeed to have her for a sister-in-law. They had ordered their meal and were talking quietly to one another whilst waiting for it to be served, when suddenly a gentleman approached their table and coughed politely.

"Do excuse me, ladies," he said hesitantly, "are you not Seeley O'Malley?"

Celia recognized the voice immediately, and as she looked up into the face of Ian Forbes, her heart felt as though it would burst with joy. Her whole countenance lit up, and a smile spread over her face as she said, "Oh, Mr Forbes, how lovely to see you." She held out her hand.

He took it and raised it to his lips, his eyes never leaving her radiant blue ones for a moment. "Forgive the intrusion, please," he said, "but I could scarcely believe it when I saw you walk in."

Celia interrupted him, "Allow me to introduce you to my sister-in-law, Mrs Elizabeth Mansfield-Brown. Lilybee, this is my very dear friend, Mr Ian Forbes, who took us under his wing when we first arrived in New York; you remember me telling you of his wonderful kindness to my father, my sister and myself. We have so much to thank him for... he was so good to us."

Lilybee smiled up at the young man and held out her hand. "I have heard so much about you from Celia, Mr Forbes. It is a pleasure to meet you. Will you not join us... or are you with someone?"

"No... no I am alone; but are you sure that I would not be disturbing you? I must apologize again for the intrusion, but I just had to come and say hello to Seeley. I simply could not believe my eyes when I saw you walk in just now," he said again, shaking his head from side to side. It was obvious that he was completely dumbfounded by her appearance.

"Oh, Mr Forbes, please do join us," begged Celia. "There is so much I want to tell you; so much has happened since the last time I saw you."

He noticed the cultured voice, but still underlying it was the soft lilting Irish brogue that was like music to his ears; and how beautiful she had grown, even more beautiful than he had remembered her, if that was possible. She displayed all the refinements of a lady, in fact she presented herself perfectly. It was obvious that she had been well tutored, possibly by her older companion, whom he considered absolutely charming. His heart was beating rapidly. He gazed at her as though she was an apparition, still unable to believe that she was sitting there in front of him. He had dreamed of her so many times over the past few years, wondering what had become of her, and longing to see her again. Her nearness took his breath away. He stammered, "Well... if you're sure I'm not intruding, I would love to join you."

"Do sit down, Mr Forbes. Your company will give us the greatest pleasure," said Lilybee.

"Thank you... and do please call me Ian, both of you," he laughed, looking directly at Celia.

He summoned the waiter, who quickly laid another place for him at the table. Then he ordered a bottle of the finest champagne. "On such an occasion as this, nothing else would be good enough," he declared.

The next two hours were like a dream for both Celia and Ian Forbes, and Lilybee was enchanted as she sat watching this delightful pair enjoying one another's company. Their interest in each other was undisguised, and it saddened

Lilybee, when the depth of their feelings became apparent to her, that there could never be anything but friendship between the two of them, now that Celia was married to her detestable brother.

Celia was anxious to know whether Ian had been informed of what had happened to her dear father; of how he had met his death in the storehouse fire. She was horrified to learn that her husband had not contacted Ian, as he had promised her he would. "Mr Hetherington and I do not have a particularly amicable relationship, for a variety of reasons," he said, glancing at Lilybee. He had no wish to offend her in any way, so he did not elucidate.

"That does not surprise me at all Ian," retorted Lilybee. "In fact, I doubt whether my boorish brother could ever maintain an amicable relationship with anyone." She put him at his ease immediately.

"I lost a considerable amount of valuable stock in that fire, Seeley, but none of it could compare with your tragic loss. I was devastated to hear of all that had befallen you after my departure for Europe. If only I had known of your suffering, if only I had known." His eyes were cast down, intent upon the remainder of the coffee in his cup, as he toyed with it before drinking it down. His face was grim as he went on, "When I returned and found you were gone, I made extensive enquiries. Gradually, I was able to piece together the truth of what had actually happened, but there was very little proof, and to save you from further distress, I decided not to pursue the matter. I knew how heartbroken you must be, and could see no justification in causing you more pain and suffering."

"I was praying for your return at that time," whispered Celia. My father completely lost his mind when Mary died. He did some very stupid things, things he would never have dreamed of doing normally. Her eyes filled with tears. "Then when he met Gilbert, I begged him..." she swallowed hard, trying to compose herself.

The young man could not bear to see her so upset. "I know... I know Seeley, but let us not talk of it any more. It is over and done, and there is nothing we can do to change it. All that matters is that you are safe and well, and I thank God for that. You have your own family now, so you must try to put the past behind you and live your life for them. I envy you so much Seeley, for I would love to have children." He could see that the two women were becoming emotional, and he wanted to raise their spirits again. "But enough of this. Now, might I be so bold as to invite you both to be my guests tomorrow afternoon... er... that is if you don't have other plans, of course? I have some business to attend to in the morning, but if you would allow me to pick you up here at midday, I'll take you out for lunch, and then maybe you could accompany me in my carriage and I'll give you a grand tour of the city. Would you like that?"

Celia looked at Lilybee, and the older woman's eyes lit up. "That would be lovely, would it not Celia?" she said.

"Oh, yes... yes it would," agreed Celia, nodding her head enthusiastically.

"Right then. I'll come for you at noon tomorrow; and now I think we should all retire, so that we'll be refreshed and ready to enjoy our excursion together. Shall we ladies?" he asked, as he stood up. He gallantly escorted his two beautiful companions from the restaurant, much to the envy of every gentleman they passed, then they each wished one another goodnight, as they separated to go to their bedrooms.

*

At noon the following day, Ian Forbes returned to the hotel in his carriage, to find the ladies ready and waiting for him. He had booked a table at Delmonico's, much to the delight of Lilybee, who could remember dining there with Percy when they came to New York as newlyweds in 1831. It was an extremely fashionable restaurant and noted for its fine cuisine. After their gallant host had wined and dined them in courteous style, Lilybee excused herself and slipped away for a few minutes. The young couple, suddenly finding themselves alone for the first time, fell into an embarrassed silence. Their eyes met, and Celia could feel her cheeks beginning to burn. It touched Ian's heart to see that she had lost none of her innocent shyness. He leaned towards her and whispered confidentially, "It is wonderful to see you again, Seeley, I'm so glad that we've met once more."

"Oh, so am I Ian. I have thought of you so many times over the past few years."

"If only I had not stayed away so long," he said sadly. "If I'd been here, I know that things would have been different. You must know how I feel about you... how I've always felt about you; but you were just a child of sixteen when I left. I would have waited for you to grow up. I could have made you so happy Seeley. I simply could not believe that you had married that blackguard Hetherington... that he of all men should take you for his wife. You deserve to be loved and cherished after all that you have suffered and I know that he is incapable of caring for anyone, other than himself, but I do promise you Seeley, that if he should ever harm you in any way, if I ever hear that he has harmed you, then he will live to regret it, indeed he will."

His face darkened, and Celia knew that he meant every word he said, but knowing how ruthless her husband could be, she hoped and prayed that Ian Forbes would never come to learn of his cruelty towards her, for she was just as concerned for his safety, as he was for hers.

As soon as Lilybee returned, they set off on their round of sightseeing. It was a beautiful day, and their young host was an excellent guide; there was nothing he did not know about this constantly changing city. They drove along Fifth Avenue to view the Italianate mansions, the French chateaux and the pseudo-gothic castles, where the rich of the city lived in luxurious elegance. He told them that these privileged people were attended by the best physicians, and their servants were carefully instructed to keep the street in front of their houses swept clean. He showed them the commercial streets that were filled with large impressive buildings, modelled in the style of Greek and Roman temples. He explained how everything had had to be re-built after the disastrous fire in 1835. Then again in 1845, yet another fire had destroyed most of the financial district, and tragically some of the last Dutch commercial buildings were lost at that time. The ladies were deeply impressed to see the new Trinity Church that had been magnificently re-built in 1839, after having been burned in the fire four years earlier. It had been the very first building in the city to use a brownstone facade, and the use of this material had now become widespread.

They went along the Bowery and saw the Bowery Theatre and the Park Theatre. Wealthy New Yorkers were fascinated by the Italian operas at the Park Theatre, and the Grand Opera House also catered for those who were acquiring a new taste for serious music. There was a whole world here of popular entertainments; theatres, circuses and exhibitions, all centred on the Bowery. The two women were shocked to hear that just prior to their arrival, the Astor Place Opera, where the English tragedian William Macready was playing, was the focus of resentment on the Bowery, because of the sycophancy of the city's elites before all things English. On the night of May 10th, a throng of people flooded the Bowery and tried to force their way into the theatre. To disperse them, the militia fired into the crowd, killing twenty-two people. Lilybee and Celia were amazed at Ian's knowledge; he even explained to them how the dam had been constructed in 1837, with aqueducts, tunnels and piping, and reservoirs that would provide water to the city.

All in all, they agreed that they had spent a most fascinating afternoon, and returned to the hotel at the end of it, in time to take tea.

Before he took his leave of them, Ian asked how much longer they intended to stay in New York, and when they told him that they should not be leaving for another two or three days, he asked if they would once again do him the honour of accompanying him to the opera before they departed. He suggested that it would make a most memorable and fitting end to their visit. Of course, they were both overwhelmed and delighted to accept his invitation, and he promised that he would take them to The Opera House, which had been built in 1833 and was renowned for its luxurious decorations in gold, red and blue, with wall to wall carpeting. How Celia wished that these days with Ian Forbes would never come to an end. She realised now how much she loved him, and she knew that she would treasure these memories always.

For Celia, there were to be two tearful farewells; the first from Ian Forbes when she and Lilybee left New York, and the second from her dear sister-in-law a few days after they had returned to 'Fortune's Hand', but they both agreed that they had had a marvellous holiday, which was made all the more enjoyable by their encounter with Celia's friend.

Unknown to Celia, he had asked Lilybee, shortly before their departure, if he might be permitted to write to her from time to time, in order to learn how Celia was and what was happening in her life.

The older woman told him that she would be more than happy to keep in touch, for she considered him to be kind and considerate, and an admirable gentleman in every respect. He had given her the address of his bank in New York, where she could be sure that her letters would be kept safely for him, should he be travelling abroad on business.

Lilybee, in turn, very graciously invited him to pay her and Percy a visit at 'White Lakes', if ever he should desire to travel to the South.

"Who knows... maybe one day I shall have the opportunity to take you up on that very generous invitation, madam," he had replied. "I thank you most kindly for it, and I shall certainly keep it in mind."

Over the following months, there were many times when they each sat and mused over their unexpected meeting with one another in New York, and of how fate had accidentally brought them together.

It was surely meant to be, decided Celia, for she had so often wondered what Ian Forbes had felt upon discovering the tragic events that had taken place at his storehouse during his absence. Now she felt at peace in her mind, although the same could not be said for her heart. She had always been extremely fond of their benefactor, from the moment he had taken her and her family under his wing, but it had been an innocent, childlike affection on her part, engendered by his infinite kindness to them all. Now she was three years older than when last she had seen him, and she had grown up, matured very quickly in those three years. She had lost both her sister and her father; she had been married and had borne two children; she had suffered untold cruelty at the hands of her despicable husband. In fact, she could scarcely believe that so much had happened to her in such a brief space of time. It was almost as though she had lived a whole lifetime, so tragic had her circumstances been. But now she knew what it was to love someone deeply, and her heart was full of the beauty of it, for that was how she loved Ian Forbes, to the very depths of her soul, so that the joy of it made her heart ache to be with him. That was how it would always be, she knew it. She would love him until the day she died.

He too realised that he could never love another the way he loved Celia O'Malley. She had stolen his heart from the very first moment he had set eyes upon her; from the moment he had first seen her on that treacherous voyage from Ireland. She filled his heart and his mind, and he had dreamed of her constantly, of what it would be like to have her as his wife. But his yearning had never reached the depths that it now reached, since he had seen her as a grown woman. He was completely captivated by her beauty, and wondered how he would be able to endure living without her, especially with the realisation that she was bound in marriage to the most vile of men. He had never ever stopped loving her, and he knew that he never would.

Lilybee too was touched by the sadness of their predicament, for she had never seen two people more destined for one another. She wished with all her heart that there was something she could do to help them, but she knew it was impossible. She also knew that she must keep in touch with this fine young man at all costs. The very fact that he had spoken to her confidentially about her sister-in-law, endeared him to her, for he had fully realised that it would be improper for him to liaise with Celia in her married state. Lilybee respected his concern for the girl she knew he had loved for a very long time; his behaviour was most commendable, particularly as he was so young. She guessed that he could not be more than twenty-five or twenty-six years old, and unbeknown to her, she had guessed correctly, for he was to be twenty-six on his very next birthday.

Ten

Celia was sitting in the shade of the trees, busily embroidering a new baby garment. She looked up and smiled, she could hear Edmund and Rosalind laughing happily, as they played with the young nursemaid, Minnie, down at the water's edge. She could hardly believe how quickly they were both growing up; Edmund's fifth birthday was just one week away, and Rosalind had turned four in February. Except for the occasions when her husband decided to return home, life at 'Fortune's Hand' was pleasant and peaceful. She loved her son and daughter dearly and happily devoted her time to their upbringing. She had become resigned to the fact that she was not to be blessed with any more children, for she had suffered two further miscarriages since that fateful New Year's Eve party in 1849, but now, three years later, miraculously it seemed, she was heavy with child once again. For the first time, she had managed to carry her unborn baby a full nine months. Her health had been reasonably good, and she had taken the doctor's advice and rested as much as possible. Now everyone in the household was looking forward to the birth with eager anticipation, wondering whether there would be a brother or sister for Edmund and Rosalind.

When the children had grown tired of playing down by the river, Celia decided to take them back to the house, as the sun was now high overhead, and the heat had become oppressive. She called to Minnie to bring them to her and they all walked back together, to make ready for their noonday meal. As she climbed with them up the steep wooded slope, Celia began to feel unwell; she started to perspire heavily, and her head was throbbing. By the time they reached the kitchen, she felt too sick to join the children for their meal; instead she retired to her bedroom to take a rest, believing that possibly she had been out for too long in the heat of the day. Beulah was there immediately, fussing over her in her usual loving way, for she was sure that the time had come for her mistress to birth her new baby.

"I knowed... I jus' knowed you shouldna gone down to that river this mornin'... no sir... not in this heat. I don', know what you was a thinkin' of... you knows you supposed to rest up like the doctor say."

"Oh, Beulah, I' m perfectly all right... stop your fussing. I'll be fine if I just rest for a while." Now Celia too was beginning to feel a little apprehensive.

"You sure ain't no perfectly all right," said Beulah, tut-tutting. "Just look at you... them clothes is all wringing wet." She went on scolding her mistress kindly. "Why you have to go sitting down there in all this heat? I jus' knowed somethin' like this'd happen. We best git that doctor man out to you straight away. There sure ain't no sense calling him when it too late now, is there?"

Celia had to agree with her, because she could already feel her contractions starting.

Jassy went to find Joshua, and sent him off to fetch the doctor immediately, because from past experience she realised that the baby would come very quickly once the mistress's pains had started. However, to the amazement of everyone, that was not so on this occasion, for the baby was going to struggle and strive for hour after hour in its relentless efforts to enter the world, and Celia too was to be forced to fight a long painful battle in her attempts to bring about the birth of her third child. The doctor stayed with her from noon that day, then on through the long night hours; and the ordeal was to continue right through the following morning and into the afternoon, before mother and baby could finally cease their efforts and collapse in exhaustion. Indeed, the doctor had never before witnessed such a gruelling delivery, when both mother and new-born infant had survived.

Jassy was to be the one to carry the long awaited news downstairs to the kitchen. She did not burst in joyfully, as she had hoped to do, but instead she opened the door quietly, and leant back against it as it closed. Everyone turned in her direction, anxious to hear that the mistress they all loved so much, had finally given birth to a strong healthy child, after so many heart-breaking disappointments. Nobody spoke, for Jassy's eyes had grown so enormous that they seemed to fill her face. "We has another baby girl," she said softly.

"Well... there ain't nothin' wrong with that," said Joshua. "Even though we's a bit short of the men now." He grinned and glanced at the other servants, who were still staring at Jassy.

"Is there something wrong... don't it look like she gonna live Jassy?" asked Maybelle.

Jassy walked to the table and fell heavily onto a chair. "I think she gonna live all right," she said sadly, "but I ain't so sure that a good thing." She hung her head and shook it slowly from side to side. "There somethin' mighty wrong with that baby... I ain't never seen nothin' like that before."

*

The doctor was sitting on the side of the bed looking at Celia, as she cuddled her new infant lovingly in her arms. She had endured an extremely difficult and painful birth, that had gone on for far too many hours, so he had not been in the least surprised when the baby was found to be brain damaged upon its delivery. At times he had even feared for the mother's life, so prolonged and agonizing had her ordeal proved to be. He realized that the child had grown far too big prior to its birth, and its head was very large, strangely out of proportion to its body.

"I am so sorry. These things happen, my dear," he said sadly, "and we have no explanation for it. Now you try to get some rest, and I'll call to see you tomorrow."

"Thank you doctor," Celia answered quietly, "but there is no need for you to apologize. So often in life things happen for which there seems to be no explanation. This child was born for me to love, and I shall love her, come what may. I had the strangest feeling of peace and contentment the whole time that I was carrying her, and I still feel at peace as I hold her now. To others, I know, she might never appear to be one of God's greatest gifts, but she is his gift to me and I am very thankful to have her."

She lifted the tiny hand to her lips and kissed it gently, then brushed it softly against her cheek. The doctor patted her shoulder and stood up. "You are a remarkably beautiful woman, Celia Hetherington," he said. "Beautiful in every sense of the word. Now you get some rest."

He turned away abruptly and strode quickly from the room, fearful that his patient might see the tears that were welling up in his eyes. Of that he need have had no fear, for Celia was already drifting off into a peaceful sleep, completely exhausted from her endless hours of wakefulness. It was those around her who were troubled, those who loved her most, but in time they too would come to realise just how special was the joy that this newest member of the household would bring them.

*

Celia's eyes were riveted upon her husband as he leant over the cradle and looked at his new born child. He had returned home just two days before Edmund's birthday, to give him the wooden rocking horse that he had bought him for a gift. His body stiffened, and the expression on his face, as he shuddered and turned away, would always remain imprinted in Celia's mind.

"Why did it have to live?" he growled callously. "What are we expected to do with it?"

Celia's revulsion for this man was far greater than any he could be experiencing for the tiny helpless infant whom he was so cruelly rejecting. Her opinion of him could sink no lower. In that moment, she felt an upsurge of inner strength, a rugged determination; she discovered an iron will that would protect her and her tragically handicapped infant from anything that might present a threat to either of them throughout the years to come. She stood up and gently lifted her from the cradle; she kissed her face lovingly and hugged her tiny form closely against her own; the need to protect her from her father's evil presence was overwhelming.

"Oh, no..." he gasped. "How can you bear to touch it, let alone place your lips upon it? What are you thinking of madam?"

Celia turned on him, her eyes blazing. "How can you be so cruel?" she demanded. "She is your daughter, your own flesh and blood. She did not ask to be born into this world, but now that she is here, let us at least care for her and show her our love and kindness in every way that we can. God knows, she will need it."

It was obvious that her outburst had shocked him. She had never before spoken to him so vehemently. She was like a tigress, courageously protecting its young.

"Daughter... daughter, you say? It's no daughter of mine, and I'll have nothing to do with it... nothing whatsoever, do you hear? It's enough that you have taken leave of your senses, but don't expect me to take part in your madness." He glared at her. "Maybe that's it," he paused, turning a thought over in his mind. "Who knows what monstrosities the peasant classes are capable of producing? But I never want to lay eyes upon it again. I'll have nothing to do with it. You do what you like madam, but keep it out of my sight."

He left early the next morning, not bothering to wait just one more day to wish Edmund a happy fifth birthday, but it mattered not to his young son, nor to anyone else, that the master of the house found it impossible to remain in his own home. They were only too relieved at his departure, for then the atmosphere returned to normality once again.

*

Celia recovered slowly from her confinement, and in so doing found a deep contentment and happiness in the rearing of her baby daughter; something of which she had never had the privilege hitherto, for she no longer needed to lie in fear of her husband's unwanted attentions whenever he returned home. In fact, his unseemly assaults upon her had ceased shortly after it had become apparent that she was once again with child. He had left her in peace for the past eight months, which she found rather mysterious, after having been made to endure his violent attacks since first they were wed. She decided that he had probably found some other place where he could assuage his desires; she had heard tell of their existence, but she had no wish to sully her thoughts with such things. She knew only that now her suffering at his hands had come to an end, and for that she was grateful.

*

Of all the servants, it was Jassy who had been the most shocked and distressed when first she had seen the mistress's new baby, but it was she who became most attached to her as she began to grow. Celia had named her Esther. She was overjoyed that for this her third child, she could choose a name herself, as her husband wanted nothing to do with her. It was a Biblical name that she had always found particularly pleasing, and she chose it for that simple reason. The baby grew robust and strong, seeming never to suffer from the minor ailments that had afflicted her brother and sister in their infancy. She was a placid, affectionate child, and was dearly loved by everyone for the happiness that she brought into their daily lives.

*

Although there was never to be another child for Celia, 'Fortune's Hand' was blessed with two more offspring in the year immediately following Esther's birth, for Maybelle and Delilah each joyfully bore a child, much to the delight of a very proud Kingston. He had never been able to make up his mind which of the two young women he preferred, for Delilah had stolen his heart with her provocative good looks, but at the same time, he simply could not resist Maybelle with her delightfully sunny nature. Fortunately for Kingston, the two women remained the best of friends, and were quite content to share his affection. The arrangement seemed to work perfectly well, much to everybody's amusement, and Delilah's son, Tobias, was born just ten days before Maybelle's daughter Bella. The two lusty, healthy babes could well have been taken for twins, as they both so strongly resembled their father Kingston, with his blue-black skin and enormous expressive eyes. As they grew, they became ideal playmates for the young Esther, and all three spent many happy hours together.

So the years drifted by, and life was good for them all. Celia was occasionally called upon to adopt the role of hostess, whenever her husband decided to return home and throw a dinner party, or entertain his business associates, but other than that, she had very little contact with him. She derived tremendous pleasure from her correspondence with her sister-in-law Lilybee, and the two of them wrote at great length to one another of all the fascinating and new changes that were taking place around them.

Eleven

The Industrial Revolution continued to gain momentum, and every part of the country, both North and South, was affected by the influences of expanding industry. Celia told Lilybee how the immigrants were continuing to pour in, and of how they were now settling, for the most part, where the industrial development was concentrated; in New England, New York, Pennsylvania and the growing cities of the mid-west. The development of roads, canals and railroads made it much easier for them to travel further afield, to where they knew they could find employment; consequently, the majority of them remained up in the North. Lilybee, on the other hand, wrote of how the wealth of the South was increasing beyond all expectation. Throughout the 1850s, 'Cotton was King', and almost four million slaves now lived and worked in the cotton belt, which covered a vast area stretching southward from Maryland and the Ohio River, right down to the Gulf of Mexico. The states of Louisiana, Arkansas and Texas were also now included in this enormous cotton growing region. But, apart from the endless acres of cotton fields, many other staple crops such as tobacco, rice and sugar cane had also been introduced. Southerners received most of their income from these crops, and they were mainly grown on large plantations such as 'White Lakes'.

Lilybee was proud indeed to point out how important her beloved cotton was, not only to America itself, but also to Great Britain, whose cotton mills entirely depended upon it; to Europe, and to many other countries throughout the world. In fact, she went on to boast, and quite rightly so, that the cotton grown, shipped and sold by the Southerners, was worth more than all the rest of American exports put together.

"What other product, grown by man," she asked, "and fashioned into such a wide variety of finished articles, affects so many people in so many different parts of the world? The answer is none," she stated categorically.

It was evident to Celia that, without doubt, the slave owners were the wealthiest, the best educated and the most influential men in the South. These same men, and their wives and families, created a way of living that was vastly different from that in any other part of America.

Tragically, and unknown to these two women, as exciting as these differing developments in the North and the South appeared to be, they were at the same time insidiously creating the most serious problems between them; problems that were eventually to bring about the most devastatingly horrific war that was ever to rage across their vast land. Men hoped and prayed that the storm over slavery would subside, that somehow compromise would be achieved, but unfortunately their prayers were not to be answered. The South's isolation was growing; their interaction with the Northern States was fast diminishing. Even their churches, in particular the Baptists and Methodists, broke away from their Northern counterparts in anger.

Lilybee was alarmed at the militant attitude that was developing in the South towards the North. The mood of the majority of the menfolk was that they should go into battle. Southerners were renowned for their fighting spirit, and it was a reputation of which they were very proud. Talk of war was commonplace, and the Northerners were becoming incensed by what they considered to be the South's arrogant actions.

The South constantly attacked the Northern way of life. They defended their system of slavery by extolling its virtues; by comparing it with the pitiful conditions of many of the white immigrants who struggled for survival in the cities of the North. Slaves were much better off, they insisted, than many of the poor immigrants, who worked for a pittance in the North, and who were hired to work only if they were fit and healthy, being ignored when they became sick or too old to work. Slaves, on the other hand, were taken care of from birth until their death, by their owners.

*

Although it appeared that the slavery issue had abated somewhat after the Compromise of 1850, which had been carefully formulated by Senator Henry Clay, there was still bitter argument between the North and South, who both believed that they had been seriously mistreated. So the dissension grew, until that fateful day, the 12th April, 1861, when at 4:30am, General Beauregard directed his Confederate gunners to open fire on Fort Sumter, which lay out in the harbour at Charleston. That bombardment set in motion the most bitter of conflicts, whose chilling battles would be savagely fought in the hills and on the plains, in the towns and villages, spilling the blood of America's sons and fathers, and leaving a shameful stain that the tears of their womenfolk could never wash away.

*

For several years, Lilybee had been toying with the idea of paying Celia a visit, to see the children before they were too grown up, but somehow she had never quite managed to find time enough to make the long journey North. Possibly, it was because she had been anxious for Percy to accompany her on this occasion, but the duties of the plantation kept him constantly occupied, so that the opportunity for him to leave never seemed to occur. The years had simply flown by and now, of course, it was completely impossible to contemplate.

The two women still found it difficult to believe that the country was at war, and whilst Celia wrote to Lilybee of her relief that Edmund was far too young to be called into the Union army, to fight for the North, Lilybee poured out her heartfelt concern for her dear Percy, who had rallied to the call and gone to join General Lee in his battle for the South.

Nobody thought that the war would last for very long, and it was generally assumed that the South would be the victors. Even Europeans could not envisage the inept North claiming a victory.

The South considered them too cowardly to fight for a great cause, without the inducement of financial reward, and the Europeans believed that the South was too large for them to defeat. Two wars in this vast country had already proven that it was impossible to defeat a widely scattered population, and in addition to that, the South had only to defend its territory, whereas the North had to fight and conquer its foe before it could lay claim to victory.

After the fall of Fort Sumter, President Lincoln urgently called for volunteers to join the army and to serve for just three months. He desperately needed to reinforce his regular army, which numbered only 17,000 men. The response was overwhelming; millions of Americans throughout the Northern Union answered the call with touching patriotism, and among that number were thousands of men, young and old, from New Jersey. As everyone was convinced that the war would be over in a month, it seemed exciting, exhilarating, to answer the bugle's call, and march to the beat of the drums. However, after the first serious battle at Bull Run in Northern Virginia, between General McDowell and his thirty thousand troops, who fought against the South's General Beauregard, with his force of twenty-four thousand, it became abundantly clear to the North that they had embarked upon a long and gravely serious war. They fled back to Washington DC in confusion, whilst the Confederates celebrated their resounding victory.

Still neither side fully realised what this bitter futile war was to cost them, for in many States, particularly those on the borders, families were torn apart, some members supporting the North, whilst others were steadfastly for the South.

Even President Lincoln's own wife had three brothers who fought and died for the Confederate army in the South; and Robert E. Lee's nephew commanded the Union naval forces on the James River in Virginia, when at the same time his famous uncle was fighting the Union army but a few miles away. These family divisions, and the tearing apart of lifelong friendships, were but a very small part of all the tragedy that was to be brought about by this war.

People were shocked and horrified at the reports of the suffering of their loved ones on the battlefields. Their conditions were appalling, and far more died from hunger and disease than were ever killed in battle.

*

The women were magnificent in their efforts to do whatever they could for the poor desolate troops. They did knitting and sewing, and wrapped parcels of home-made foods, to bring them cheer as well as sustenance, and many were the tales of their bravery in their endeavours to assist their menfolk. One woman in particular, was Clara Barton, who stood barely five feet tall, and was unmarried. She began her war work among homesick troops from her native Massachusetts, by collecting and distributing brandy and tobacco; lemons; soap; sewing kits and home-made preserves. Then, when she heard of the thousands who were left wounded and dying at Bull Run, she realised that her place was in the battlefield itself. So she followed the troops, wherever their battles might take them. She cooked over open fires for the sick; she dressed their wounds, and was even known to dig bullets out of flesh with her penknife. She ably ministered to the wounded and the dying at Cedar Mountain, Second Bull Run, Chantilly, South Mountain, and at Antietam, where, when rebel artillery seemed sure to hit the field hospital, and all the male surgical assistants scurried for cover, she stood her ground and held the rolling operating table steady, so that the surgeon could complete his work. This gentleman afterwards wrote of Clara Barton's valour to his wife, and called her a true heroine of the age, the 'Angel of the Battlefield'. So she became known, and women everywhere revered the name.

Reports of such exploits appeared daily in the New York Tribune, for war correspondents travelled with the regiments and sent sensational photographs and stories back to Horace Greeley, the Editor, for publication.

Twelve

The war had been raging now for two whole years, and the horrors of it all made Celia's blood run cold. She and her friends in the Sewing Circle were still organizing rallies to raise funds for the poor fighting boys, and continually sending home-made provisions, in order to reassure them that they were not forgotten by their loved ones and friends. Despite the fact that many families in Asbury had to bear the grief of parting from their menfolk, when they joined the Union army, and Celia knew that several of her closest friends had made the heart-breaking sacrifice, she was deeply thankful that her own son had remained at home, for she knew that she could never have borne to see him go.

Then, one beautiful spring afternoon, her worst nightmare was realised. Her husband returned from one of his mysterious business trips, to announce that President Lincoln was calling for a further three thousand troops to replenish his Union army. As the volunteering had fallen off so dramatically, the Government was being forced to enact a conscription law, in order to acquire the additional men that were so desperately needed. They should be between twenty and forty-five years of age, and were to serve for a term of three years. Gilbert Hetherington was greatly perturbed, for his forty-fifth birthday was still a few months away. He paced back and forth across the terrace, where Celia sat rolling bandages with the help of Rosalind and Jassy. She often wondered at the constant demand for these bandages and dressings that were packed and sent off; so many, that she had long since ceased to keep account of them.

"Of course, I can't possibly go into the army, not now… I'm far too busy with keeping up their supplies. What would happen to my business if I should be called away?"

Celia guessed at the kind of business in which he was likely to be involved; most certainly it would not benefit anyone as much as it would benefit him. Her heart lurched as he went on, "But where is Edmund, I'd like a word with him?"

What could he possibly want with her son? Even as the question arose in her mind, she had the gravest misgivings, but she hoped and prayed that she might be wrong.

"He is down by the river I believe… but why do you ask?"

He ignored her question and hurried off in search of the boy.

Edmund was sitting on a fallen tree, sketching, when his father approached him. "Oh, there you are, your mother told me that I might find you here."

He stood looking down at the drawing of some Canadian geese that lay on Edmund's lap. "Is that all you can find to do with your time boy?" he demanded.

"I have finished all my school work, sir, and Mama told me that I could spend a little time on my sketching."

"Well now, I think we should find something more worthwhile for you to do, now that you're so grown up. Did you know that President Lincoln is desperately calling for more soldiers? What do you say to joining a regiment? It will do you good to get away from your mother's apron strings…

make a man of you. Now you give it some thought, and tomorrow I'll take you down to sign on."

The boy could not look at his father as he turned and strode away. He sat for a very long time gazing into the gently flowing river, and wondering how he could bear to leave the peace and serenity of this place he loved so much.

He could hardly sleep that night. Every time he closed his eyes, he could see his mother's tear-stained face, and hear her pitifully pleading with his father, but he knew that in the morning, he must bid her and his sisters farewell, for his father was determined to send him to the war.

*

The whole household shared in Celia's grief, after she was forced to part with her son. Jassy and Beulah loved all her children as though they were their own; for had they not been involved with the births of each of them? They were just as horrified as their beloved mistress, that their master could inflict such a dire punishment upon so young a boy, for punishment it would most surely be. No one was in any doubt of what misery and hardship the troops had to endure, and it was blatantly obvious that Edmund had been sacrificed as an act of bravado, to cover his father's cowardice. There was a special exemption for any man who did not want to serve his country; he could either pay a 'commutation fee' of $300, or find a substitute to serve in his place. At last Gilbert Hetherington had found a use for his only son.

Edmund wrote to his mother twice during the first few weeks of his military training; brief letters in forming her that he was well and would soon be sent to join the troops in battle. Celia could sense his sadness, and she was heartbroken, hardly able to bear the thought that he could be wounded or killed, and she might never see him again. The battlefield was no place for any sixteen-year-old boy, she thought sadly, nor for any of the courageous men who had so valiantly answered the call to arms. Her tears fell yet again, as she recalled a passage that had been reported the year before, during the Seven Days' War for Richmond; that bloody, bitter week of fighting in which it was said that at least fifteen thousand bleeding men were carried into Richmond, where every house had been opened to take the wounded. Both sides had also suffered thousands of deaths, yet on the 4th July, Independence Day, one Southern private had written:

"There are blackberries in the fields, so our boys and the Yanks made a bargain not to fire at each other, and went out in the field, and gathered berries together and talked over the fight, and traded tobacco and coffee and newspapers as peacefully and kindly as if they had not been engaged for seven days in butchering one another."

Would it ever be possible for anyone to fathom the madness of war? she wondered; or begin to understand what drove men along the path of self-destruction?

Celia received no further communication from her son, but she prayed with all her might that he would be returned home safely to his family.

Everyone tried to reassure her that, of course, he must be alive and well, although she had had no word of his whereabouts, and she knew, for it was common knowledge, that the deliveries of mail were very unreliable. All she could do was wait patiently, and try not to give up hope, but this she found to be exceedingly difficult, when so many wives and mothers in Asbury had received notification that their men folk had been killed in battle.

Altogether, one hundred and two militia, both cavalry and infantry, had gone to fight in the Union army from the small town of Asbury, but only twenty-nine of them were ever to return. This took an enormously heavy toll of the sparse population. Even Doctor Robert Brown, who had practised in the town for some fifteen years, since 1846, had volunteered in 1861, realising how desperately he would be needed to tend to the sick and wounded on the battlefields.

*

Very gradually, the tide turned in favour of the North, and the battles at Gettysburg, Vicksburg, and Chattanooga were proclaimed as resounding victories. The army of the North grew in strength and numbers, whilst that of the South diminished and grew weak from hunger, until it was no longer able to continue the fight. Then came the final hour; with his army dwindling, and the South without enough food to feed its starving people, General Lee was forced to surrender.

In Appomattox, on Sunday, 9th July 1865, General Lee went to meet General Grant, in the front parlour of a civilian house that belonged to a Mr Wilmer McLean. There the two men, who had once fought on the same side in the Mexican war, sat down to sign the articles of surrender. General Grant provided food rations to feed General Lee's starving troops, and the two men shook hands. The war was over.

At twelve noon, five days later, Major Robert Anderson stood at the foot of the flagpole in Fort Sumter, ready to haul up the same ragged banner that he had been forced to lower, when the first shots had been fired in 1861. The war that had wrought such destruction, and would never ever be forgotten, had lasted exactly four years.

The killing was not yet over, however, for that same day, Good Friday, President Lincoln was shot through the head and killed, whilst he sat watching a play in Ford's Theatre, in Washington. The assassin who fired the pistol shot, John Wilkes Booth, was eventually trapped in a tobacco barn in Virginia, where he himself was shot through the back of the head and killed by an army sergeant.

Once the country had mourned the tragic death of Abraham Lincoln, Andrew Johnson was duly elected to take his place. Then came the job of re-building all that had been destroyed during the war years.

*

The relief shared by everyone throughout the country, both North and South, that peace had at last been restored, was greatly overshadowed by the sorrow of those whose hearts would always ache for their loved ones who were never to return. Celia was among those who mourned, for apart from one brief official report, stating that her son was missing, 'his whereabouts unknown', she had no knowledge of what had happened to him. She had done everything she could to glean more information, but in the turmoil and chaos of the war, she had never been able to find out whether he was dead or alive. All she knew was that he had been fighting with

127

General Ambrose Burnside's troops at Petersburg, and that thousands had been killed or taken prisoner by the rebels.

When the war ended, she once again began hoping for news of Edmund, but week after week went by without a word. Then, when she had almost come to accept that he was no longer alive, she received a much-crumpled letter from Lilybee, that had been written the year before. It was the first she had received from her sister-in-law for over three years. By some miracle, it had finally found its way to 'Fortune's Hand'. In it she read the words for which she had been yearning since the day he had left. Her son was alive and safe. He had not been killed, as so many other thousands of mothers' sons had. Celia clutched the precious letter to her breast and shouted at the top of her voice, "He is alive he is alive... my son is alive... thank God."

She ran to the kitchen and told the wonderful news to the servants; they all rejoiced together, hugging one another, laughing and crying at the same time. When they had all quietened down, Celia read Lilybee's letter aloud, for every one of the servants knew her sister-in-law as well as she did herself, and she knew that they were deeply interested in any news that ever came from their former home in North Carolina. Lilybee wrote of how Edmund had been seriously injured, and had been brought to her at 'White Lakes' in the summer of 1864, by Mose, Percy's manservant. She was nursing him back to health, and would write again later, to tell of his progress. Then she went on to say that her dear husband, Percy, had been tragically killed in action. It was not a long letter, for which Lilybee begged her forgiveness, but it was all that she could manage to write in her great sorrow. She promised to write again as soon as it became easier to do so. Celia was devastated by the news of dear Percy's death, and her heart went out to Lilybee, for she knew how devoted they were to one another. She sat down immediately and wrote to Lilybee, pouring out her heartfelt gratitude that her son was alive, together with her deepest condolences that Percy had died. She was also longing to know by what miraculous coincidence Mose had encountered her son, for she found it almost beyond belief. She concluded that it was, undoubtedly, a miracle, for how else could it possibly be explained?

A week later yet another letter arrived, and again it had been written the previous year. In it Lilybee gave a much fuller account of all that had happened, and then Celia was horrified to learn of the circumstances in which Percy had lost his life, and also that her young son's leg had been amputated to save his. She received the news with mixed feelings, still hardly able to believe that he was alive, yet shocked and saddened at his tragic plight. At the same time she thanked God that he had not been taken from her for she fully realised how fortunate she was that he had survived.

The two women resumed their correspondence with one another once again, much to their mutual enjoyment, and Celia watched anxiously for every report that came from Lilybee of Edmund's progress. She longed for him to come home, but unfortunately it seemed that he could not face the prospect of meeting his father. Lilybee explained his delicate mental state, which his mother fully understood, particularly as she knew how difficult had been the relationship between father and son. Lilybee also urged that Edmund be allowed time to recover from all that he had suffered during his war service and Celia, in accepting her sound advice, resolved to be patient for a little longer.

Sometimes she felt that she was never to be blessed with peace of mind, for having finally overcome all the sadness and pain that she had endured, not knowing whether her beloved Edmund was alive or dead, she was once again to be tormented by what her husband had so cruelly arranged for the fate of her young daughter Rosalind. He had spoken time and time again of marrying her off to an elderly widower, the most despicable of men, and now he proposed to announce their betrothal at Rosalind's eighteenth birthday party, which was being held in just two days' time, but she was determined that the marriage would never take place... never, never. She simply could not tolerate any more of Gilbert Hetherington's callous manipulation of their children. He had forced their only son into the army when he was still but a child, and he had nearly lost his life; now her daughter was threatening to kill herself rather than marry the hateful man her father had chosen for her. Well, she had had enough... her mind was made up, he must be stopped. She had formulated a plan, but if it failed then she would be compelled to take drastic action. She must remove this monster once and for all. She would end his life, to preserve the lives of her children, for she knew that there was no other way of saving them.

Rosalind 1866

One

Rosalind slammed the heavily carved door behind her and fled up the wide staircase and along the passageway to her bedroom, stumbling in her haste; she could feel the tears pricking the back of her eyes as she burst through the door and flung herself onto the bed in despair, her father's words still ringing in her ears. She felt nauseated at the very thought of what he had said, despite the fact that she had known for almost a full year exactly what this coming night would bring.

She would be eighteen years old tomorrow and there was to be a special dinner party this evening in celebration, to which around thirty guests had been invited. She recalled her pleas and protests to her father and shuddered at what his reaction had been. Her pleading simply angered him more and finally he had dismissed her from the room, bellowing an order that she should go upstairs immediately and make ready for the coming party, without any more of her insolent behaviour.

Her tears now fell unchecked as she raised her head and turned to find the loving black face of Minnie her maid peering intently into her own. The two girls automatically fell into each other's arms and their tears mingled as they wept silently together.

Finally, Minnie pulled away, noticing as she did so that there was no difference in the taste of their salt tears, even though her skin was as dark as Rosalind's was fair. How she loved her mistress, and what would she not give to make her happy, but she was powerless to help her. As she had done so many times in the past, since she had first come to take care of this girl when she was just a baby, she now placed an arm around her shoulders and gently pulled her head down on to her breast, at the same time fondly caressing her copper-red hair and crooning softly to her. They rocked to and fro for several minutes before Rosalind blurted out, "I won't marry that dreadful man. I can't Father can't make me. I'll kill myself first, I will…I will…"

"There, there," crooned Minnie. "Don' you git frettin' like dat Miss Rosalind, it ain't gonna do you no good. You jus' knows your pappy al'us gets what he wants in the end honey-child, so you jus' let Minnie git you all prettied up for dat party. You jus' come on now."

"Oh, Minnie, what am I to do? I would rather die than marry that horrible man, I hate him, I hate him. How can father even think of such a thing? He's so old Minnie, and he has all those children! I can't… I can't…"

Again, Rosalind clung to Minnie and sobbed as though her heart would break. She thought of what her life would be married to Henry Youngman; she thought of the eight children he already had and wondered how many more she would be expected to bear him. She felt the nausea rise up into her throat and clasping her hand across her mouth, she ran into the closet which joined her bedroom to Minnie's and there released the fear and the overwhelming emotion brought about by what her father was forcing her to do. As always, Minnie was at her side and she gently bathed her mistress's forehead and face with a cool damp cloth; she too felt horror and revulsion at the thought of what was lying ahead for her beloved Rosalind.

Gilbert Hetherington was a cruel man who would stop at nothing to gratify his own desires, or further his ambitions. Minnie was well aware of his cruelty, for she had suffered at his hands so many times over the past seventeen years. She had been terrified of him since their first meeting, which was no wonder, for he had torn her from her mother's arms when she was just nine years old and bundled her into the coach which had brought her north from Carolina to this small town in New Jersey. On that occasion too, her mother had sobbed and pleaded with him not to take her little child, but he had struck her across the face with the back of his hand and roughly snatched Minnie as her mother had stumbled on to her knees, burying her face in her hands and crying pitifully.

Too terrified to utter a sound, after witnessing this brutal treatment of her mother, the child was thrown on to the seat of the coach as though she were a mere bundle of clothing. So her new life had begun; she was being taken to the Hetherington household hundreds of miles away from everything that she knew and loved, to become a nursemaid to Gilbert Hetherington's eight months' old daughter Rosalind.

Minnie pushed to the back of her mind the memory of what had happened on that fateful day, as she had forced herself to do for the past seventeen years, for now it was her job to prepare Rosalind for the coming night's ordeal. She knew only too well that punishment would be meted out to her in the dark night hours if her rebellious mistress did not adhere to her father's commands. She busily prepared Rosalind's toilet and pulled out the beautiful dress that she was to wear, together with all the finery that accompanied it. The material was the finest that money could buy, a rich emerald green velvet, which enhanced Rosalind's beauty even more, as she slipped it over her shapely young body. Minnie dressed the vibrant copper-gold hair and lovingly coaxed it into place, then stood back to admire the breath-taking beauty of this vivacious girl; how could she become trapped in a marriage such as the one her father had arranged for her? The very thought of Henry Youngman sent shivers down Minnie's spine, he and Gilbert Hetherington were cast from the same mould.

Like the ripples on a pond, once a stone has been cast in to it, so the misery of Rosalind's plight was to spread throughout the household, enveloping them all. She had brought down the fury of her father upon every one of them, and in particular her mother, for after the heavily carved door of her father's study had slammed shut behind Rosalind, Gilbert Hetherington turned upon his wife, his face purple with rage, "What have you to say to your daughter's behaviour, eh? Have you taught your children nothing of how they should behave and what is expected of them?" He paced angrily back and forth across the room. "How dare that girl take it upon herself to question what I have instructed her to do; and might I ask what you have been doing these past months? You knew full well that I had made an agreement with Henry Youngman long since, that he should have Rosalind's hand in marriage; it was your duty to prepare her for this. I will not tolerate her objections; she is promised to Henry Youngman and that is the end of the matter."

Celia did not lift her eyes from her embroidery, for she knew full well the picture her husband would present at this moment. He simply could not tolerate anyone questioning his decisions, or daring to oppose him. How she despised him and the loathsome arrogance he displayed. She answered him quietly, "I have spoken to her on the subject several times, but Rosalind does not care for Henry Youngman. It is quite understandable Gilbert; he is, after all, old enough to be her father. Have you not thought of how unhappy she would be, forced into such a marriage? Won't you reconsider, for her sake please?"

Gilbert Hetherington swung around abruptly, not able to believe that his normally subservient wife had dared to make such a proposal, especially as she knew for how long he had nurtured the thought of what this alliance would bring. He strode towards the quietly composed figure and leaned menacingly over her; how she infuriated him as she sat steadily pushing and pulling the needle through that wretched piece of cloth. It had long seemed to him that she cared for nothing as much as her precious needlework. Indeed, Celia never failed to enter her husband's study without a piece of handiwork whenever he summoned her, for it provided her with a perfect excuse for not raising her eyes to his. Now he thrust out his hand and snatched it from her in an endeavour to force her to look at him. "How dare you make criticism of what I have spent so much time in trying to arrange," he thundered. "It is time for that girl to be disciplined and made to realise that we all have responsibilities to bear. Hers are to me and she will be made to accept them." Celia kept her head bowed and closed her eyes tightly. 'Responsibilities' he had said; oh how well she realised that everyone had responsibilities; she needed no reminding; look at how seriously she had taken her own and the misery she had endured since she had shouldered them. If only she had known what she now knew; if only she had been older and more experienced, how different her life might have been. Now she thought sadly of the party for Rosalind that very evening. It should have been such a joyous occasion, one of happy celebration, but instead it had been marred by her husband's determination to force their daughter into a totally disagreeable marriage, purely to gratify his own desires, as always.

She now rose slowly from her chair and picked up the embroidery which he had thrown to the floor in his anger, and watchful as ever that her husband was at a safe distance from her, she made for the door. During the years that she had been married to this repulsive man, she had learned how carefully she must tread when his uncontrollable temper had been aroused, and now, whilst her husband was pouring himself a very large measure of his favourite brandy, to help assuage his anger, Celia discreetly slipped out of the room and hurried away to prepare herself to meet their coming guests. She was trembling inside after this latest confrontation, but knew that she must regain her composure before she welcomed the first of them. She had mastered the art of concealment so well, that no-one observing the serenity of this beautiful woman would ever have detected her inner turmoil. On the contrary, everyone admired Celia Hetherington's seemingly calm demeanour, and marvelled at how well she tolerated this insufferable man.

She started to climb the stairs, then suddenly remembered that she should look in upon the servants who had been working from early morning preparing all the delicacies that were to be served that evening. She re-traced her steps and went into the kitchen; it was a hive of activity and a mouth-watering aroma from the variety of delicious dishes filled the air. Celia walked slowly around the large central table where they were laid in readiness, looking at every one of them in turn. "The food looks delicious; you have done really well, all of you," she said. Then she made for the large dining room, where two more maids were busy completing the lavishly impressive table settings.

Her youngest daughter Esther was in there watching the activity, and as soon as she saw her mother at the door, she ran to her with outstretched arms. Celia received her with a warm hug and kissed her several times on the forehead and cheeks. "Are you being a good girl and behaving yourself my darling?" she asked.

The girl nodded her head vigorously, causing a small trickle of saliva to escape from her open mouth. "I helping Jassy," she replied.

"Oh, I see. You do as Jassy tells you then, and don't get in the way, will you?"

Jassy looked around and her face broke into a wide smile. "She ain't makin' no trouble ma'am, we is almost done here now, then I's gonna take Miss Esther upstairs to her room."

"That's fine Jassy. Thank you."

Having thus satisfied herself, Celia once again started up the stairs, thinking as she did so how ironic it was that of her three children, Esther was by far the most fortunate, locked away in her own simple and carefree world, for she knew nothing of the fear and misery that her father engendered in her older brother and sister.

From the moment Gilbert Hetherington had first discovered that his third child would never be normal, he had had an abhorrence of her; for him it was as though she did not exist. She was never allowed in any part of the house that he might use; he had never laid eyes upon her and he never would. It was her birth fourteen years ago that had brought about the final severance of any relationship between her father and mother, and Celia had welcomed this with gratitude, as theirs had never been a loving union from the very beginning, but now she was being forced to witness the same tragic fate befalling Rosalind. She could not bear to think of her daughter suffering the same intolerable existence as she herself had from the moment she agreed to marry Gilbert Hetherington. If only there was something she could do to prevent this disaster. Oh, if she could just think of a way to spare her child this misery.

She gripped the rail at the top of the staircase and leant heavily against it in despair. She bowed her head and prayed silently, "Dear God, please help me to find a solution to this dilemma. Please don't let my child be forced to suffer the same fate that I have please, please."

Would her prayers be answered? She had prayed for the safe return of Edmund, her only son, when his father had banished him into the Union army. "To make a real man of him," as he had said. Her pleas and protestations had been ignored, as always, despite the fact that the boy had barely reached sixteen years of age. Yet her prayers had been answered in that her son had indeed survived the war, but it had almost broken her heart to learn of his near fatal injuries from her sister-in-law Lilybee, after Edmund had been taken to her plantation in North Carolina, soon after he had been injured. Later, she had also learned that one of his legs had been amputated to save his life and oh, how she had longed for him to return home to her at that time, so that she could give him the motherly love and comfort which he so badly needed, but the boy could not endure to face life in his father's house again.

How much more of his destructive manipulation would her children be able to tolerate from their father, thought Celia; and for how long must she be expected to tolerate his unspeakable malice? She could feel within herself a new force awakening; a burning hatred that she could no longer restrain. It was as though all the years of unhappiness and sub-servience, to which she had been subjected at the hands of this man, were erupting inside her and she was powerless to control her actions.

Almost without realising it, Celia had bathed and dressed and was now sitting before the mirror watching her maid brush and comb her hair into the latest style for the coming evening's celebration. She really must take hold of herself she thought; she must not allow herself to become consumed with the hatred she had always felt for Gilbert Hetherington. Lately it was as though it drove all normal thoughts from her mind and she realised that if she did not make every effort to control herself, then the most tragic and disastrous events could be unleashed. Of late she had feared for her sanity, so intense had her loathing of her husband become. She could not stand by and watch him destroy her children's lives as he had destroyed her own.

Throughout the whole time that she was attending to her toilet and making herself ready, Celia's thoughts had been of her three children: dear Edmund, her eldest, Rosalind, less than one year younger and dear little Esther now almost fourteen years old. She loved them all dearly and it saddened her to think of the dreary life they all endured because of the dominance of their father. She leaned towards the mirror and gazed at her reflection, trying hard to concentrate her thoughts on what she was doing. "That will be fine now Beulah. Thank you. Would you just clean up here?"

"Yes 'm...you sho' looks a picture, you sho' does."

"Why, thank you Beulah. Yes, this is a pretty dress, isn't it? I loved the colour just as soon as I saw it, and Mrs Day made it up just beautifully from the pattern I gave her."

Celia stood up and smoothed the skirt of her dress over her thighs, held up her head and pulled back her shoulders, then, with a deep intake of breath, she left her bedroom and descended the stairs in readiness to meet the guests who had been invited to her daughter's party. As she did so, she could hear the first of the carriages arriving and coming to a halt outside the front door; she consciously flicked back her head with the slightest movement and gently smoothed an imaginary stray wisp of hair at her left temple, then assuming a relaxed smile she stepped into the role of perfect hostess, as was expected of her.

It was not long before the whole company was making its way into the beautiful dining room and there were gasps of admiration as the guests surveyed the lavishly set table. Gilbert Hetherington felt fit to burst with pride, and his wife's appearance had not gone unnoticed by him either.

Despite their disastrous relationship, he could still appreciate her undeniable beauty; in fact, it was her comeliness that had made his 'arrangement of convenience' so pleasurable. Now though her youthful attractiveness had been replaced by a rare beauty, and her child-bearing had moulded her figure into softly rounded contours. She looked radiant in the dark wine red dress that she was wearing and her raven-black hair shone like silk in the glow of the candles, which had been lit everywhere. What a pity that her deep blue eyes never once met his own, he thought. Then he remembered why he had orchestrated this evening's hospitality; where was his truculent daughter? That girl had better pay heed to what he had told her earlier in the day; he would not tolerate any nonsense from her that might jeopardise his intended manipulation of Henry Youngman. She was growing more and more difficult to handle; she was a spirited individual, to be sure. If only his son had exhibited half the character that she did, then maybe he could have taken to the boy; but he was like his mother, sensitive and quiet. It never failed to amaze him how little they had in common with one another, despite the fact that they were father and son.

Up in her room, Rosalind realised that she could delay the fateful event no longer. She clutched Minnie's hand. "Come to the top of the stairs with me, please Minnie," she begged. "My legs are trembling so that I fear I shall fall."

The two girls made their way along the passage, Minnie sidling along behind her mistress to give her the comfort she so desperately needed. From the top of the grand staircase, Rosalind could hear that the guests had arrived and her stomach churned once again; she glanced around at her maid for reassurance, then very slowly descended the stairs, making a determined effort to conceal how wretched she was feeling. After all, she thought, Father was only going to announce her betrothal to Henry Youngman this evening and if she could somehow manage to delay the actual date of the proposed wedding, then that would afford her the time she needed to try to persuade her father to change his mind. Failing that, then she vowed silently that she would take drastic steps to free herself from this contract. She knew that she could never marry the man her father had chosen for her; never, never, never!

All eyes were upon her as she entered the dining room, for she was an exceptionally beautiful girl, lithe of body, with a natural exuberance that captivated everyone who met her. Indeed, nobody was more captivated than Henry Youngman had been since the first moment he had set eyes upon her. She had visited his house many times in the past, as she and his eldest daughter, Eunice, had become bosom friends when they had both attended Pine Lodge, the town's elite establishment of learning for young ladies. Since the death of his late wife, Henry Youngman's smouldering desire had burned more intensely, occasionally whipped into flames by the promises of Gilbert Hetherington. Of course, he needed a wife; how could a man of his standing in the community be expected to live his life in solitude? He could not endure the celibate life which had been forced upon him since his wife's death and he was not disposed to partaking of the delights which were so obviously enjoyed by men such as Hetherington. Indeed, he very rarely travelled to the cities where every conceivable form of entertainment could be found. His thriving business occupied much of his time, but at the end of the day, his thoughts were free to wander to the joys of more leisurely pursuits, and those thoughts became more and more enraptured by the delightful Miss Hetherington.

Once the guests were all seated, the servants quickly busied themselves in serving the delicious foods. Celia noticed how fresh and attractive they were looking in their new blue check dresses with the crisp, white frilled aprons and the paler blue cotton squares tied turban-style around their heads. The two menservants carefully pouring the drinks looked equally handsome in their immaculate royal blue livery. It was obvious that those who had been invited to the evening's festivities were suitably impressed with the grandeur of it all. That is exactly what her husband had intended; it was all part of his elaborate scheme to ensnare Henry Youngman. No expense had been spared in his endeavour to convince this prominent and wealthy townsman that Gilbert Hetherington was a man of equal substance. There were oysters and champagne to begin with, followed by tender chickens and fat ducks, pheasants and succulent roasted hogs, all served with the freshest of vegetables. In fact, the gardeners had handpicked the potatoes, turnips and cabbages that very morning from their own kitchen gardens.

Then the cooks had surpassed themselves with their fancy desserts, and the guests murmured their appreciation in turn as they devoured the sweet coffee cakes and fruit cakes, together with light sponges and stewed apple sauce, accompanied by the mellow currant wines, of which the ladies were particularly fond. All this mouth-watering food, washed down with generous measures of good wine, soon had the gathering affably relaxed and chatting animatedly.

The most exciting topic of conversation was, without doubt, that concerning the bank robbery which had taken place earlier in the month on the 14th February, St Valentine's Day to be exact, shortly before two o'clock in the afternoon. Eunice Youngman, Henry Youngman's eldest daughter, was enthralling everyone seated around the table with her graphic account of the daring deed. She had read the full report of it in the 'Tribune' and was repeating almost word for word how a dozen horsemen had ridden into Liberty, Missouri, in broad daylight, all of them wearing long soldiers' overcoats and some with six-shooters strapped outside their coats. Three of the riders had dismounted in the deserted town square, taking up posts from which they could watch the surrounding streets, while the others reined up in front of the Clay County Savings Association. Then two of them had dismounted and stepped into the small bank. Inside a clerk and a cashier were labouring over the accounts at desks behind a wooden counter. The cashier, a Mr Greenock Bird, saw the two strangers stop to warm themselves at the stove. His son William, the clerk, went on writing. Nobody had ever robbed a bank before, not during business hours. It was even more alarming that the raid had been carried out in broad daylight.

The eyes of everyone were on Eunice as she related this absorbing piece of news; everyone, that is, except her father, whose eyes were devouring the guest of honour, Rosalind. She suddenly became aware of him ogling her from across the table and she felt intense revulsion welling up inside her, as it had always done in the past whenever she met him. His lecherous behaviour and unwanted attentions to her had, in fact, marred the friendship that she had long enjoyed with his daughter, Eunice, and as a young girl she had felt uneasy whenever he was in the room with her. There was something about his manner that had made her fearful of him, although as a naive youngster she had not fully realised exactly what it was. Now she realised only too well why she could never bear to be near him, and the realisation made her shudder. He repulsed her in every way. The very thought that she should ever be bound to this man in wedlock was completely abhorrent to her, and it was monstrous of her father to demand that she accept him as her spouse. Once again, she vowed that it would never happen, and she knew that she must take drastic action to prevent such an unimaginable fate befalling her.

The meal was now almost over and Gilbert Hetherington had gauged the moment well. His guests had consumed enough good food and wine by now to put them in the most convivial of spirits. He felt confident that this was the most favourable time for him to play his next card. He stood up unsteadily and toppled against his chair as he raised his freshly filled glass high into the air in an over-exaggerated manner. "May I have your attention ladies and gentlemen?" he said loudly. "This party tonight happens to be a double celebration, as I am pleased to announce, not only my daughter's coming betrothal to Mr Henry Youngman, but also the subsequent merger of our two companies, Youngman's Haulage and the Hetherington Trading Company. I will not deny that I have for a very long time dreamed of such a partnership with Youngman's and with the merging of our two families, what more appropriate time could there be to realise that dream? So, my friends, if you would care to raise your glasses with me, we shall drink a toast to those two most important forthcoming events."

Henry Youngman's face suffused with colour and it did not go unnoticed that he seemed rather taken aback at Gilbert Hetherington's announcement. His obvious embarrassment was not due solely to the fact that he was old enough to be Rosalind Hetherington's father, but more so that her father had so cunningly manipulated him in this way. Over the years, in his business dealings with the man, he had become well aware of just how devious he could be, but to venture this far; he had no right, no right whatsoever. The conversation around the table became excited and congratulations were being proffered on all sides to both men, so that Henry Youngman was forced, albeit unwillingly, to accept them with good grace, but he could not allow Gilbert Hetherington to coerce him in this way; he would have to have a serious discussion with him to establish exactly what had prompted him to make such an outrageous claim. Certainly they had more-or less agreed that upon Rosalind's acceptance of him as her husband, then an arrangement could be entered into which would afford Hetherington a much more beneficial arrangement concerning the transportation of his goods to the docks, a special concession for his bride's family, but a partnership, never! It was a preposterous notion absolutely preposterous! Everyone knew that Hetherington was a gambling man, but this time he had taken things a little too far.

Henry Youngman was not the only one sitting at that table to suffer extreme embarrassment at Gilbert Hetherington's outburst, for his wife could not avoid noticing the volume of alcohol that he had been imbibing throughout the meal, and now his drunken performance was the final humiliation for her. How could he behave so despicably before their guests? She cast a glance towards her daughter and saw how mortified she was by her father's exhibition. Celia was consumed with hatred for him. As it was obvious that everyone had finished eating, she rose and said, "Should we not adjourn now, ladies and gentlemen?" She simply had to remove herself from the proximity of her husband and she was also anxious that the misery she knew Rosalind was suffering should not be prolonged. "Coffee is to be served for you in the study gentlemen; and perhaps the ladies would care to accompany me to the drawing room." So the gathering dispersed, the men to enjoy brandy and cigars with their coffee, and the ladies to indulge in their usual small talk.

There were loud exchanges and guffaws of laughter as the men proceeded into the study; Hetherington, without a doubt, knew how to entertain his guests. Generous measures of brandy were being poured and the finest cigars handed around.

Through the smoke filled atmosphere, like a cat watching a mouse, Henry Youngman was watching Gilbert Hetherington proudly playing the beneficent host. He felt instinctively that this overly generous hospitality was designed purely to impress, not least of all himself, for that was the nature of the man. Others might be taken in by his blatant showmanship, but not he. Hetherington was up to something and Henry Youngman was determined that, before this night was over, he would know exactly what he was scheming. He could hardly concentrate on what those around him were saying, yet normally he would have been the focus of everyone's attention, for he enjoyed nothing more than the cut and thrust of lively debate. He relished constructive argument, which afforded him the opportunity to air his views on the latest market trends and commercial developments. "What have you to say about that eh, Henry?" A firm slap on the back brought his attention back sharply to the topic which was under discussion. "How about this cable that's to be laid under the Atlantic then. Can you believe what it'll mean? No more waiting upon the fastest packet to dock in New York with the news bulletins from Europe. I hear that Horace Greeley of the *New York Tribune* is talking of opening his own European News Bureau in London, the first to be set up by an American newspaper. Just imagine that." George Thompson went on. "Huh, I reckon we'll see another cent on the copy again. We've already had the price of the *Tribune* jumped up from two to three cents during the war, and now with the local reporters getting thirty dollars or more per week, when they were only earning fifteen or twenty prior to the war, it's obvious that the readers will have to foot the bill." As always, when Horace Greeley's name was mentioned, the conversation gathered steam, for since he had founded the *Tribune* in the winter of 1840-41, just about every published issue from the 1830s onwards had been forcefully discussed by him in his own publication. Controversial though he was, he had played a central part in all the major political and social moves of the Civil War period. Firstly, he had been a leading Whig; then a pioneer Socialist; next a co-founder of the Republican Party. Why, he had even been influential in swinging the party's 1860 nomination to Lincoln. He had been a pacifist, then a Civil

War militant, so it needed no more than the mere mention of his name to spark heated exchanges.

Henry Youngman was far too preoccupied with his own personal deliberations to become embroiled in this latest round of argument. He drew slowly on his cigar and swirled his brandy around in the bottom of the hand-blown balloon. "Aw, surely you don't expect to git any sense outa him tonight, George," retorted Cyrus Aitken. "His thoughts ain't likely to be much taken up with politics tonight. More'n likely they's on that lovely gal that he's about to be a-marryin'. Ain't that so Henry?" Cyrus Aitken's homespun humour brought forth raucous laughter from all the men in the room and Henry Youngman's face reddened for the second time that evening.

His host, anxious to ingratiate himself with his future son-in-law and to keep him sweet-tempered for the discussions which he knew would arise after the rest of the company had departed, hastily brought attention to the lateness of the hour. "Come now gentlemen," he said. "How about emptying your glasses and leaving us to discuss the formalities of Henry's betrothal to my daughter? He can well do without your ribaldry at this time of night, and as you can imagine, there are many things that we need to discuss." This had the sobering effect that was desired, and the gathering soon dispersed.

After their appreciative farewells, Gilbert Hetherington returned to the study, where he had left Henry Youngman. He knew that he would have to call into play all his guile and cunning to appease this more than normally astute businessman, but he also knew that he could play his hand with dexterity, because he held a master trump in the form of his beguiling daughter Rosalind. He had been quite taken aback himself by her appearance tonight, he could scarcely believe that she had matured so rapidly, and he had not failed to notice her effect upon Henry Youngman. In fact, he had kept a very watchful eye upon him. Oh yes, he held the master trump all right, of that he had no doubt. He cursed silently to himself as he recalled the unfortunate turn of events that had befallen him recently, and because of his run of bad luck at the gaming tables, he fully realised that he desperately needed this association with Henry Youngman to save him from ruin. He also relied heavily upon his daughter's ability to captivate this wily individual. He hoped that he had not over-estimated just how much the man was in need of another wife, although he felt reasonably confident of his deductions in that direction. After all, Youngman had never been lured to the 'fleshpots' of the cities, as he himself had. How the man resisted the temptation he would never understand. Now he needed to hook, net and land his quarry and to this end he would spare no effort.

"Another brandy, Henry?" he asked in a most conciliatory tone, as he lifted the decanter and refilled his own glass.

"Not for me, I've had enough for tonight. What I would like though, is an explanation of what you think you're about in making such an outrageous announcement during dinner. What's the meaning of it Hetherington? We have never discussed any merger of our two companies. Where did you get such a preposterous notion? I'll have none of it, do you hear me?"

Gilbert Hetherington tipped back his head and drained down the last of his brandy before turning his bloodshot eyes upon Henry Youngman. "Come, come now Henry, surely you didn't think that you were going to get the hand of my young daughter without first making a fair trade with me, did you? Who do you think you're dealing with here? I take it that you have eyes in your head, and if you do, then you'll have noticed just what a beauty she is becoming. She's young and untouched. Now do you think that I'm going to give away a prize like that for nothing; well, do you?"

"All right, all right, yes I'll admit that over a drink or two, I have more than once agreed that if Rosalind would marry me, then you would certainly receive considerable reductions in your tariffs for the cartage of your goods to the city, but that was as far as it went. There has never been any discussion of a partnership. What has led you to think otherwise?"

"Before you get on your high horse, you just think what's at stake here; and tell me what would be so wrong with you and I becoming partners? It makes a whole lot of sense if you will just consider it carefully. Now listen to what I have to say and don't be so hasty. I refuse to believe that you are not aware of what is going on in New York right now. Why, that city is simply booming. If you just took yourself out of this town occasionally, you'd see for yourself all the opportunities to be had. Men have been making fortunes during the years of crisis in the war, but you can't imagine all the changes that are taking place there still. There are new streets appearing; new mansions; new fortunes to be made everywhere, and we could have some of that together Henry. Don't you see? Remember A T Stewart, who made $5 million with his department store in the war year of 1864? Well, he's about to move into his new white marble palace that he has had built for himself on Fifth Avenue. Then there's Pierpoint Morgan, still in his twenties, who has made a fortune in gold speculation and his sales of munitions. And how about Jay Gould, that small foxy looking man? Everyone fears him with his ruthless operations on the stock market. Then Jim Fisk, fat and flamboyant, covered in diamonds; what was he, but an ex-pedlar from Vermont who made a killing out of war contracts and cotton deals across the lines? These men can be seen on any fine Sunday, riding up Fifth Avenue, past all the newly built mansions with their friends and associates. Then they ride through Central Park on the outskirts of the city; it has just been freshly landscaped and everybody of note can be seen riding there in their gleaming carriages, wearing all their finery. Now why don't you come into New York with me on my next trip, to get an idea of what I'm talking about? You should see the avenues north of 42nd Street now. What were once straggling roads, which simply ran off into open country between odd clusters of houses, are now brownstone fronts. They're pushing along into 57th Street and beyond it. My God, there is even talk of a new elevated railway being built to carry fast traffic above the crowded streets. In fact, financing railroads has now become the downtown fever. Don't you want some of that? I do! There'll be no stopping us if we pool our resources."

"There's nothing stopping you Hetherington; you can do exactly what you like, but I'm quite happy with the way my business is flourishing. I have as much as I can handle, and more, right now. As a matter of fact, my young nephew, my sister's boy, is about to arrive from England. He's coming over here to work for me until my own boys are old enough to come in. I'm anxious to see how that young fella shapes up, because I'm not at all sure that he wouldn't make a suitable beau for Eunice. It's high time that she gave some serious thought to settling down. That girl is as wild as an untamed colt. I don't know what they taught those girls at that fancy school they were at. She's got some rare notions in that head of hers. To be quite honest with you Hetherington, I'm just not interested in any of these money-making ventures you're so steamed up about, I'm satisfied with what I've got, and that's the end of the matter."

Gilbert Hetherington was not about to give up. He realised that he now needed to play his hand more skilfully than he had ever done and this was what he enjoyed most. Nothing thrilled him more than the game of chance, the taking of risks, the gamble. He suddenly changed tack. "You haven't had a chance to speak with Rosalind this evening, have you Henry? Let me fetch her in for a few moments before you go." So saying, he was out of the room before the other man could make any response. He hurried along to the drawing room, but all was quiet. "Dammit," he muttered, as he realised that the female guests must already have departed. He poked his head around the open door and saw that Celia was still there. "Where is Rosalind?" he asked.

"She has gone up to her room for the night."

"Get her down here at once. I want her to have a few words with Youngman. Don't just stand there, do as I say and bring her down... now!"

Celia swept past her husband and went up to fetch her daughter. She couldn't believe that he would drag the girl from her bedroom at this hour of the night. She tapped on

155

Rosalind's door and called softly to her as she entered the room. "My dear, are you in a decent state? Your father has asked that you come down to have a word with Mr Youngman before he leaves."

Rosalind had already removed her dress and let down her hair. "I can't Mother, I'm in a state of undress. Whatever is Father thinking of?"

"Please don't argue child, just do as he says. He is in no mood to be disobeyed; it will be better for us all if you just come quickly. Slip on your new robe and pin back your hair; that will be perfectly all right."

Minnie ran to the closet and snatched the frilly garment that Rosalind had just received from her mother for her birthday, she noticed how softly feminine it was as she helped her mistress to put it on. Then she brushed out her hair and pinned it back loosely. Mother and daughter slipped quickly along the passage and down to the library without another word.

As the girl entered the room, Gilbert Hetherington knew that he had won this game. She looked adorable in the cream-coloured silky gown with her hair tumbling around her shoulders soft and golden.

What a master-stroke he had played. He knew that Henry Youngman would not be able to resist her. He took just one look at the man; as always, he was enraptured by her. His legs felt weak as he stepped towards her and took her hand. Lifting it to his lips, he planted a fervent kiss upon it, "You look beautiful my dear, just beautiful." He breathed heavily. Rosalind lowered her eyes demurely, or so it seemed to him, but in truth she could not bear to look upon this fleshy face that was being pushed so close to her own, and she could scarcely control the shudder which was sweeping through her body as her nostrils caught the odour of his breath. It was an odious mixture of decaying teeth and stale cigar smoke, overlaid with brandy. She simply could not tolerate him. "I hope you will excuse me, sir," she whispered inaudibly. "For I feel extremely tired after such an evening of entertainment, and the hour is very late. I was just about to go to my bed, so may I bid you goodnight and retire?"

"Why, of course, you dear girl, you will be feeling quite exhausted by now, but you must promise to pay me a visit in a day or so. There is much that we need to discuss concerning our future together." He had not released Rosalind's hand for one second and again he raised it to his hot sensual lips. Oh, to think that she was soon to be his, he mused. He was nobody's fool and he knew only too well that Hetherington was using his daughter in the most advantageous way possible to cajole him into this merger of their two companies, but he had his desires and he had long desired this delightful creature with her burnished copper hair and confident manner. She had captivated him from the first moment he had laid eyes upon her and now his fervour had reached such a pitch that it tormented him night and day and drove all sane reason from his mind. Whatever the cost, he must have her, of that there was no doubt, none whatsoever.

No sooner had the ladies retired, than Gilbert Hetherington once again pressed Henry Youngman for an agreement on the matter of the partnership. He dared not lose this golden opportunity now that he could see the devastating effect his daughter was having on the man, and in his euphoric state, he would no doubt agree to almost anything that was suggested to him. He approached with outstretched hand.

"Well Henry, shall we seal the bargain here and now dear boy? Anyone can see how fond you are of my girl, now what do you say? I don't give a damn for your contentment with what you already have. Can't you see that you will be needing a far greater fortune to provide for the enlargement of your family once you're wed again. With a young wife like Rosalind, who's to know how many more mouths you'll need to feed? Oh yes, you'll have to increase that fortune of yours, without question."

Hetherington was chuckling heartily and beaming at Henry Youngman, enjoying the coarse intimation of his remarks. The other man needed no lurid description of what his marital state would procure for him; at last his dreams would become reality. The object of his desire would be his, all his. He took the hand that was being proffered to him and shook it enthusiastically.

"All right then, you have my acceptance. You certainly know how to drive a hard bargain, but maybe what you are saying does make sense. Nothing would please me more than to add to my brood and in that case I shall certainly need to increase my personal fortune. Who knows how many more children Rosalind will bear me, as you say, so yes, you're right, now is a most propitious time for me to make extra provision for them." He nodded his head thoughtfully. "Well then Hetherington, now that the matter has been decided, I shall ride into Flemington shortly and have a word with Horace and Wilbur Samuels; they deal with all my legal and business affairs, so I'll get them to draw up the agreement. How does that suit you? Of course, it will all be dependent upon that girl of yours marrying me. That's how our bargain has been agreed and that is how it will be drawn up."

"That will suit me fine Henry; the sooner the better, as far as I am concerned, you know that." So saying, Gilbert Hetherington made a move towards the door and the other man followed, anxious to be away to his bed where he could dream his dreams and pander to his fantasies, happy in the knowledge that they were soon to become reality.

As he saw him off, Gilbert Hetherington rubbed his hands together and smiled gleefully, for he knew now that he would have no difficulty in warding off his creditors, nor in preventing the bank from foreclosing on him. It had been a good night's work, and oh how masterfully he had played his game. He was still not done either. All he now needed was the opportunity, and he could once again turn the tables of good fortune his way. No matter that Lady Luck had not been smiling kindly upon him of late, he could soon recuperate his losses with the benefits that Henry Youngman's alliance would afford him. He was fully confident of that.

Two

Early the following morning Rosalind lay in her bed half awake, her eyes still closed; she had slept fitfully, drifting in and out of dreams that were continually woven around Henry Youngman. Several times in the night she had awoken to find herself weeping. She doubted that she would ever sleep peacefully again. How could she, when her mind was filled with the dreaded thoughts of her betrothal to such a man? Now she stirred sleepily and stretched her limbs. She could hear Minnie moving quietly about the room. Then she heard the silver tray holding her warm coffee being placed on her bedside table. She half opened her eyes, and through the haze of her eyelashes, she could make out the form of her maid bending over her.

"Is you awake Miss Rosalind?" asked Minnie. "Come on now, you sleepy gal. You jus' drink yo' coffee while it still warm. Then I is gonna git you all prettied up to go down to breakfast with yo' mama; she is awaitin' on you downstairs, 'cos today is special, has you forgotten? Happy Birthday Miss Rosalind."

By now Rosalind had raised herself up on to one elbow and was rubbing the sleep from her eyes. Then she held out an arm towards Minnie, who sat down immediately on the edge of the bed and wrapped both her arms around her mistress in a warm embrace. The two girls adored each other, and for as long as she could remember, Rosalind had clung to

160

her nursemaid whenever she was in need of comfort. They hugged one another silently for several seconds.

"Thank you Minnie, but I don't know how happy a birthday I shall have with the thoughts of Henry Youngman filling my head. I can't marry him... and I won't, and that is all there is to it. Oh, what shall I do Minnie? Please help me to find a way out of this dreadful dilemma."

"Now don' you git frettin' yo'self again Miss Rosalind. We'll think of somethin', never you mind. Now come on and git yo'self out of that bed. Yo' mama and sister is a-waitin' on you downstairs, so we ain't got no time for talkin' 'bout that jus' now."

At Minnie's insistence, Rosalind was soon out of bed and dressed and running down the stairs to join her mother and sister in the special celebration breakfast that they were to share together, just the three of them, for her father never joined in the family meals.

"Happy Birthday" rang out as she came into the room and Esther could hardly contain herself with excitement as Celia led her older sister around the table to where there were several small gift packages waiting to be opened. "Oh, Mother, really you shouldn't have," said Rosalind. "You have already given me a beautiful robe."

"They are only small items my dear, to make your birthday breakfast more special. Esther helped me to wrap them for you, and there is a special one from her, perhaps you should open it first."

Rosalind quickly undid the parcel indicated by her mother and found inside a lovely black marten cap. "Oh, how beautiful, thank you Esther," she said, planting a kiss on the younger girl's cheek. "I shall wear it this morning when I go down into town with Minnie. It is just what I need on a cold day like this."

Clapping her hands, Esther jumped up and down. "A hat a hat," she was chanting in her baby-like manner. Rosalind opened her other packages one by one, exclaiming her delight at each of the gifts in turn: lace handkerchiefs, hand-sewn by her mother; some new silk ribbons for her hair; a new pair of fur mittens to match Esther's cap, and some stationery in a fancy box. She hugged her mother fondly.

"Thank you, Mama, they are lovely, every one of them."

"Well, come on now girls, let us eat before the food gets too cold. Your father left a message that you may visit Mrs Day and have a new dress made up, that is his gift for you. He is leaving today for New York on another of his business trips."

"Oh, may I call in to see Mrs Day this morning then Mama? I know she has recently received some new materials and patterns from the city, Yoonie told me last night; she is going to Mrs Day herself this morning, so maybe we shall meet there."

"Of course you should go and see Mrs Day this morning, my dear. Choose something especially pretty for yourself, and I shall hear all about it when you return."

The happy trio enjoyed their breakfast, and as soon as it was over Rosalind and Minnie hurriedly made ready for their outing into town. It was a bitterly cold day, and when they had climbed up into the trap, they snuggled up against each other under the bearskin rug to keep warm. The pony took off at a slow trot and they rolled gently down the lane and on to the iron bridge across the Muscanetcong river leading into Main Street. The river was beginning to freeze along its edges and the naked branches of the trees, which lined its banks, were covered with the silver white rime of the hoar frost which had crept over them in the chill night. "Isn't it beautiful Minnie?" breathed Rosalind, as a small flock of wild geese descended in formation just in front of them and landed in a white rippled spray on the deep blue water. Except for their brief appearance, nothing disturbed the landscape, which looked exactly like a gigantic painting, so vivid were its colours on this clear winter's day; brilliant blue of sky, which was reflected in the wide expanse of the river as it flowed along its course, lined on either side by thick undergrowth and tall trees, whose topmost branches appeared to be etched in charcoal against the skyline. Once across the bridge, the girls passed the Post Office on the right and Smith's Horse Barn on their left. Rosalind knew that her father envied the lucrative business that William Smith and his son had with the farmers of Warren County, for they frequently drove to Ohio with horse, buggy and collie dog, to buy sheep, as many as four to five hundred at a time, which they then drove back overland to their barn to sell.

The Smiths were renowned throughout the area, as they had one of the few businesses of its kind in the whole of the eastern United States. The pony was now trotting along briskly, its breath forming white clouds of vapour on the icy air; past School Street on the left, where Rosalind and her friend Eunice had been taught by Mrs Violet Yates and her daughter, Alice, at Pine Lodge. Finally they drew up outside Mrs Day's dressmaking establishment in the middle of town and the two girls quickly made their way inside, pleased to get out of the cold. Mrs Day greeted them and drew them close to the stove which was throwing out a welcome heat.

No sooner had the seamstress produced her latest catalogue of patterns for Rosalind to see, than Eunice Youngman appeared at the door, much to the delight of her friend.

The two girls chattered excitedly as they thumbed through the patterns and sipped the hot coffee that Mrs Day always supplied to her clientele. Then they spent considerable time in making up their minds over which materials they liked, and how Mrs Day should make up the dresses for them. Their business done, the two girls finally bade farewell to the dressmaker, and as they left Eunice asked Rosalind if she would care to accompany her to her home for a brief visit. The other girl was not too anxious to meet up with her betrothed until it was absolutely necessary, so she declined politely, promising Eunice that she would call upon her within the next few days, as she knew full well that she would not be able to delay the dreaded visit for too much longer.

"Oh yes, do come soon Roz," said Eunice. "My father is leaving for New York tomorrow morning for he is to meet my cousin who is coming from England. His ship is expected shortly after midday and father is anxious to be there, when it docks.   Do come and see me while he is away, then we shall be able to enjoy a nice long chat without interruption."

Rosalind made a mental note that she could visit her friend within the next day or two without fear of a meeting with Henry Youngman, then the two friends went their separate ways.

On the way home, Rosalind recounted to Minnie all the details of the previous night's happenings, and of how her father was using her to coerce Henry Youngman into becoming a business partner with him. "Can you believe that any father could do such a thing to his own daughter, his own flesh and blood?" cried Rosalind.

"Yes 'm, I sho' can, when that father is yours, Miss Rosalind," replied Minnie ruefully. "There ain't nothin' that he wouldn't do to please himself, you always know'd that."

Minnie hated him with a vengeance, the same as everyone else in the household did, but she had even more reason than anyone else for the deep hatred she felt.

Night after night, whenever her master was at home, he would steal into her room, sometimes long after she herself had fallen asleep. His nocturnal visits had started long ago, when she was just an eleven-year-old child, and she could well remember how terrified she had been the first time he had awoken her as he climbed into her bed, reeking of the brandy that he always drank so greedily. As her pitiful cry had emitted from her mouth, he had stifled it by roughly clasping his hand across her small face and pressing her head hard back into the pillow, at the same time whispering his coarse threats into her ear of what would happen to her if she dared to utter another sound.

Afterwards, as he crept stealthily back to his own room to sleep off his drunken stupor, there was no one to love or comfort the small child he had left afraid and alone, as she lay sobbing and trembling, not able to understand what had happened to her, or why. Then, as the years went by, his treatment of her had become more unbearable, as he took his pleasure of her whenever he felt the need to satisfy his unnatural desires. Oh yes, Minnie could believe anything of her cruel master, anything at all.

As the pony and trap drove back through the town, it began to snow, and by the time it reached the impressive gates of 'Fortune's Hand', the enormous soft white flakes were beginning to cover every inch of the dark, lifeless landscape,   and magically transforming it into a winter wonderland. It was obvious that this was to be a really deep fall and the girls hurried into the house as quickly as possible, to warm themselves with the hot soup that they knew would be served for lunch. As soon as they had removed their outerwear, Rosalind went into the dining room to join her mother and sister, Esther, who were already seated at the table, whilst Minnie slipped into the kitchen to take her meal with the other servants. As Rosalind sipped at the piping hot liquid, she regaled her mother and young sister with an account of her trip to the dressmaker and told them of her meeting with her friend Yoonie. Inevitably, the name of Henry Youngman crept into the conversation and Rosalind told her mother of Yoonie's invitation to call whilst her father was away on a trip to New York during the next few days. "It would be pleasant to spend a few uninterrupted hours with Yoonie, Mama, so I think I shall accept her invitation. Certainly I have no desire to meet up with her father, but how shall I avoid it when he returns? He is expecting me to call upon him shortly and I simply cannot bear the thought of it. Oh, what shall I do Mama? I could never marry him, no matter what father says."

"Now listen, my dear child," replied her mother. "I shall do everything in my power to prevent such a disastrous event, never you fear. Just be patient for a while, and don't do or say anything to incur the wrath of your father."

"But he will insist on me marrying as soon as possible; he will force me to it, I know he will. Whatever can I do to dissuade him from making the arrangements with Henry Youngman?" At the very thought of being trapped for the rest of her life with this odious man, the young girl ran fearfully around the table to her mother. She fell on to her knees and laid her head on to her mother's lap, crying, "Oh, I cannot bear it Mama, I just cannot bear it. I shall kill myself first. I mean it. I really shall."

"No you won't, my darling, for I shall never allow your father to sacrifice you in this way. Trust me, I shall find a solution to this dreadful dilemma, never fear. For a start, I shall insist that no plans are made until the winter is over. That is one way in which we can delay the proceedings. Then another is, if you insist that you will not wed without Edmund being in attendance. Your father cannot refuse to allow your brother to be present, and I shall support your request very strongly. We shall both insist upon Edmund coming home for the ceremony. You see, already we have managed to create obstacles for your father to overcome. At least they will afford us more time to think of a way in which we may prevent the whole affair from taking place."

"Oh Mama, you're wonderful, you really are," cried Rosalind. "Do you think that we shall be able to persuade father though? He seems so anxious to be rid of me, and I cannot think why."

"Don't you concern yourself with that my darling, it has always been impossible to fathom out what your father is scheming, but this time he shall not succeed, I swear it."

Rosalind jumped up and flung her arms around her mother's neck, at the same time planting a noisy kiss on her cheek. "Oh Mama, do you really mean it. Do you think that you could make Papa change his mind? I couldn't face life with that dreadful man. It would be the end of me."

Celia nodded her head thoughtfully, for she realised exactly what would become of her young daughter if she did not put a stop to her husband's selfish plans; maybe even more than Rosalind herself did.

Three

The snow continued to fall steadily for the rest of the day and when night closed in, the temperature plummeted, freezing the deep layers into beautiful solid crystal-like formations. By morning, it looked almost as though a giant hand had been laboriously sculpting them throughout the dark night hours. Then, as the sun rose brilliantly in a clear blue sky, it cast its golden rays over every tree and bush, so that their snow-ladened branches glistened and sparkled as though they were encrusted with diamonds. The whole landscape was breath-taking in its splendour as the first welcome light of day caressed its contours.

Henry Youngman had risen early on this glorious morn, and was not in the least perturbed at the prospect of venturing forth upon his journey to New York in such hazardous conditions. He was a man of great determination, and having once decided that he would meet his nephew when his ship docked, then, come what may, nothing would prevent him from so doing. He was just finishing his breakfast as his eldest daughter, Eunice, came into the dining room with the two youngest boys, nine-year-old William and six-year-old George. Their father noisily drank down the last of his coffee and wiped his thick moustache vigorously with his table napkin. "Now you children, behave yourselves while I am away and do as your sister tells you," he commanded, as he rose from the table. "I shall see if I can find something for you in New York, but only if you are good."

Eunice stepped towards her father and gently brushed some stray crumbs from the lapels of his jacket. "You know I shall take good care of us all while you're away, Papa. Have a good trip and mind the roads in this snow. Do you think you will be able to get all the way into New York today? The snow looks very deep."

"I'll manage perfectly well, don't you worry my girl I want to be there to meet your cousin when the ship docks. I had intended to go all the way by road, but in these conditions I think it might be advisable to take the train from Ludlow. They do try to keep the line clear, so I'm sure everything will be fine. Good-bye now."

Henry Youngman left the room just as the twins, fifteen-year-old Charlotte and Edward, arrived downstairs for their breakfast. "I'm just off, do as your sister tells you," he repeated again.

"Oh Papa, we will. You know that," they chanted in unison, jostling one another playfully as they made their way to the dining table.

They were beautiful children, with silver-blonde hair and deep blue eyes; they took after their mother, there was no doubt of it. The last to arrive were Susannah, almost twelve, Emily, thirteen and Lydia sixteen; then all eight children began their breakfast. They laughed and chatted together as they ate and talked of what fun they would have in the snow after school. Despite the rigours of the New Jersey winters, it was impossible for them to resist its magical allure. Eunice watched them all carefully from where she sat at the bottom end of the long table, making sure that they all partook of a good meal. She gently cajoled and coaxed little George to eat some more of his food, as it was such a cold day. He had always been a small weakly child and seemed forever to be suffering from some ailment or other. Even though Eunice had not yet reached her eighteenth birthday, she lovingly shouldered the responsibility of motherhood for her brothers and sisters, and had done since the demise of their poor mother. In fact, the burden of that particular role had been forced upon her when George, the youngest, was little more than a year old, for their mother had died on Christmas morning five years ago, painfully trying to give birth to her ninth child. Eunice was just twelve years old when their mother had been so suddenly taken from them, and she had desperately clung to her mother's hand as she drifted into unconsciousness, but not before fervently imploring her eldest child to love and foster her younger brothers and sisters. This heartfelt plea had had a profound effect upon Eunice and she had loved and fostered her family to the very best of her ability. Despite the fact that she herself was only a child, the younger ones had always clung to her for whatever love and comfort they needed. In fact, it was not so unusual for her to take care of the smallest children, for her mother had borne them in such quick succession. She had always, it seemed to Eunice, either been struggling to recover from the difficult birth of a child, or heavily encumbered with another pregnancy, and apart from her eight live children, she had also endured three miscarriages, so it was little wonder that her health had been so seriously undermined, and that she had finally succumbed. Indeed, Margaret Youngman's short life had been an arduous one, for she had been forced into marriage shortly after her seventeenth birthday, and she had died before she reached her thirtieth. It had sadly fallen upon Eunice to explain to her brothers and sisters that their mother was no longer with them. Lydia and the twins had taken the news the hardest, but mercifully the younger ones did not fully comprehend the situation; after all their beloved Eunice was still there for them, as she had always been. Immersed as she was in the care and well-being of her family, and having witnessed the devastating effect that so much childbearing had had upon her mother, Eunice had long ago decided that she would never marry and be made to suffer the same fate. She nurtured thoughts of independence and freedom, and expounded her beliefs at every available opportunity, much to the consternation of many of the older women with whom she socialised. She had heard tell of Mary Ashton Livermore, a prominent reformer and pioneer of women's suffrage, and she devoured every word of the articles which were written by her, but she lived for the day when she could actually attend one of her lectures, for she was a distinguished public speaker. Eunice loved to discuss her heartfelt commitments with her best friend, Rosalind Hetherington, as the two girls had always shared each other's confidences without embarrassment. She very much hoped that Roz would call upon her during her father's absence, despite the inclement weather, for they so much enjoyed each other's company. Even though Eunice was just as perturbed as her friend at the marriage arrangements that their respective fathers had agreed upon, she would have welcomed the company of a woman like Roz, to share the burden of the day-to-day management of the household. She could think of no one she would rather choose as a companion, but the very thought of such a vivacious young girl being trapped into marriage with a man as old as her father, was repugnant to her.

How could any young girl endure the restrictions that such a marriage would impose upon her? But it was all too commonplace; young women in their prime, bound to men old enough to be their fathers. What selfish beings the males of the species were, she mused, seeming only to concern themselves with their own needs and desires: never giving a moment's thought to the opinions of their womenfolk. It was almost as though they thought of them merely as another of their chattels, with no consciousness at all worthy of consideration.

The children had now finished their breakfast, so she rose from the table, clapping her hands to quieten their noisy chatter. "Come on now all of you, it's time you were on your way," she said. "Make sure that you wrap up warm today, and take care on the roads. No stopping to play in the snow or you'll be late for school. I promise that you shall play out in it when you come home this afternoon." As they left the room, they each planted a kiss on Eunice's cheek; she knew that she had replaced their mother in their affections, and she loved them in return, as she knew her mother would have done.

*

The house soon became quiet once the children had left, and after she had been to the kitchen to dispense her instructions to cook and the other servants, Eunice settled herself by the window in the front parlour, where she had a good view of

Main Street. She adored this large rambling house that she had grown up in, with all its interconnecting rooms leading off the long central passageway. Her father had constantly added to the original building, both on the ground floor and the upper level, but the extensions had been expertly carried out by master builders, so that the finished effect was much to be admired by all who visited the Youngman's home. It was a cosy house with an abundance of wood-panelled rooms, which were immaculately kept by the servants. It stood at the far end of the town, right on Main Street, and there were two acres of land to the side and rear of the property, with a variety of mature trees which shaded the neatly clipped lawns.

Asbury was a flourishing town, one of the most important in the area. It was a growing community and its industries were growing too. The first Post Office had been established fifteen years ago, in 1851; and in 1852 the Summerville-Easton Railroad had extended its line from Whitehouse to Easton. This company later changed its name to the Central Railroad of New Jersey. As better ways of travel were introduced, the travellers through Asbury increased, and two nice hotels had been opened. Iron mines were in operation, also several blacksmiths, as well as wagon and carriage shops. There was a tailor shop at the south end of town, several dressmakers and a millinery shop; a butcher's shop and two lovely churches. Then, of course, there was the flour mill on the other side of the bridge. Eunice could well remember when she was a small girl, that every year, as the river Muscanetcong flooded in the spring, the people had had trouble crossing the bridge; then they had to pay two or three cents to be ferried across. Eventually though, the old wooden bridge had been replaced by the new iron one. The Hetheringtons lived on the other side of the bridge in 'Fortune's Hand' the grand looking mansion which stood up on the high ground overlooking the river. Eunice had spent many happy hours there with Rosalind when they were younger, especially in the summer months when they would play out in the grounds which ran down to the river's edge. She recalled how pleasant it was on a hot summer's day when they removed their shoes, hitched up their skirts and waded in the cool shallow water. She was suddenly brought back from her reverie as she caught sight of a sleigh jingling merrily along Main Street; she was delighted to see that it was her friend, and she ran out to the front door to welcome her. "Oh Roz, how lovely to see you," she cried. "Come in, come in. You must be frozen. Here, give me your cloak and sit there by the fire, I'll ring for hot coffee with rum in it to warm you."

Rosalind sank into the large comfortable chair that her friend had indicated to her, close to the fire. She raised her skirts a little, so that the warmth from the fire could reach her legs. Eunice soon returned to the parlour and tugged the bell-pull to order their warm drinks, then the two girls relaxed in the cosy atmosphere to enjoy one another's company. They had been bosom friends since their first day at school together, although they were not at all alike in appearance, exact opposites in fact, for Eunice was quite heavily built, tall and dark like her father. Her nose was the dominant feature of her face and she tended to over-exaggerate its proportions by always wearing her thick dark hair pulled back tightly into a neat chignon. Her manner of dress too was exceptionally austere; she wore only the plainest of dresses, which were always in dark practical colours with little or no adornment. Rosalind, on the other hand, was a true beauty with a beautiful figure, pretty copper-gold hair and enormous eyes that were flecked with green. Her manner of dress greatly complimented her beauty, for she always wore glowing colours that enhanced her vibrant hair; this too was always dressed in style with some delicate ribbons or lace. In no time, the two girls were chatting happily, each totally engrossed in what the other had to say. Then Eunice laughingly suggested to Rosalind that she would really enjoy having her as a stepmother, to help with the children and the daily running of the household. "It would be such fun Roz," she said. "Don't you agree?"

The other girl spluttered into her coffee cup. "Yoonie, what a suggestion! How could you? I would rather die than marry a man who is old enough to be my father, even if he is wealthy. How would you feel if our positions were reversed? Could you bear to be tied for the rest of your life to an old man with decaying teeth and thinning hair?"

"Not I! You know that I shall never marry, no matter whether the man be young or old. It is not my desire to follow my mother to an early grave. The very thought of childbirth terrifies me, so I shall remain a spinster all my life. Anyway, I have enough family to keep me occupied, so I have no need for more."

Henry Youngman could hear the raised voices of the two young women as he walked through the front door. He immediately recognised that of Rosalind Hetherington and his heart pounded. He had been feeling extremely miserable until that moment, because he had not been able to travel to

New York as planned. The trains had been halted because of the heavy snowfall, so he had been forced to abandon his trip, at least until the following day. The thought of his betrothed now lifted his spirits; he could not wait to see her again. He hovered outside the parlour as he removed his hat and coat, and the excited conversation of the two girls carried through the closed door. His chin dropped and his face burned with embarrassment as Rosalind's words caught his ear. His hand rose involuntarily to touch his balding head. His heart felt leaden in his chest. He turned from the door, hoping to steal away quietly. Maybe he should not intrude at that moment. He hesitated for a few seconds, but his desire to see the idol of his dreams swept aside all rational thought. She was here in his home, he must see her, talk to her. He turned back to the door and took hold of the doorknob forcefully, so that its rattle would announce his entrance. The two girls turned in surprise, wondering who had intruded upon their privacy. Believing that they were alone, their most intimate secrets unwitnessed, they had felt no need to observe caution. The warm rum had had an effect upon them, being young and unused to strong alcohol, and in their excitement their laughter and talk had become louder and louder. They glanced furtively at one another, not knowing whether they had been overheard. Eunice leapt to her feet. "Why Papa, what are you doing here? I thought you would have been well on your way to New York by now. What has happened?"

"All trains have been cancelled today, due to the heavy snowfall, but the line should be cleared by tomorrow morning, so I have been told. I hope that your cousin will be all right. Fortunately, I had written to his mother long before he left England that, should I not be at the docks to meet him when he arrives, he should book into the St Nicholas Hotel and wait there until I call for him. That will compensate for any disappointment that he may be feeling, to find that there is no one to meet him, as arranged. The St Nicholas is really palatial, with plush-lined marble halls, and the fact that there are seven hundred beds, should easily ensure his comfort and well-being until I am able to go and fetch him. Although I have never yet visited the place myself, it is highly recommended by all those who have."

He now turned his attention to Rosalind. How radiant she looked as the flames from the huge log fire flickered upon her golden hair and set her dewy complexion aglow. He stepped towards her, hardly able to check the impulse to throw his arms around her and hold her close. "So you have called, my dear, as I asked; I am so sorry that I was not here to receive you. There is so much that we must discuss; arrangements to be put in hand. I'm sure that you are just as anxious as I to talk of what has to be done. I assure you that just as soon as I have dealt with my nephew's arrival and settled him in, then we shall have as much time as is necessary. Mind now, we don't want to delay the proceedings for too long. I would like our marriage to take place as soon as possible, and I know your father is in full agreement with me on that." He conveniently forgot what he had overheard just a few minutes ago.

Rosalind felt as though she was on fire; she could hardly breathe. The heat of the room after she had come in from the bitter cold, combined with the hot rum drink that she had consumed; then the recollection of what she had been saying about Henry Youngman as he had burst in upon them so unexpectedly, all added to her extreme discomfort. She must get away from this man; she had the same feeling welling up inside her that she had always known whenever he came near her. She loathed and despised him and here he was talking of marriage. She now leapt to her feet in fright, as her friend had already done. "You are mistaken, Mr Youngman," she cried. "I came only to see Yoonie today, I had no other purpose, I can assure you." She felt panic-stricken, she must escape his attentions. She edged around him in order to make for the door.

"Oh, surely there is no need for you to go just yet, my dear," he said imploringly, at the same time catching hold of her arm and drawing her against him. "Do please sit down here by the fire for a little longer." He would not allow her to leave, he could not. "Eunice has to go and attend to the servants for a while, I am sure," he went on, "so we may have the opportunity for a quiet confidential chat with one another." Henry Youngman was determined to make the most of this unexpected meeting with his heart's desire. He must be near her, to touch her, hold her, maybe even to steal a kiss. He had never felt this way in his life before. The girl fired his blood as no other female had ever done. He was like a young lovesick boy, he could not get her out of his mind. It was as though a madness had befallen him, as though he was bewitched. He was completely out of control, his desire burned fiercely.

Rosalind sensed his passion and she feared him. She wrenched her arm from his lecherous grasp and blurted out, "Please let me go, sir. I must leave right away. I have other errands in town and Mama is expecting me home for lunch."

Eunice could see how alarmed Rosalind was becoming and she quickly joined in. "Yes Papa, we were both about to go along Main Street to Amy Perkins. We need to order some new bonnets to go with the dresses we're having made. I'll just bring our cloaks Roz."

She ran to the door and hurried away to fetch their outer-wear. Rosalind was terrified of being left alone with this man, she made to escape, fast on the heels of Eunice, but suddenly she felt herself being grasped from behind, for Henry Youngman could not believe that they were at last alone, and his desire overwhelmed him. His arms tightly enveloped her small, slender waist, pulling her backwards, and he pressed his face into her neck, groaning in ecstasy at the very nearness of her. The girl pummelled her clenched fists against his forearms, screaming in horror. "Leave go of me... leave go of me. I hate you."

His behaviour appalled her and she buried her face in her hands, not able to bear the thought of him touching her. Suddenly Eunice was beside her, pulling her father away from the terrified girl. "Father, what are you doing?" she asked incredulously. "Take control of yourself. Can you not see that Rosalind wants none of this?"

Her father came to his senses abruptly, stammering in embarrassment. "Oh my dear, forgive me... I don't know what came over me. What must you think? I am sorry, so sorry." He fled towards the door and left the two girls clinging to one another, his daughter trying to calm her friend. "Oh my dear Roz... what was he thinking of? I am so sorry... please try to calm yourself. Come now, let us put on our cloaks and I shall take you home. There, there, it's all over now. Try not to think of it."

Once she was safely tucked into the trap beside Eunice, Rosalind began to calm down and she welcomed the icy chill of the air to stop the burning in her cheeks. Then, as she recalled all that had taken place, a new fear gripped her heart, and she prayed that her father would never come to hear of this encounter. She voiced her fears to Eunice. "Oh, if my father comes to hear of what has happened today, he will be most displeased with me. Is it possible that your father will tell him of my objection to him? I feel so afraid. Why did it have to happen? If only I hadn't come to visit you. What do you think I should do?"

Eunice placed an arm around her friend's shoulders and squeezed her reassuringly. "My dear Roz, never fear that my father will breathe a word of it, for I am sure he will not. I know him and he would never risk further embarrassment by recounting what has happened between you today. Give it not another thought. I am sure that your father will never come to learn of it; certainly not from my father anyway. It is an unfortunate incident which should be forgotten. It is over and done, so that is the end of the matter."

The trap pulled into the drive of 'Fortune's Hand' and Eunice asked her friend if she would like her to escort her into the house.

"No thank you, Yoonie, I can manage perfectly well. I do not want Mama to know of this, for she will be most upset. It will appear more normal if I just step down from the trap here and go in alone. I am so sorry for what has happened, and I hope it has not spoilt what would otherwise have been a most pleasant visit for you. I shall see you again soon, no doubt, and thank you for bringing me home. You are my true friend Yoonie."

Eunice smiled broadly. "And you are mine, dear Roz. We shall never speak of this again, that I promise. Now take care and mind you don't slip on the steps. I shall see you again soon; goodbye."

Rosalind stood for a few moments at the front door and waved to her friend as the trap slowly disappeared down the long drive. When she turned to go into the house, a feeling of despair swept over her. She felt doomed and she began to doubt that her mother would ever be able to intervene on her behalf in the matter of her arranged marriage.

*

When Eunice arrived home, her father avoided her; in fact, he remained in his study, going over and over in his mind the occurrences of that morning. He sat motionless in his favourite armchair beside the fire, his head resting back, his eyes closed, as he once again recalled the thrill of holding Rosalind Hetherington's lithe young body against his own. The sweet smell of her still lingered in his nostrils and he sighed deeply with longing. What would he not give to hold her near at this very moment; he could hardly endure the waiting until they were wed. He was just a little perturbed at her violent reaction to his advances, but once they were man and wife she would become his property, she would belong to him alone, then her objections would be of no consequence. He savoured the thought. There was no doubt that she was a spirited individual, he liked that. A smile played upon his lips as he recalled how desperately she had fought against him when he held her tightly in his grasp, but a little resistance made the game all the more tantalizing.

Suddenly, her words re-echoed in his ears; the words he had accidentally overheard through the parlour door. He stood up abruptly and peered at his reflection in the large mirror over the mantelshelf. He gingerly ran his hand over the top of his sparsely covered head, then stroked his moustache into shape. On the whole, he was not too displeased with his appearance. Then he parted his lips in an artificial smile; it occurred to him that maybe he should think about improving his teeth. He could remember reading an advertisement somewhere, giving the particulars of tooth extraction and the fitting of false teeth. He was sure he had seen it in the newspaper recently. He returned to his chair and thumbed through the publications that were lying on the occasional table beside him. He selected one and quickly scanned the advertisements. Yes, there it was:

DR D M SWAYZE   DENTIST.

Best and Handsomest sets of teeth:
$15 to $18 Plain or Common sets: $10 to $12
Fine Gold Fillings: $1.50 to $2.
Teeth extracted without pain by the use of gas or chloroform.

He must make an appointment with Dr Swayze soon he decided.

His eyes travelled on down the column of print and fell upon yet another advertisement. This was for a book that greatly intrigued him. He felt it would be very much in his best interest to acquire it. He read of what it promised to contain:

Mind Reading, Psychomancy, Fascination, Soul-Charming, Mesmerism and Marriage Guide, showing how either sex may fascinate and gain the love and affection of any person they choose, instantly.

    400 Pages by Mail 50¢.
    HUNT & CO.,
    139 s 7th Street, Philadelphia.

There was a time, when to resort to such idiocy would have been beyond his comprehension, but now he would do anything to enhance his chances of ensnaring the delightful Miss Hetherington. He felt a surge of excitement at the thought of reading this particular publication, and he could not wait to put its claims to the test. He must obtain a copy... he must... he must. He would send for it at once. He never doubted for one moment that with its aid he could captivate his love and he would stop at nothing until he had done so.

Four

A week elapsed before Rosalind and Eunice met one another again. This time it was in church on Sunday morning. Rosalind always accompanied her mother, together with Minnie, to the Sunday morning service at the Methodist Church on Main Street. She walked in and glanced around at the congregation; the pews were quite well filled, even though the weather was so bad. She espied Eunice in her customary pew down on the left towards the front of the church, alongside her brothers and sisters, but there was a stranger with them whom she did not recognise. A broad shouldered young man with dark curly hair sat beside Eunice at the end of the pew by the aisle. They were talking quietly to one another as Rosalind approached them. Suddenly he became aware of her as she hesitated to greet her friend before taking her seat on the opposite side of the aisle beside her mother and Minnie. Eunice looked up and her face broke into a broad smile. "Hello, Roz, it's good to see you again. Allow me to introduce you to my cousin Benjamin Richmond. Do you remember my father spoke of him? He has been here for just over a week now and is to help my father in the business. This is my best friend Rosalind Hetherington, Ben; we were at school together."

Rosalind held out her hand, noticing how handsome the young man was as he stood up and took it gently in his own.

He was very tall and she had to raise her eyes to his. He was gazing intently at her and Rosalind caught her breath as a delightful tremor ran through her body. His hand tightened momentarily on hers, and he too took a deep breath as a pleasurable sensation swept over him. He could not take his eyes from the face of this beautiful young girl; her radiance captivated him. "I am very pleased to make your acquaintance, Mr Richmond," she whispered dreamily.

"And I am very pleased to make yours er, Miss..." his voice trailed away.

"Please do call me Rosalind." She tried to remove her hand from his ardent grasp, although she felt most reluctant to do so.

Suddenly realising that he was still holding her hand in his own, Benjamin Richmond released it guiltily.

"No doubt we shall meet one another again," Rosalind said, smiling sweetly at him.

"I sincerely hope so, Rosalind," he murmured quietly, as he watched her step gracefully across the aisle to take her seat beside her mother, just one row in front of the Youngman's pew.

Throughout the service, Benjamin Richmond's eyes were drawn to Rosalind Hetherington's fascinating profile again and again; he wondered what had overcome him; and Rosalind herself had purposely stepped along the pew past her mother and Minnie, so that as she turned towards them from time to time, she could more easily cast a surreptitious glance at the handsome young stranger to whom she felt so deeply attracted.

The service was brought to an end more quickly than normal, in order that the congregation should not suffer from the cold for too long, and very soon everyone was filing out of church and bidding goodbye to friends and relatives, anxious to be home to the warmth of their firesides. Rosalind and Eunice took the opportunity of having another little chat with one another, and once again Benjamin Richmond was the subject of interest. Rosalind asked him about his sea voyage from England and he was more than happy to inform her of all the details. Celia and Minnie were already tucked up inside the trap, and the Youngman children had all scrambled into their family carriage. Rosalind and Benjamin could have gone on talking to one another forever, oblivious to the cold and to the many pairs of eyes that were watching them. "Come along Rosalind, my dear, we should be getting home now," called her mother. "Don't keep Yoonie and her family waiting around in this cold for too long."

Rosalind smiled sheepishly at Benjamin. "Oh, do forgive me," she said, "I hadn't realised that I was delaying everyone, but I find it so interesting to talk to you."

"Don't apologize, please. The pleasure was all mine, I am so happy to have met you, and I hope we shall meet again very soon."

The young man held out his hand to assist Rosalind into the trap which had pulled up right beside them, and he inclined his head deferentially to the occupants as it drove off. Rosalind could not resist turning her head for one last look at him as he joined the Youngman's for the short drive home along Main Street in the opposite direction.

His heart felt light at the pleasure of meeting such a charming girl, and he looked forward with renewed eagerness to the life that he might build for himself in this strange and wonderful new world. He was completely entranced by the beautiful young friend of his cousin, and he spoke not a word as the carriage made the short journey back home; he thought only of her and of how soon he might see her again; but once they were all seated around the table for Sunday dinner, he could not wait to question Eunice about her closest friend. He wanted to learn everything that he could about her. Fortunately, thought Eunice, her father had not come in to take his meal with them, for he had been suffering from a heavy cough and cold for several days, that he had decided were due to the severe wintry conditions to which he had been exposed when attempting to meet his nephew in New York. He was spending the day in bed, in an effort to recover, for he was loath to take time away from his business, no matter how poorly he might be feeling.

*

Eunice had been very much aware of the immediate attraction between her cousin and her friend, and she now wondered what his reaction would be when he learned that Rosalind had been promised to her father in marriage. She too had taken an instant liking to him; he seemed to her to be a fine sensitive young man, and for that reason she would not like to see him hurt in any way. She knew that it would be difficult to break the news to him, but for his own sake she thought it better to acquaint him of the situation now, in order to save him embarrassment should he inadvertently disclose his interest in Rosalind to his uncle. Benjamin had been questioning her about the girl throughout the entire meal, and it was obvious that he was extremely captivated by her; she thought it such a pity that his dreams were to be thwarted, for they would indeed have made a perfect couple, and she would have so much enjoyed encouraging an alliance between them, but somehow or other she must prevent her cousin's interest from developing any further, because she knew the rage it would engender in her father should he ever suspect what was happening.

She waited until the rest of the family had finished their meal and promptly dismissed them from the room, so that she could have a quiet word with their cousin. She did not know how to begin, for she knew that what she was about to tell him would come as a tremendous shock. She cast down her eyes to the scraps of food that remained on her plate and gently poked at them with her fork. There was no easy way to say what she knew she must. She began, "Ben, I think there is something you ought to know." He looked at her with curiosity, his attention caught immediately by the serious tone of her voice.

"What is it?" he asked.

Eunice swallowed hard, then went on quietly, "Rosalind is betrothed to my father." She could not make the statement more easy for him to bear and she could not look at his face as the words left her lips, for she knew how horrified he would be by her disclosure.

The young man was indeed stunned; he could not believe what he had just heard. It seemed to Eunice an age before he finally spoke. "Surely not. It cannot be true Yoonie; not your father and that beautiful young girl. Tell me it is not true."

Eunice forced herself to lift her eyes to his face. "I wish I could tell you that it is not true Ben, but it has all been arranged between my father and Rosalind's. Believe me, I wish it were not so."

"What does Rosalind think of it; is she in agreement?" he asked incredulously.

"No, she is not. She is most adamant that she does not want the marriage to take place, but you know how these arrangements are agreed upon between the menfolk. I strongly suspect that it is a pure business arrangement on the part of Roz's father; he is a very devious man and it is obvious that he has offered his daughter's hand to my father to further his own ambitions, as far as I can see, and my father has been a very lonely man since my mother died. In fact, he cannot wait for the wedding to take place. I feel so desperately sorry for Roz, as you can well imagine, but knowing her father, I cannot see that she will be able to put a stop to it now that everything has been agreed."

Benjamin stood up. "Please excuse me, Yoonie," he said hoarsely, as he hurried from the room. A dark cloud had suddenly cast its shadow over his life. He went straight to his room and flung himself on to the bed despondently. He lay staring up at the ceiling, his head cradled in his hands. He simply could not believe that Rosalind Hetherington was betrothed to his uncle. He was strongly attracted to her himself, but that was normal, he was just three years older than she, but his uncle was more than thirty years her senior. Disgust arose in him at the very thought of them together. It was obvious that she would come to live in the house if they were married. He could never remain there, feeling the way he did about her. It would be too much for him to bear. From what he had seen of the small town of Asbury, in the short time that he had been there, he had already decided that he could quite happily settle there, but now he had encountered an insurmountable problem and he did not know what to do.

Five

The Youngman's haulage business was situated along the Bloomsbury Road and as it was but a short distance from their house on Main Street, Benjamin had taken to walking to the yard every morning. He enjoyed the exercise, and was also very interested in coming to know the inhabitants of Asbury, many of whom he met on his way. As he was about to make his life among them, he wanted them to accept him and become his friends.

He always set off early, so that when he came to the yard, he would have the time to stop for a chat with the men who worked for his uncle. There was a goodly workforce and he was determined to acquaint himself with every one of them.

Youngman's premises were impressive and were established well beyond the last of the houses that had been built along the Bloomsbury Road; they occupied a large area of land and considerable care had been taken in planning their layout. Strong wooden buildings had been constructed to the sides and the rear of the property, and the yard was secured from the road by huge iron gates. On the right of the entrance were the stables, with spacious haylofts above them; well stocked with fodder for the teams of horses that were used to haul the heavy wagons. To the left were the huge barn-like structures where the wagons were housed when not in use, or under repair. Henry Youngman had had various workshops incorporated within these buildings, and he kept his own well-skilled workforce to carry out all the work that was necessary in the efficient running of his business. He was a very astute man and had realised well in advance the benefits to be gained from employing his own repairmen; these included wheelwrights, saddlers and blacksmiths, in addition to all his loaders, drivers and general yard hands.

Then arrayed along the rear of the spacious flagstone courtyard were the storage buildings with a strong, wide loading bay built to the front of them, and steps at either end. The offices were situated above the storage area, and these had large windows right across the width of the building, providing a perfect view of the activity in the yard below. There was a spiral iron staircase at one end of the building, leading to the upper level, and Benjamin was always greeted enthusiastically by the men on the loading bay, as he climbed this stairway to reach his office. He found the work most interesting and had begun to settle into the daily routine very well. In the few weeks that he had been there, the men had taken a great liking to him, and this had not gone unnoticed by his uncle. In fact, Henry Youngman was more than satisfied with the way in which his nephew conducted himself, and had already concluded that he had found a most promising suitor for the hand of his eldest daughter. He decided that he must lose no time in discreetly sowing the seeds of this particular notion in the minds of both youngsters, before any other attractive female caught the eye of this eligible young man. He appreciated that Eunice was not the most desirable of women in appearance, but she had a lovely disposition which had always made her popular among her friends. More importantly, she was a Youngman, with all the wealth and advantages that her father had assured for her. If the youngster had any intelligence at all, thought his uncle, then he would surely realise the benefits to be gained by such a marriage. His future would be secured; he could not fail to see that.

When Henry Youngman arrived at the office, Benjamin was already busily checking through the inventory of goods to be despatched that day. Due to the recent bad weather, a number of wagons had still not been able to make their scheduled journeys, but now that the roads were improving, it would soon be possible to clear the backlog and get the goods moving again. Benjamin had noticed a 'HOLD BACK' notice attached to one consignment of goods, and he took it over to his uncle as soon as he sat down at his desk. "Is there any reason why these goods cannot be sent out now, sir?" he asked. "They have been held back for quite a while. Should I release them today?"

"No Ben. I don't want those goods to be carried just yet. They are from Hetherington's and there is a large account still outstanding. We will not ship those items until Hetherington settles his debt; it has been outstanding now for several months, and I mean to have it settled. You should know, my boy that we are going into partnership with Hetherington's Trading Company soon; in actual fact, I am to marry the man's daughter, Rosalind, and it has been agreed that our two companies shall be amalgamated upon our marriage. Despite all that, I don't see any reason why that account should not be settled. The man is incorrigible, and that debt has been outstanding for long enough. Tell you what Ben, why don't you take the account along to Hetherington by hand. It will be an opportunity for you to make his acquaintance. It would be a good thing for you to come to know him, as we shall all be working together soon. Now you go along and introduce yourself to him; tell him I sent you. Take my trap and drive up to Fortune's Hand now; he never leaves too early in the morning, so you should just catch him. Will you do that my boy?"

"Er... yes, uncle... of course... but where exactly is Fortune's Hand?"

Benjamin received the instructions from his uncle with mixed feelings. He was not sure if he should be pleased or not, but as soon as he had been given the directions to Hetherington's mansion, he lost no time in setting off with the overdue account safely tucked into his jacket pocket. His heart had leapt at the thought of visiting the home of Rosalind Hetherington; the very thought that he might catch another glimpse of her made his pulse race. On the other hand, it all seemed so futile. She was betrothed to his own uncle, and the realisation of that plunged him into the depths of despair; so why should he feel any joy in beholding her face again? But it was such a beautiful face, he recalled.

He slapped the reins enthusiastically, to urge the horse to quicken its pace, excitement mounting in him at the very thought that he now had an unexpected opportunity to visit the home of the girl who had constantly haunted his dreams since he had first met her. Now he hoped and prayed that he might meet her again.

*

Rosalind was just coming out of the dining room when the door chime sounded. She hesitated at the foot of the stairs, to see who had come to call so early in the day. As the manservant opened the door, she caught sight of Benjamin and her heart too missed a beat as he stepped into the hall.

"I have come to see Mr Hetherington on business," he said politely.

"Massa, he ain't home today, sir," came the reply.

Rosalind quickly intervened. "It's all right Tobias, Mr Richmond is a friend, I'll take him into the library. Do take off your things and come in Ben."

He handed his hat and coat to Tobias, never once taking his eyes from her face. His undisguised admiration caused her to blush deeply, and this made her appear to him more beautiful than ever. She led him into the library and turned to close the door, brushing softly against him as she did so. He could smell the sweetness of her and his mouth felt dry. How could he tell her what had brought him there? "Please sit down; I'll ring for a drink, would you care for some coffee with rum, to warm you?"

"That would be most enjoyable, if it is not too much trouble."

She indicated that he should take the chair close to the fire. "I am so sorry that my father is not here. He has been in New York on business for quite a while and we never know when he will be returning. Do you need to see him urgently, or can it wait?" She was not really interested in what had brought him there, just glad that he had come. She was completely enamoured by his presence; she studied him closely. She admired his open honest face, his thick curly hair, the firm set of his chin. There was nothing about him that displeased her.

Benjamin sensed her liking for him and it touched him deeply. He could not bring himself to tell her the nature of his visit. "Oh, I was just delivering an envelope for my uncle, but I am sure that it can wait until your father's return." He realised with pleasure that he would have another opportunity to call, if he was unable to deliver it on this visit. "My uncle wanted me to acquaint myself with your father, as he will shortly be forming a partnership with Youngman's."

He looked steadily at her and she lowered her eyes. Dare he mention her betrothal to his uncle, he wondered? He leaned forward on his chair, asking earnestly, "Is it true that you are to marry my uncle, Rosalind?" There, he had said it. He must hear it from her own lips before he could really believe it, although it pained him even to think of it.

Rosalind could not look at him. Her hands lay in her lap and she clasped and unclasped them nervously. "My father and Mr Youngman have made some sort of business agreement, Ben; my father is trying to force me into a marriage with your uncle." It was difficult for her to speak of it, Benjamin could see that. She took a deep breath, then went on, "I have had no say whatsoever in the matter, and I cannot bear the thought of it." She could not go on any longer; she pressed her hand over her mouth and looked up at the concerned face before her. The tears which had welled up in her eyes, now spilled down her cheeks. She sobbed. "It would be unbearable... I could never marry that dreadful man... never, never. I have told my mother so, and if my father tries to force me to it, then I shall kill myself; I really shall."

Benjamin was on his knees before her. He took her hands in his own. "Oh, Rosalind... no, no. Please don't. You must never even think such a thing," he pleaded. "I cannot bear it and neither can I bear to think of you married to my uncle. I refused to believe it when Yoonie told me. I could not imagine a girl as young as you being tied to such an old man. You are right, it would be unbearable. How could your father consider such a monstrous idea?" He shook his head in disbelief.

"You have no idea what my father is capable of. He thinks only of himself, no one else matters to him. Mama has vowed that she will not allow him to use me in this way and I know she will do everything in her power to prevent it, but I fear that my father will never allow her to stand in his way. He is a ruthless man... it is impossible to reason with him. He will stop at nothing to further his own interests." Their conversation was brought to a halt by the arrival of their drinks. They sipped at the hot rum coffee in silence; it helped to restore their spirits and they relaxed for a few moments, just happy to be together, even if only for a short while. Benjamin knew he must return to the yard as his uncle would be expecting him, but he had lost his heart and wanted nothing more than to stay with Rosalind.

"I shall have to leave you now," he said sadly, "but would it be possible for us to meet again soon?" He rose to go.

"I would love that Ben, but where should it be?" She stood up and stepped towards him hesitantly. He opened his arms to draw her close and enfolded them around her. She felt warm and safe, this was where she belonged. She lifted her face to his and he kissed her tenderly on the lips. He had never before kissed any girl, but it seemed the most natural thing in the world for him to do.

Rosalind pulled gently away and her fingers drifted up to her lips, to catch and hold fast the beautiful sensation of his lips upon her own. "You are so beautiful," he whispered, "I must see you again."

"That would make me so happy Ben, but it will be difficult. We must be careful." She thought for a moment. "I always go down to Main Street with Minnie on Saturday mornings, between ten and eleven o'clock, to browse around the store. Perhaps we could meet there. I usually see Yoonie, so if you could accompany her, then I shall be able to invite you both back for coffee. You could tell her that I have suggested it."

"What will she think of it though? Will she not disapprove, because you are betrothed to her father?"

"No... never. She is a trusted friend and we have no secrets from one another. She is just as perturbed as I am at what our fathers are trying to arrange. She is a very good sort and you need have no fear that she will betray your trust."

"Very well, I shall do as you say, but now I really must go." He took her hands placing them together and lifting them to his lips.

"Until Saturday then, I shall look forward to seeing you. Please try not to worry... I want to help you Rosalind. Maybe I could speak to my uncle. Perhaps if he knew how much you are opposed to marrying him, then he would not insist upon it... surely he could not."

"Oh, no... no... please don't say anything to him, Ben. He must not know of our meeting," she begged. "My mother has asked me not to anger my father for the present, but to be patient and give her the opportunity of trying to find a solution to this dreadful dilemma. It would be better if you did not mention the matter to your uncle... please." Rosalind felt very afraid. She thought of her recent encounter with Henry Youngman; Ben knew nothing of that, and she could not bring herself to tell him of it. She was anxious to avoid any further incidents for the present. She dreaded to think of what her father would do if he suspected what had happened. "You are very kind and I appreciate your sympathy, but promise that you will wait awhile, to see what will happen when my father returns. If he ever came to hear of our association, there is no knowing what he would do."

Benjamin could see how alarmed she was. "All right, all right," he assured her. "You know that I shall do only what is in your best interest. Now please calm yourself; promise me that you will not worry. I could never do anything to cause you distress."

"Oh Ben, I know that you could not."

They clung together once more before he left. She watched him drive away in the trap and turned to go upstairs. She could not wait to tell Minnie all that had happened between them, and how it had so suddenly changed her whole life.

*

Minnie's eyes grew wide with alarm at her mistress's outpourings. "Does you know what you is doing Miss Rosalind?" she asked. "Has you gone mad? What you think your father gonna do when he knows about this?" She held her head in her hands and shook it from side to side in dismay. "Lordy... Lordy now I knows youse lost your mind."

"No Minnie, just my heart, I have never felt like this before. It's the most wonderful feeling as though I am alive at last. This is what I have been waiting for, although I did not know it. Can't you understand Minnie? I want to be with Benjamin Richmond more than anything in the world... just to see him, to be near him is enough. I can't explain it to you, it is indescribable." She felt elated.

Minnie had never seen her mistress like this before, but she was afraid for her. She must reason with her. "Now calm yourself, is you thinking about this? What your father gonna say if he gits word of it? You just be careful Miss Rosalind... please."

"I am being careful Minnie, but that doesn't change the way I feel. There is nothing I can do about it. Oh, please be happy for me," she begged.

Minnie's arms were around her mistress immediately. "Oh Miss Rosalind, you knows all I wants is for you to be happy, you knows there ain't nothin' I wouldn't do for you, but you heading for trouble, and I don't want to see you hurt."

Minnie could see that it was no good trying to reason with her mistress, and she wondered what was to become of her. In fact, she could see nothing but trouble ahead for all of them, she mouthed a silent prayer.

Benjamin was no less smitten than Rosalind, for he too had never before felt this way, but he realised that he should be extremely careful not to disclose his feelings to his uncle just yet, although it was inevitable that he would have to be told eventually. He wondered just how to approach the situation, but for the moment he must keep his promise to Rosalind and remain silent. Little did he know how difficult that would prove to be.

*

The meeting that had been secretly planned for the following Saturday, took place exactly as arranged, without any problems whatsoever. It was the first of many such meetings, although Eunice was not at all happy with what Benjamin and Rosalind were doing. She sympathized deeply with their plight, but at the same time she warned them both to be very careful. She too could foresee nothing but trouble ahead.

Her father had not the slightest suspicion of the web of intrigue that was being spun around him. In fact, when he accidentally encountered his daughter and nephew whispering secretly to one another, he felt sure that they were simply behaving covertly as young people were apt to do when forming a romantic alliance. When they looked at him a little guiltily, he would smile benignly at them and assure them that all was well, and that they should pay no heed to his presence. He enthusiastically encouraged them in what he supposed were their hesitant attempts at courtship, fully convinced that his subtle hints had been acted upon by the innocent young pair. He congratulated himself upon his clever orchestration of what appeared to be their obvious interest in one another.

*

It was not long before Benjamin and Eunice realised with dismay that their constant outings with one another, together with their continual intimate conversations, were being completely misconstrued by him, but they dared not disclose their true meaning. However, their betrayal and guilt would soon be brought to an end; so too the newfound joy of the innocent young lovers, for Gilbert Hetherington arrived home unexpectedly one afternoon, to find the downstairs parlour alive with the sound of excited voices and laughter. Lydia, Charlotte and Edward had accompanied Benjamin and Eunice on yet another visit to 'Fortune's Hand' on the very day that Rosalind's father had chosen to return home, and it was their joyful laughter that greeted his ears as he stepped through the front door. He quietly entered the parlour to witness for himself the cause of all the hilarity. He stood watching the group for several minutes before they became aware of his presence, and it took him no longer than that to observe with horror the undisguised attraction between his daughter and the strange young man who was sitting beside her. They were completely oblivious to all that was going on around them; their eyes never left one another. He could see exactly what was going on between them and it infuriated him. He wasted no time in disbanding the youngsters. "So, this is what happens when my back is turned," he declared at the top of his voice. The room fell silent immediately and several pairs of eyes were riveted upon his irate countenance.

Rosalind could not face him; she felt deeply ashamed that Benjamin should have to witness her father's uncontrolled anger. "My friends were just about to leave, Papa," she said, almost inaudibly.

"Yes, we should be getting home now, before the light fades," agreed Eunice, endeavouring to ease her friend's obvious embarrassment.

"I shall see you in the library when your friends have left, my girl," said Gilbert Hetherington sternly, as he turned and strode away.

Rosalind felt deeply humiliated; her face was afire and her eyes filled with tears. *How could he?* she thought dejectedly.

There was a flurry of activity as the younger children fetched their coats and hats. It took but a matter of minutes before the group had departed. Benjamin tried to take Rosalind's hand for just a second, to reassure her of his feelings for her, but she quickly withdrew from him, terrified lest her father should be watching, unbeknown to them. "Thank you for coming, all of you," she whispered. "Have a safe journey home. I am so sorry..." Her voice faded away. She kept her head bowed as she closed the door, then walked slowly back along the hall to the library, dread filling her heart.

As she had suspected, her father had left the door ajar, obviously so that he could see and hear what was happening. She hesitated before entering, but he was watching for her. He drained down the last of the large brandy that he had poured himself and thumped the glass on to the table. "Come in and close that door," he thundered. Before she had had time to seat herself on the chair that he had indicated, he went on, "What do you think you are playing at? Is that the behaviour you think becoming to someone who is betrothed to be married? What you need is a good thrashing, my girl." He paced the room, hardly stopping to draw breath. "Is your mother aware of what you are up to? Who is that young upstart anyway, and where did you meet him?"

"He is Mr Youngman's nephew recently arrived from England Papa. He is a fine man, a gentleman, and we... we..."

Her father did not allow her to finish. He swung around.

"You mean to tell me that you have the temerity to conduct a dalliance with the nephew of your own betrothed? I cannot believe it, my own daughter. Have you been to see Henry Youngman whilst I have been away?" Rosalind kept her eyes averted; she bit her lip and shrugged her shoulders. "Well, have you or have you not? It was my understanding when I left for New York that you should pay him a visit in a day or two, to discuss details of your coming marriage. Now tell me, have you seen him since I left?"

Rosalind could not divulge to her father the disaster of her recent meeting with Henry Youngman, so she chose not to mention it, but she was her father's daughter after all, and under his constant bombardment, her fighting spirit was roused. She was determined to have her say, no matter what the consequences.

"I have no wish to marry that dreadful man, Papa. I can't, I can't, I hate him and you cannot force me to it. Oh please... please, won't you understand?" Her voice rose louder and louder; she was becoming almost hysterical in her pleading.

Suddenly his hand struck out and hit her full force across the face; her head jerked violently on her neck; she felt the painful impact, she heard the resounding thwack. It reverberated through her head. She felt sure that her jaw had been broken. She gasped in agony, then buried her face in her hands, sobbing uncontrollably. "That settles it; you will be married to Henry Youngman as soon as it can be arranged. Do you hear? There will be no more meetings with that young upstart, and I shall tolerate no more of your insolence. Now get out of my sight."

As she fled from the room, he poured himself another generous measure of brandy and gulped it down before going in search of his wife.

*

Celia was upstairs in her own room with Esther. She liked to spend as much time as possible with her youngest daughter, and they were in the habit of taking tea with one another every afternoon. It was their special time together. The girl always showed great delight at being in her mother's room, and Celia would keep her amused by looking at picture books with her, or playing childish games. Despite the fact that her youngest child would never be normal, Celia loved her dearly and always took it upon herself to ensure that she was protected and well cared for. Jassy usually took charge of her during the day, and the other housemaids would take it in turns to sleep in Esther's room at night, just in case she should wake and need attention. This simple girl brought much love and warmth into what would otherwise have been an extremely gloomy household, for despite the fact that the mistress always treated the servants with kindly consideration, the same could not be said of the master, and they all dreaded the times when he returned from his business trips. He brought an atmosphere of misery and fear into their midst.

Celia and Esther had enjoyed their tea and the small fancy cakes that Jassy had set out upon the tray for them. Now it was playtime, and Celia was hiding inside her closet among her dresses, calling softly to Esther, "Come and find me... where am I?" The child never tired of this particular game; it was one of her favourites. She ran towards the closet, where she knew her mother was always hiding, and Celia caught her hands as she groped among the array of long skirts and dresses. "Oh...here I am... you have found me. You clever girl." She grabbed Esther and hugged her, and she squealed with delight. It was always exactly the same sequence of events, but she loved the repetition of it.

They were dancing to and fro and laughing together, their arms tightly clasped around one another, when Gilbert Hetherington burst in upon them. "What is going on here, has everyone gone mad today?"

Two startled pairs of eyes were turned upon him and immediately the room became darkened by his presence. Esther positioned herself behind her mother for protection, sensing instinctively the hatred that her father felt for her. She was always kept as far away from him as possible. All the servants were aware that he would not tolerate the girl anywhere near him. "Come to my study, we need to talk," he snapped.

Celia could see from his expression that something had caused him extreme displeasure. Normally, he never sought her out when he returned home. In fact, it was only by word from the servants that she ever knew when he was there. He had not entered her room, but stood menacingly by the door, barking his orders at her. Now he turned around and was gone. Celia bent over Esther and gave her a reassuring hug.

"Come on now darling, let us go and find Jassy downstairs, shall we?" Her daughter was dribbling uncontrollably, as she always did when frightened. "Come along dear... come with Mama." Celia placed an arm around Esther's shoulders and guided her out of the room. She left her in Jassy's care, then went to fetch her sewing before joining her husband in the study. Wondering what could have caused his latest outburst, she walked in and seated herself, then quietly proceeded to work on her embroidery.

"Do you have to take that damned handiwork everywhere with you... do you never go anywhere without it? I have a matter of extreme seriousness to discuss with you, and here you are, as usual, giving all your attention to that unimportant frippery. It's no wonder that I find everything in uproar when I come home. It's intolerable. There are many things that I find intolerable in this household, and I mean to remedy them. Do you understand? It seems that as soon as I turn my back, my daughter is indulging in an association with Youngman's nephew..." He paused. He could see Celia was taken aback. "Yes right here under your nose and you do nothing to stop it. Are you aware of what they were doing down here in the parlour while you were idling your time away with that idiot child? Well I'll have no more of it. Before I take another trip, Rosalind will be married to Henry Youngman... I'll see to that. No more dilly-dallying. You will start to make the necessary arrangements immediately. Is that understood?"

Celia could feel tears smarting her eyes, but she was determined that this brutal man should not have the satisfaction of knowing how deeply he had hurt her, how deeply it always hurt her when he made his cruel references to their youngest child. She blinked rapidly to dispel her tears. "You must be mistaken, I am sure you are Gilbert. I know nothing of any association between Rosalind and Henry Youngman's nephew. What gives you cause to make such wild accusations, especially against your own daughter?"

"There, there I knew it. You have no idea of what is going on around you. Ask her... ask her what kind of behaviour she was indulging in with those friends of hers. Anyway there shall be a stop to it. I intend to see Youngman in a day or two and I shall tell him to set a date as early as he sees fit."

Celia became alarmed. Could these accusations be true? She suddenly recalled how interested her daughter had seemed to be in the strange young man who had accompanied Eunice to church not long ago. She desperately needed time to delay these disastrous proceedings. Could she cajole her husband into agreeing to some form of compromise? She must try anything to prevent her daughter from being used in such a despicable way.

"I have no doubt that Mr Youngman is anxious for the wedding to take place as soon as possible, that is understandable but at the same time he will surely appreciate that it would be a far more enjoyable occasion if the weather was better. Do you not think that it would be advisable to wait until spring is here? Think how delightful it would be when the blossom is on the trees and the countryside is fresh and green. Besides that, it will take a few weeks to have all the dresses made. Firstly there is the bridal gown and I should imagine that Henry Youngman's daughters will want to be bridesmaids. Do please allow time enough for everything to be arranged properly. Let it be a wedding for the townfolk to remember. And have you thought of Lillybee? She might also like to come. Do you realise that we have not seen her for many, many years, so I feel sure that she would love to pay us a visit for a short while and what better opportunity of inviting her than for the wedding of her niece? Rosalind has already asked that Edmund should be here, so perhaps they could travel north together." Celia glanced up furtively to see what effect this suggestion had had on her husband. Knowing how much he disliked his son, she was unsure of how he would receive this suggestion.

He thought careful for a moment or two. He had never considered inviting his sister, she was so far away, but of course it was a possibility. As for his son... well, if it would help to appease his rebellious daughter and encourage her to accept the marriage arrangement more willingly, then he may have to comply. Anything to trap Youngman into a partnership. He dared not risk his daughter raising too many objections, for fear that she might deter the man from entering into their contract. Nothing must endanger that, not now, his situation was becoming desperate. He had suffered another devastating run of bad luck on his latest trip to New York. What a fool he had been. For the first few nights everything had gone his way, his winnings were mounting so high that he felt sure he could not lose, but as always his initial success had made him over-confident, and certain that he was on a winning streak, he had thrown caution to the wind, had become more and more foolhardy. Fighting against all odds to reclaim as much as possible of what he had so recklessly lost over the past year or more, he had finally wagered every penny that he had won on the first few nights, hoping against hope that it would restore his fortune. Then, as always, Lady Luck had abandoned him and he had come away from the gaming tables even more in debt. He could not understand it. Why had he not quit while he was ahead? He had been doing so well, but once again the fever had gripped him. It was a madness that overcame him; it controlled him, he just had to go on and on, positive that he could make that one big win, convinced that he could grab back all that he had lost in the past. Then came the final realisation, the despondency, the degradation of knowing that he had overstepped the boundaries of good sense yet again.

He looked at his wife. "All right then, a Spring wedding it is. I shall write to Lilybee at once, but you must make sure that there is no more nonsense from Rosalind. Let that be agreed."

Celia breathed a sigh of relief;   she could not believe that her ploy had worked so successfully. "I shall go and speak to her at once," she said, anxious to put an end to the discussion and make her escape.

She found her daughter sitting quietly in her room, not moving, just staring out of the window, her back to the room. She called softly to her. "Rosalind... Rosalind my dear, I have just been speaking to your father."

The girl turned to face her, without saying a word. The left side of her face was swollen and bruised and her eye half closed. The corner of her mouth had been split open against her teeth, and the blood had congealed around it. It was not her face, it was contorted out of recognition. Celia gasped in horror when she saw what her husband had done and anger welled up inside her. She took her daughter lovingly into her arms and moaned softly, "Oh my dear... my dear, what has he done to you... how could he... why? Is it true that he found you with Mr Youngman's nephew when he came home today? Is it true Rosalind? Tell me, please my dear, tell me."

"Yes Mama, it is true. Benjamin Richmond has been here to visit me several times, we have fallen in love with one another... we just want to be together, is that so wrong?" She broke down and cried bitterly.

Her mother led her to the bed and seated her gently on it, then sat beside her. "Why did you not tell me of this, why my dear?"

"I knew you would be worried Mama and you had asked me not to do anything to anger Papa. We didn't plan it; it just happened so suddenly. We have done nothing wrong... we have never behaved improperly. We just wanted to be with one another. Yoonie always brought Ben with her when she came to visit, so that we could see one another, that was all. Today she brought him with Lydia and the twins, and Papa heard us laughing and talking together when he arrived home. We were doing no harm Mama, I swear it. Papa was angry, you know how he is, and my friends were afraid of him, I could see that. He humiliated me, he ordered me to his study, and when I tried to explain to him that I could never marry Mr Youngman..." She could not go on... she broke down again and sobbed.

"There, there, try not to upset yourself again, my darling. I told you before that you should never be sacrificed in this way, and I shall keep my word. Trust me."

They sat together in silence for a very long time, each deeply engrossed in her own thoughts. They fully realised that for the next few weeks, albeit unwillingly, they would be forced to feign interest in the wedding preparations. However, they also realised that this would afford them the time that they each so desperately needed to put into operation their own individual plans, for they were both equally determined that this fateful wedding should never ever take place.

Six

Henry Youngman sat in his office nursing his swollen jaw. He was beginning to think that he had done the wrong thing in going to see Dr Swayze. He had had several teeth removed and had never before known such excruciating pain... the violent throbbing... the interminable ache. It was unbearable agony. Worse still, his suffering was not yet over, for once his gums were healed, he had to undergo the ordeal of having his false teeth made and fitted. The very thought of having to endure any kind of pressure upon his torn and ragged gums was more than he could bear. He was beginning to wish that he had never heard of Dr Swayze.

He was sitting at his desk holding a very large white linen handkerchief to his bleeding mouth when Gilbert Hetherington arrived. "Why, my dear fellow, what on earth has happened to you?" he asked. He was unable to determine from his muffled sounds, exactly what the other man said in reply, but from his gesticulation it became obvious exactly what was ailing him. "You have my deepest sympathy, and, I would never have bothered you had I known that you were in such a bad way, but as you know, I returned only yesterday from New York and it is on a matter of extreme urgency that I have called upon you today. I feel sure that you can have no knowledge of it, and that it will shock you as much as it did me when you hear what I have to tell you."

Henry Youngman felt wretched and certainly was not at all interested in anything that he thought Gilbert Hetherington might have to tell him. Why did the man have to come bothering him today, he wondered. He felt so ill, that the last thing he could face was this individual confronting him with problems. He just wanted to be home as soon as possible. He breathed a shuddering sigh and removed the bloodstained cloth from his mouth. "What is it Hetherington?" he asked wearily. "Couldn't it wait another day or two until I am feeling more like my old self?" His words were still barely intelligible.

"Afraid not Henry... afraid not. This personally concerns not only you, but my own daughter, and I think you should know about it right away."

Despite the fact that he was feeling so wretched, Henry Youngman's ears pricked up immediately. Gilbert Hetherington went on, "If you mean to wed Rosalind, then I advise you to do so at the earliest opportunity. That is, if you don't wish to lose her."

"Lose her? Whatever do you mean, lose her? I don't understand you Hetherington."

"Well, it would seem that your own nephew is becoming strongly attracted to your betrothed Henry; I actually found them together in my parlour when I returned from my trip yesterday afternoon. Have you any knowledge of his interest in Rosalind?"

Henry Youngman could not believe what he was hearing, in fact, he did not believe it at all. "What are you talking about, are you out of your mind? You are completely mistaken Hetherington, and I know that for a fact." He was in no mood to sit listening to such outrageous nonsense. Just as soon as he had cleared up a few minor items of business that required his attention, he would be away to his home, where he could recover from his devastating encounter with the dentist. He wanted peace and quiet and the chance to rest, not to have to sit here listening to what this unpleasant man was fabricating. What was he up to now?

"Oh, I am mistaken am I? My wife said exactly the same thing when I spoke to her about it yesterday." Gilbert Hetherington's voice was raised in anger; he did not like to be opposed. "What is the matter with you, can't you see what is going on under your very nose? I have seen them together; have you? I think not, or you would not be so quick to dispute it. How can you be so sure that it is not true, eh? I'd like to know what makes you so sure."

Henry Youngman once again removed the handkerchief from his mouth, and with a deep sigh he tried to answer as coherently as possible. He said very slowly and concisely, "Because Benjamin is interested in Eunice, his cousin, that is why." He closed his eyes; his patience was wearing thin. "They have been out and about everywhere together this past couple of weeks and they are never out of one another's sight at home. It's no secret, they are constantly engaged in intimate whispered conversations together; what do you think that indicates? It is exactly what I had hoped would happen, and I have encouraged them as much as possible. They will make a perfect match for one another. Now, if you don't mind, I just want to finish what I am doing here and get home, so that I can take something to stop this pain." He was feeling really ill now and this man was aggravating him beyond all endurance.

"All right… all right, but don't say I didn't warn you. I thought we had struck a bargain with one another over this marriage. Now you just ask that nephew of yours what was going on in my parlour yesterday afternoon. See what he has to say for himself, will you? I can see I haven't chosen the right moment to inform you of this, you are not feeling yourself and I can understand your reluctance to believe what I am telling you about your own kin, so I'll be off, but you come up and see me in a day or two, when you have recovered, and we'll discuss this further." He placed his hat on his head, gave it a firm tap, and strode towards the door, calling back over his shoulder, "I'll bid you good day now, and you'd better tell your nephew to keep away from my daughter."

His every step resounded on the iron staircase as he stamped down angrily into the yard, where his trap was waiting. Benjamin had been working in the warehouse and he came out onto the loading bay just as Gilbert Hetherington drove off through the gates. He could guess what he had come to tell his uncle and he was deeply saddened. It was not his intention to cause trouble, but he knew now that it could not be avoided. He walked slowly up the stairs to the office, wondering what was going to happen now that his secret had been revealed. In a way it was a relief that he no longer had to deceive his uncle, although he knew that the truth would anger him, but he and Rosalind loved one another and there was nothing anyone could do to change that. No matter how much opposition they had to face, they were determined to be together always, and they both realised that their greatest difficulty would be in trying to persuade his uncle and her father to accept it.

As he entered the office, his uncle glanced up at him. "I have had Gilbert Hetherington here, making the most outrageous accusations," he said. "I don't know what has come over the man, but I can't talk about it now, I just want to get myself home. I'll see you later, carry on here for me, will you?" He found it a great comfort to know that he could trust this young man to take over the running of the business in his absence. He had fulfilled every expectation, as far as he was concerned, so how could he believe what that fool Hetherington had told him?

Benjamin could see how much his uncle was suffering and he sympathized. "Of course I'll carry on here. You get along home, you don't look at all well. Get to bed and rest awhile, don't worry about anything, I'll make sure that it is all taken care of."

The older man nodded gratefully, then put on his hat and coat and left without another word, still fully convinced that Gilbert Hetherington had made a ridiculous mistake.

*

Eunice was on her usual Monday morning trip along Main Street to replenish the family's provisions for the week. She had finished browsing around the store and had given a list of the items she needed to Robbie Groves, the young shop assistant, for delivery later in the day. The bell jangled loudly as she opened the door to leave, and it was then that she espied Gilbert Hetherington driving by in his pony and trap. She could guess from the direction in which he was heading that he might possibly be going to see her father at the yard. A wave of apprehension swept over her as she remembered his violent reaction the afternoon before, when he had found her and her family making merry with Rosalind in his parlour. She had always thought him an abominable man, and now she wondered what fate had befallen her friend after they had all left so hurriedly. She had a feeling of foreboding, so on the spur of the moment, she decided to go up to see Rosalind for a quick visit, before returning home, especially now that she knew her tyrant of a father would not be there. She felt more comfortable about calling when she knew that he was not at home. She paused for a moment or two before leaving the shop, then when he was out of sight she hurried to her own pony and trap. It took her but a few minutes to drive over the bridge and up to 'Fortune's Hand' and she was soon being shown into the parlour once again by Tobias, the manservant, before he went to fetch Rosalind. She did not take a seat, for she was not intending to stay for very long, but she was most concerned about her friend and just wanted to make sure that she was all right. She stood looking out of the window while she waited, and she turned immediately she heard her voice. "Hello Yoonie, how kind of you to come."

As she caught sight of her friend's face, her heart lurched. She ran to her and wrapped her arms around her in a loving embrace. "Oh no... no..." she cried. "Oh, the monster. He has done this to you, hasn't he?" Rosalind did not answer, but hung her head in shame, as though she herself were to blame for her ghastly appearance. Eunice placed her hand gently under her friend's chin and lifted her face. She looked intently at the swollen countenance, with its dark bruising and painful cuts, then she kissed Rosalind's right cheek very softly. "Oh, I am so sorry that this has happened my dear friend. I knew that there would be dire consequences, but this is unspeakable. I have just seen your father driving along Main Street, and I supposed he was on his way to see my father. What on earth will happen when he too learns of the association between you and Benjamin? I am so worried for you both. There is bound to be even more trouble when my father finds out what has been happening. What will you do now?"

Rosalind recounted all that had happened after her friends had left the previous day, and Eunice was deeply moved. "Now my father has forbidden me to see Benjamin again. He is insisting that I wed your father as soon as possible. He said that I am to prepare myself for the wedding, but I can tell you that it will never take place." Her manner became defiant. "No indeed... it will never take place; I can assure you of that."

"What do you mean Roz? I don't understand."

"My mother and I have discussed it, but we need a little time to make our plans, so to appease my father, we shall start making the wedding arrangements, just as he said. My brother is to come, together with my Aunt Lilbyee, from North Carolina. I must see Edmund... on that I am determined; but then I shall leave. I shall have to go away to escape from my father, if I want to live my life as I please. My mother is to ask my aunt if she will help us; it seems that she has some influence over my father, being a much older sister."

Eunice was aghast, but she realised that what her friend said was true. It was the only solution to this unbearable problem. "Is there anything I can do for you Roz? You know I will help in any way that I can."

"Yes, there is something, if you will. I must see Benjamin. We shall have to meet in secret somewhere, so if you could carry a message for me."

"Of course... of course... anything. What shall I tell him?" She watched her friend walk to and fro, her hand held to her forehead, trying desperately to decide what to do.

"Yes, that's it." She took hold of Yoonie's hands. "Please will you ask him to meet me tonight? It must be late, so that my father will not know of it. Would you ask Ben to come around to the back of the house at 9 o'clock tonight? Tell him I shall be waiting for him in the stables. Will you do that for me Yoonie?" she pleaded earnestly.

"Consider it done. Benjamin will be there, never fear. Oh, Roz... I wish there was something more I could do for you."

"No... no, that is enough Yoonie. I don't want to involve you any more than is necessary, but I have no other way of contacting Benjamin, so what you are doing is of tremendous help, and I very much appreciate it."

The two girls held one another close for a moment and then walked together to the front door. "Thank you again for coming. We shall see one another again soon, although I shall not be able to come down into town for a while, not until my face is a little more presentable. I couldn't show myself looking like I do, I cannot bear the thought of Benjamin seeing me like this either, but I need to talk to him as soon as possible. I know I shall be able to withstand anything if I have his support... anything at all. Now you ought to go Yoonie, before my father returns. I don't want to arouse his suspicions and anger him again, for fear that he might imprison me upstairs for disobeying him. If he thinks that I am complying with his instructions, then I shall more easily be able to slip out later this evening to meet Benjamin."

Eunice could understand her friend's fear, so she departed without further delay, saying quietly, "I shall keep in touch Roz; somehow I shall find a way, so take heart from that."

True to her word, Eunice delivered the message to Benjamin as soon as he returned from the yard in the late afternoon. Her task was made easier because her father had been tucked up safely in his bed since he had returned home earlier in the day. She told Benjamin what Roz had suffered at the hands of her father, and his overwhelming concern for her increased. He had hardly slept the previous night for worrying about her, but this news was almost more than he could bear. He ate little of his meal and could hardly wait until it was time for him to go out and meet Rosalind. He left early, eager to see her again. She filled his thoughts from morning until night and all he wanted was to be with her.

After his uncle had left the yard earlier that day, he had decided that he could no longer tolerate the deceit, nor hide his love for Rosalind. It was a natural, beautiful thing, so why should they be forced to hide it? He wanted to shout it to the whole world. His mind was filled with these thoughts as he hurried through the town in the dark of the night. He had decided to walk, so that he could slip in quietly, unobserved. He was over the bridge now and soon on his way up the sweeping drive of 'Fortune's Hand'. Although he was not familiar with the buildings to the rear of the property, he had no difficulty in finding the stables. He slowly pulled open the heavy wooden door, standing slightly ajar. As he entered, he heard Rosalind call softly to him, "Ben... Ben I am here." He could make out her shadowy form in the last of the stalls. She had brought a small lamp with her; it was turned down so low that its dim light was hardly enough to penetrate the gloom, but just enough to guide him in the right direction. He hurried to her and took her in his strong arms.

She made a low agonized sound as his face brushed against her swollen cheek. His concern was immediate. "Oh my love... my love. I am sorry. Forgive my clumsiness. I couldn't see. Yoonie told me what your father has done to you. It is despicable... unbelievable."

She was glad that he could not see how ugly the wounds were. He held her more gently, brushing the top of her head with his lips. "I love you so much Rosalind, I cannot bear to think of you suffering in this way. I have decided to tell my uncle of my feelings for you, just as soon as he is fit and well again. I wanted to tell him today, after your father had called upon him, for I am sure that they were speaking of us, but he was so unwell after his visit to the dentist, that he had to go home. However, I have resolved that just as soon as he is recovered, then he shall learn the truth. I hate all this deception... I have to tell him. He does not seem to be an unreasonable man; maybe he will try to understand."

"Oh no Ben... please don't... please. First let me tell you what my mother and I have decided. If you aggravate the situation now, then all our plans will be ruined. You must have realised that it is not possible to reason with my father, we have both tried to do so and failed, so my only hope is to go away somewhere. That I am determined to do, I have made up my mind. I just need a little more time to get everything arranged; do you understand?" She could not mention the abhorrence she had of his uncle, nor the fear she had always felt in his presence. Being a man, how could he begin to comprehend that the very thought of Henry Youngman made her flesh creep?

"Roz, if you really mean it… if you are of a mind to go away, then we shall go together. I want to take care of you, keep you safe always. I want to make you my wife… you know that, don't you?"

"I hoped so very much that you would want to come with me Ben, and I told my mother that I thought you might. Only then could she accept my decision to leave, but of course I could not force you against your will and if you should have refused…"

He did not let her finish. "How could you ever doubt me Roz? Surely you know that I would go with you to the ends of the earth, if needs be. As long as we can be together, nothing else matters; but I don't know how I shall avoid discussing it with my uncle. I hate to go on deceiving him. It pains me to have to do so, but if it is to keep you safe, then I suppose I have no alternative but to do as you ask."

The young lovers talked together in subdued whispers for a very long time, formulating their plans. Rosalind told him that her mother was to ask her aunt for help. They might even be able to go south to her plantation, if she was in agreement. She gradually persuaded Benjamin that it would be prudent to wait awhile, so that they might make their escape safely. He knew that the coming weeks would be difficult, but to alleviate her fears, he promised that he would do everything he could to give the impression that he fully accepted her coming betrothal to his uncle. How he would manage that, he did not know, but he gave her his word that his uncle and her father would learn nothing from him of their intended abscondment. They both agreed that the sacrifices they were being called upon to make now, were necessary to ensure their freedom and happiness for the rest of their lives.

Suddenly they heard a sound; it was the stable door being opened quietly. "Miss Rosalind... Miss Rosalind is you there?" It was Minnie calling urgently as loudly as she dared, without causing alarm. She was terrified that they might be discovered by her master.

"Yes Minnie, it's all right, I'm here."

"Then you jus' better git back to the house right now... quick... before your pappy finds out you ain't in your room." She turned and hurried away.

"I have to go now Ben, it's not safe for us to stay here for too long. Yoonie will help us to keep in touch, but we must be careful not to arouse any suspicion. Go now my love and please take care of yourself. My heart belongs only to you, and remember, that no matter what arrangements I am forced to make in the coming weeks, concerning my supposed marriage to your uncle, they mean not a thing. Just look forward to the day when we can be together, and be patient my darling... be patient."

"You hold my heart too, Roz," he whispered, "and be assured that you may rely on my complete agreement to any plans you have to make to secure our future together. My only regret is that you are the one having to carry that burden, if I could spare you, I would. Never doubt me my love... never ever doubt me."

They crept stealthily from the stables and went their separate ways, each deeply concerned for the well-being of the other. They were happy in their newfound love, but wondered how they would survive the uncertainty of the coming weeks, or how they would endure the interminable separation.

Seven

By the following morning, Henry Youngman had recovered enough to return to the yard, and as usual Benjamin was hard at work when he arrived at the office. He had not slept at all well, because of his throbbing, aching gums, and in his hours of wakefulness, Gilbert Hetherington's accusations against Benjamin returned to haunt him again and again, so that he had longed for the morning when he would have the opportunity to speak to the boy, to find out why he should have been so maligned. He sat down wearily at his desk and looked across at his nephew, who was seemingly engrossed in checking down a long list of some sort. He had purposely waited until coming into the office to speak to him, for there he knew they would have privacy. He wanted to get this unpleasant task over and done with, so he cleared his throat noisily, then blurted out, "Were you in Hetherington's parlour on Sunday afternoon with his daughter?"

Benjamin felt his face reddening. He had been dreading a confrontation with his uncle and he wished that he could just tell him the whole truth and be done with it, but he knew that was not possible; so despite his embarrassment, he looked his uncle straight in the eye and replied, "Yes sir I went to visit her with Yoonie, Lydia and the twins."

This statement seemed to puzzle his uncle somewhat. His brow puckered and he sat quietly for a few moments, twirling his pen in his fingers and digesting what Benjamin had said. "Oh... so you were there with Eunice and the others were you?"

"Yes sir."

Henry Youngman reflected on what Gilbert Hetherington had told him. The man had never mentioned that any of the others were there. In fact, he had given the distinct impression that his nephew had been alone with Rosalind. He was completely puzzled. "Then why would Gilbert Hetherington be so perturbed about it?" he asked. "It doesn't make sense, does it?" He noticed his nephew's embarrassment and attributed that to the fact that he was coy about his relationship with Eunice. He decided to put the boy at his ease... encourage him a little. "I have noticed that you and Eunice appear to be extremely fond of one another. Is that so?"

"Oh yes, sir. We enjoy one another's company very much," Benjamin answered without hesitation, but he wondered where this line of questioning would lead.

"That pleases me Ben, it pleases me a great deal." The boy's enthusiastic response encouraged him. He continued more confidently, "I told Hetherington that he was mistaken when he suggested that you were interested in his daughter. I told him that you had eyes only for Eunice. The man's a fool. I knew it all along. I'll tell you now, my boy, that I had been hoping for someone like you to come along and wed that daughter of mine. You'll be set for life if you do, I'll make sure of that." He was staring intently at his nephew. "Nothing would give me greater pleasure than to see you two settled in wedlock. Just as soon as you feel ready for it, let me know." He nodded contentedly.

Benjamin hardly knew what to do. He had to speak out right now. He could not allow his uncle to continue with this train of thought. "Forgive me, sir, but I think you have made a serious mistake. I am very fond of Yoonie, she is a fine young woman, who would no doubt make an excellent wife for somebody one day, but she and I are just friends, very good friends, nothing more. Please don't misinterpret our friendship. There could never be anything more between us."

Once again his uncle became puzzled. He smoothed his moustache over and over again with his forefinger and thumb, unable to comprehend what these two youngsters had been up to of late. He would get to the bottom of it now though, he was determined of that. "But the way you two are always together... it's obvious to anyone that you are fond of each other. You'd make an ideal couple, a perfect match. As far as I'm concerned, she couldn't wish for a better suitor, one from her own family; especially from the business viewpoint. Keep it in the family eh? Now what do you say Ben?"

The boy shook his head from side to side in dismay. "No sir, no. I've told you we are just good friends."

The older man was not to be deterred. He wouldn't listen to a refusal. "Good friends? Well that's a solid enough foundation for a marriage. I've known many that were built upon far less. I'll talk to Eunice... I'm sure that you must have realised by now that it would be a good deal for you. You'd be wise to give it some more thought. Just leave it to me."

He knew that his daughter was a strong-minded individual with the most outlandish views; enough to deter even the most stalwart of men, but it was high time he rid her of those nonsensical opinions she was always spouting. He would point out to her that she would never induce anyone to marry her and settle down if she did not modify her way of thinking. What were women coming to these days, he'd like to know?

Benjamin felt uneasy; he tried again. "Look Uncle, please… I cannot permit you to go on with this. I simply do not love Eunice, and that is an end of it, I could never marry her and I know full well that she would not wish to marry me either. It would cause tremendous embarrassment if you ever mentioned the subject to her."

Henry Youngman was growing impatient. He was not interested in Ben's objections. "You don't love her? What do you mean, you don't love her? What has that to do with anything? I've never heard such balderdash in my life. What do you know of love, a mere boy? You get rid of all that romantic nonsense and keep your feet firmly on the ground if you want to get ahead in this world." He thumped the table with his fist. "And let me tell you, that so called love you're going on about, is no more than lust, make no mistake about it, pure lust, and Eunice would be just as good between the sheets as any other female. You have a lot to learn… oh yes, indeed you do boy."

Benjamin was sickened by what the older man was saying. How could he speak of his daughter in that way? And worse still, the thought of his beloved Rosalind being traded by her father to such a loathsome man was unthinkable to him. His emotions took hold, he said gruffly, "I may be a mere boy, sir, but I hope that I have more sensitivity and concern for women than you are exhibiting with your tasteless remarks; and I know only too well what it is to fall in love."

"Hah! So you think you do, eh?" His uncle was ridiculing him. "And who do you suppose you have fallen in love with... who is this fortunate female? Come on then, let's hear about it."

"It happens to be Rosalind Hetherington, sir. She stole my heart the very first time I met her, and that is not lust... my love for her is pure and true, and I would never have it compared with lust." He realised immediately what a foolish disclosure he had made, but his emotions were running high and he simply could not stomach the lewd remarks that this man was making.

Henry Youngman sat bolt upright, as though he had been dealt a blow. "What did you say? What did you say?" he spluttered. "I hope my ears are deceiving me." He was livid. "How dare you sit there and admit that to me, knowing that I am about to marry the girl. So, it seems Gilbert Hetherington is not half the fool I had imagined. What did he witness between you and his daughter that threw him into such a rage, eh?" He jabbed a podgy forefinger at his nephew and exclaimed wildly, "You had better take care boy, I'm warning you; you're treading a dangerous path. I didn't bring you over here to go philandering around with my future wife. You'd better get any such ideas out of your head straight away, do you hear me, or you'll be out of that door a good sight quicker than you came in... do I make myself clear? You just thank the Lord that your mother happens to be my sister, or by thunder I'd kick you out myself, right now."

Benjamin realised that his imprudent disclosure would bring down the wrath of his uncle upon him, but he had never dreamed to what extent. He was deeply shocked at the older man's outburst, his uncontrolled fury. He was raging, and Ben quivered at the very thought of what Rosalind might have been made to suffer at the hands of such a violent man. He knew now that his uncle was no better than her own father. What fate would have befallen her he wondered, had they not met and fallen in love with one another. He was afraid of jeopardizing her position any more than he had already, so he would have to comply with his uncle's demands, at least for the time being, but he would take comfort from the knowledge that one day soon he could take her away with him to safety.

"I'm waiting boy," bellowed his uncle. "Can you give me your assurance that I shall hear no more of this nonsense from you? Can I trust you not to speak of it again? If so, then for the sake of your dear mother, I shall keep you gainfully employed here as I promised her. Now, let me have your word that you will forget this conversation ever took place... I don't want to hear you mention Rosalind Hetherington again. Is that agreed?"

Benjamin had no difficulty in making such a promise. He had no intention of ever mentioning Rosalind's name to this despicable man again. Now he must bide his time until she was good and ready to leave with him; until then, their secret was secure.

Ben picked up the list that he had been checking and hurried out of the office. He wanted to get away; he needed to breathe some fresh air and allow himself time to calm down before going into the warehouse. He stood at the bottom of the iron stairway and took several gulping breaths. The cold air felt good, it refreshed him and helped to clear his head before he went in to talk to the drivers about their consignments.

As soon as he had gone, his uncle snatched pen and paper and scribbled a note to Gilbert Hetherington. He had to see the man as soon as possible, to expedite the wedding arrangements. He opened the window and called down into the yard to Oscar Holz, one of the general hands, to come up to the office. When the man came in, he handed him the note, carefully sealed in an envelope, and instructed him to go up to 'Fortune's Hand' and make sure that Gilbert Hetherington received it without delay. "Should he be down at his storehouse along the river, then you take it to him there. Don't come back until you have delivered it, and wait for a reply; is that understood?"

"Yes sir."

The man left and headed straight for the stables to get one of the horses. He scrambled astride its bare back and trotted off on his errand.

Henry Youngman sat down at his desk again, brooding over what had taken place between himself and his nephew. He found it difficult to believe what the boy had told him, but at the same time he could well understand how the heart of any red-blooded man would be captured by Rosalind Hetherington. He drifted off dreamily into a reverie, thinking of what it would be like when she became his wife. He must marry her, and very soon, or as Hetherington had warned him, he might lose her.

Oscar Holz did not find Gilbert Hetherington at home, so he rode along the river to his storehouse, where he found him deep in discussion with his Indian agents. Oscar jumped down from the horse and handed over the note. He stood patiently waiting for a reply, as he had been instructed. He watched the other man nodding approvingly; he was obviously pleased to read what had been written. "Good... good," he said. "You can tell Mr Youngman that I shall call upon him this evening, at around 7 o'clock. It will be my pleasure."

As the clock chimed the hour, Gilbert Hetherington was being shown into the study where Henry Youngman sat waiting for him. He lifted the brandy decanter and looked enquiringly at his guest, who nodded his head in acceptance. As he handed over the drink, Henry Youngman motioned the other man to sit. "I think I owe you an apology," he said. "It would seem that your suspicions were well-founded concerning that young nephew of mine, but I have taken him to task over it and I can assure you that he will not be bothering Rosalind again... no sir, I couldn't believe my ears when he admitted that your accusations were true, but I have taken care of it now, so let that be an end of the matter."

"All right Henry, if you say so, I'll not interfere. Although I cannot understand why you did not make it your business to see my daughter during my absence. Had you done so, then maybe her attention would not have wandered elsewhere."

"I appreciate that I have been neglectful in that respect, but you know I had terrible difficulty in bringing the boy from New York. The weather was atrocious and I came down with a heavy cough and cold afterwards. It took me awhile to get over it. Then I thought to get something done about my teeth, in readiness for my coming betrothal, you know how it is... and that put me out of circulation again. It was just unfortunate that these things happened one on top of the other. It couldn't be helped, I'm afraid, but just as soon as I have done with Dr Swayze, I shall make it my business to see Rosalind and finalize all the arrangements. Has she mentioned a special date that would please her? I shall be happy to agree to whenever she chooses, although I hope that it will not be too long delayed."

"Well, she and her mother seem set on a spring wedding; something to do with the weather being more settled. They are making a start on the arrangements, ordering dresses and suchlike, and I am inviting my older sister from North Carolina. I hope she will accompany my son Edmund on the journey, because Rosalind is anxious for her brother to be at her wedding."

"Of course, of course... that is only natural, I fully understand. These things are best left to the womenfolk. I daresay Eunice would like to be of assistance too, it'll take some organizing. We'll leave everything in their hands. That will be fine."

"You haven't forgotten our bargain, have you Henry? I'm looking forward to the signing of the documents in connection with our partnership, on the day the wedding takes place."

"I'll have them ready for you, don't worry, exactly as we agreed. A bargain's a bargain."

The two men looked steadily at each other, raised their glasses in salute, then tipped back their heads and drained down the last of the fiery liquid in one gulp.

Grace 1838

One

Mose urged the horses into a gallop and the wooden cart lurched from side to side over the rough unmade road. The young girl in the back spread her arms to steady herself and Mose called over his shoulder, "Is you all right back dere? We soon home now and then we is gonna git you sump'n ta eat." The girl didn't answer, but just looked out over the sides of the cart, anxious to see where she was being taken to start her new life. She had been sold on the auction block earlier in the day to a Mr Percy Mansfield-Brown and he had paid the grand sum of $1,250 for her; she was a 'best brown girl' and the bidding was always high for the choicest slave. Mose felt sorry for his lone passenger, she was no more than a child really, small and slim with wistful eyes, but she would certainly be a beauty in a year or two, he could see that. Massa had bought her special for his wife, to be a 'house girl', so she had to be a 'best'.

Percy Mansfield-Brown was riding up ahead in the pony and trap with his wife's young brother Douglas Hetherington, whom he had taken with him to the auctions today, because this nineteen-year-old wanted to learn everything there was to know about the running of the plantation, and that included the buying and selling of the slaves. Douglas knew that there was a lot to be learned, but as far as he could see, it was to prove fascinating in the extreme.

He could scarcely believe that it was but a few months since he and his brother Gilbert had been met by their older sister Lilybee as their ship had docked in New York. He had no wish to recall the unpleasantness of the sea voyage from England, nor indeed the circumstances which had prompted their father to despatch them in such haste to Lilybee and her husband in America. However, Douglas was feeling, at last, that perhaps he was not so unfortunate as he had at first believed. Indeed, his life since coming to his brother-in-law's plantation in North Carolina, had certainly taken a turn for the better. He thrilled at the numerous opportunities he had of wielding his power over the slaves who worked the plantation, and he made sure that he never missed a chance of exerting that power.

His brother-in-law slowed the pony and trap as it turned into the driveway of 'White Lakes' his plantation home. It was an imposing mansion of great elegance, set well back from the road, with close-clipped lawns, sweeping down to a gently flowing river. The house itself, shaded by tall trees and surrounded by beautifully kept gardens, looked cool and inviting with its wide verandahs and its white Grecian pillars supporting the roof. This picture of grandeur also met the eyes of the newest arrival, as Mose brought the heavy cart to a lumbering halt behind his master. "Take the new girl down to the cabins," called Percy Mansfield-Brown. "Let her feed and rest tonight and bring her up for Madam to see her in the morning."

"Ye' sir," replied Mose, as he flicked the whip lightly over the horses and drove his young charge the last short distance down to the cluster of log cabins which housed all the slaves, and which lay on the far perimeter of the plantation, near to the fields where most of them worked. The cabins were dark and dingy with no windows, and there was a communal dining room in which they all took their meals. This was where Mose finally drew to a halt, then he jumped down and strode quickly around to the back of the cart to help his young passenger down. As he placed his large strong hands under her armpits to swing her to the ground, he noticed how thin and under-nourished her body felt beneath the torn cotton dress that she was wearing. It occurred to him that at least now she would be fed regularly and given a decent dress to wear. She cast down her eyes ashamedly, almost as though she was aware of what he was thinking. He smiled broadly at her. "Has you got a name Missy? I'll take you in to Angelique, she one of the cooks here and she soon git yo' sump'n ta eat. You mus' be real hungry 'bout now, 'cos likely you ain't had nothn' ta eat since sunup. Ain't that right Missy?"

"I is called Grace," said the young girl, catching hold of the sides of her shabby dress and simulating a slight curtsy. To this brow-beaten scrap of humanity, Mose in his bright checked shirt and tidy pants presented a personage of privilege, and she knew how to behave when the circumstances arose.

Mose bent his broad muscular frame towards her and gently lifted her chin with his enormous forefinger. "You don' never have to go a curtsyin' to old Mose now, little missy. There ain't no need for you to do that. Does you understand?" Again she cast down her eyes. Suddenly he felt as though he wanted to gather her into his strong arms and protect her from everyone and everything that might ever present a threat to her innocent young life. What was it

241

about her that made him feel this way, he wondered? He took her gently by the arm and led her into the kitchen of the dining room where Angelique was stirring an enormous cauldron that was simmering over the fire. The mouth-watering smell from the stewed meat and vegetables filled the log cabin. "That sho' smells good Angelique," said Mose. "You got enough in that pot to feed us two? This 'ere's Grace and she gonna work up at the house for the Lady Lilybee. She had a long day, so jus' soon as she done eatin', she better git to sleep. I's jus' gonna put them horses to the stable, then I be back for some o' that food myself."

"Sit yo'self down honey-chile, and you can git some of Angelique's gumbo inside of youse," called the kindly-looking old woman over her shoulder. "It' sho' looks like you is in need of it. Why, you ain't nothin' but skin and bone. Where is you from chile? It don' look like youse been looked after, no how. We is sho' gonna have to git you cleaned up some before you goes up to the house to see the Lady Lilybee in the mornin', but don' you go mindin' about that now; you jus' eat."

Grace picked up the spoon that Angelique laid on the table beside the large bowl of steaming gumbo, and set about eating it with great relish. She could not remember anything ever tasting so delicious and her benefactress smiled pityingly down at her, at the same time ladling out another generous measure of the stewed meat and vegetables on to her plate. As she was scraping her bowl clean, Grace thought lovingly and longingly of her mother. Would she ever see her again, she wondered? She thought not, for her mother was very sick and had been for some time. Her former owner was not one of the privileged rich planters, as was Percy Mansfield-

242

Brown; on the contrary, he had worked in the fields alongside the few slaves that he owned, trying to eke out a living from his meagre crop. Frequently, there had been insufficient food to eat, and it was not unusual for Grace and her mother to go to bed hungry. The young girl could not help comparing this heavily-built, over-weight, seemingly happy-go-lucky woman, with the painfully thin, semi-starved image of her mother, that she carried in her mind, and she could hardly recall her father, although her mother had constantly spoken of him and told her of how, when Grace was just a small child, he had been sold at auction because he was an expert field hand, and as his owner had fallen into insurmountable debt, he had been forced to sell Daniel, his most valuable slave.

For Daniel, the pain and heartache of being separated so tragically from his wife and child had been too much for him to bear, and one day, overcome with longing, he had just slipped away from his new owner and tried to make his way back to his former home and his wife Chloe and his daughter Grace. He had almost reached them when, as so often happened with runaway slaves, the bounty hunters with their hounds had tracked him down.

Upon his recapture, and to prevent him from attempting to escape again, they had brutally chopped off half of his right foot, and then he had been dragged back unconscious to his rightful owner. After the inhuman treatment to which he had been subjected, it seemed that the spirit simply ebbed out of Daniel, and he never recovered, but just died a lingering and painful death from his injury, which never healed. When word of her husband's fate eventually reached Chloe, a part of her died too, and she never overcame her grief.

Suddenly, the exhaustion of her arduous day engulfed the young girl and, coupled with the recollection of her mother's tragic life and now their final parting from one another, it was simply too much for her to endure. Without warning, her head fell with a jerk down on to her chest and she started to sob uncontrollably, just as Mose reappeared at the door of the cabin. Immediately, both he and Angelique were beside the distraught figure; the older woman gathered her small frail body into the bounteous fullness of her own and tried to comfort her as only a mother could. "Dere, dere, honey-chile, you is gonna be fine, jus' you see. There ain't nothin' for you to fret about no more. We is gonna see to that, ain't we Mose?"

He was down on bended knees beside Grace and the kindly face of this enormous man was peering up into the tear-stained face of the small lonely child who had captured his heart, and his voice was hoarse as he spoke, "Mose is gonna take care of you from now on missy, so you jus' dry them tears and then we is gonna git you to bed. You is jus' tired out, that's all." So saying, he lifted her gently from Angelique's voluminous embrace and cradled her as though she were a baby in his strong arm. Indeed, it occurred to Mose that she felt just as small and fragile as a baby as he strode through the door of the cabin and made his way along the dusty path to the sleeping quarters, with Angelique padding heavily along behind him in her big loose shoes, her breath coming in short gasps.

She opened the door of the first cabin that they came to and peered into its dark interior; there were four bunk beds inside, but only two of them had occupants, so she beckoned Mose quietly inside, pressing her forefinger to her thick full lips, to ensure that he did not disturb the other two girls. There was not too much danger of this, for they were both field hands and had long since gone to bed, having been worked until they had dropped.

Angelique and Mose quietly fussed and comforted Grace, as Mose laid her to rest on the rough bunk which was to be her sleeping place from now on, and stroking her forehead lightly, he murmured, "You jus' git to sleep now, missy, and Mose'll come for you in the morning after breakfast, when you is ready; then we go on up to the house to see the Lady Lilybee. No more cryin' now, 'cos you is gonna be all right."

Grace sank thankfully on to the crude bunk bed and looked up into the two concerned faces above her. She had never before experienced such kindness from anyone, other than her mother, and she was completely overwhelmed by it. "Thank you, thank you both," she whispered, as her eyelids slowly closed. Her last thoughts were of her mother and she drifted off into a deep slumber before she had even had time to finish her childlike prayer for her mother's safety.

Mercifully, she did not know, and she was never to find out, that her beloved mother had already departed this life to join her father, for when Grace had kissed her goodbye in the early morning hours, the last small glimmer of light had finally gone out of Chloe's world and she slipped peacefully away.

Two

Shortly after daybreak the following morning, Angelique once again shuffled along the dirt path to the cabin where she had helped to put Grace to bed the previous night. She pushed open the door and a weak shaft of light filtered into its gloomy interior. She could scarcely see the two sleepy faces of Eliza and her granddaughter Ophelia, but she called softly to them to get up, and told them to wake the new girl and bring her with them when they came for their breakfast. Then she was gone, anxious to get to the kitchen to prepare the first meal of the day for the rest of the field hands. There were three cooks for the mammoth task of serving meals for more than one hundred and thirty workers. Most of the house slaves took their meals in the slaves' kitchen up at the house, but there were still more than enough mouths for Angelique and her two assistants to feed. The kitchen of the long cabin was her domain and everyone respected her authority for the running of it.

She had been at 'White Lakes' plantation for as long as she could remember; long before Mr Percy Mansfield-Brown had owned it. In fact, she and her mother had been bought by the previous owner at an auction of slaves, horses and other cattle; here the mother and child had been purchased together with sixty sheep and a strong work horse for one hundred and fifty dollars. She had come there when she was just a tiny baby and whilst her mother had worked from dawn to dusk in the cotton fields, she had been cared for by the younger children who were not old enough to work. The infants were placed in baskets with ropes tied to their handles, then they were suspended from the trees and the younger children set to swinging them. Although she had never married, when Angelique was seventeen years old, she had borne a baby daughter whom she named Eulalia. The young slave girls were greatly encouraged to bear children, and they were often rewarded with a new dress when they did so, because for many planters, their most profitable product was the slave who could be sold. Then when young Eulalia had just turned fifteen years old, she herself had given birth to a daughter, whom she called Ophelia. Less than a year later, however, Eulalia was sold at auction, because as a sturdy young woman, she could fetch a good price. When she learned that her daughter was to be sold, Angelique had wept for days. She thought that her heart would break, and had it not been for her baby grand-daughter, she would have been completely inconsolable, but to help overcome her grief, she devoted herself to little Ophelia, who was to grow up never knowing her own mother.

Following Angelique's instructions, Eliza and Ophelia awakened Grace and took her with them down to the long cabin to get their breakfast. On the way, as young girls do, they plied this interesting new arrival with questions of how and why she had come to 'White Lakes'. Grace, being naturally quiet and reserved, answered their childlike questions with as few details as possible. It was not that she resented their friendly interrogation, but simply that she had never been used to company of her own age. In fact, when she came into the enormous communal dining room, she was quite taken aback at the hive of activity which met her gaze. Never before in her young life had she seen so many people congregated together at one time, not even in the poor country church that she and her mother had attended with the family who owned them. She felt lost and alone, despite the fact that so many people were milling around her and she longed for the quiet comfort she had known with her mother, even though their life had been so very poor and deprived.

Suddenly, all the workers were filing outside and assembling into 'gangs', and a smaller group of men were taking instructions from a white 'massa', who had just arrived on horseback. Grace was later to learn that he was their 'overseer', a man whom they all feared and hated. He was telling the smaller group of men, the 'slave drivers', what work their gangs were expected to do that day. He came every morning to assign the various jobs to the slaves, such as tending the cotton, hoeing the corn, cultivating other food crops, cutting wood, hauling water, and feeding livestock, apart from all the household chores.

There was always much work to be carried out on a plantation of this size, as cotton growers also raised most of the food that was eaten by their family and slaves. Once they had received their orders, all the workers set off either towards the cotton fields, or to wherever else their labour was required. As they filed slowly along the dusty paths, a few deep melodious voices began to sing softly, to be joined gradually by others of different tone, until the voices of men and women in unison were filling the early morning air with the most beautiful sound that Grace had ever heard. There was no musical accompaniment, but none was needed when voices of that magnificence blended in harmony. The sweet resonant sound echoed over the shabby cluster of log cabins, and then trailed off into the distance as the long shambling line of field hands reached their place of work. Grace would eventually come to know and love every one of those negro spiritual songs that were so much a part of this new community she had been brought to.

As quiet once again descended on the long cabin, Grace was fascinated to see several quite small children line up in front of Angelique, their round innocent faces staring up into her large kindly one. She was carefully explaining to them what kitchen chores they were to carry out. These children were quarter-hands, and they were employed only part-time until they grew old enough to become full hands. Suddenly she heard a deep voice boom out from the open doorway.

"Is you ready to come on up to the house now, Missy?" She turned around to see Mose smiling broadly at her.

"Now you jus' hold yo' hosses Mose," said Angelique, "she ain't going nowhere looking like she does, no sir she ain't. You jus' come on over here to Angelique honey-chile and I is gonna git you cleaned up some 'fore you goes up to see the Lady Lilybee." Angelique took a huge iron pot filled with hot water from the top of the stove and poured some of it into a large tin bowl on the table in front of her. Then she plunged a piece of soft cloth into it, wrung it out and applied it to Grace's upturned face. Next she placed her ample hand on top of the girl's head, pressing it down on to her chest, and slapped the soggy cloth around her neck, back and front. With several deft movements, she succeeded in freshening up Grace's appearance to her satisfaction. "Now you give yo' hands a good wash in that bowl, and then you is ready," she said contentedly.

Grace did feel fresher after her encounter with the warm wet cloth, so she and Mose then made their way up to 'White Lakes' Mansion, her small delicate hand tightly clasped in his strong reassuring grasp. Any nervousness that Grace had been feeling as she walked towards the palatial residence, through its immaculately kept grounds, was magnified a thousand fold as she was finally led in by one of the attractively dressed housemaids, to be inspected by the lady of the house. She was dumbfounded and her eyes grew wide in wonderment at what now met her gaze. In all her young life she had never beheld such opulence, nor could she ever have imagined the magnificent style in which the rich Southern planters lived. Their homes were places of distinction and beauty, full of old world luxuries, and Grace was now privileged to see one of the most impressive of them. There was fine old furniture, exquisite silverware gleaming atop highly polished surfaces, tapestries hung from the walls and magnificently carved cabinets displaying curios and a collection of rare books. The Lady Lilybee herself was dressed in the prettiest gown of lavender silk and hand sewn lace, and she was smiling at her, yes, she was actually smiling at her. Grace was entranced by her beauty. To the naive girl, she looked exactly like the angel in the picture she had seen in the small country church that she used to attend with her mother. She never dreamed she would ever see a real one down here on earth. She thought that they all lived up in heaven with Jesus. The angel spoke, "Why, come in child and let me look at you."

Grace felt a firm poke between her shoulder blades from the housemaid who was standing just behind her; this propelled her towards the mistress and she fell forward awkwardly and tripped as she tried to regain her footing, but once she had steadied herself, she took hold of the sides of her shabby dress and curtsied as her mother had taught her to do. She cast down her eyes and kept them riveted on her bare dusty feet. "What is your name child?" asked Lilybee.

"I is called Grace ma'am," she stammered.

"Grace? Mmm, that is a pretty name, I like it. Now Grace, you are to work up here in the house for me, so you will try to learn all that there is to know from the other house girls, do you understand?"

"Yes ma'am."

"Good. That is fine; they will tell you what your duties are, but first I think we must clean you up and then dress you properly. Will you take care of her Mattie? Take her over to Mercy, so that she can measure her up for some dresses, will you?"

"Yes ma'am," answered Mattie.

"Oh, and don't forget to find her some shoes. Isaac should have some in the servants' stores to fit her. Now you may run along. Go to Hannah so that she can give you a bath before you have the fitting for your dresses, won't you?"

The two girls bobbed a curtsy and left the elegant room with its elegant occupant, then quickly made their way back to the slaves' kitchen which was at the rear of the house. On their way, Mattie found time for a chat, which was her favourite pastime. "Ain't she pretty?" she said. "Has yo' ever seen a lady like that before?"

"No, never," whispered Grace, still overawed from her encounter with the Lady Lilybee. "She look jus' like an angel, and I thought they was only up in heaven with Jesus."

"She really kind too," said Mattie. "She don't never talk mean to nobody, not nobody. Everyone say she the best mistress they's ever had."

Grace could not believe that she was to become part of all this splendour. How she wished that her mother could be here with her to see it all too. She was now longing to go and see Mercy to be measured for her dresses, then later on she would be given some shoes. It was like a dream; was it really happening, she wondered?

Once back in the kitchen, Mattie could not wait to impart to Hannah all the instructions that she had been given, with particular reference to the bath that Grace was to receive before being taken over to Mercy for the fitting of her dresses. No sooner had the word 'Bath' been mentioned, than Hannah set about the task with enthusiasm. Motioning to Grace to follow her, she departed through a doorway at the end of the kitchen, which led into a large stone floored washroom, where several slaves were busy with the household laundry. There were a number of enormous wooden tubs arrayed on benches along one wall and some of the laundresses were energetically agitating large volumes of clothing up and down in hot soapy lather, sweat streaming down their faces and dripping off to disappear beneath the soapy foam that was frothing up over the sides of the tub. The atmosphere in the washroom was hot and oppressive, and a smell of soiled clothing and pungent soap pervaded the air. Again Hannah motioned to Grace; she poked a finger in the direction of an empty wooden tub of enormous proportions, which was standing on the floor in a corner.

"You jus' git a pail and pour plenty of water in that tub gal," she said, "and you can help her," she called out to Mattie, who had been following Grace like a shadow ever since she had been assigned to take care of the new girl earlier in the morning. "Come on now, we hasn't got all day." The two girls struggled back and forth with their pails several times to a huge copper full of hot water, and gradually managed to almost fill the giant vessel. When Hannah decided that they had put in enough water, she said, "Git outa that rag yo' is wearing and put yo'self down in there."

As the self-conscious girl stepped gingerly into the steaming water, Hannah placed her hands on to her shoulders and pressed down firmly. Grace disappeared almost up to her neck and she grabbed at the rim of the tub to right herself, whereupon Hannah began to lather and scrub her vigorously all over with a giant-sized bar of laundry soap and a large piece of soft cloth.

She plunged it in and out of the warm suds, then held it aloft and wrung it out, so that the copious foam cascaded all over her captive's head; this too was rubbed with great fervour and after several minutes, having satisfied herself that her job was now well done, Hannah called for Mattie to bring another pail of clean water for the rinsing. Soap suds had trickled down into Grace's eyes and ears and she was bending her head forward with her screwed up fists pressed tightly into her eye sockets, trying to prevent the sting of the strong caustic soda. She had never received a cleansing like this for as long as she could remember, but afterwards, as she assisted Hannah to dry her off with a large coarse towel, she felt as though she had experienced a rebirth. Suddenly, it was as though all the hardship, toil and tragedy she had known in her young life, until that moment, had disappeared, along with the dust and grime that had been so thoroughly removed from her exterior. Having taken such trouble in the cleansing of her body, Hannah was determined that Grace should not become soiled again by the torn dirty rag of a dress that she had removed prior to her bath, but it was obvious that she could not walk around stark naked, so she sidled over to one of the women who was carefully ironing all manner of garments and had a whispered conversation with her. When she came back to Grace, she handed her a large, red checked, cotton tablecloth and promptly set about instructing her on how to make an attractive sarong-style dress by swathing it around her body. In an instant Grace became transformed into the beautiful young woman she really was, and Hannah and Mattie could not disguise their admiration. "Yo' sho' is a beauty," said Hannah, shaking her head from side to side in amazement. "Or yo' will be when yo' gits some flesh on that half-starved body yo' has under that cloth." A wave of pity had swept over her when she had seen how undernourished Grace was as she had removed her torn shabby dress earlier. "Sho' can't wait to see how good looking yo' is when Mercy gits yo' all dressed up in them special dresses she gonna make yo'." Grace sensed that she looked radiant. The warm water and over generous applications of soap had had a magical effect upon her. She was glowing from head to toe, but she had no conception of just how beautiful she really appeared to others. Her mother had been a mulatress and Grace had inherited her mother's exceptional beauty. Her skin was a delightful smooth, golden

254

brown and her features were finely moulded, but from her father she had inherited the most enormous black eyes, which sparkled like diamonds and illuminated her whole face. The combination was captivating. Mr Percy Mansfield-Brown had chosen her very carefully from the slaves on the auction block yesterday, and now it became apparent that he had chosen well.

Mattie was thoroughly enjoying her role of chaperone for the day, and she was strutting along like a peacock beside this delightful girl who had just emerged from the washroom like a butterfly emerging from its chrysalis. They were making their way over to Mercy the dressmaker. Grace too was walking with her head held high, now that she had on a pretty new dress, even if it was only a borrowed tablecloth. She felt strangely different and she was aware of the admiring glances that were being cast in her direction by the workers that they passed. Suddenly, they came upon Mose who was bringing the pony and trap around to the house for the massa; he slowed to a halt and looked down at the beautiful young girl who stood before him. He could not believe the transformation that had taken place since he had last seen her just a few hours ago. He raised his battered straw hat and with a wide sweep of his arm, brought it around to his chest, at the same time bowing his head in a most deferential manner. He looked up smiling broadly. "Who is this fine lady yo' has with yo' today Mattie?" he asked jokingly. "She sho' is a good looker, ain't she?"

Grace's face crumpled into a shy smile and she lowered her eyes demurely, embarrassed at his fine compliment. Mose felt his heart miss a beat, then it began thumping again so loudly that he felt sure Grace would notice. She really was the most captivating girl he had ever met. Why did she touch him so deeply he wondered?

"Where is you going now then, Missy?" he asked, his voice catching in his throat as he struggled to hide his emotion.

Before Grace could say a word, Mattie answered, "We is going over to see Mercy, so Grace can git some dresses fitted; ain't that so Grace?"

Grace nodded her head. "Yes," she said coyly.

"Well, I best let yo' ladies git on with yo' business then," said Mose. "That sho' is some important job yo' is about. I see yo' later Missy, when it time for us to eat."

Then with a soft slap of the reins on the pony's back, he continued on his way.

"I likes Mose," said Grace softly. "He the kindest man I ever knowed."

"He sho' is," replied Mattie. "He Massa's favourite. He been here since he a small boy, and when he growed up, he a 'slave driver' for a long time, but not no more. Now Massa have him to work up at the house most all the time."

"A slave driver?" queried Grace. "What a slave driver?"

"Don' yo' know nothin'? A 'slave driver', he most important. He take charge of a gang and he keep 'em working for the overseer. Everyone like Mose. He a real good man, but Master Douglas and the overseer, Mr Clayton, is real jealous, 'cos Massa Mansfield-Brown like him so much." Oh yes, Mattie was really enjoying herself today, and she chatted non-stop to Grace in her high-pitched voice, recounting every scrap of gossip that she could remember. They finally arrived at the seamstress's cabin, to find her door wide open. Mattie poked her head inside and called to her.

"Come on in then, come on in," answered Mercy cheerily. The sewing machine didn't stop whirring for a second, and Grace watched in fascination as the hands of the tall, thin woman deftly lifted and pushed, lifted and pushed, and the cloth moved rapidly through the machine as the needle sped up and down, in and out, never ceasing in its task until it came to the end of the neat straight seam. Grace was enthralled. The only form of sewing she had ever witnessed was always done by hand. She looked all around the cabin; it was lined with shelves, which held a large quantity of different coloured cotton cloth, most of which Grace recognised as that she had seen the female slaves wearing. She felt a surge of excitement at the thought that she was going to have a new dress. She could only remember having worn second-hand dresses in the past, which her mother had cut down and altered to fit her, and they had been very few. Now she was to have a new dress made specially for her. Again she wondered if she was dreaming; it all seemed so unreal.

Mercy left the garment she was sewing and turned her attention to her visitor. "I can see who is needing a new dress," she said, eyeing the tablecloth that was so attractively swathed around Grace. "Now yo' jus' tell me where you is gonna work and then I make you a dress the right colour."

As usual, before Grace could open her mouth, Mattie provided all the information that was necessary. Mercy turned to one of the shelves and lifted down a length of pretty pale green cotton. It seemed that only the house girls wore dresses of that particular colour, whereas the field hands and rough workers wore dresses of a much coarser grey-coloured cloth, and the cooks and kitchen maids wore brown and white check. Grace had her measurements taken, and Mercy told her that she would add a few inches here and there, to allow room for her to grow. The older woman too had noticed how under-fed the new arrival was, and she fully realised that she would soon put on weight once she started to eat regularly. "Yo' can come and git the dress after breakfast tomorrow," she said, then she unrolled the cloth and spread it across her cutting table ready to make a start on it.

Grace was grateful when it was time for the long noon rest, and she was able to return to the slaves' kitchen for her meal. Once she was seated, she found herself watching the door intently, waiting for Mose to appear. She couldn't wait to tell him all that had happened to her that morning, because she knew that he would listen to her with interest.

She felt that in him she had really found a friend. He was her anchor in this strange new world; someone with whom she felt safe, someone she could trust. Then she saw him strolling through the door, hat in hand. His enormous stature dominated the room, and as his eyes searched along the tables for her, a feeling of pride swept over Grace, something she had never experienced before in her under-privileged upbringing. It was obvious from the way that they greeted him, that everyone liked and respected this giant of a man, and it was not just because of his obvious strength, but more because of his gentle manner. He was kind and courteous to everyone, and Grace could not believe that a man of his standing would ever befriend her. He had no difficulty in finding her among the other girls, and it was not only the red checked tablecloth that made her stand out from the rest of them. He strode over to where she was sitting and placed his hat beside her on the long wooden bench. "I be back in jus' a minute," he said, as he went to fetch his food.

While he was eating, Grace related everything that had happened to her since he had dropped her at the house first thing that morning, and as she talked it surprised her to realise that she had never talked so much to anyone in her life before, particularly a man. Although she was not aware of it, in this man she had found the father figure that she had never known, and it was a most pleasurable experience for her.

Mose listened intently to every word she spoke with such enthusiasm. He enjoyed the soft tone of her voice and the way she had of explaining the smallest detail. One moment she seemed childlike in her naivety, and then in the next she assumed the maturity of a much older woman. This was no doubt due to the fact that she had grown up in almost complete isolation, deprived of the normal protection of her father; then when her mother's health had failed, she had been forced to adopt the role of her protector, despite the fact that she was so young and inexperienced herself.

Mose was completely bemused by her, and almost without thinking, he asked, "Does yo' know how old yo' is Grace?"

"I is fifteen this harvest," she said without hesitation. She knew her age exactly, because over the years her mother had told her every time the anniversary of her birth came around. "My mammy said that it was the hard work that she was at with the harvest that birthed me so quick." Grace went on. "She and pappy was working in the fields from sun up 'til sundown every day. The massa, he didn't have nobody else, jus' my mammy and pappy, and his own kin, to do all the chores, so my mammy couldn't rest up when she about to have me. I was birthed right there in the field by my pappy."

Mose encouraged her to talk of her family, wanting to know everything he could about her. She told him of how her father had come to die so tragically when she was not much more than a baby. Then how her owner had been finally forced to sell her too, in order to reduce his mounting debt. Mose listened sympathetically as she described how she had come to be roused long before daybreak on the previous day, and taken on a very long journey to a place the like of which she could never have imagined in her wildest dream. She had been taken away from her mother for the first time in her life; away from everything that was familiar to her.

It was little wonder, he thought, that her eyes were staring in such bewilderment at everything around her. He felt a tightening in his throat, as her out-pourings brought back memories of his own sad childhood. He himself had been one of five children, all of whom had been sold by their owner when they were old enough to fetch a good price. The planter who had bought his mother when she was a young girl, was not in the least bit interested in planting crops. A slave girl's value to her master was, in part, measured by her capacity for bearing children, and this particular master bred from his slaves as quickly and as cheaply as he could, because since the law was passed in January, 1808, prohibiting the importing of slaves into the United States, there were only two sources of supply left open. One was the bootleg importations from abroad, and the other the domestic trade, namely, slave breeding or rearing for the market. It became increasingly difficult for slavers to import slaves, but even so the importations still continued as an illicit traffic. This illegal trade was even worse and far more brutal than the authorised trade had been.

Then in the year 1820, Congress placed the importation of slaves on the same footing as piracy, and it was made punishable by death. However, with the development of the new cotton states, Alabama, Mississippi, Louisiana and Texas, an increasing slave labour was necessary, in order to keep pace with the opening up of these new lands. With the additional huge demand for slave labour, the unscrupulous planters, who were fully aware of the earnings to be had, entered into the business of breeding them, and they were greatly encouraged by the professional traders, speculators and dealers, who were also assured of enormous profit. In fact, it became far more lucrative for planters, whose lands had become less productive, to enter into the slave breeding business.

That this type of trading brought unimaginable hardship for the slaves, is not to be denied. Thousands of negroes, in degradation and misery, were driven along the highways in coffles, marching and bivouacking in chains, urged on by whip and pistol, herded in stockades or slave pens, torn from their families and sold on the auction blocks as so many cattle. These downtrodden beings were taken into regions where plantations were larger, where tasks were heavier and where their bonds were at once more irksome and more permanent.

It was the intolerable distress brought about by such practices, by being torn from his mother, and his brothers and sisters, at such an early age that had prevented Mose from ever forming a close bond with any other person. He had never before been attracted to anyone, or shown any

261

romantic interest in the other female slaves at 'White Lakes', but this was different. Suddenly he had no control of the situation, and it had taken him completely by surprise. This young innocent girl had unwittingly broken down the defences he had built up around himself over the years, and she had completely stolen his heart. He simply did not know how to cope with the overwhelming depth of feeling he had for this comparative stranger who had come into his life, but he knew that he could never acquaint her of his feelings, for he could not betray the trust which she so obviously placed in him, and which he found so disarming. However, he vowed that he would always guard her as best he could, and try to give her the protection that she had never before known in her young life.

*

When the long noon rest was over, Mattie once again appeared, to take charge of Grace. She herself had spent her rest time with her man Zac. They were planning to marry at some time in the future, and she took great delight in telling Grace of their plans, as the two girls made their way over to the servants' stores, where Grace was to be given some shoes. Isaac was a kindly old man with white hair and a back bent over from years of hard toiling the fields. Now he had a much easier job, more suited to his declining strength. He never tired of telling anyone who would stand and listen to him, of what a good massa Mr Percy Mansfield-Brown was to his workers. As they grew older and more feeble, he always found less arduous tasks for them to do, and for this reason the slaves on 'White Lakes' plantation seldom found reason for complaint. Now Isaac was entrusted with the care of the servants' stores, and he did his job most conscientiously. He took a long hard look at Grace's feet, which he could see had never before had to endure the constriction of footwear, then off he went to rummage amongst his stock. He soon returned, beaming all over his wrinkled, weather-beaten face, and handed Grace a pair of extremely soft black leather boots, which had obviously been worn before, and which he knew would be easier and more comfortable for her to wear, as she was not used to them. "Yo' try dis pair young lady," he said, rubbing them vigorously against the sides of his trousers, to remove the film of dust that had accumulated on them.

Grace's heart leapt in her breast when Isaac held forth the coveted footwear, and she took hold of them eagerly, hardly able to wait to place her feet inside them. She sat straight down on the floor and began the arduous task of pulling them, one by one, over her feet and up her legs, for they had quite high sides. When her feet were firmly encased in them, she stood up and looked down upon them in wonderment, unable to believe that they were her feet projecting from beneath the folds of her newly acquired raiment. The old man stooped down very slowly, and gently pressed his gnarled finger on the end of one of the boots; there were at least two inches to spare. "Yo' got plenty room in there for yo' toes, but that don't matter none, 'cos they soon fit when yo' grow."

"Yes, that don't matter," replied Grace immediately, worried that they might be taken back again. She had never seen such grand boots in her life before, and she was determined to keep them, no matter how much too big they might be. "Is I gonna keep these; is they really mine?" she asked.

Isaac nodded his grey head and laughed at Grace's disbelief. "They sho' is," he answered her kindly. "Now jus' let me tie them for yo', or yo' might go fallin' over them laces." He deftly threaded each of the boots, showing Grace how it should be done. He fastened them as tightly as possible, because her legs were so painfully thin that he feared she might lose them as she walked. Then she turned around and stepped out through the door with Mattie, her head bent forward so that she could enjoy watching her feet as she struggled to walk in the too large boots, which would be her most treasured possession from that moment on. That night she could not bring herself to remove them when she went to bed. Instead she lay on her back, having carefully arranged her thread-bare cover so that it did not reach to her feet, and she gazed in admiration at the soft, black leather boots until her eyes finally closed involuntarily upon the most exciting day she had ever known in her life.

Three

As the days and weeks gradually lengthened into months, Grace found herself settling contentedly into her new life. She had passed her fifteenth birthday during harvest and in so doing had seemed to become far more grown-up than when first she had arrived at 'White Lakes', her newfound happiness made a marked difference in her, which was apparent to everyone. Gone was the lost bewildered child whom Mose had brought into their midst. She had slowly grown and ripened, just as the crops in the fields grew and ripened, and exactly as Hannah and Mercy had predicted, with regular nourishment, her young body had now fully developed from that of an immature girl into that of an attractive curvaceous woman. Even the new dresses which had completely enveloped her when she first wore them, now fitted to perfection. She presented a most delightful picture when she arrived at the house each morning, her pale green dress set off by the fresh white frilled cap and apron. Her feet had still not reached into the extremities of her black boots, but Grace's delight in them had not diminished.

The Lady Lilybee had taken a great liking to the new young girl that her husband had so kindly bought for her. He had made a wise choice, as she very soon discovered. There had been something about this forlorn human being that had reached out to him when, as she had stood upon the auction block, the auctioneer had ripped down her dress at the pressing demands of the prospective bidders, and despite the fact that she had obviously been half-starved and neglected, Percy Mansfield-Brown had seen her potential and had upped the bidding until no others would match his price. Grace had not disappointed him, she had fulfilled her hidden promise, for she had proven to be bright and intelligent and very quick to learn, and that pleased her mistress, who monitored her progress most carefully. She had also been delighted to note how quietly and gracefully this young newcomer conducted herself, and it often occurred to Lilybee that she had been named well, for 'Grace' suited her admirably.

Once the harvest had been gathered in, all the workers were assigned the chores that would keep them gainfully employed during the long winter months which stretched ahead. After the livestock had been slaughtered, they were set to mending the fences and clearing the land in readiness for the following Spring's planting. Up at the house, the talk was constantly of the approaching Christmas season, and Grace was absolutely enthralled by everything that she saw and heard. The grandeur of her master and mistress's lifestyle was completely unbelievable to her, and she never ceased to be astounded by all that she witnessed in the daily routine of the household.

That she had become great friends with Eliza, and Angelique's granddaughter Ophelia, with whom she shared her cabin, was of untold joy to her, and because they both worked out of doors as field hands, they never tired of listening to everything that she had to tell of her wonderful new experiences up at the house, of her different duties and of what happened there each day. The three girls spent many happy hours during the long winter nights, chatting and laughing together, as they lay in their bunks. In fact, Eliza and Ophelia waited eagerly for Grace to return every night, because their working day ended when the daylight hours ended, which was long before Grace finished her duties, and her accounts of life up at the house enchanted them. When listening to her, they could transport themselves from the drabness of their own dark windowless cabin, for they found her tales quite magical; it was as though they were being read chapters every night from a never-ending book. They could not wait for Grace to come to bed to continue her accounts of the day's happenings, and because it compared so unbelievably with their own lowly state, it became even more enchanting to them.

As well as her valued friendship with Eliza and Ophelia, Grace also found considerable enjoyment in her association with Mose. First thing every morning, they walked together up to the house, exchanging snippets of information about their duties and what was happening from day to day in the household. Mose had watched her blossom over the months and he derived untold pleasure from his innocent friendship with her. It pleased him to see how happily she was settling in at 'White Lakes' and how well she looked now in comparison with when she had first arrived. Grace, in turn, found tremendous comfort in the knowledge that Mose watched over her, for true to his word, he took care of her as best he could and tried to ensure that she came to no harm. It was obvious to everyone that they had a tremendous fondness for each other.

One morning, just a few days before Christmas, Mose told Grace that the brother of Master Douglas was due to arrive at any moment from the North, and that he was coming to visit his sister Lilybee and her husband for the holiday. Then Grace told Mose about the arrangements that were being made for the big party to celebrate Christmas Eve, and of how the whole household was at fever pitch with all the preparation. Every one of the house servants would be on duty that night, and Grace could hardly contain herself with excitement as she told Mose that she was to wait on table for the first time, and that she was afraid she might do something wrong. "You'll do jus' fine Missy, so don' yo' git frettin' yo'self' bout that, no siree," he assured her.

Grace smiled coyly at his words of encouragement. She loved him for the gentleness and concern that he never failed to show her.

Finally, Christmas Eve arrived, and Grace set off from her cabin freshly attired for the special dining room duty to which she had been assigned. She bade farewell to Eliza and Ophelia, who had long since finished their work, promising them that she would tell them of everything that happened when she returned later that night. Her excitement was contagious, and they both assured her that they would wait up for her until she came back to the cabin, no matter how late it might be.

All the servants stood in line along the spacious kitchen, and Hannah walked slowly in front of them, carrying out her inspection, and giving them their orders, one after the other. After all the laborious preparations, she was determined that nothing should go wrong with the serving of the grand fare, the cooking of which she had been supervising since early morning.

Suddenly the dinner gong was being sounded and Grace beheld a sight the like of which she had never before witnessed. All the guests were filing into the dining room and seating themselves around the sumptuous table, and the servants began their tasks. It was not just the delicious food which astounded Grace, but the elegance of the clothing worn by the guests. Then there were the grand adornments upon the table: the cutlery, the fine china and glass, the silver candelabra. Everything was just magnificent, and she could imagine the delight of Eliza and Ophelia, later that night, when she described for them how gracious was the life up at the house. Her eyes shone as brightly as the candles which glowed all around the room, and her face too reflected the joy of what she was witnessing.

The guests talked and laughed; ate and drank, and no one to such an extent as the newly arrived guest, Gilbert Hetherington. He was being made to feel welcome by his older sister Lilybee and her husband, as well as his young brother Douglas, whom he had not seen since they parted company in New York shortly after their arrival from England many months ago.

When Douglas had left for Carolina with his sister, Gilbert had decided to stay in New York to try his hand at setting up in commerce in the North. Douglas had been very regretful at their parting, and had missed his brother sorely at first, for the two boys had never been apart before. There was not much difference in their ages, Gilbert being the older by little more than a year. The younger boy had always depended upon his older brother and been led by him; often into serious trouble, which was why their father had finally despatched them in such haste to their sister and her husband in America. However, upon his arrival in North Carolina, Douglas had soon discovered how good life could be down in the South for the prosperous planters; their lifestyle very much resembled that of the gentlemen in their mother country. In fact, the plantations of the South were reminiscent of the country estates in England. They were, in a sense, part of England which had been carried to the New World. Wealthy planters dressed and spoke and acted much like country gentlemen in the mother country. Their religion was essentially protestant, their traditions western European, and their language, law and governmental structure English. Socially, as well as economically, the plantations played an enormously important role in Southern life, which was soft, dreamy and deliciously quiet; a life of repose, or so it seemed; but hidden behind this facade were also the hard repulsive aspects of plantation life. There was a prevalence of drinking and gambling, and the covert relationships of masters with the women slaves. There were a great many abuses of the institution of slavery, and the latter was one of them.

Fortunately for Grace, thus far in her innocent young life she had never been exposed to the wanton attentions of the opposite sex. On the isolated farm where she had been born and reared, she had been completely unaware of problems of this nature that normally beset so many young slave girls on the bigger plantations.

Now, as she busied herself around the table, her graceful movements, the extraordinarily unusual beauty of her features, and the delicate golden-brown colour of her skin, were being lasciviously observed by Gilbert Hetherington. He had, in fact, noticed this delightful young girl immediately he had entered the dining room, and became completely captivated by the way in which her enormous dark eyes gazed in awe at all that was wonderful and new around her. Indeed, every time she had occasion to come near him, his longing intensified. He noticed how the soft green cotton dress that she was wearing, clung provocatively to her firm young figure as she leant carefully between each guest whilst serving their food; her slim waist beneath the band of her white frilly apron; the smooth contours of her neck and arms. It was all he could do to keep from taking hold of her, so greatly burned his desire.

He missed not one minute detail of her shapely young form, and as his blood warmed in response to the potent wines, so did his ardour. He was determined that he should have her before this night was over, and the sooner the better. He had heard many a tale of the sensual delights enjoyed by the slave owners of the South, and he intended not to miss any opportunity that might present itself.

His brother Douglas was perfectly well aware of what was passing through Gilbert's mind, and he smiled inwardly. It was obvious to him that his older brother was still up to his old tricks, despite their father's warning. He fancied that there would be some sport a little later that night, and he thrilled at the thought of it.

When they had finished their meal, the men adjourned to the study to enjoy their brandy and cigars. The two brothers tarried for a short while, chatting confidentially to one another, then, on the pretext that he needed some fresh air, Douglas made his excuses and stepped out on to the

271

veranda. This immediately gave his brother the opportunity to leave too.

"What a good idea, Douglas," he said. "I'll keep you company." Once outside, and unobserved, they lost no time in disappearing in the direction of the kitchen, where they concealed themselves behind some shrubbery, to watch and wait for their unsuspecting victim. "This reminds me of old times. Oh, how I've missed you," Douglas said laughingly.

"Ssh… I think somebody's coming," his brother warned.

The servants began to leave as soon as they had finished their particular jobs; they hurried on their way back to their cabins, for it was late and they felt weary from the extra duties and long hours they had been called upon to do that day. From early morning they had been working on the final preparations, and then returned later in the evening to tend to the guests at the party itself. They were all anxious to be away to their beds, not bothering to wait about for one another as they normally did, for there were not many hours of the night left for sleep.

Eventually, Grace stepped through the kitchen door; she was one of the last to leave. Douglas Hetherington nudged his brother, as he caught sight of her silhouetted against the bright light from the kitchen. They heard her bid goodnight to the few servants who remained, and watched as she hurried along the path towards the cabins. Grace felt so happy, and she smiled to herself as she thought of all she would have to tell Eliza and Ophelia of the grand spectacle she had been privileged to witness that night. They would have to wait to hear her story though, for she was completely worn out, and almost falling asleep on her feet. The path, that wound its way through the extensive gardens, was bordered on either side by trees and shrubs, so Grace did not notice her two pursuers keeping abreast of her, but well hidden behind the thick foliage.

Then, just as she was about to turn off the path in the direction of the cabins, they leapt out, and before she realised what was happening, they had pulled her in the opposite direction, into the shrubbery. As she opened her mouth to scream for help, a large hand was clamped roughly over her mouth and nose, so tightly that she could hardly breathe. She was petrified with fear. "Now you stay quiet and you'll not be hurt," growled Gilbert Hetherington. "Do you understand?"

Grace tried to nod her head, but it was being held rigidly in a vice-like grip. It was not difficult for these two strong young men to lift her bodily and carry her slight frame between them, and as soon as they were well away from the path, and secluded by the shrubs and bushes, they flung her to the ground and Gilbert Hetherington fell heavily upon her before she had time to try to make her escape. Grace felt his urgent clumsy hands ripping at her clothing, and she struggled to be free. Like a trapped animal, she lashed out with her arms and legs in one enormous burst of effort, and as she tried to scream aloud, her cry was stifled by her attacker's hand once again being clamped over her mouth. As his powerful hand squeezed her cheeks painfully, she bit ferociously into his flesh, and heard him groan in agony.

Suddenly, his anger was aroused, and in a blinding upsurge of rage, he rained blow after blow upon her face, almost rendering her unconscious. He did not cease until she was forced to surrender to his superior strength.

For as long as she lived, Grace would never forget the horror of this frenzied attack, nor the evil expression on the face of the man who had so mercilessly violated her. Now she moaned pitifully as she tried to move, for every part of her body ached. She lay whimpering in pain, as she curled herself up, her tears falling silently upon the bloodstained earth beneath her. She wanted to die from the fear and shame of what had happened to her.

She did not know for how long she had lain there when she heard movements around her. In her confusion, she thought it was her attackers again. She cried out in terror, and tried to cover her head with her arm. "No... no..." she screamed.

Mose crouched down beside her and spoke softly, reassuringly. "Sshh ...sshh... Missy, it's all right, it's only me Mose. Don' be afraid girl. You is gonna be all right now."

She could not look at him. She did not want him to look at her. She did not want anyone to look at her ever again. She felt dirty, in a way that she did not understand. She heard a woman's voice, then another answering. Soft comforting sounds. Eliza and Ophelia were beside her, talking quietly as they tried to cover her nakedness with what was left of her torn clothing. Then Mose lifted her gently and held her in his strong arms, swaying her slowly, as though she were a tiny baby in need of comfort and love. She rested her head against his broad shoulder, as he carried her to her cabin. She could feel his tears falling on to her bruised flesh, and hear the sob in his voice as he whispered against her head. "Oh, Missy... my Missy...what has they done to yo'. Who gone done this to you?" He wished with all his heart that he could get his hands on whoever had hurt this innocent young girl so badly. He wished that it was within his power to do that for her, but he knew what would happen if he ever tried.

Slaves belonged to their masters, and they could do with them whatever they wanted.

It was fortunate indeed for Grace that Eliza and Ophelia had been trying to stay awake to hear her account of what had happened at the grand Christmas Eve party. They had both nodded off to sleep in the darkness of the cabin, as the hours crept by, but had awakened intermittently, to see if Grace had yet returned. Eventually, Ophelia had become worried; she could tell that it was well into the early morning hours by now, for there was not a sound to be heard around the slaves' quarters, just the dead silence... the still in the air, that only came when everyone was slumbering deeply. She crawled from her bunk and groped her way in the darkness to awaken Eliza, who had dropped off to sleep again. "Eliza wake up. Eliza." She called her friend urgently as she shook her shoulder.

"Ugh... what? What?" Eliza propped herself up on her elbow. "What wrong, 'Phelia? Is it Grace? Is she come back?"

"No... no, she ain't, and I don' like it. I got a feelin' sump'ns wrong. It nearly morning she shoulda bin back long since. Come on, 'Liza, git y'self outa that bed... we is gonna see where she is." Eliza reluctantly left her bunk, and the two girls pulled on their work dresses before setting off in search of their friend. They were frightened, and clung arm in arm with one another as they made their way slowly along the shadowy path to the house. Almost at the same time, they heard the pitiful sounds coming from deep within the shrubbery, and stopped abruptly, straining their ears, trying to make out what it was. Their eyes were like saucers as they stared at each other, too frightened to investigate any further.

Again they heard a muffled groan, but they could not see anything from where they were standing.

"Quick... we best git my gran'ma," said Ophelia. Eliza needed no second bidding, she could not wait to be gone. They fled together, back along the path, the way they had come.

Angelique was awake immediately, and she lost no time in going to fetch Mose from his cabin; then, whilst her granddaughter and Eliza took him back to the place where they thought Grace might be, she retreated into the kitchen of the long cabin, her special domain, where she stoked up the fire to heat a large cauldron of water. It was the only thing she could think of doing at that moment; the most natural thing for her to do, to try and allay her fear. All the while, she kept one eye on the open door, and when she saw Mose approaching, carrying Grace in his arms, she plodded out as quickly as she could and waved him past, saying, "You git her to her cabin Mose. I'll be there just as soon as I gits a pan of hot water."

She bathed and gently cleansed the bruised battered body that lay on the crude bunk. Ophelia had lit the small oil lamp, and was holding it aloft, so that her gran'ma could see what she was doing. For all her bulk, Angelique's deft movements could not have been more gentle. As Grace flinched and whimpered in pain, this kindly woman spoke comfortingly to her; it was obvious that she had dealt with such cruelly inflicted wounds many, many times before this. She could not bear to recall the number of occasions on which she had gently bathed the bloody lacerations caused by the whippings and beatings of Ralph Clayton, their savage overseer, upon the bodies of any slaves who displeased him.

When she was done, she stroked Grace's head lovingly. "Now you try to git some sleep honey-chile," she whispered. "Angelique'll come and see to you in the mornin'." She motioned Ophelia and Eliza to get to bed and departed with her pan of water.

She almost collided with Mose, as she stepped out into the dark night. "Now you git to your bed... ain't no use in hangin' round here," she scolded softly.

"Is she gonna be all right Angelique?" She could hear how concerned he was.

"Sho' she is... I'll see to that, don't you go mindin' yourself."

"How did it happen... why... why her?" he asked. He was following Angelique slowly back to the long cabin; he was too shocked and upset to think of sleep.

"'Cos she jus' a black slave girl...that's why Mose. Now you forgit about it, you hear me? Aint no good makin' no trouble now... you knows that."

"I ain't about to make no trouble Angelique, but that don't mean I ain't a-mindin' it. It ain't right, no sir, it jus' ain't right. She ain't nothin' but a child; whoever done that to my Missy, well he wants whipping, yes sir he does."

Angelique was worried about the way Mose was acting; she had never ever seen him angry before, not like this; not in all the years they had known one another. They had arrived at the long cabin, and Angelique pushed open the door; she had left it slightly ajar. She was anxious to calm Mose. "Does you want a cup of coffee with me, Mose? I got some good coffee... I hidden it away, if you does."

Mose nodded his head and followed the old woman through the long cabin to the kitchen. He would not be able to sleep any more that night, he knew it, so he accepted her offer of hospitality gratefully.

While she was preparing the coffee, Angelique chattered, "You know Mose, Grace ain't a child no longer… she a beautiful grown young woman. You can see that for yourself, can't you? It ain't no excuse for what happened to her tonight, but that's the reason why it happened. She ain't the first… and she sho' won't be the last. Ain't nothin' we can do about that."

Mose felt choked by his frustration, the futility of his anger. He fell heavily on to the bench beside the table and covered his face with his enormous hands. His broad shoulders heaved with his uncontrolled sobs. Angelique almost dropped the pot of boiling water that she was gently pouring on to her freshly crushed coffee beans. She scurried across to Mose and pulled his head against her ample body. She was deeply shocked to see this giant of a man reduced to such a pitiable state. He was the solid rock to whom so many of them had clung when their troubles had borne them down. She could not believe that he too could succumb to such profound emotion.

"Oh… Mose… don't, don't fret yo'self honey." She spoke soothingly to him and stroked his head gently, as though he were a young child. "I ain't never seen you like this before; don't take it so hard. Grace gonna be fine, sho' she is… ain't gonna do no good if you gives in like this." She knew, as they all did, how carefully he watched over Grace; how fond of one another they were, but she was still touched to see how badly he was taking what had happened to her.

"I can't help it Angelique. I jus' can't stand to think of what they done to her." He tried to compose himself. "I loves that little gal more'n I ever loved anythin'. If she growed up, why I'd ask her to be my wife… but she no more'n a little chile."

"Let me git our coffee," said Angelique, shaking her head sadly from side to side. As she brought the strong sweet brew over to the table, she sat down opposite Mose and looked at him thoughtfully. "I jus' done told you Grace ain't no child any more Mose; she soon be woman enough to be a' marryin' if that's what you has a' mind to."

Mose sipped noisily at his coffee, then leant across the table towards the old woman. He asked her confidentially, "How old you say I is Angelique?"

She thought carefully for a moment, then lifted her podgy fingers and tapped those of her right hand with the forefinger of her left, counting slowly to herself. "I says you mus' be 'bout twenty-nine," she replied solemnly.

"That little gal don't want a old man like me then," said Mose sadly. "Is you sho' I so old Angelique?"

"Sho' I's sho'," she snapped back. "But that don't make no matter. You jus' be patient for another year or two, and she gonna catch up with you a bit. Then she see what a fine catch you is…yes sir, she sho' will." She nodded determinedly, and Mose bit his lower lip and cast his eyes upwards, giving her words of wisdom serious consideration. They finished their coffee in silence, then Mose took a slow walk back to his cabin, just as the light of day began to appear in the sky.

Word of what had happened to Grace soon spread around the plantation, but not a living soul knew who had carried out the attack, for Angelique had warned Grace not to breathe anything to anyone. "Don't you say nothin' about this honey-chile; you hear what I is sayin'?" she whispered to her patient, as she smeared her wounds with a thick layer of her home-made balm. "You jus' forgit all 'bout what happened... that's the only way there is. You jus' find yo'self in a whole heap of trouble if you tells anyone 'bout this."

There was no need of Angelique's dire warning, for in her terrified state Grace had retreated into a shocked silence, and her painfully swollen features engendered such deep pity in the other slaves, that they could not bring themselves to speak to her of what had happened. Instead, they tried to help in the only way they knew how, by carefully concealing her absence from the Master and Mistress. For several days, whilst Angelique gently nursed her, the house servants shared her duties between them, and because the normal routine was completely disrupted by all manner of Christmas festivities, with guests coming and going at all hours, the young girl's presence was not missed.

When Angelique was satisfied that Grace was well enough, she urged her back to work, and watched with concern as she walked slowly beside Mose up to the house. She could not raise her eyes to his, nor did she answer when he spoke to her. Mose was heartbroken and felt as humiliated as did Grace, for he could not rid himself of his guilt at having failed her. When she needed him, he had left her unprotected, or so he believed, and what was worse still, now he was powerless to do anything to put matters right. He wanted to find whoever had carried out the attack and make him pay for his vile crime, but he knew that that was an impossibility. Instead, he could only accompany Grace day after day, as he had always done, and wait patiently for time to heal both her body and her mind.

At the beginning of summer it became obvious that Grace was carrying a child, and this fact did not go unnoticed by the Lady Lilybee. Because of her fondness for the girl, she was more concerned than she might normally have been. She spoke to Percy over breakfast one morning. "Who do you suppose is the father, my dear?" she asked. "I have never noticed Grace spending her time with any of the young boys, have you? She always seems so quiet and withdrawn. I must confess that it has come as quite a shock to me. Could you try to find out who might be the culprit? She is such a child really." Lilybee tut-tutted and gently brushed the corners of her mouth with her serviette. She raised her eyebrows and smiled sweetly at her husband.

"I'll see if Mose has any idea who it might be. He has taken the girl under his wing since she came here; if anyone knows anything, I'm sure he will… but these things happen my dear, you know how the slaves are." He kissed her forehead, then went in search of his manservant.

Mose took a deep breath and his nostrils flared. "No sir, Massa Percy," he said emphatically. "Grace ain't had nothing to do with none of the young boys… no sir she ain't. She ain't never looked at nobody since the day she came here, and I's took care of her like I's her own pappy… I sho' has."

"Well… someone is responsible for her condition Mose. Haven't you any idea who it might be?" coaxed Percy.

Mose kept his eyes glued to the ground and shuffled his feet uneasily.

"It's just that the Lady Lilybee has taken a particular liking to the girl Mose, and she's concerned about her because she's so young. It's quite all right, there's nothing to fear… we know these things happen, but the Mistress would just like to know who is responsible. Is there anything you can tell me?"

Mose hesitated, kicking the dust to and fro thoughtfully; then, very quietly, he murmured, "Shouldn't done that to her... she just a child. No one should done that to my Missy."

Percy Mansfield-Brown leant towards Mose, cupping his ear in his hand. "What's that you say? Come now Mose... tell me what happened."

His master was a kind man, a good man, Mose knew that, so he repeated what he had just said, more slowly and clearly. His master nodded sympathetically. "Now tell me exactly what happened Mose. I want to know." He had always liked his manservant; he knew that he was trustworthy.

Slowly and painfully Mose explained how he had found Grace on the night of the Christmas party, and that she had not spoken a word to anyone about it since. He emphasized that none of the slaves had had anything to do with the attack though. Percy was deeply perturbed by the story, and so was Lilybee when her husband recounted it to her later that day.

"If it wasn't one of the slaves, then it must have been..." her voice trailed away.

"What... what, my dear?" asked Percy, concerned by his wife's worried frown.

"Oh, no, if I thought for one moment..." again she stopped in mid-sentence.

"What... what is it?" asked Percy. "I can't make any sense of what you're trying to say."

"Leave this to me, Percy dear, I'll not say another word until I'm absolutely sure." Lilybee hoped against hope that her suspicions were unfounded.

She made it her business to speak privately to Grace the very next morning. The girl was greatly distressed and would not utter a word about what had happened to her, but whilst Lilybee was questioning her, Douglas came into the room to speak to his sister. He was completely unaware that Lilybee was otherwise engaged, and was quite taken aback when he caught sight of Grace. The reaction of the young girl, when she saw him and heard him speak, told her mistress all that she wanted to know. Her worst fears were confirmed. She dismissed Grace from the room immediately, with a few kindly words, and waited until she had fled before confronting her brother. Despite her abhorrence of what had happened to the innocent young girl, she was determined to question him.

It did not take her long to establish who had been responsible, and she warned Douglas of the consequences, should she or Percy ever come to hear of any such incidents in the future. She had already suspected that he was not the true culprit, the one who had carried out the brutal attack, but she shuddered at the realisation that he derived the utmost pleasure from witnessing such crime. She had never been able to understand the evil natures of her two younger brothers, and she was deeply troubled.

Four

Mattie had wanted her wedding day to be a memorable one; she and Zac had planned it for a very long time. So it was, memorable indeed. She had chosen it to be on a Sunday, towards the end of summer, and every slave from the plantation, who did not have to work on that day, was in attendance. They had all helped with the preparations, to ensure its success, and were now congregated down by the river where a flowered arbour had been erected for the happy couple. The gardeners had provided foliage and blossoms in abundance, from their careful pruning of the shrubberies surrounding the house, and the women had even managed to produce a beautiful bouquet for the delighted bride. Jasmine's seven-year-old twins, Clarissa and Clarence, were her chosen attendants, and old Blossom Junior was officiating, as was usual on such occasions.

When the bride and groom had followed him along the dusty path down to the river for the special ceremony, all the slaves had danced along behind them in twos and threes, singing joyfully and clapping rhythmically, so setting the mood of the whole proceeding. Once there, Blossom Junior had arranged the couple under the arbour, the twins directly behind them, and then with magnificent gestures of his right arm, he ensured that the congregation were correctly arrayed, as he saw fit. He coughed loudly to bring the gathering to order, and then began his impressive performance. There was no doubt that any couple fortunate enough to be married by old Blossom Junior, could be considered well and truly married by the time he had done. He did not strictly adhere to the original wording, as written in his King James version of the bible, but everyone was duly impressed with his enthusiastic rendition.

Clarissa and Clarence gazed up in awe at the old man as he stood, bible in hand, before the happy couple. Clarissa turned to look at Clarence, and as their enormous brown eyes met, they collapsed in a fit of giggling. Their mother, Jasmine, bent towards them and scolded softly, "Sh... sshh, behave yo'selves." She gave them a warning look and straightened Clarissa's flowered headdress, which had fallen down over one ear during the giggling fit.

Blossom Junior paused and glowered at the two children, then continued with his own flowery interpretation of the wedding vows, for although his eyes travelled intently back and forth over the printed pages of his beloved Holy Bible, he was not able to read one single word of it. Nevertheless, it was his most treasured possession, and he proudly produced it at every conceivable opportunity. It was a large black leather-bound volume, which had no doubt been of considerable magnificence in its former days, but now its binding was cracked and mildewed, and many of its pages had long since disappeared. It had been handed down to Blossom Junior by his old pappy, Blossom Senior, and it was as necessary a part of his wedding and funeral regalia, as were the frayed, patched, long black tail-coat and shabby battered top hat that he wore for all such occasions, over his old checked shirt and worn trousers. It was little wonder that the seven-year-old twins could scarcely control their laughter.

Blossom Junior stuck out his tongue and licked the middle finger of his right hand, before solemnly turning over to the next page of his bible, then peering intently at Mattie and Zac, he intoned, "Does you Zaccharius, take this gal Matilda as your lady wife?"

Zac grinned broadly and shyly replied, "I sho' does."

Blossom nodded in approval, raised his eyebrows and fixed his gaze upon the bride. "And does you, Matilda, take this handsome man here as your husband?"

"I sho' does," replied Mattie enthusiastically.

"Then I declare before all these good people that you is now man and wife, for as long as you is both alive… and we all hopes that to be for a very long long time. Now I is done here, so we can all git to eat that good food that's been waitin' for us back in the long cabin. Bless us all Lord."

Every voice rang out together in a melodious "Amen," and the celebrations began. The children danced and sang and twirled around amid the grownups, as they all made their way back to the long cabin, anxious to partake of the food and drink that had been laid out in readiness for all to enjoy.

Grace had never before witnessed such a spectacle, and although she did not join in the lively dancing, she was enthralled by the antics of those who did, and by the wonderful singing that carried on long into the night. Mose sat beside her throughout the whole proceedings, smiling broadly and tapping his feet to the rhythm and clapping. It was the first time he had seen Grace really happy and enjoying herself since the attack upon her the Christmas before, and he was overjoyed. She looked up at him and thanked him shyly when he fetched a plate piled high with all sorts of delicious food, and she took hold of his hand and pulled him down beside her, so they could eat together. Mose thought his heart would burst.

There was only one thing that could have made him happier, and that was if he and Grace could have changed places with Mattie and Zac, and been wed in their stead. Once again, he recalled Angelique's words of wisdom, as he had done many times during the past few months, and wondered if she could be right, that maybe one day Grace might consider him a 'fine catch' and agree to become his wife. He chewed at his food and sighed deeply. He knew that he would have to remain patient for a very long time.

Five

Shortly after her sixteenth birthday, Grace was to experience the miracle of bearing her first child. She began to feel unwell during the afternoon, whilst she was working up at the house. There was no doubt in anyone's mind of what the cause might be. Hannah sat her down on one of the benches in the slaves' kitchen and sent Mattie to find Mose. He fetched the old cart immediately, and tenderly lifted Grace up into it to take her back to her cabin.

As he drove her slowly along the path towards the cluster of cabins, she asked Mose if he would drive her down to the river, for that was where she wanted to be. Mose was a little alarmed; he wondered why she was so anxious not to return to her cabin.

"Is yo' sure Missy… don't you think yo'll be better where you can git some help if you needs it?" he asked.

"Please Mose… just take me down to the river. Please," Grace groaned pitifully and clutched at her stomach as another pain welled up and then subsided.

Mose could see the beads of perspiration glistening on her brow, hear the urgent pleading in her voice. "All right… all right, sho' I take you Missy. Don't you go frettin' now." He was so worried about her that he would do anything she asked of him.

The cart lumbered to a halt and Mose lifted her most lovingly and carried her to where she was pointing. Grace had been to this same spot many, many times during the past few months, and she had decided that this was where her baby would enter the world. She would not have her born in the darkness of the cabin, where she had lain and suffered hours of horrifying recollection of what had happened to her nine long months ago. The big man's strong arms lowered her gently to the ground.

"Now you stay quiet while I goes for one of the women to help you Missy... you hear me?" She nodded and closed her eyes, thankful that he was leaving her, so that she might relax between the agonizing pains that seemed certain to rend her immature young body asunder.

Grace was not too aware of what was going on around her during the next few hours, when the pain was at its merciless height, only that voices and hands were gently reassuring her and providing all the assistance she needed to bring her baby safely into the world.

Then, when at last she found herself drifting dreamily in a blissful pain free haven, Jasmine placed her tiny daughter in her arms and stood smiling down at her as she gazed in wonder upon the most beautiful sight she had ever beheld. In all her young life she had never before known the overwhelming joy that now filled her being. It was completely unexpected, it astounded her, so unaware had she been that this moment could bring such supreme happiness. She pressed her lips lovingly to the tiny rounded cheeks that were still wet with her own body fluids, and blinked back the tears that welled up in her eyes. "My baby... my own baby," she whispered.

For hours Mose had kept at a discreet distance whilst Jasmine and the woman who had come to assist her were attending to Grace, but when their job was done, and the young mother had fallen into an exhausted sleep, he approached quietly and whispered to Jasmine that he would stay close by and watch over mother and baby through the night, what little there was left of it. Jasmine laid her hand on his arm and nodded, smiling kindly at him.

"Sho' Mose we knows she be safe with you. You try to git some rest too... you needs it as much as we does. Goodnight."

His concern could not have been greater had he been the child's father. "Goodnight Jasmine, and thank you for what you done for Missy," he said softly.

Grace awoke at first light and looked around to find her guardian slumbering peacefully a short distance away. She smiled contentedly to herself; his nearness was always a source of comfort to her. The baby whimpered again, the same small muffled sound that had awoken her a few minutes earlier. She removed the light cover that had been placed over them both and brought the child to her breast, crooning softly as its small quivering mouth began to suckle noisily. Her heart was filled to overflowing with the love that she felt for this, her own child, an all-consuming emotion that she would never have believed existed. She sat entranced, closely studying the tiny miracle that lay in her arms. She was sublimely happy, completely oblivious to everything around her.

Mose was awakened by her singing, he blinked and rubbed his eyes. He in turn was entranced by what now met his gaze. Grace had never looked more lovely than she did at that moment, silhouetted against the light of the early morning sun, as its soft, golden rays filtered through the leafy trees around her. He brought himself up on to one arm. "Mornin' Missy," he called softly. He felt a pang of guilt at imposing himself upon her obvious reverie.

She smiled at him. "Has you been here all night Mose?"

"I sho' has. I told Jasmine I gonna watch over you and the baby. Couldn't leave you here all by yo'self now, could I?"

"Thank you Mose. Youse a good man. I wish there something I could do for yo'."

"Ain't no need Missy... jus' long as you is all right, then I's happy... you knows that." He was watching her closely. "But you sho' had me worried, wanting to come down here by the river for the birthing. Why you do that?"

Grace frowned. "That dark cabin ain't no place for my baby to be born, that's why. The shadow of that devil-man is in there... he been in there ever since that night." She shuddered. "I jus' wanted to git far away from him... far away as I could."

It was the first time Grace had ever spoken of what had happened to her all those months ago, and Mose nodded in agreement.

"I can understand that... you wanting to git away from what bin' troublin' you, but what 'bout the baby ain't she to do with that too?"

Grace drew the baby close, clutching the tiny head protectively against her as she leant towards Mose. "No she ain't," she said angrily. "She mine Mose... jus' mine. She ain't nothin' to do with him, nothing at all. I ain't never gonna think of him no more never... and I don't ever want to talk about it again, you hear?"

The baby cried fretfully. Grace was clutching her a little too tightly. She looked down at her and rocked her gently to and fro. "Sh... ssh... don't you cry honey-chile, there ain't nothing to be afraid of." She turned to Mose. "She my little angel... she special, and I is gonna love her like no mammy ever loved her baby... you see, you see."

Her eyes filled with tears. Mose quickly edged himself towards her, he couldn't bear to see her distressed. He knelt up in front of her and placed his enormous hands on her shoulders reassuringly. "I knows you will Missy... why you'll be a real fine mammy, the best mammy that little gal could have. I'll watch over her too, same as I has yo'. She's gonna be jus' fine."

Grace looked at the concerned face that was peering intently at her. "I'd like that Mose having you to watch over the two of us. You bin' jus' like a real pappy to me like I always thought my own pappy would have bin', if I'd knowed him."

Mose's heart lurched and he dropped his eyes, lest this innocent young girl might suddenly become aware of his true feelings for her. He was fearful of what effect that might have upon her. Grace bent her face below his, trying to see into his eyes. She whispered softly, "What yo' mammy called Mose? Youse never told me."

He was puzzled. "What yo' ask that for?"

"Well... my baby need a name, don't she? And I wants to do something special for yo' Mose... for all that yo' done for me. Now what yo' mammy's name?"

Mose swallowed hard. "She always called Minnie, but her name was Mignonette. She was real proud of her name, 'cos it was French... she said that it was a plant with sweet smelling flowers, it a French word that mean dainty. That's what was told to her anyway."

Grace's face lit up. She beamed down at the sleeping infant and said softly, "Ain't that a lovely name my little angel... Mignonette, what you think of that then? If Mose agrees, then you is to be called after his mammy... what you say Mose?"

Grace could see that he was moved. She reached out and brushed his cheek with the back of her hand. "Does you agree then Mose?"

He nodded, "That's jus' fine Missy... makes me feel real proud."

*

Life was good for Grace. The joy she had felt at the first sight of her baby daughter had never diminished. She had become enraptured by her, and as the child grew it pleased her to notice that her skin was dark, much darker than her own. It was obvious that she took after her grandfather Daniel, because Grace could remember her mother telling her that he was a pure negro. Grace was delighted, in fact, she could not have been more so; above all else, she did not want the white blood of the man from whose seed Minnie had sprung, to be apparent in her.

She loved her daughter, she fussed over her; she spent as much time as possible with her. When it was time for the long noon rest, she would hurry away so that they could be together. The young child would watch for her mother to come when her work was over, and she would run with outstretched arms to be gathered up, and the two would hug and kiss as they clung to one another, spinning around and laughing. Then in the evening Grace would croon softly to the child, teaching her all the beautiful sad songs that were so much a part of the life of the plantation slave. In fact, it seemed to Mose that Grace never stopped singing, so contented had her life become.

She had learned all that there was to be learned about the duties up at the house, and she now spent most of her time caring for the Lady Lilybee, who had developed a great fondness for her. Grace too loved her job of personal maid to the mistress, and she considered herself fortunate indeed to have been chosen for that particular role. She no longer had to wait at table, or do the more menial tasks around the house. Instead, she spent most of her time attending to the Lady Lilybee's toilet, and taking care of her wardrobe and all her personal needs. Consequently, she very seldom came into contact with the house guests, who frequently came and went at 'White Lakes', so it was little wonder that she managed to avoid Gilbert Hetherington on the very few occasions that he paid a visit.

Then, inevitably, one beautiful summer's day, she encountered him quite unexpectedly. She was carrying her mistress's afternoon tea out on to the verandah, and there he stood, talking quietly to his sister. Grace felt her legs weaken, she almost dropped the tray she was carrying, for despite the fact that she had striven, over the past few years, to suppress the memory of his violent assault upon her, this sudden confrontation, his actual physical presence, immediately brought back the horror of it in all its terrifying detail. As her eyes met his, her hands began to shake, the fine bone china rattled noisily on the beautiful silver tray. She could scarcely control herself as she poured the tea for her mistress; she could sense his eyes following her every movement. He could not believe the exquisite beauty of her, the way she had matured.

"Would you fetch another cup for Mister Gilbert, Grace?" said Lilybee.

Grace removed herself immediately, glad of the opportunity to regain her composure. As soon as the girl was gone, Lilybee lost no time in confronting her brother. She had noticed the alarming effect he had had on her maid, and she was perfectly well aware of what effect this seductive young woman was having on him.

"I would advise you to forget any designs you might have upon my maid, Gilbert," she said sternly. "I warned Douglas long ago of what would happen should Percy or I ever come to hear of any more of your intolerable behaviour towards any of our servants. Do you understand?" How she despised him.

"Surely you wouldn't spoil a fellow's sport now, would you Lilybee? Why, you Southerners are renowned for your hospitality up in the North, and I was under the impression that that hospitality embraced every aspect of what it takes to entertain a gentleman hereabout. You are not trying to tell me, are you dear sister, that your plantation is any different from all the others?" He laughed derisively, ridiculing her. "That's not what I have heard from Douglas... not at all," he added, enjoying her obvious embarrassment.

Grace appeared again with the extra cup and saucer, and immediately poured the tea for her mistress's guest. He was watching her closely. Her cheeks were deeply suffused with colour, and her extreme discomfort excited him all the more.

He was put out by his sister's remonstration, and leant back in his chair defiantly, ogling her maid unashamedly.

Lilybee was furious. "Thank you Grace," she said quietly. "That will be all, you may go now."

She leant towards her brother, her loathing of him evident. "I'm warning you Gilbert, I shall not tolerate any more of your abominable behaviour here at 'White Lakes', is that understood? Father gave you warning enough too, when he despatched you here, and I shall make it my duty to inform him, as he requested I should, if you ever step out of line again. The financial provision he made for you and Douglas when you came here was more than adequate for your immediate needs, but if you have it in mind to lay claim to the additional monies he promised you, then I strongly advise you to make an effort to settle down in a decent respectable manner, for you'll not receive another penny until you do. Now if you do not pay heed to what I am saying concerning your future behaviour towards the slaves here at 'White Lakes', I shall see to it that Father is informed. He is adamant that you mend your ways, and I mean to ensure that you do, or you shall live to regret it." It was not in Lilybee's nature to be testy, but her brother Gilbert always managed to try her patience to the extreme.

She finished her tea and stood up abruptly. She simply could not endure his presence for a moment longer. "I hope that it will never be necessary for us to have a discussion of this nature again, Gilbert, for I find it most distasteful," she said icily, as she swept along the verandah and disappeared into the house.

*

For the next day or two, Gilbert Hetherington brooded over what his sister had said. He seethed inwardly, deeply resenting her interference, but at the same time, he knew that it would be to his distinct disadvantage to ignore her threat. Just wait until he could lay claim to the additional monies his father had promised though; once they were his, he would no longer need to placate her, nor anybody else for that matter. His face broke into a malevolent smile. He was beginning to tire of his stay in North Carolina, and decided that he would leave the following day. If his enjoyment was to be so curtailed here, then he might as well return to New York. He had had his noonday meal and was walking through the gardens towards the river. He would sit for a while in the shadow of the trees that lined its banks. He found a fallen tree and sat motionless upon it watching the water as it flowed and rippled peacefully along its course. He had been there for several minutes before he heard voices; he listened intently, he could hear a child laughing happily... water splashing. He was curious, he wanted to see who it was. He made his way quietly along the bank, careful that he should not be seen. His pulse raced as he caught sight of Grace with a small child. They were both standing barefoot in the cool, clear water, their cotton dresses drenched and clinging to them, as they splashed and played together, totally absorbed in one another. He guessed that the child must be about three years old.

He gasped as the realization that he was most probably its father overwhelmed him. Douglas had informed him of everything that had happened when their sister Lilybee became aware of Grace's condition; of how angry she was that her favourite house girl had been used in such a way. He was bemused at the effect this slave girl had on him, and even more so·now that he was observing her with the child he had fathered. She really was a beauty, there was no denying it, and he was overcome with longing for her. Never before had any woman fascinated him as did she. He felt an overwhelming desire to be near her, to speak to her.

Grace caught Minnie under the arms and lifted her high into the air, twirling around in the water as she did so. The delighted child squealed and threw back her head, and Grace laughed aloud, happy to be sharing this special time with her.

As Gilbert Hetherington pushed aside the thick foliage and stepped into view, Grace's expression froze. She lowered her arms, clutching Minnie against her. The child wound her legs around her mother's hips and buried her face in her neck, sensing that there was something wrong. Grace did not move, she could not, she was paralysed with fear.

"I heard you laughing. It must be lovely and cool in there," said Gilbert Hetherington. "Please don't let me stop you."

Grace cast a glance in each direction, looking for a means of escape. She felt trapped, and became alarmed. "I has to git back... it soon time for work again," she stammered. She stepped towards the bank and fell forward, steadying herself with one arm as she tried to scramble up the slope with Minnie clinging on to her precariously.

"Careful... here, allow me to help you."

Grace felt him clasp her free arm tightly, as he pulled her to the top of the bank. He stood close and put out his hand, trying to lift Minnie's chin, but the terrified child pressed her face even more closely into her mother's neck.

"Let me see if you are as beautiful as your mother," he said. "She is your child, is she not?"

"Yes sir, she mine." Grace kept her head bowed and stared at the ground. She wondered how he had found her here; no one ever came to this place, it was special for her and Minnie. She desperately wanted to get away from him. He could see how afraid of him she was and her vulnerability made her all the more appealing to him. He found her completely irresistible, wanting to touch her. He clasped her upper left arm again with one hand, whilst trying to raise her face to his with the other, his thumb and forefinger spread on either side of her chin. Grace jerked her head and sank her teeth deep into the soft flesh. She leapt back in terror at the loud howl of pain that rang out. Minnie too started to cry loudly as this stranger struck out at her mother.

"You vixen," he yelled. "You'll not get away with this. Look what you've done." He quickly found a handkerchief and was trying to bind it around his hand.

Grace could see the blood oozing from the wound. She turned and tried to run from him. He grabbed at her again. Minnie was screaming. Grace kicked at his shin with her bare foot; her only concern now was for the safety of her child.

"You leave us alone," she hissed, "or I tell the mistress..."

He had already freed her and was bent over rubbing his tender shin. As she made her escape, she could hear his violent curses.

"I won't forget this," he called after her. "I'll make you pay... you see if I don't."

That threat was to haunt her time and time again before she would finally suffer its effect, but she could never have guessed at just how cruelly he would exact his revenge.

Six

Grace was now twenty-five years old, and Mose had long since ceased to foster the hope that one day she might become his wife. All the love she had to give, she gave to her daughter Minnie, who had grown into a beautiful child. Mose was almost as fond of her as was her mother, but Grace's complete preoccupation with her had always worried him. He had, on occasion, tried to advise her that she ought not to devote all her time and attention to her, but Grace was not to be persuaded to do otherwise. He had even once ventured to ask her if she had ever considered sharing her life with a man. "Youse a beautiful young woman Grace, any man would be proud to call you his own," he had said tenderly.

Grace had laughed self-consciously. "What I want a man for Mose, when I got Minnie and you? You two is all I need. I don't want nobody else."

He realised with great disappointment that it would never enter her head that their relationship was anything other than friendship, so he had become resigned to playing the part of protector to her and Minnie, just thankful that he was able to be a small part of their lives. He had never found the courage to divulge to her his true feelings, fearing that she might reject him. That possibility was far too devastating for him to contemplate, for he adored her too much.

Maybe it was the secret knowledge of just how much he loved her that provided Grace with the solace she so desperately needed when her world was violently torn asunder.

Mose's grief was deep and heartfelt. It was almost as if he had expected the tragedy to happen, had somehow foreseen it, for had he not tried to warn her so many times that she ought not to devote all her time and attention to her small child? He knew, he had always known that it would destroy her if ever Minnie was taken away. He had been torn apart from his own family, from his mother, and the brothers and sisters that he loved. Now he was being forced to re-live all that heartache once again, as he watched helplessly whilst Grace suffered the same cruel fate.

Grace had been uneasy, nervous and watchful for the past month, ever since she had learned that Gilbert Hetherington was once again visiting 'White Lakes'. This time he was accompanied by his wife and their two young children. The atmosphere up at the house had been one of excitement and laughter, for the massa and mistress were enormously fond of the young Mrs Hetherington and her two little ones. Although she had not caught a glimpse of Gilbert Hetherington, the very knowledge that he was somewhere around the house threw her into a panic, his very presence menacing her day after day. So, when Mose brought the news that the visitors were making ready for their departure, relief flooded over her. At last she might feel safe once again. Little did she suspect that her beloved child was to become the focus of her tormentor's evil intent.

She was busily tidying her mistress's dressing room when, quite by chance, she happened to overhear the massa telling his wife that he had decided to make a present of one of the young slaves to their sister-in-law. "Celia needs a nursemaid with those two infants to contend with," he said, "and it would seem that she'll soon have another on her hands, if I'm not very much mistaken."

He twirled the side of his moustache thoughtfully. "There are several young children running around the plantation, who would be just the right age, one of the small girls should do ideally. Why, she could be a nursemaid and playmate for little Rosalind. What do you say my dear?"

Lilybee took a final peep at herself in the mirror, turning her head from side to side to make sure her hair was exactly to her liking before going down to breakfast. "Why, that's a lovely idea Percy... how very thoughtful you are my darling." She brushed his cheek with her lips and swished past him towards the door. "I'm sure Celia will be delighted." A slight frown creased her brow. "Gilbert is absolutely insufferable," she said quietly. "That dear girl has hardly had time to recover from Rosalind's birth, and here she is carrying again." She shook her head disapprovingly as they went out, accompanying one another down to breakfast.

When the door had closed behind them, Grace set about tidying the bedroom. The massa's words were still ringing in her ears. "One of the small girls." Her heart began to pound in fear. She felt sick with apprehension at the thought that her child might be the one who was selected. She clasped her hands together tightly, fingers entwined. "Oh, no," she breathed. "Please God don' let the massa give my Minnie away... please God... please." Somehow she knew, she had a horrifying premonition that that was exactly what would happen.

She stopped what she was doing and stood in the middle of the room, unable to think coherently. Her mind was in a turmoil. Suddenly she knew that she must go to her daughter; find her without delay. She fled from the room and down the stairs. There was no one about, the family were all taking breakfast. She ran through the slaves' kitchen without stopping, and out along the path towards the long cabin. Mattie and Hannah stood looking with mouths agape as she rushed past them, wondering what was wrong. Grace did not stop running until she came to the long cabin. She was gasping for breath as she called urgently through the open doorway to Angelique. "Is Minnie with you?" She could see several little ones carrying out their chores around the kitchen.

"No, she ain't here."

Grace broke in, imploring, "Where is she... I must find her, where is she?"

Angelique became alarmed. "She down at the fields, taking care of the babies today... I think."

Grace had already turned and was on her way there before the last words had left Angelique's lips.

By the cluster of trees that bordered the plantation, she could see Minnie with another small girl. They were gently swinging the babies in their coarse baskets that had been hung from the lower branches of the trees. Grace could hear Minnie's melodious voice as she sang the lullabies she had taught her. The smaller child would join in with a child-like tuneless burst whenever she thought she recognized a particular passage of whatever song Minnie was singing.

Grace stopped running, careful not to alarm her daughter. As she drew nearer, Minnie caught sight of her and her face lit up in a broad smile. "What you doing down here Mammy? It ain't time to eat yet?"

Grace could not speak, she just gathered her bewildered daughter in her arms and held her close. She pressed her lips to the top of her head and swayed gently to and fro. She felt that her heart would burst with the love she carried within her for her only child.

"You gonna come with me Minnie quick now."

She took hold of Minnie's hand and turned to re-trace her steps, hoping that she could hide her somewhere safe. If she could keep her out of sight, perhaps one of the other children might be chosen. Minnie could hardly keep up with her mother as she raced back towards their dingy cabin.

"What wrong Mammy... why is you so afraid?"

"You got to keep in the cabin and stay there until I comes for you, you hear?"

Grace could not speak of what she feared would happen to the child. "Don't you make no noise. You stay quiet... does you understand?"

The bewildered child did not understand, but she nodded her head, her eyes wide with fright. Whatever it was that her mother was afraid of was certainly, by now, scaring her too. They had almost reached their cabin when, approaching them from the direction of the house, Minnie saw the tall man, a fair-haired stranger, slowly walking towards them. Her mother gasped and stopped suddenly, rooted to the spot. She reached out her arm protectively and pushed Minnie behind her, trying to keep her out of sight.

"Ah, there you are," said the stranger... "and you have your child with you... good. I thought it would take me longer to find her. She is coming with me, we are in need of a nursemaid and playmate for my young daughter."

Minnie was overcome with curiosity and was peeping out from behind her mother's skirt. "Here child, come, let me take a look at you," he said. He stepped forward and reached out his arm.

Grace spun around and crouched down, gathering her daughter into her arms. Her heart was in her mouth as she blurted out, "She too young to be a nursemaid... to be taken away."

Gilbert Hetherington gazed down at her, a cruel glint in his eye. "Nonsense, she'll make a fine nursemaid, as well as a playmate for my daughter. Now let her go." He pulled roughly at Grace's shoulder, at the same time catching hold of Minnie' s arm. He wrenched her away from her mother and was about to set off towards the house with her, when Grace threw herself on to him, grabbing at his free arm. She clung to him crying, "No... no...you can't take her away... please, please." She was completely distraught. Gilbert Hetherington was livid, his temper flared. He shook free of her, but she pulled on his arm again. "No please... you can't take her, you can't," she wailed pitifully.

He had had enough, he shook her off once again and turned to face her. She saw the hatred in his eyes as the back of his hand struck her full force across the face. She fell to her knees sobbing. He strode off, dragging Minnie beside him, her small bare feet hardly touching the ground. She was terrified... too terrified to utter a sound, and so she remained when he bundled her into the coach that was to take her to the North. There she crouched, cowering in the corner,

Friday: 25th July, '14.

Dear Pat,

Here it is at last m'darlin'... and
I am quaking in my shoes in case
you think it's a load of rubbish!
Honestly I am!   However, it comes
with much love; now I'm going to
crawl under a stone somewhere!

OH, yes ... Thank you very
very much for all the "info" you
so kindly sent me ... and I have
contacted the publishers to tell
them about my book being shown
under "Catherine F. Andersen." They
are correcting it (so they said!)

Now dear, I shall let you know
when the little "celebratory"
buffet is to be held up at the
"mitre" (I have told Andy that
you and Kathy will probably come).

                                        PTO...

No pressure though ... we'll
have a natter about it later...ok?

In the meantime, take care...
don't work too hard!

God bless you darlin' ...

Paddy xxx

x   x
x I LuV YA! x
x   x   x   x

trying to seek refuge behind all the luggage that was piled high around her.

*

As soon as he heard what had happened, Mose lost no time in making his way around to the slaves' kitchen in search of Grace, and his apprehension grew when Mattie recounted to him what she and Hannah had witnessed. He left quickly and ran along the path towards the long cabin to ask Angelique whether she knew anything. She could not tell him very much either. In his desperation, he asked all those he met if they had seen Grace, or if they knew her whereabouts.

Piece by piece, he managed to glean enough information to trace her down to the river, to her favourite place. Why hadn't he thought of it before? He found her lying face down on the ground, sobbing bitterly, her head nestled on her arm. He knelt down beside her and placed his hand gently upon her shoulder, hardly able to speak, for he could not find the words with which to console her.

"Grace… don't… don't," he murmured softly. "This ain't gonna do you no good." He struggled to hold back his own tears. He bent over her and raised her up, enfolding her in his strong arm.

She buried her face against him and emitted a long pitiful wail, "My baby. Oh, Mose… he took my baby," she cried.

Mose stroked her head, trying to comfort her. "I knows. I knows, but ain't no use you frettin' like this. The Lady Lilybee, she soon gonna be missin' you and wonderin' where you is. Now you come on back to the house, 'fore you finds yo'self in more trouble. Come on now, you come back with me." He stood up and pulled her up beside him.

"What I gonna do without her Mose? She all I cared about, and now she gone."

"Least you knows where she gone and you knows what family she with. T'ain't like she been sold at auction, like you was and like I was, and all my family. I never knowed where my brothers and sisters took, and I don't s'pose I ever gonna see dem again." He tried desperately to lift her spirits. "Why, who knows, one day you might git to see Minnie…the mistress, she might go up to the North a'visitin' her folks and who say she ain't gonna take you along with her? That way you git to see Minnie again, sho' you will." He nodded his head convincingly, just trying to reassure her a little.

Grace did not know how she lived through the rest of that day, her thoughts were constantly woven around Minnie, wondering what was happening to her, and knowing that she would be desperately unhappy at being so violently torn away from her mother. Several times her sadness engulfed her and she succumbed to silent tears. Only once did her mistress notice her distress and ask, "What is it Grace?"

Grace's tears coursed down her beautiful face and she hurriedly wiped them away with her hand. "I jus' thinkin' of my baby, ma'am," she answered quietly. "Worried 'bout her."

"Oh, my dear girl, there is no need for you to worry… not at all," said Lilybee cheerily. "Why, she will have a lovely home up in New Jersey… of course she will. My sister-in-law will see to that. She is to care for her baby daughter… be a nursemaid and playmate for her. Would you not rather that than have her sold away later on to heaven knows where?"

Grace nodded her head obediently. "Yes ma'am," she murmured.

"Of course you would. Now you cheer up, there's a good girl. She'll be with the other servants from 'White Lakes', or had you not thought of that? Jasmine and her twins Clarence and Clarissa... why she'll be fine, and no doubt news of her will come from my dear sister-in-law from time to time... you'll see. Now dry your tears and fetch me some tea, will you?"

No matter what anyone said, the pain in Grace's heart did not ease away; she knew it would never ease away. She could not envisage life without her daughter. She ached with longing for her, and prayed that she would come to no harm.

When the time came for her to have her evening meal, Grace had no appetite. She could not go to the slaves' kitchen, but instead she wandered down to the river where she could be alone in her grief.

That was where Mose found her long after sundown. He sat down quietly beside her; neither of them spoke, but Grace was glad that he had come to be with her. After they had sat in silence for a very long time, he asked, "Don't yo' think yo' oughta git back now? Yo' needs to git some sleep."

She didn't answer. He put his arm around her shoulders. "Grace... does yo' hear me?" He shook her gently. "Come on now, yo' needs to git some sleep."

She turned her face to his and her large sorrowful eyes filled with tears. "What I gonna do without her Mose... and what she gonna do without me... who gonna hold her when she scared? Ain't nobody gonna love her like me."

Mose was burdened down with pity for her. "She be all right... don' forgit she be with ol' Jasmine and her twins...

and Beulah. Yo' knows they take real good care of her. Yo' try and remember that, and don' go frettin' all the time. It jus' make yo' feel bad, that's all."

"But I loved her more'n anything… and she loved me… now I ain't got nobody, Mose, nobody."

She turned and flung her arms around him, burying her face in his neck. He felt her despair. "Yo' got me Grace," he whispered quietly, "Don' yo' never forgit that… yo' got me, and I loves you more'n I ever loved anythin' in all my life." She could hear the emotion in his voice, feel his arms tremble as they drew her close. She looked up into the dear face that she knew so well, and her eyes met his. Then, for the first time, he revealed to her all the love he carried in his heart, it shone from his eyes, so that she realised at long last the true depth of his feelings for her.

She felt a true constriction in her chest, and the pain of it forced her to gasp for breath. "Oh, Mose… Mose," she breathed tenderly.

"Missy… my Missy," he answered hoarsely, his voice catching in his throat. He had not used that special term of endearment for longer than he could remember. "I loves yo', I always loved yo' from the first day I brought yo' here in that big old cart." He sighed as he took her face between his giant hands and kissed the tears from her eyes. She felt his lips on her cheeks, first one, then the other, kissing away her tears. Then he placed his lips firmly upon her mouth, to stop its trembling. He kissed her fervently, and she responded to the intensity of his passion, for it seemed perfectly natural for her to do so. Mose was overcome with desire, he was swept along by the tide of his emotions, and he carried Grace with him, gathering her up into the shelter of his love, vanquishing all her sorrow so that she might forget, just for a brief moment, all the heartache that was threatening to destroy her life.

*

Their newfound joy in one another, the strength of their love, helped Grace and Mose to come to terms with the loss of little Minnie, and Grace desperately clung to the hope that one day she might see her beloved child again. She continually reassured herself with the words of Mose and her mistress, that at least she knew of her child's whereabouts, and she had to admit that she was indeed more fortunate than many thousands before her, whose loved ones had been sold away, never to be heard of again.

Through her own sorrow, Grace suddenly became painfully aware of how great had been the misery visited upon her own kind for generation after generation by their cruel owners. It was misery of an immeasurable degree, brought about by their brutal and inhuman treatment. She failed to understand how it could be allowed to happen. Of course she knew, as all the slaves on the plantation knew, that moves were afoot to bring about radical change. They had heard tell of the secret organization that existed, that had been in existence, for some fourteen years now, which was run by anti-slavery people. It was known as the 'underground railway', and had been set up to secretly assist fugitive slaves to escape to the Northern states or Canada. It was talked about covertly, in subdued whispers, and only when a few slaves might happen to arrange a clandestine meeting with one another. When Grace made mention of it to Mose he became alarmed. He fully realized how great had been the effect of Minnie's loss upon her, and he was afraid of the lengths to which she might be driven, in order to be reunited with her. "Don' you never git yo'self mixed up in that," he warned. "Hasn't you heard what they does to runaways? They tracks 'em down and they's lucky if they gits to live afterward. Now you jus' promise me you won' t go tryin' to run away; please Grace promise."

"Oh, Mose… course I won't. You think I don' remember what happened to my own pappy? Why, mammy told me 'bout it so many times, it was like I was there to see it for myself." She shook her head sadly. "Anyways, I ain't plannin' to take no risks at all… not for quite a while I ain't, 'cos I wants to make sure this baby gits birthed here, where I knows it safe." She glanced down to where she had placed her outstretched hands on either side of her abdomen, then peeped up mischievously under her eyebrows, to catch Mose's reaction to her momentous news. "Can't go havin' no baby where we has to keep looking over our shoulders all the time… or has to keep movin' on."

She saw his look of puzzlement change to one of complete joy and excitement. He smiled broadly as he asked incredulously, "Is you tellin' me…?" his voice trailed away. He snatched off his battered straw hat and flung it to the ground, jumping up and letting out a wild howl. "Oh, Missy… I can't believe it," he cried, as he gathered her into his arms and spun her around and around.

"Well, you jus' better git used to it, 'cos you is gonna be a pappy for sure, and now we best git back to the house, 'cos I reckons the noon rest must be over by now." As much as they would have loved to tarry longer by the river, they knew that they must now get back to their usual chores, but their spirits were soaring at the expectation of their new child.

*

A few weeks later, Mose's joy was complete when Grace and he were given permission by the master to be married by old Blossom Junior, and there was great rejoicing at 'White Lakes'. The master saw to it that Mose and Grace were allotted a small cabin of their own, as befitted his most favoured manservant, and Grace's happiness was marred only by the fact that Minnie could not be a part of it all. She was even more saddened when the Lady Lilybee suddenly announced that she was to take a trip up to see her sister-in-law in New Jersey, for her heart had leapt at the thought that she might have the opportunity of seeing Minnie again, but her mistress quashed her hopes by refusing to allow her to travel in her delicate state. Despite Grace's heartfelt pleas and protestations, she finally had to accept that it would be absolute folly for her to undertake such an arduous journey just a few months prior to her baby's birth.

"Far too risky, my dear," said Lilybee. "It would be impossible for you to endure such a journey. Besides, how do you imagine Mose would feel at your leaving just now?"

So Grace had to console herself with the hope that maybe, just maybe, at some time in the future, she would see Minnie again, and she knew that she would never ever give up that hope for as long as she lived.

*

The following August, as the sun rose gloriously above the horizon, Grace presented Mose with a baby son, and made him the proudest man on earth. He had spent an extremely worried, wakeful night with her down by the river, once again, as she was so insistent that the baby should not be born in their cabin. It brought back memories of that night ten years ago when she had given birth to Minnie, except that this time Jasmine's place was taken by Mattie, who was herself now a mother of three fine children. When Mose had hurried to fetch her in the middle of the night, fearing that Grace's time was near, she had asked Ophelia to come along to assist her, but when they discovered how difficult a time Grace was having, Mattie sent Ophelia to bring her grandmother without delay, for the older woman was far more experienced with prolonged and complicated births. Mose was beside himself with anxiety; he wrung his hands and prayed loudly to the good Lord to bring Grace safely through her ordeal.

"Oh Angelique, what I done to her?" he moaned.

The old woman shooed him away. "Now Mose, youse jus' gittin' in the way. We's got enough to do here tryin' to git this baby born, without you a frettin' and fussin' so you jus' git," she said testily.

He moved out of sight, but within earshot, and despite his profound fear for his wife's safety, those three able assistants finally managed, after a considerable amount of effort, to coax Grace's fine lusty infant safely into the world. Just as soon as the baby's first cry rent the air, Mose was on the scene, unable to contain himself for a moment longer.

The undisguised joy of the three women immediately set his mind at rest; their faces were wreathed in smiles.

Before he had time to ask, Mattie blurted out, "It a boy Mose... a beautiful boy... biggest baby you ever did see, ain't that so Angelique?"

"He sho' is," agreed the old woman, laughing and shaking her head from side to side. "He a son you can be real proud of... you jus' go take a look."

Mose approached mother and baby apprehensively, and fell to his knees where they were lying. He gazed in awe at his son, as he lay contentedly snuggled in the crook of his mother's arm.

Grace smiled up at him, she knew that he would be bursting with pride. He asked, "Is you all right... youse had a real bad time birthing that little fella, ain't yo'?"

Grace could hear his concern; he looked tired and drawn from his all-night vigil. "He ain't so little," she said laughingly. "It seem like he gonna take after his pappy."

Angelique bent towards them and said softly, "We be goin' now; she be fine Mose, yo' jus' let her git some rest, and you looks like you needs some too."

"Yes oh, yes... thank you, thank you for what you done Angelique, and you two gals," he said.

Grace glanced up at her three friends. "Thank you for what you done for me," she whispered.

When they were alone, Mose kissed her long and hard. "I loves yo' Missy," he said softly. He flung himself down and lay flat on his back beside her, propping his head on his arm. He could not believe how fortunate he was to be blessed with such a beautiful wife, who had now borne him a fine son. "In't this some kind of a day?" he asked jubilantly. "Gotta be... 'cos it the day our son bin born." They both lay gazing up at the heavens above them. The sky was a brilliant blue, and the sun's rays blazed in golden splendour across its vast expanse. "Feels like I flying up there... up where it sunny and blue," said Mose. "Free as a bird." He laughed and turned his attention upon Grace and the baby. "What you a thinkin'?" he asked her.

"When the baby was birthed Mose, when the pain was at its worst, that all I could see; I couldn't take my eyes away from that sunny blue sky, no sir... there it was above me, a peaceful, sunny, blue heaven." She paused in thought for a few moments. "That's what I'd like to call our baby... 'Sunny Blue', 'cos that's what I'll always see when I remembers the day he born. Does you like it?"

"I sho' does... that a special kinda name, jus' the kind of name he should have, 'cos he a very special boy. Ain't nobody ever had that name before, I's sure of that. Sunny Blue... Sunny Blue," he repeated slowly. "I likes it jus' fine." He chuckled and raised himself up on one elbow. "Now then Sunny Blue, I best git myself off to my chores... you stay here with your mammy 'til I gits done, and I be back before you knows it."

"Yes... you git now Mose, so we can rest some," Grace chided him. He kissed her noisily on the forehead, stroked the baby's cheek gently, and left them to recover from their night's ordeal.

*

From the moment he entered the world, young Sunny Blue became somewhat of a celebrity at 'White Lakes', for he was, and indeed remained, the largest baby ever to be born on the plantation, and to add to his renown, he was also the son of the most revered of slaves, Mose, that gentle giant of a man whom everyone loved and respected. The boy became as popular with the other children as was his father with their parents, and his very name could not have been more aptly chosen, for his temperament was never anything other than sunny. He stood head and shoulders above his playmates, being large in stature like his father, and he was blessed with the innate good looks of his mother, who absolutely adored him. Much to Mose's great consternation, she was determined that her son's fate would never follow the same path as that of her daughter. She had vowed when he was born that one day he would be a free man, and she had whispered to him of freedom since the moment he was first able to comprehend its meaning. Despite his misgivings, despite his constant urgent warnings to Grace of her foolhardiness in making such rash promises to the boy, Mose too nurtured the hope, deep within his heart, that one day Sunny Blue would gain his freedom. It mattered not that he himself, as countless generations of slaves before him, had been forced to accept the inevitability of his own situation, for had they not witnessed the futile attempts of so many who had tried to escape, and had they not trembled in fear at the horrific tales of what had happened to those who were recaptured; still there burned within him a small glimmer of hope that one day all slaves would be free. For years that small glimmer of hope had been kept alive and, in turn, almost extinguished, only to be rekindled yet again by the men who so valiantly fought to abolish slavery.

Famous was the abortive conspiracy of Denmark Vesey in Charleston as early as 1822, and then Nat Turner's failed rebellion nine years later, when sixty whites had been murdered. Tragically, not only had the perpetrator been caught and hanged, but also scores of innocents too, who had played no part in his rebellion. Now it seemed the whole country, both North and South, was in fearful contention, and shocking reports of John Brown's attack at Harper's Ferry on the Potomac greatly intensified the situation. He, together with eighteen followers, had carried out his rebellious attack with the intention of inciting a revolt, in which he imagined that all slaves would join him to be organized into an army, then destroy the institution of slavery once and for all. However Colonel Robert E Lee of the United States army soon forced this handful of men to surrender, whereupon Brown himself was taken to Richmond in Virginia, then tried and hanged.

Mose had long since accepted that never in his own life would he know the joy of freedom, but he would never give up the hope that someday things could change for his son, and his son's sons.

Seven

Ralph Clayton had been more than usually aware of Sunny Blue since the first morning he had put him to one of the gangs as a 'full hand'. His cold steely eyes watched him constantly from beneath their half-closed lids; watched and waited, as any other predator watches and waits for its prey.

Because of his extraordinary stature and strength, the boy had not been allowed to remain a 'quarter hand' for as long as the other children of his own age. Instead, he had been considered perfectly well able to toil from sun up to sun down in the cotton fields alongside the men. He was a handsome boy, with a fine physique, and his popularity with the other workers became apparent immediately, not only because he was industrious, but because he constantly entertained them with his magnificent singing voice. Wherever he was working it could be heard; it rang out, filling the air with melody. Since he was in the cradle, Sunny Blue's mother had crooned to him all the negro spiritual songs that were forever to be heard around the plantation, and he had grown to know and love every one of them. The men too would join him in their own particular favourites, in an endeavour to alleviate the tedium of their chores, and to lift their spirits.

At the end of the day, as soon as it was sundown, the workers would shuffle back along the dusty path towards their cabins, more than ready for their evening meal and a well-earned rest. Quite frequently they came upon Ralph Clayton sitting astride his horse, to the side of the path; he would cast his eyes over the slovenly shambling groups, searching their number as they drifted past him. Not one of them met his gaze; they kept their eyes averted in an attempt to become inconspicuous to him. On one such occasion, without ceremony, when he caught sight of Sunny Blue, he leaned down, thrusting his folded whip in his direction.

"You... boy," he blurted out hoarsely. "Here, over here, by me."

The group disintegrated to allow the boy space to step out, then re-formed hurriedly, anxious to be on its way. It was obvious that they were not unaccustomed to what was happening, but the lone boy was bewildered, his eyes full of puzzlement as he looked up at the overseer.

"Come with me boy... and keep up," he growled, swinging his horse around and setting off for his own quarters. Sunny Blue ran beside the trotting horse until they came to Ralph Clayton's place, not too far distant. It was a large wooden cabin with shuttered windows and a wide stoop across the front of it. Ralph Clayton dismounted and nonchalantly tossed his horse's reins around the wooden rail as he climbed the steps, all the while glancing furtively behind him to see that there was no one about. He grasped Sunny Blue by the arm, pulling him roughly up the steps and in through the door.

The boy could hardly see inside the gloomy interior, but Ralph Clayton lost no time in lighting the single lamp that stood on a cluttered wooden table in the centre of the room. Everywhere was in disarray: odd items of clothing were draped haphazardly over the chairs on either side of a large open fireplace; books and papers lay strewn about and the bed along one wall remained unmade. A strong smell of liquor hung in the stale atmosphere, and Sunny Blue did not fail to notice the collection of empty bottles and unwashed glasses that stood on a small table beside the bed.

The overseer kicked the door shut and flung his hat on to the large hook behind it. "Pour us a drink, boy," he ordered.

Sunny Blue uncorked a part-filled bottle and tipped a measure into a glass.

"Pour one for yourself."

He replaced the cork. "I don't drink massa," stammered the boy.

"I said pour one for yourself."

Ralph Clayton picked up the glass and emptied it in one gulp. His fist banged the table, the glasses rattled. "... and pour me another."

The boy nervously refilled the glass and poured a small measure for himself into another one.

"Drink up."

Sunny Blue slowly raised the glass to his lips and sipped the fiery liquid. He coughed and spluttered as it slid down his throat.

He was not sure what happened next, just that when the hated overseer tried to make his assault upon him, he fought with all his might to prevent it, finally delivering a resounding kick where he knew it would hurt him most. As the groaning man fell to his knees the terrified boy leapt to the door and was through it and away before his attacker could regain breath enough to stop him. He ran faster than he had ever run in his life before, not towards the cabins, but up towards the house, where he knew his mother and father would still be at work. He reached the kitchen and burst through the door relieved to find Hannah and several of the other servants busily working there.

"Why Sunny Blue, what happened to you?" asked Hannah. The boy stood trembling and gasping for his breath, his hand cupped around his bleeding lip, his left eye swollen and closed.

"Has you had some kinda accident... what happened? Come here and let me take a look at you."

Sunny Blue collapsed against Hannah's motherly form and sobbed, "I's lookin' for my mammy," he cried.

"All right... all right... we'll find her, now you jus' sit yo'self down and let·me clean yo' up some." Hannah flapped her hand at one of the younger kitchen maids and motioned her to go and fetch Grace from the Lady Lilybee's rooms upstairs, then she took a small pan of warm water and a soft cloth and bathed the painful looking wounds, comforting the distraught boy as she did so.

Grace was hurrying along the passageway towards the kitchen, close on the heels of the young messenger who had been sent to fetch her, as her mistress came out of the dining room.

"What is wrong Grace... what is it?" she asked. One look at her maid's worried expression told her that something was amiss.

"It my Sunny Blue... he hurt ma'am," Grace gasped breathlessly, as she hurried towards the kitchen. Lilybee paused for a moment and watched as the two disappeared through the kitchen door.

She decided to find out for herself what had happened. She entered the kitchen quietly, to find a very distressed

Sunny Blue enfolded in his mother's arms and haltingly relating what Ralph Clayton had done. She was appalled at the boy's tale, as were his mother and the other onlookers. Several of the servants had gathered around mother and son, and were muttering sympathetically; they dispersed immediately they heard their mistress's voice. "Poor child... oh, you poor child," she said kindly. "You go Grace... go now... take care of him and get him cleaned up." She shook her head disbelievingly. "He's had a nasty shock, he'll need to rest. Bring him with you up to the house tomorrow morning, will you? I'll speak to the master, see if he can't use the boy up here around the house, in the gardens maybe. Now off you go."

"Thank you ma'am, thank you," said Grace gratefully, as she ushered her son towards the door.

Lilybee went in search of her husband immediately; she knew where to find him. She tapped gently on the door of his study and opened it slowly. He leapt to his feet as her head appeared.

"My dear... come in, come in. Won't you join me in a glass of something?" He guided her over to a comfortable chair and went to pour her a drink. He himself was enjoying his usual measure of brandy with his after-dinner coffee.

"I believe I shall Percy, maybe just a small glass of port dear. Heaven knows I need it after what has happened."

He listened intently to what she had to tell him. "Why don't you get rid of that beastly man, my darling?" she pleaded. "You know how the slaves fear him, and it's little wonder. Could you not manage the plantation yourself now... with the help of Douglas? I have always disliked him since the first moment I set eyes on him, you know that. Why can't we be rid of him?"

Percy grew thoughtful. With a deep intake of breath he replied, "Because he is a fine overseer Lilybee. I have to consider that. I am fully aware of his brutality and I do try to keep a check on him, but it is difficult for me to interfere too much in his running of the gangs. It is essential to maintain discipline; you know the delicate issues at stake. Just think of how many slaves are trying to abscond from their owners now. No matter what my personal opinions are, I must not lose sight of the fact that I am, first and foremost, a planter, a slave owner, and I have invested substantial amounts of capital in them. We all know how urgent the slavery issue is becoming... and who knows what will happen at the election in November. It is strongly rumoured that the Republican 'rail splitter', Abraham Lincoln will win, and what then? Our worst fears could be realized my dear... supposing he persists in abolishing slavery, how would we manage? If we were forced to free our blacks, they might well abandon our cotton fields... and supposing they insisted on working for themselves, what do you think would happen to us?"

Lilybee could see from her husband's grave countenance just how serious the problems were, and she sympathised deeply.

"Right you are, Percy dear, keep him on if you must. I do fully realise our predicament, of course I do, but could you not, at least, remove that poor child from that evil man's control! His behaviour is abominable, and there is no knowing what harm might befall a young boy in his hands. I have told Grace that you might find him a job around the house... maybe in the garden... do you think so my darling?"

Her husband could not refuse her heartfelt plea. "Of course... of course. I'll see to it that Ralph Clayton has no more dealings with the boy. Leave it to me."

If only Percy Mansfield-Brown had been able to resolve all the problems that irked his wife as easily as he resolved this latest one concerning the hated overseer and his young victim, but they were soon to be beset by a turn of events whose tragic outcome they could never have foreseen, for in the November election of 1860, Percy's suppositions became a reality. With the Democrats' voters calamitously split between Douglas, Beckenridge and Bell, Abraham Lincoln swept to victory, and despite hardly winning a vote in the Southern states, he decidedly won every single state in the North, with the exception of New Jersey. Now this six feet four giant of a man was the President Elect, and when the news was received down in Charleston, South Carolina, their plans to secede from the Union gathered momentum. In December they formally seceded from the United States, and Mississippi, Florida, Alabama, Georgia, Louisiana and Texas followed their lead. They formed their own alliance, and drew up a document on the 4th February 1861, to announce the formation of the Confederated States of America, to be known as the Confederacy. The political situation continued to deteriorate, culminating with General Beauregard's crucial attack on Fort Sumter on the 15th April, which signalled the outbreak of war, for the President was forced, albeit unwillingly, to respond without hesitation by issuing a proclamation that there was to be a blockade of all the Southern ports.

He called for a force of 75,000 volunteers to restore federal authority in the South. Upon the issuance of this proclamation, Virginia, Arkansas, Tennessee and North Carolina also joined the Confederacy, thus creating a most dire situation for the newly elected president. He had clung steadfastly to the hope that war could be avoided, tried continually to calm the troubled waters that divided the North and the South, and had urgently enjoined the Southerners in his carefully worded inaugural speech:

"In your hands, my dissatisfied countrymen, and not in mine, is the momentous issue of civil war."

But it was all to no avail, for now the twenty-three states of the North, with a population of twenty-two million, were drawn into conflict against the eleven states of the South, whose population numbered just nine million, of whom almost four million were slaves. This disparity in numbers did nothing to deter the South, who never once doubted their superior military strength. They fired that first shot, and in so doing, plunged the whole country into the most savage war of its entire history.

Eight

Grace felt that her heart would surely break, as she kissed Mose goodbye. She could not accept the injustice of what he was being called upon to do. Here was the massa going off to war, taking with him one of his slaves, to fight against the men who would have all slaves free. "It ain't right Mose, you knows it ain't," she sobbed bitterly. "S'posin' you gits killed or sump'n...what Sunny Blue and me gonna do then?"

"I ain't intendin' to git killed... no sir I ain't, 'cos I won't be doin' no fightin', so don't you go frettin' yo'self 'bout nothin' like that. I's jus' goin' as Massa's body servant, that's all. Anyways, Massa he say we be back again in no time, 'cos we is soon gonna whip them Yankees up North. I heard him tellin' that to the Lady Lilybee jus' yesterday so you dry them tears... you hear Missy?"

Grace broke down and wept all the more at his special term of endearment.

"And you Sunny Blue... you be a good boy while I's gone and take care of your mammy 'til I gits back."

"Yes Pappy... I will...I will." Sunny Blue brushed each of his tear-stained cheeks hurriedly with the palm of his hand. His father dropped his small cloth bundle to the ground, grabbed his wife and son, one in each of his arms, and pulled them close. They clung together in a final heartfelt embrace, then, swallowing hard, Mose pressed his battered hat resolutely upon his head, grabbed his bundle and strode away, not daring to look back at the small gathering of friends who had joined Grace and Sunny Blue to bid him farewell outside their cabin.

He came up to the house just as the Lady Lilybee too was bidding her husband an emotional farewell, before he set off to join the troops of General Robert E Lee.

The two men set off slowly, and Percy Mansfield-Brown waved his hat gallantly in the air before his horse began to quicken its pace. Mose followed closely behind him, astride a sturdy mule, leading another heavily laden with baggage. Both men secretly nurtured the hope that it would not be too long before they could return home to their grieving wives, although Percy was more than confidently optimistic of that, for he, along with every other Southerner, had been tremendously encouraged by the resounding victory of Beauregard's troops on the 21st July, 1861, at the first Battle of Bull Run, when the Union army, under the command of Irwin McDowell, had been sent running in panic back to the bridges of the Potomac. On that day the North had become a laughing stock, as they fled in terror from the Confederate troops, the debacle witnessed by the residents of Washington, men and women alike, who had ventured out in their droves on that scorching mid-summer's day, taking their picnic hampers with them, to enjoy the fun and to speculate on who would be the first to retire. The tide turned in favour of the rebels when one of their commanders spurred on his men by pointing to the troops further along the line, who faced the foe unflinchingly. "Look at Jackson's men, standing like a stone wall," he had shouted. So did that illustrious general come by his never-to-be-forgotten name.

Hostilities had not begun again in earnest until the following spring of 1862, when the South tried to break the blockade of her ports by the use of an ironclad ship. This vessel, formerly of wooden construction, had fallen into their hands when they had captured the naval yard at Norfolk, Virginia, and by cladding it with iron, they set in motion a furore of activity in the shipyards of Europe and England, for wooden ships immediately became obsolete. They were not successful in breaking the blockade, however, because the North, with its vast resources, hurriedly produced enough ironclad vessels to maintain their supremacy on the water.

Then, at the beginning of June, General Robert E. Lee was appointed the new commander of the army of Northern Virginia, to replace General Johnston, who had received a near fatal wound at the Battle of Seven Pines the previous month. Upon taking up his new command, he realized that it was imperative to strengthen the fortifications around the Southern capital of Richmond in Virginia, if its safety was to be maintained.

He immediately sent an urgent plea to the Carolinas and Georgia for the reinforcements he so desperately needed, and when the call came, Percy had not failed to answer it even though his dear wife fervently begged him not to do so. Thus had he and Mose ventured forth on their heroic journey northwards, joining up with the countless others who, like himself, were anxious to fight for the independence of the South. When they finally came to their destination, neither man was prepared for the awe-inspiring spectacle that met their eyes; nothing could have prepared them for it. They were both equally dumbstruck as they surveyed the consolidated forces of General Lee and 'Stonewall' Jackson's men, the latter recently arrived from the Shenandoah Valley.

It was a magnificent sight to behold, as Percy proudly related to Lilybee in his first letter home. He was resting outside his tent, his eyes travelling over the regiments of men whose collective mass spread farther than the naked eye could see. "When I sit here and view this vast army of men, kindred souls, fighting for a common cause, I cannot doubt that we shall prevail. If you could but see them for yourself, my darling," he wrote, "it would cheer and reassure you as wholeheartedly as it does me." Maybe it was fatigue, but to Percy the whole scene seemed unreal, eerie even, with the smoke from the cooking fires slowly rising and drifting in cloud-like wisps, creating a dreamlike, vague quality. As if to add to the illusion, was the incongruity of the soldiers' attire; regiments of men in a variety of differing uniforms, not uniforms in many cases, but an odd assortment of garb that they had thought would serve the purpose. This caused mayhem and confusion in many of the battles that were fought, for it was not always possible to distinguish between friend or foe.

The profound effect that this experience was having upon Percy Mansfield-Brown was as nothing compared with its effect upon his servant. Mose had never witnessed anything of the like in his life before. What a tale he would have to tell his wife and son when he returned home. As he too sat gazing at the magnificent scene before him, he quailed inwardly, for no matter how virtuous the cause of the North, the awesome spectacle of this Southern army mustering for battle completely annihilated any hope he might have of ever being free. To him this mighty army appeared unconquerable, and he could never imagine President Lincoln's men able to bring about a change.

Lilybee read Percy's first letter to Grace, knowing full well that she too would be greatly relieved to learn that her man was safe and well. However, when she heard how strong and powerful the Confederate army appeared to be, Grace was deeply saddened, for there was not one slave at 'White Lakes', or in any of the Southern states, for that matter, who would not wish to see General Lee's army defeated. She thought of Mose constantly, and longed for him to come home, for she and Sunny Blue missed him more and more with each passing day.

Life on the plantation was changing dramatically, and feelings of unrest were growing amongst the slaves. Rumours of Northern soldiers deliberately encouraging them to desert the plantations were rife, because the Northerners fully realized that the loss of their workers would be crippling to the planters, and this would, in turn, seriously affect the South's economy. Additionally, with an ever-increasing number of slave owners being called to join Lee's army, the hold of master over slave fast eroded.

General Lee took a month to enlist reinforcements, and to provide him the time he needed to gather together a sufficient number of troops to counter the Union's attack, another officer, Brigadier General J. E. B. Stuart, carried out a sortie of attacks upon their supply lines, but by the end of June, Lee felt that he had now procured as many troops as was possible, with which to meet the Northern advance upon Richmond, and despite the fact that he was greatly outnumbered, he embarked upon what was to become known as the Seven Days' Battle, during which he was to lose twenty thousand men. The death toll for the Union army was a devastating seventeen thousand, but although their losses were fewer they were driven back towards Washington. The South were once again proclaimed the victors, having secured the safety of their capital, and more importantly they had managed to capture thousands of small arms and fifty heavy artillery pieces from the enemy, which they desperately needed. For the duration of this war, the South would be continually forced to plunder the enemy's military supplies, because of their own inadequate resources. Furthermore, their loss of troops in battle would prove far more critical to them, for they had not the necessary number in population to continually provide replacements. It was not difficult to establish how devastating the loss of twenty thousand men would prove to the Rebels; far more devastating, in fact, than the loss of seventeen thousand from the massive Union army's one hundred thousand in this latest battle.

*

Mose sat near his master, quietly watching and waiting for him to awake. He studied the face that had aged almost beyond recognition during the horrific fighting of the past week, and to his utter disbelief he was overcome with pity for this fine Southern gentleman, who had been reduced to such a pitiable state.

Mose had grown to like and respect his master over the many years that he had served him, but never once had he imagined that he would ever be moved to pity him. Yet now, as he lay completely exhausted and saddle-sore, his features masked by the grime of the battlefields, his hair matted and unkempt, Mose experienced the deepest sense of compassion for this dishevelled old man. When he finally awoke, Mose was beside him in an instant with a steaming mug of coffee, and then he immediately returned to the fire to fetch a deep pan of hot water, so that his master could cleanse himself.

Percy gazed at his reflection in the small mirror as he slowly and carefully shaved off the coarse growth that had accumulated on his cheeks. He became thoughtful. How had he ever believed that his response to the fighting call had been heroic? Where was the heroism in killing and maiming his fellow men? He closed his eyes tightly as the bloody scenes from recent battles vividly crowded into his mind. He tried desperately, unsuccessfully, to blot them out, but he knew that the noise and confusion, the pain and suffering he had witnessed over the past week, would remain with him for the rest of his life. "Why?" he asked himself sadly. There could be no sane reason for such an appalling loss of human life, nor for the ruinous destruction of the country for whose development so much sacrifice had already been made. He was in a state of profound shock at all that had happened. Having become so accustomed over the years to the dreamy tranquillity of life at 'White Lakes', he was ill prepared for such violent devastation. The smell of death hung in the air and now, after witnessing so many thousands of those deaths, Percy realised how soon he too could become one of their number. He thought lovingly of his wife and his home, and wished with all his heart that he had never left them. How old and weary he felt now.

He suddenly became aware of Mose moving around quietly, attentive as ever to his master's comforts, as much as was possible in these appallingly dire conditions. As he finished his ablutions he called to him, "Mose... I want a word with you. There is something I need to tell you."

"Yes sir, Massa Percy... I be right there." Mose hurriedly discarded the pan of dirty water and hurried back to the tent.

Percy indicated the stool close to his own and waited until his manservant was seated. He looked concernedly at the bowed head before him and was once again compelled to acknowledge the inhumanity, the insufferable injustice of subjecting any man to slavery... this man in particular, with his massive strength and his gentleness of spirit. How long had he felt it? "Look at me Mose," he said quietly. The large sorrowful eyes met his own. "When this war is over, when the fighting is all done, you shall have your freedom. I want you to know that."

Mose was stunned; a puzzled frown creased his brow. "You are to be a free man... do you understand?"

"Er... yessir Massa Percy, I think I does." He was deeply confused. Mose was hardly able to grasp what he had heard. The full realisation of it would take him time to assimilate.

"I shall write to the mistress to tell her, so that if anything happens to me, as well it might, then when you return to 'White Lakes' she will be able to carry out my wishes."

He spoke resolutely and Mose became alarmed. "Ain't nothin' gonna happen to you Massa, why, you said yo'self we is soon gonna whip them Yankees. We be gittin' back home in no time."

His master shook his head disconsolately. "I'm afraid I took far too much for granted my man. It would seem this could be a long and bloody battle... and at the end of it, in truth, I fear that neither side will ever feel that a victory has been won."

Both armies, Union and Confederate alike, constantly manoeuvred their positions in a bid to outwit each other, but although their battles were courageously fought, time and time again serious blunders and errors of judgment caused devastating loss of precious lives, particularly for the South, who could ill afford the losses. Invariably, the regiments of the North greatly outnumbered their own, but by carefully dividing his army, when he felt it necessary, and carrying out rapid surprise attacks, General Lee managed to maintain the morale of his troops.

In early August, Percy and Mose found themselves fighting with the twenty-four thousand men, under 'Stonewall' Jackson's command, at Cedar Mountain, where they soundly defeated a segment of the Northern army. Then by the end of that same month they were plunged into the second Battle of Bull Run. Once again the fighting was savage, and the assaults so numerous that several of Jackson's units ran out of ammunition with which to fight their foe. In sheer desperation, and determined not to give in, the Confederate troops used their muskets as clubs with which to defend themselves. Miraculously, Major General James Longstreet's corps arrived at an opportune moment to come to their aid, thus ensuring another Confederate victory.

So the war continued and the bitterness grew, particularly when scores of slaves began to desert the plantations to follow the Union army of the North. At first they were put to work as cooks, drivers and navvies, but it was not long before they were accepted into some regiments as soldiers. On the 27th September, 1862, at New Orleans,

General Ben Butler began to organize a regiment of free black 'Volunteers': the First Louisiana Native Guard. More bloody battles ensued, Antietam standing out as the most bloody of the war, when both sides each lost a quarter of their fighting force. After it, Lee retreated to Virginia to replenish and reorganize his army, whilst President Lincoln issued his Preliminary Emancipation Proclamation. In it he outlined his intention of freeing all slaves on or after the 1st January, 1863, in the rebellious states.

Lincoln was bitterly criticized by his political opponents, who considered that he was seriously overstepping his power of authority, but he remained firm in his desire to eventually bring about harmony between blacks and whites.

Nine

It was the year of 1863, and Percy could not believe that he had been away from his beloved wife for almost a year. He had written to her so many times during his months of absence, constantly reassuring her of his love, and careful to avoid any mention of the privations and suffering that he, along with thousands of others, had to endure in this relentless war.

As he had promised Mose, he did not forget to inform her of his intention to free his manservant when the war was over and he knew, without doubt, that she would carry out his wishes should he not return. With the losses that were sustained in the continual fighting, Percy was becoming more and more convinced that he would never again return home to 'White Lakes', and to add to his despondency came the death of their magnificent General Stonewall F Jackson, after the battle at Chancellorsville in May. Tragically, he had been fired upon inadvertently by his own sentries, who in their confusion had mistaken him and his horsemen for a detachment of Union forces, as they returned to camp after dark. In conditions as appalling as they were, with insufficient medical assistance and very little food, he died a lingering death from complications and pneumonia, as so many other brave souls had. Shock waves reverberated throughout the North and South when the news was received, and his men deeply mourned his loss.

Just two months later, Lee relentlessly urged his troops northwards yet again, this time into Pennsylvania, to carry out the invasion that he had been planning for so long. His army came upon the enemy unexpectedly in the small town of Gettysburg, which was not exactly where he had intended to engage them. Nevertheless, battle ensued and this would prove to be the greatest, the most devastating battle he had ever undertaken. It raged for two whole days, and resulted in the combined loss of a further fifty thousand men, killed, wounded and missing, from both armies.

In the aftermath of battle, General Lee was forced to retreat with his depleted army, leaving his dead to be buried by the foe. The corpses were afterwards said to be so many in number that they completely covered the battlefield in which they had fought so valiantly.

Percy could not help but marvel that he was still alive, but for how much longer would this destructive war rage on, he wondered; and for how much longer could he continue to survive? Every time he returned from battle he felt unbearable guilt that he was not lying dead with all those who had perished. It was almost as though he would welcome death as a blessed relief, for he had grown to dread every new assault, every charge that they made upon the enemy. He was deeply ashamed at the recollection of that final charge on the 3rd July; his stomach had churned, causing him to retch violently as Major General James Longstreet had resignedly agreed to Major General George Pickett' s request for permission to attack.

Pickett's Virginians had been chosen to lead that last fifteen thousand man charge, together with Pettigrew's North Carolinians, Percy's own attachment. Longstreet's countenance was grave for he fully realised that he was sending his men to certain death. He had opposed Lee's strategy from the very start, knowing that it would be suicidal for the men to attempt their attacks uphill; the enemy held the stronger defensive positions on the hills and ridges which lay to the South of Gettysburg.

As he called the retreat of his army, what little there was left of it, Lee too realized the gravity of his mistake... just he, and he alone, had brought about the mass slaughter of his men by an appalling miscalculation. He met them as they returned, beaten and dejected, to assure them that responsibility for the defeat was entirely his, not theirs, for they had fought unflinchingly, and far more courageously than any commander would ever have expected of them, and now all he could do was to effect their escape back across the Potomac river, aided by the torrential rain and dismal conditions, which mercifully deterred their reluctant, exhausted foe from pursuing them.

*

Throughout that same year of 1863, many battles were also being fought in the western theatre around the Mississippi river, and none as bitter or more savage than those at Vicksburg where the town was laid to siege by the Northern army, which brought unmerciful suffering to the civilian population, as well as the Confederate soldiers who were defending it. Ulysses Grant and his men successfully prevented any supplies from reaching his starving foe, and as their fresh water and food dwindled away, they were forced to eat stewed mule, rodents and cane shoots in order to stay alive; and with no coffee or flour, they had to make use of many strange improvisations. Finally, after more than half a year of fighting, the Southern army had no alternative but to surrender Vicksburg to the North.

This dealt a bitter blow to the Confederacy, but the Union were jubilant, because they had turned the tide of war in their favour. They now felt that victory was within their grasp at long last. The battles of Chickamauga and Chattanooga followed, and Longstreet's troops joined the army of Tennessee to assist in bringing about a victory for them in the first battlefield, greatly encouraging the weakening South. This restored their sagging spirits temporarily, but they were soon to be dashed by the resounding Northern victories at Chattanooga, and as the year neared its end, Longstreet drew back to the border of North Carolina where he could set up camp for the winter.

In the May of 1864, as the war moved into its third year, Grant marched the army of the Potomac southwards, down to the dense woods of Virginia, where he intended to launch yet another attack upon the Confederate capital. His troops numbered one hundred and twenty-two thousand, as opposed to the South's sixty-two thousand. Even so, Lee ordered the advance of his magnificent men to engage this mighty fighting force, and the two armies encountered one another just west of the Wilderness Tavern. Hence the Battle of the Wilderness ensued, and it was fought with great ferocity across the same terrain as that of the Battle of Chancellorsville less than a year earlier. Whilst the fighting raged, Longstreet's Corps, as they had done in the past, arrived to reinforce Major A Hill's men, who were succumbing to the superior strength of the Union army, but as the South launched their renewed attack, one of their own units accidentally fired upon Longstreet and his staff. That bravest of generals sustained a serious injury to his neck in this unbelievable repeat of the disaster that had befallen 'Stonewall' Jackson the year before, but although severely injured, fortunately he did not lose his life. When the news reached Lee he was completely devastated, to the extent that he contemplated discontinuing the battle. However, he finally managed to reorganize his troops and continued to counter-attack. As success became imminent for the Confederates, their bitter fighting was halted by the outbreak of a ferocious brush fire, which spread rapidly between the two opposing forces. As always, there was the most horrific loss of life on both sides, and thousands of men, some mortally wounded, others unable to escape the raging inferno, were burnt to death. The screams of the dying were said to have resounded to the furthest perimeter of the fighting lines, and those who managed to survive, afterwards described the macabre spectacle as "a true hell on earth."

The ensuing battles at Spotsylvania Court House and Cold Harbor, just served to inflict more brutal punishment upon the two armies, with the Union's casualties rising to an alarming fifty-five thousand, and those of the Confederates reaching a crippling forty thousand. Northerners were appalled at the staggering loss of young lives, and Grant had still not taken the South's capital, Richmond.

Now Lee entrenched himself and his drastically reduced army to the South of Richmond at Petersburg, where they were barely managing to survive under the pressures of the Northern army's siege, but they held out with rugged determination, stubbornly refusing to be ousted. Here their courage was stretched beyond endurance as they were forced to fight an even mightier battle. No longer did the war of North versus South play the most vital role; in its stead came the all-consuming struggle against pitiless hunger and disease.

*

Percy had grown weak from lack of food. He knew that he did not have enough strength to survive these rigorous conditions for very much longer. The ravenous pain in his stomach completely obliterated all other senses of body and mind, and he knew full well that he was soon to die. He could not believe that they had been reduced to living in trenches like so many animals, watching their enemy in parallel trenches just a stone's throw away. This dismal state of affairs had persisted throughout June and July of 1864, and the deadlock seemed set to continue without hope of relief. That was until the dawn of the 30th July, for at four forty-five in the morning came the most almighty, earth-shattering, explosion. The magnitude of the blast, the total devastation it caused threw the Confederate army into absolute confusion. The destruction was horrifying as enormous masses of earth, tons of it, were violently projected skywards, carrying with it the massacred bodies of men and horses, guns, carriages and fortifications.

Mose searched frantically through the rubble praying aloud to God that he would find his master. Sobs racked his body, his teeth chattered uncontrollably at the horror of what he was seeing as he groped his way through the mounds of mangled corpses. Furiously he scraped and dug away the earth where he detected the slightest sign of movement or life, and heaved with all his might to free those who were screaming for help. He worked for what seemed like an eternity, along with the scores of others who were desperately trying to save the wounded; he lost count of the number he carried to the field hospital, not really a hospital, but a make-shift area crudely set up, where the sick and dying might receive some kind of medical attention. Now the numbers of wounded had grown to so many that they were simply being lain side by side on the ground around the medical tents, with scarcely a hope of receiving the attention that they so desperately needed. As the day wore on and still more were being rescued, the numbers grew alarmingly. Mose returned time and time again to the scene of the carnage, and just as he was beginning to lose all hope of ever finding Massa Percy, he caught sight of him bloodied and staggering around on the perimeter of the huge crater that had been ripped in the earth by the explosion. At first he was not absolutely sure who the bedraggled figure was, thinking him to be just another of the injured who needed help, but as he came closer and recognized his master, his relief was overwhelming. Percy was on the point of collapse, and as Mose's strong arms encircled his body his legs buckled beneath him.

"Mose is that you Mose?" he muttered.

"I'se here Massa... you jus' take it easy now. I'se gonna git you to a doctor." Mose waved to another of the rescuers who was hurrying close by with a rolled up stretcher. "This gen'lman is needing some help," he called urgently.

Percy clenched his teeth with the pain; he could feel every movement as the two men struggled to carry the stretcher over the uneven ground. Then again it accelerated as they lifted him from the stretcher and laid him upon the hardened earth alongside all the other wounded.

"I be right back, Massa," said Mose. "You jus' rest here and I be back real quick."

Then he was gone, and Percy drifted off into oblivion. It seemed no time at all before Mose returned, carrying a tin mug filled with water. "The doctor man he say he come as soon as he can. Here... you drink this." He lifted his master's head gently and moistened the parched lips.

"You're a good man Mose... loyal. I don't know how I'd have managed without you these past two years." Percy's face contorted in pain. "Stay here with me will you?"

"Yessir Massa Percy... I sho' will. I ain't figurin' to go nowhere... not without you I ain't. Now you jus' git some rest, and I be right here." He poured a little of the water from the mug onto a piece of cloth and gently applied it to the blackened face of his master; it was a useless gesture, but there was nothing more that he could do to alleviate his suffering. Then he sat on the ground beside him, his knees drawn up to his chest, his arms folded across them, so that he could rest his weary head. All around him men were dying, he could hear their agonized cries for help, but none came, for the medical teams simply could not cope with the enormous task that had been thrust upon them.

A rescuer arrived carrying another of the injured over his shoulder. He laid the figure to rest on the other side of

Percy, then disappeared again. Mose raised his head to look at the new arrival, who was muttering incoherently, with an occasional loud outburst of garbled words. Mose could see that he was only a youngster, not much more than a boy really, and his clothes were in tatters, so that it was virtually impossible to tell to which army he belonged. What did it matter, thought Mose, he was in pain and needing help just as much as the next man. The young boy cried out yet again, more urgently, and raised himself unsteadily on to one elbow. His eyes stared ahead, unaware of those around him, a terrified look on his face.

"Mama... Mama," he called, then in a smart military manner, "Hetherington, sir... New Jersey... yes, sir." He struggled to get up on his feet and screamed in pain; blood was pouring from a wound to his left leg.

As he fell back on to the ground, Mose leapt up and went to him. "Careful now... you take it easy young massa." He spoke quietly, trying to reassure the boy.

Suddenly the eyes were looking steadily into his own, focussing upon his face. "Is that you Joshua... where's Clarence? I haven't seen him all day. Minnie said he would come fishing with me down..."

His voice trailed away. Mose tried to make him comfortable, and gently stroked his forehead, brushing back the tangled hair. He was a good-looking boy and much too young to be fighting in this savage war; Mose was deeply moved by him.

He continued to mutter deliriously, repeating various names. Suddenly Mose began to connect what he was saying; his mouth dropped open in disbelief. Surely he must be imagining it, but no, he heard them again.

"Joshua, where's Clarence? Minnie said... Rosalind... Rosalind... yes sir. Hetherington, sir... New Jersey. Here Mama... Mamma... I'm here Mamma."

Percy was stirring; Mose turned to him, "How you feelin' now Massa?" The old man was ghastly pale. "You think I ought to go for that doctor man... see if he coming?"

Percy nodded. "Need something for the pain Mose... see what you can do, will you?"

Mose was gone immediately, and finally managed to locate a medic who was on his way to the area where Percy was lying. He administered morphine to those in the worst pain, and cleaned and dressed their wounds to make them more comfortable. Percy's external wounds were superficial, but it was obvious to the doctor that he had severe internal bleeding, which would necessitate surgery. He chatted to the elderly man as he treated him, careful to avoid mentioning that he would need surgery very soon. He then turned his attention to the young boy, and asked Mose to keep a steady hold of him as he cut away his bloodstained trousers from the injured leg. The wound was deep and obviously extremely painful, but he dressed it as best he could, then continued on his never-ending rounds, doing what little he could to ease the suffering of his patients.

Very soon warm soup and drinks were being brought around, and Mose marvelled at the number of women who volunteered their services in the field kitchens. Hundreds of them had continually served throughout the war, following the armies, both North and South, to nurture and succour the fighting men and the wounded. Mose tried in vain to encourage his master to take a little nourishment, but Percy wanted only to rest. He then went to the boy and fed him, baby like, with the warm soup. Once the youngster had nodded off to sleep, Mose was able to attend to his master again; he wanted to tell him what he had heard, although he could scarcely believe it himself.

"Massa... Massa... is you awake?" He bent towards the old man, talking confidentially. "Ise got sump'n I thinks you oughta know."

Percy's eyes opened. "Yes Mose, what is it?"

"That boy, Massa... he say his name is... er... Hetherington. I heard him loud and clear, more'n once, sir. Then he start a' sayin' all kindsa names I know... yes sir Massa Percy. Joshua and Clarence, his twin boys... and then Minnie. I thinks he your kin Massa... can't be nothin' else, not with all dem names he a callin', what you think Massa? Maybe you oughta ask him, if he wakes again."

Percy became thoughtful, trying to absorb what he had been told. Everything seemed so unreal to him, could he have misunderstood?

"What's that you're telling me Mose? Oh, no... no... you must be mistaken."

"Well I heard him plain as day Massa... he called out his name loud and clear... he say Hetherington... New Jersey, and then like I done told you, all the names of the folks used to be a workin' down 'White Lakes' plantation. Can't be no mistakin' that... no sir. You ask him when he wakes... you hear for yo'self Massa, 'cos I is sure what I heard."

Eventually the boy did awake, seeming much better for the rest and the medical attention he had received. Mose spoke softly to him:

"How you feelin' now young massa, better is you?"

The boy rubbed his eyes and stared around him at the vast number of troops who lay everywhere. "Where am... where am I?" he stammered. He looked fearful; he could sense that he was in the enemy's camp.

"Ain't nothin' to be afraid of... you is safe here," Mose said reassuringly. "Massa Percy... Massa Percy... he awake now."

He shook his master gently and Percy turned to look at the youngster. "Who are you boy... where are you from?" he asked quietly. He could see that the boy was very afraid, and hastened to allay his fear. "My man here says that you were calling the name of Hetherington when you were delirious. Is that your name?"

The boy was too scared to answer, for if this man was a Confederate, then he was in danger. Percy went on, "If you're a Hetherington from New Jersey, then surely we must be related. My wife's brother, Gilbert Hetherington, lives there with his wife Celia, and his children Edmund and Rosalind, oh, yes... and young Esther."

The boy's countenance changed to one of complete astonishment. "I am Edmund Hetherington sir," he whispered. "Gilbert Hetherington is my father." He smiled, relief flooding over him. Perhaps he was safe after all.

"Well, well... upon my word; I'm Percy Mansfield-Brown, your Uncle Percy from North Carolina. This is truly remarkable, is it not?"

Mose was grinning broadly, almost unable to believe such a coincidence... although he had seen many other Union soldiers brought here throughout the day.

Percy and Edmund were weak, and the excitement suddenly overcame them; they each lay back in repose, their features more relaxed after their pleasant and unexpected encounter.

*

Soon the night closed in and the light from camp fires and lanterns glowed brightly against the darkened sky. Mose had found some blankets with which to cover his two patients, and settle them both comfortably. He remained wakeful, lest they should need him. Percy was worried about his nephew, he realised that he would be in danger if it were discovered that he was a Union soldier. Feelings were running high in the Confederate camp, particularly since the news of Sherman's siege of Atlanta had filtered through. It would seem that he was intent upon the destruction of that city; and now this bombardment today, so near their capital, Richmond, causing even more devastating loss of life. When all seemed quiet, he called softly to Mose to come near.

"The boy won't be safe here, Mose, you know that don't you? I want you to get him away if you can. Take him back to 'White Lakes' where he'll be looked after until all this fighting is over. Go now... try to find a cart... something you can both travel in. Go...go now, before sun up. You must get him away. See if you can find a cart, then fetch it nearby, so that he can reach it with your help... careful you're not seen. Hurry now... there's no time to lose."

Mose made off and was indeed soon able to find a wooden cart. In all the confusion, it was not difficult to move around without being questioned. He looked for a suitable horse and hitched it up, then led it stealthily to where he could conceal it. He returned to fetch Edmund, exactly as his master had instructed him to do, but after hiding him safely in the bottom of the cart, he went back to fetch Percy.

A pitiful argument ensued, as the sickly old man tried to persuade Mose to leave him behind, but his manservant was adamant that he would not. "You must go without me Mose... I couldn't...travel anywhere...I'm dying, don't you understand? Now just leave me and go... let me die in peace... it's more important to save the boy."

Mose could not hold back his tears. "I can't leave you Massa Percy, not here. I ain't goin' nowhere without you. If youse gonna die, then it ain't gonna be here, no sir, it ain't. Please Massa, I always done everythin' you told me, but now come the time that I ain't a-listenin' to you no more, 'cos I knows I'se right 'bout this. I'se takin' you back to Carolina, where you belong. Ain't nothin' you can do 'bout that, so you jus' hold on, I'se gonna take care of yo' 'cos I knows the mistress'd want me to take you home."

He placed his arms under the dying man and lifted him as gently as he could. Violent pains rent Percy's body, and he tried hard to stifle his groans. Mose soon had him lying as comfortably as was possible in the cart beside Edmund, then he led the horse quietly away, in the direction of the North Carolina border.

They could only travel under cover of darkness, so just as soon as it was daybreak Mose had to find somewhere to hide, for he was not at all sure what reaction he would invoke should he, a black slave, be discovered travelling abroad unaccompanied, or seemingly so. It felt mightily strange for him to be acting independently at all, unaccustomed as he was to being completely in command of his own situation. Never before in his life had he known such a privilege, and it was presenting great difficulty. Their progress was slow, and he foraged for food and water as they went, always careful to ensure that the cart was well hidden when he had to leave it. The condition of his master, as well as that of the boy, deteriorated as the days went by, and Mose was not able to provide the medical attention that they so desperately needed. They drifted in and out of delirium, throwing Mose into a panic when they did so, for he was terrified that somebody might hear their cries.

On the third night they left Virginia and crossed the border into North Carolina, and Mose reckoned that they could be about half way home by now. As he slowed the cart, in order to search for a safe hiding place before dawn broke, Percy called to him. The old man knew that his final hour had come; he was desperately weak, he no longer had the strength to fight on. He had long been expecting death, had thought about it constantly during the past two years, and now that it had come, there was no fear in him, just complete acceptance of it.

"What is it Massa…?" Mose could hardly bear to look at his master, for he too knew that the end was very near. His heart was heavy with grief.

"You'll have to leave me here Mose."

His manservant broke in, "Oh, no Massa Percy, no… I gonna git you to 'White Lakes' like I said."

Percy closed his eyes tightly and gasped for breath, he had never felt so tired. "No time left," he whispered almost inaudibly … "but save the boy… too young… to… die." His breathing became laboured, rattling in his throat. Mose took the skeletal hand of his master between his own and felt the fingers close weakly in fond acknowledgment, before falling limp as Percy withdrew from the final fight, to take his well-earned rest.

"Oh no... Massa... no." Mose enclosed his arms around the lifeless form and drew it up against him. He could not believe that this stalwart old man had finally succumbed, after all the rigours of the past two years. Their shared experiences together, the trials and tribulations they had endured day after day, had drawn them close, so that now their parting caused him intense pain. Mose was completely exhausted after the night's exertions; he had often been forced to walk, leading the horse when the terrain had been difficult, and now with his master gone, he too felt his will to live slipping away. An overwhelming desire to lie down and die swept over him, he was on the point of collapse. How easy it would be, he mused, just to give in, give up the fight.

How long he sat there, he had no way of knowing, but suddenly he became aware of the sun's first rays filtering through the branches of the trees, bathing every leaf with its golden light. He rubbed his eyes in disbelief... was that his wife silhouetted against a distant tree? He blinked several times, then looked again. She had disappeared. No matter, Mose had seen her, as he had seen her all those years ago, silhouetted against the light of the early morning sun. To him, she had never looked more lovely than at that moment, and now she had come to him again, to remind him of how much he loved her, to call him home.

There was much that he had to do; he knew that he needed to find cover during the daylight hours. As soon as they were well concealed, he crawled beneath the cart to snatch a few hours of rest; he must regain the necessary strength to dig a secure grave for his master. He drifted off to sleep content in the knowledge that he could, at least, lay him to rest in his own beloved state of North Carolina.

Several hours later, Mose was awakened by the loud buzzing sound of the flies which were swarming all over his master's corpse. He knew immediately, although it was not yet dark, that he could not delay the burial for a moment longer. He took the pick and shovel from the cart, and went in search of a suitable place, somewhere sheltered, that might remain undisturbed.

Sweat poured from him as he carried out his unhappy task, and when it was done, he was careful to ensure that there was no evidence of a grave, nor the slightest indication that anyone had been there. Then, before leaving, he felt it necessary to offer up a prayer for Percy Mansfield-Brown. He mouthed a few simple, but appropriate, words, stooped to pick up his tools, and reluctantly left him at peace in his final resting place.

Ten

Mose could not believe that young Edmund Hetherington was still alive as they came within sight of 'White Lakes'. He drove the cart around to the kitchen, anxious to get him the care that he needed. The joy at his homecoming was completely overshadowed by the sad news he had to convey to the mistress of the house. He banged loudly on the kitchen door; it was apparent that everyone had gone to bed. He called out and banged on the door again. A small glimmer of light appeared under the crack of the door, and a concerned voice questioned, "Who dere, who is it?"

"It's me... Mose... quick, call the Lady Lilybee... I'se got her nephew here, and he hurt real bad."

There was a short pause and Mose could hear whispered exchanges, then the sound of the bolts being drawn back. The door opened an inch or two, and Hannah peeped out. As she caught sight of Mose, she flung the door wide and let out a long, joyful wail.

"Mose Mose... it really you." She threw her arms around him and swayed him back and forth enthusiastically. "I don' believe it, you home... you home." She laughed excitedly. "Does Grace know you here?"

Mose shook his head. "Not yet... no."

Hannah turned to the young black girl, who was standing behind her, a dazed expression on her face. "Quick Lavinia, you go fetch her... quick as you can... now run."

The girl disappeared in the direction of the slaves' quarters, barefooted and dressed only in her night shift. Mose was ushered inside and plied with questions. He did not answer; he was too full of sorrow.

"You must fetch the Lady Lilybee, it can't wait Hannah," he urged. "That young boy... he gonna die if he don' soon git some help."

The old woman pointed to a chair. "You sit there Mose... I fetch the mistress right now."

Before he knew it, everything was in turmoil. First came the mistress, overjoyed at his arrival, but curious to know why he was there.

"Percy... where is Master Percy... oh Mose, how is he?"

Even before he spoke, she could read in his face the news he was about to give her.

Mose could hardly utter the words, "I done all I could to bring him home to you ma'am... but he... he..."

Lilybee broke in, "I know, Mose... I know." She fought to control herself, she could see that he was in no fit state to talk about it. More than anything, he needed to rest, for he was in a state of collapse. She laid her hand on his arm. "We'll talk later... not now. See, here comes Grace... you go with her, get to your bed. I'll see you tomorrow."

Mose pointed towards the door. "Out in the cart ma'am... your nephew, Edmund Hetherington; he need help real bad. Massa Percy, he done told me to bring him to 'White Lakes' ma'am." He looked at her helplessly.

"All right... all right Mose, you shall tell me everything when you have rested. Go now, I'll take care of the boy."

Mose turned to his wife who was standing just inside the door, she had not yet spoken a word, her heart was too full. He walked towards her, almost unable to believe that they were united at last. She fell into his arms and they clung together for several moments, weeping silently. She pulled away from him and gazed up lovingly into his eyes. "Oh, Mose, Mose... it been so long. I thought I never gonna see you again," she sobbed. "Thank the Lord you is safe... thank the Lord."

"Aaamen... Aaamen," sang Hannah, quickly brushing a tear from her eye. "You git him to bed now Grace... he look like he need a good long rest."

Grace nodded, and gently pulled Mose with her out of the kitchen door. Lilybee followed, anxious to attend to the injured boy. She was puzzled by what Mose had said about him; about the boy being her nephew. She did not fully comprehend, surely he must be mistaken. Nevertheless, if he needed help, then she would take care of him; that was the first priority. Her heart felt heavy at the news of her dear husband, but she tried not to think of it, not for the moment, at least. She must concentrate upon the task at hand. She called to Hannah to come with her and fetch the lamp, and when its light fell upon the injured occupant of the cart, they gasped in horror. Lilybee feared him dead, so corpse-like did he appear, and it was obvious that his life's blood had been fast oozing away, for it had saturated the rags covering his wounds, as well as those upon which he was lying.

"Oh, Hannah... we need some of the men to help us with this poor soul... quickly, quickly."

Hannah once again sent the young Lavinia scurrying towards the slaves' cabins, to bring two or three of the men. Then she and Lilybee disappeared into the house to arouse some of the housemaids from their quarters below. Lilybee called for plenty of hot water to be made ready, and for sheets to be brought to cover the kitchen table, so that they could clean the boy, and administer first aid. Fortunately, he was in an unconscious state when the men carried him in, which made the job of soaking off his badly soiled clothing, and cleansing his wounds, much less difficult.

Afterwards, a room was made ready for him, and once he was comfortably settled in bed, Lilybee dismissed all the servants and told them that she would stay with the boy, watch over him through the rest of the night. She knew full well that she would never be able to fall asleep again now, not after the shock of hearing that dear Percy was no longer alive. She needed time to sit quietly and think about what had happened, to come to terms with her tragic loss. As she sat in the stillness of the night, the lamp glimmering low, she could easily imagine that this was but a bad dream, that when she awoke, the ache in her heart would melt away; but with the break of day came the cruel realization that all the horrors of the night were true, that she was never ever to see her beloved husband again.

*

Lilybee was not the only one to remain awake as the night hours slipped stealthily away, for Grace too found that sleep eluded her. She could hardly contain the joy in her heart; she had never felt more alive. She was happy to lie beside Mose's

357

recumbent form once again, careful not to move, lest she awakened him... scarcely able to believe that he was actually there. Her happiness at her husband's return was in stark contrast to the sadness being experienced by her mistress, and she was fully aware of just how fortunate she had been.

Shortly after dawn, Grace woke Sunny Blue; she bent over him and whispered in his ear that his pappy was home. As he was about to let out a loud yell, she clamped her hand over his mouth. "Shs shh, he fast asleep. He jus' about all tired out, so don' you git wakin' him 'til he good and ready."

Sunny Blue crept from his bunk across to the big bed on the opposite side of the cabin, to peer at his father. He turned to his mother, his face creased in a huge grin; his heart too was full of joy at the safe return of his father, after two whole years. When he had made himself ready, he set off to take his breakfast in the slaves' kitchen up at the house.

"You tell Hannah I be comin' with your pappy, jus' soon as he ready, Sunny Blue. The Lady Lilybee, she wanna talk with him 'bout the massa, so we both be comin' late... you go now... git your breakfast."

Normally they walked to their work together every morning, as they had done ever since the mistress had arranged for the boy to work in the gardens, and around the house, and Grace always tried to keep him well away from Ralph Clayton, to avoid his unwanted attention.

"Don' you git stoppin' nowheres Sunny Blue. You keep goin' all the way up to the house, you hear?"

"You know I will Mamma... I ain't figurin' on stopping nowhere." The boy knew that his mother was greatly afraid of the malicious overseer, as were all the other slaves at 'White Lakes' but they knew that the future now held hope for them, and they dreamed of a life free from the tyranny of men like Ralph Clayton.

*

Later that day, Grace told Mose of all the changes that had taken place at 'White Lakes' whilst he had been away, and then as they walked together up to the house, he was shocked to see for himself the evidence of neglect everywhere. The growth of cotton had been abandoned, fields turned to producing food crops, and many of the able young slaves had been called by the Confederate government to work in factories, or as building labourers, blacksmiths and suchlike, with the result that the plantations had rapidly deteriorated, their livestock diminished, and their fields overgrown with weeds. Mose noticed too how many of the slaves' cabins had been deserted, and how derelict everything looked with fences broken down, and equipment in disrepair.

Grace went in search of her mistress as soon as they arrived at the house, and Lilybee asked her to bring Mose to the master's study, where they could talk to one another uninterrupted. "You come in too Grace," she said quietly, and do sit down, both of you." Despite their fond regard for their mistress, both Mose and Grace felt intensely ill at ease at being afforded such a privilege. Lilybee detected their discomfort immediately, and did her best to dispel it.

"I want you to know how deeply grateful I am for all that you did for Master Percy, Mose," she began. "In every letter I received from him, he told me of your unswerving loyalty, your constant courageous support. He held you in the highest esteem, and I thank you for it, from the bottom of my heart. It is indeed a consolation for me to know that he had you to rely upon, that you were beside him throughout his darkest days. It could not have been easy for you, but I am sure that my dear husband could never have wished for a more devoted companion. Now… that being said Mose, I would like you to acquaint me with all that has happened since you went off to this perfectly dreadful war, or as much of it as you care to remember, and feel disposed to tell me."

By gentle persuasion, Lilybee managed to glean, bit by bit, the details of how Percy and his manservant had been engaged for the past two long and dreary years. Both she and Grace sat dumbfounded as Mose, in his simple, decent manner, poured forth everything he thought it fitting to tell his master's widow. He took care not to distress her unduly with too many harrowing details, but at the same time, he ensured that she was left in no doubt of her husband's undaunting valour. He told her too of how it had come about that her young nephew was discovered in the field hospital, lying alongside his uncle; of their joy at the discovery that they were, in fact, kinfolk, and how amazed they had been at the unbelievable coincidence. Finally, in a voice choked with emotion, Mose relived the most painful moments of all, when he had reluctantly laid his master to rest, peaceful at last within the borders of his own state, North Carolina.

Lilybee wept unashamedly, as did Grace, at Mose's sensitive account of his master's sad passing, and when he had finished, she remained silent for several minutes, trying to compose herself before she spoke again; then, heaving a deep shuddering sigh, she said, "Thank you Mose, thank you… I am deeply indebted to you, as my dear husband must surely have been, God rest his soul."

"Aamen," whispered Grace and Mose in unison.

"And to that end, I am now going to carry out his heartfelt wishes concerning you Mose, and, of course, your wife and son. He wrote to me long since, that for your devotion to him, you were to be granted your freedom as soon as the war was over, and that should he not survive it, then you were to be freed upon his death." She bent forward, as though to give greater emphasis to what she was about to say. "Mose, I have the greatest pleasure in telling you that you are now a free man... as from this moment, you and your family are free, as Master Percy desired you must be, should he not return from the war. There, it is done, and I shall give you the necessary written confirmation of it just as soon as I am able to put pen to paper." She stood up and stepped towards the bewildered man, proffering her hand.

Mose leapt to his feet and quickly wiped his hand down the side of his trousers, before timidly taking the delicate pink fingers into his own. Lilybee smiled and glanced towards Grace, whose mouth was agape; she had had no idea that Mose was ever to be given his freedom. "Thank you ma'am... I don' know what to say," he stammered. "Massa Percy, he done told me long time ago he gonna make me a free man but I can't believe it gonna happen, no sir I can't. Thank you ma'am, thank you."

Lilybee raised her hand to stop him. "All right Mose you've thanked me enough," she laughed. "You have more than earned what Master Percy has given you, but now I want to ask you to give me something in return."

Mose looked puzzled. "What you want me to give you ma'am? I's sure I ain't got nothin' you want."

361

"That's where you're wrong Mose… you see, I would be very very sorry to lose Grace, or you for that matter… not to mention Sunny Blue, for what he does here in the gardens and around the house. You must have seen how the place is deteriorating and what I had in mind was that you should remain here, work here for me. What do you think? You talk to Grace, give it some thought, and let me know your decision."

"Oh, ma'am, I couldn't leave you… not now Massa Percy's gone," cried Grace.

"I am so happy to hear you say that," replied Lilybee. She stepped towards the door and opened it: "Now I'll draw up your document Mose, and we'll discuss your employment here a little later, that is if you decide to stay. Oh, and by the way, we shall see if there isn't something we can do about that cabin of yours… make it more comfortable, perhaps… yes I'm sure you could make a nice little home there."

Grace felt that she was floating as she and Mose made their way back towards the kitchen; she was in a state of euphoria. Could she be dreaming, she wondered? Hannah was alone, busily preparing food, as usual, but Grace spoke not a word to her as they passed through.

"We see you later Hannah," said Mose.

The older woman smiled and nodded, "Sure Mose… you take it easy for a bit; find your way around again. Things here has changed some since yo' been gone."

As soon as they were away from the house and alone, Grace turned to Mose and flung her arms around him, hugging him tightly. "Oh, Mose… Mose… I don' believe it; I don' believe it happenin' to us." She threw back her head and laughed loudly, almost hysterically. Mose lifted her from the ground and twirled her around, joining in her laughter.

"What Sunny Blue gonna say when he hears we free?" asked Grace. "Now my promise comin' true... he gonna be free, jus' like I always told him."

"What you think 'bout stayin' here Grace?" Mose became suddenly serious. "Mebbe it be best if we stays awhile, 'cos this old war ain't over yet, and it mighty dangerous to go a-wanderin' 'bout the countryside right now. I sure don' want nothin' happenin' to you and Sunny Blue. To tell the truth Missy, it feel real good jus' bein' home with you again... yes sir, it sho' does."

So it was settled, they decided to stay, for as Grace had already told the Lady Lilybee, she couldn't go leaving her, not now Massa Percy was gone.

*

After Lilybee had written the note of manumission for her slave Mose and his family, carefully stating that it was in accordance with her husband's dying wish, she left the study and went to see how her nephew Edmund was coming along.

She could tell, as soon as she entered the bedroom that his condition was worsening, he was extremely feverish and becoming delirious again. "Oh, my dear boy," she gasped. She turned to the housemaid who had been sitting with him. "Quickly girl... go and find one of the men to fetch Master Douglas. Tell him he has to come immediately... we need a doctor, tell him it's urgent. Now go and find someone to bring him here without delay." The flustered girl ran to Hannah, who in turn sent her scurrying away to tell one of the stable boys, for it would be quicker for one of them to take a horse to find Master Douglas. It was common knowledge to everyone that he could usually be found well away from the house, down at Ralph Clayton's place.

Lilybee wasted no time in despatching her young brother in the pony and trap, warning him as she did so, "Don't you dare show your face here until you have found a doctor, do you hear?" She knew how little he could be trusted to act on his own initiative, and he was fully capable of lying to her, should it prove difficult for him to find a doctor in town. She prayed that he would do as he was asked for once, as their young nephew's life depended upon him.

It took Douglas some time to locate a doctor when he reached town, for so many of them had joined the army where they were desperately needed to tend the sick and wounded. Eventually, however, he managed to trace one who was home on a short furlough, after having spent more than two years in the Confederate field hospital. When he heard what Douglas had to tell him of Edmund's condition, he feared the worst. "We have no time to lose if the boy's wound has turned gangrenous," he said gravely, "and from what you have told me, I suspect that it has."

Upon his arrival at 'White Lakes', his suspicions were confirmed, after he had examined Edmund, and Lilybee almost collapsed when he advised her that the boy's leg would have to be amputated if his life was to be saved.

The kitchen table was to be used for the operation, and the doctor asked for two strong, able-bodied men, to be summoned to hold his patient during the surgery. Just Lilybee and Grace were to remain, in order to assist with fetching and carrying whatever might be needed, then the gruesome task began. Lilybee was sure that she would faint; the very thought of what was about to happen turned her legs to water, but the young doctor's command of the situation, the speed and dexterity with which he performed the vital operation, allowed not the slightest opportunity for anyone to fail him. Before she knew it, Edmund was resting peacefully once more in the bedroom, and the doctor agreed to stay overnight in order to keep an eye on him, until the worst danger was passed. Before he left, he promised to return once more to check his patient, but then he must rejoin the Confederates wherever they might need him.

For the next few months, Lilybee spent her every waking hour nursing Edmund back to health; whilst her mind was fully occupied with her nephew, she had not the time to dwell on the loss of her beloved husband. Grace did all she could to help her mistress, but she was greatly concerned about her, fearing that she too might fall ill, so seldom did she take any rest. Eventually, their constant nursing brought about the desired improvement in the young boy's condition, and they were able to encourage him to leave his room.

Mose would help him downstairs, where he could sit in the study, quiet and undisturbed; or sometimes he would decide to go out on to the verandah, just to gaze at the tranquil beauty of the autumn landscape. It soon became apparent to Lilybee that Edmund's injuries were not confined to his physical being, but that the war had had a far more drastic effect on him mentally. She realised that his recovery would be a long painful process, but she was determined to do everything in her power to heal him both in body and mind.

Eleven

Since his return, Mose had been kept busy in carrying out repairs and trying to restore the grounds immediately around the house. The mistress had put him in charge of a small gang, which included his own son, and together they had brought about unbelievable improvement.

In addition, he had renovated and extended his own small cabin, and added a separate room, so that Sunny Blue would no longer have to sleep in with his parents. He utilized the wood from other cabins which stood deserted, and even made his wife some simple items of furniture, a few chairs and a table, some shelves for the wall. They were happy and content with their new existence, with what seemed to be the new order of things. Indeed, Mose could still scarcely believe his good fortune, for he had never dared to hope that one day he would be given his freedom.

*

Christmas came and went, but there was little cause for celebration in the South. News of the war could not have been more dismal. The stories of Brigadier General Sherman's relentless destruction were horrific. In Atlanta he had laid to ruin the few remaining factories, and left the city on fire before setting forth on his infamous march through Georgia to the sea. He had boasted that he would give the city of Savannah to President Lincoln for a Christmas present, and that is exactly what he did do, but in his wake he left a trail of total devastation sixty miles wide. Having ravaged Georgia, he then turned his sights on South Carolina. It was now clearly apparent that the Confederates were no longer in a position to withstand the enemy's strength; the army of the South would very soon be defeated. The civilian population, both North and South, longed for the war to be over, for every day it continued brought more hardship and suffering.

Then, mercifully, on Palm Sunday, 9th April, 1865, General Robert E Lee finally surrendered, and brought all the barbaric destruction to a bitter end.

The jubilation of the slaves was unbelievably short-lived, for just five days later, they learned of the assassination of their 'Great Emancipator, 'Mr. Linkum'. His death enraged the North, and their heartfelt grief was shared by every negro in the land, for had not this 'Messiah' freed his children from their bondage?

To him they owed their thanks that Congress had finally passed the Thirteenth Amendment, outlawing slavery forever. Despite all this, they had no land of their own, no income, and no work other than that provided by their former owners, and the Southern planters, made even more bitter by defeat, were determined to deal with the negro in the way they thought best.

They could never treat them as equals; they considered them their inferiors, therefore, they must be kept in a thoroughly subordinate position. They were to remain illiterate and unskilled, with no legal protection or rights of their own. Laws were eventually passed to this effect, known as the Black Codes. Free he may be, but in reality the negro was still little more than a slave. Douglas Hetherington and Ralph Clayton let this be known to every one of the workers at 'White Lakes' and even though this once magnificent plantation would never again enjoy the thriving prosperity that it had in the past, everything possible was being done to restore it and utilize its barren land in the most profitable way.

One morning at breakfast, Douglas upset his sister by suggesting that Mose and his son should be set to work on much more gruelling tasks than those of maintaining the gardens and caring for the livestock. "There is heavy work to be done, far more important work, and we could do with some extra strength," he said. "Ralph Clayton has asked for more hands Lilybee... and I can't refuse his request."

"Those two men do the work of four around here," cried Lilybee, "and it certainly isn't easy work either. Why, they produce every morsel of the food that we all eat... the fruit and the vegetables, not to mention the meat. The animals and chickens are thriving since Mose returned... we have only him to thank for that."

Douglas was filled with loathing for Sunny Blue and his father; he had always been envious of the high regard in which his brother-in-law had held his manservant, and now he was gone, here was his sister still singing the praises of this worthless darkie. He found it quite intolerable. "If you want my opinion, dear sister," he said loftily, "I think that slave needs taking down a peg or two. He has far too high an opinion of himself, and that boy of his is arrogant; a good whipping wouldn't come amiss in this case. For the life of me I shall never understand how you could have considered granting him his freedom. It's becoming more and more difficult to manage things around here, without encouraging them to think of themselves as our equals."

Lilybee almost exploded. "For a start Douglas, I have not asked for your opinion, so I should thank you to keep it to yourself; and do I have to remind you that slavery has been abolished? As for Ralph Clayton, I have no doubt that he has put you up to this. Don't think that I am to be fooled by him. I am perfectly well aware of his activities, and they do nothing to commend him. He is the most insufferable man I have ever had the misfortune to meet, and I shall not tolerate his interference, do you understand? Maybe if he had not treated our hired hands... and remember that they are hired hands... so cruelly, they would not have been so eager to abscond. He must surely have treated them abominably if they found it preferable to run away, for that too puts them in the most appalling danger." Her brother looked sullen, but she was not to be deterred. "I suggest that you take yourself off now, and tell Mr Clayton that I have no intention of losing one of the most loyal workers we have ever had here at 'White Lakes', and, furthermore," she banged her clenched fist on the table, "I do not intend to assign him to any other job, when he and his son are working perfectly satisfactorily on what they are already doing." She rose from the table. "Agh," she groaned impatiently, "I have far more important things to be attending to... and so should you have."

Ralph Clayton did not receive Douglas' message at all well, and he vowed that one day he would have his revenge on Mose and Sunny Blue. He had never forgiven the boy for daring to fight back on that occasion more than two years ago, when he had forced him into his cabin. The boy would pay for what he had done; he would not escape his punishment.

*

Summer was nearing its end, and Sunny Blue had passed his sixteenth birthday, although from his stature he could well have been mistaken for a full grown man. His mother smiled fondly at him as he was leaving the cabin to go and spend a few hours with his young friends. It amused her to see him beside the other boys and girls of his own age, behaving in the same youthful way; because of his mature looks, he looked peculiarly out of place. Nevertheless, it was good for him to enjoy young company, she thought, to do the things that young boys normally did. She called to him as he went, "Now don' you go gittin' into no trouble... you behave yourself, you hear? And don' be too late coming back."

"No Mamma... I won'... I won'." He raised his large brown eyes upwards; his mother said the same thing every time he went out on his own, but he knew that she meant it kindly. He made his way along the path towards the other cabins, looking for his friends.

"They's all gone down to the river, Sunny Blue," called an old man who was sitting outside, enjoying the balmy evening air. "Ain't bin gone long though."

The boy nodded and carried on along the path towards the river to a favourite meeting place. He soon caught the sound of their happy voices talking and laughing; he could hear water splashing. He knew that his friends were bathing in the river, and he hurried to join them.

"Come on... come on... where's you bin?" his friends called. Sunny Blue wasted no time at all in pulling off his clothes, and plunging into the water. They played for a very long while, innocently unaware of how quickly the time was passing, until one of the younger boys suddenly remembered that he should be getting home. He clambered up the bank and grabbed his clothes, holding them against his wet body, not bothering to put them on. He called to the others in the water as he left, waving his hand in goodbye. The other boys decided that they should be leaving too, so they emerged from the river one by one. It was as they were picking up their clothing that they heard the small cry, the scuffling sounds coming from a short distance away. The boys looked from one to the other fearfully.

"What that?" whispered one.

"You think it Nathan... maybe he in some kinda trouble?" asked another.

They pressed together and went to find out what was happening, still pulling on their clothing as they did so. Sunny Blue hurriedly led the way, the others clustered behind him for protection. They came across Nathan's clothing strewn about haphazardly, and very soon they saw him ahead; he was struggling against two men, his arms and legs flailing. They were trying to constrain him as they pulled him along. The boys immediately recognized the overseer and Massa Douglas, and they stopped dead in their tracks.

"What we gonna do?" asked one small boy, starting to whimper.

"We gotta help him, tha's what we gotta do," said Sunny Blue. "We can't jus' leave him, can we?"

"I's scared of that bossman... he real bad," said the small boy.

"All right then... you git along home... youse too little to do much anyways," said Sunny Blue reassuringly. "But go tell my pappy will you, quick as you can now?"

The small boy nodded his head vigorously, and made off, followed by several others who were also glad to escape. Sunny Blue hurried to help his terrified friend. As he neared the battling trio, he called loudly, "Leave him alone... leave him alone. He ain't done nothin' wrong."

Ralph Clayton spun around, unable to believe what he was hearing. His countenance darkened as he saw who had come to the rescue of his latest victim. He leered as he spoke. "Well look who we got here... ain't that something. What you think you gonna do boy?" he drawled menacingly.

"Let him go." Sunny Blue's tone changed. "Please Massa," he begged. Suddenly confronted with this most vile of men, his courage deserted him.

"Please, is it?" sneered the overseer: "What if I don't... eh, nigra boy? Here Douglas... catch ahold of this one." He thrust the small writhing child away from him, and made a grab for Sunny Blue. Nathan saw his opportunity and leapt in terror away from the second man, then took off before he could be caught again, running for his life back along the path towards home.

Ralph Clayton's anger flared. "Right" he yelled. "You bin askin' for it boy. About time you was taught a lesson." He had grabbed hold of Sunny Blue's arm in a vice-like grip and wrenched it behind him.

"We gonna have us some sport tonight Douglas. Here... grab a hold."

Sunny Blue cried out in pain as his other arm was clasped. He mustered all his strength and lashed out with his leg at the second man, catching him squarely on the shin. Douglas howled, and promptly released his hold.

"Why you..." Ralph Clayton swung a punch with his clenched fist against his captive's neck. As the boy fell forward on to his knees he felt a heavy boot in the small of his back. "You gonna be sorry you spoke outa turn nigra," growled Ralph Clayton. "Now you git up on your feet... you comin' with me."

"Oh, no he ain't... no sir... he ain't goin' nowheres with you."

In all the confusion and noise, no one had noticed Mose approaching along the dark, dusty path. He lunged at his son's attacker, grabbing him by the shoulder; as he yanked him around to face him, he delivered a resounding punch to the hated overseer's disbelieving face. Under the force of Mose's gigantic strength, he fell to the ground like a rag doll. Mose's anger welled up and overflowed. It was as though all the misery and degradation, every inhuman act he had had to endure throughout his life, was epitomized in this contemptible, immoral human being; he could not bring himself to acknowledge him as a man.

He stooped down and hauled him to his feet, one enormous hand supporting his neck. He drew the stupefied face close to his own, so close that he could feel his very breath against his cheek, and he threatened, "If you ever lays a finger on my son again, I gonna kill you bossman." Then, once again, Mose drew back his fist and smashed it with full ferocity between the cruel steely eyes. Ralph Clayton felt his nose squelch before he hit the ground and sank into unconsciousness.

It had all happened so quickly, and Douglas Hetherington had stood by helplessly, his face ashen. Now he dropped to his knees beside the prostrate form of his friend, trembling in fear. He was absolutely aghast at what this black slave had done, for as far as he was concerned, and a great many others like him, all blacks were slaves, always had been and always would be.

Mose grabbed Sunny Blue's arm, concerned. "Is you all right son?" he asked.

"Yes Pappy... I thinks I is," came the terrified reply. He had never before seen his father enraged in this way.

"Come on, we best git outa here quick." The two started to run back towards the slaves' quarters, Mose almost having to carry his son for he had not yet recovered his strength after the brutal attack he had sustained.

When they came to their cabin, Grace was standing by the open door, anxiously watching for them. "Quick, git inside," urged Mose.

Once the door had closed behind them, he turned to his wife, his face gravely concerned. "We's gotta leave here... we's gotta git away tonight. That man's dangerous... ain't no knowing what he gonna do when he wakes up."

"What happened, what you sayin'?" Grace cried in horror.

Mose explained exactly what had taken place when he had found his son in Ralph Clayton's clutches. Then Sunny Blue broke in, telling all that had happened previously with little Nathan. His parents fully understood his concern for his friend's safety, and did their best to dispel his anguish at the trouble he had brought upon them by his action. Mose took Grace by the shoulders. "We mus' git away... me and Sunny Blue, you knows that don' you?" Grace nodded sadly, her eyes filled with tears. "There ain't nothin' for you to worry about, 'cos I knows exactly how we can git to safety. I learned a lot when I travellin' with Massa Percy them two years. I knows how to live off the land, and I knows how to stay alive." Grace's tears were flowing fast. Mose heaved a sigh and went on, "Yo' always said your son gonna be a free man one day... when he growed, ain't that so?"

She nodded her head. "Well, I gonna take him the only place he ever be free, away from them like Ralph Clayton; right up in the North across the border to Canada. I heard tell of it long time ago, when I's away with Massa Percy, and that's where I's gonna take our son."

Grace gasped, and Sunny Blue's eyes grew wide in amazement.

"Now Missy... you listen... and listen good. I gonna leave you here for a while, 'cos we gotta git away fast as we can, ain't no other way... but when I gits to Canada, I gonna fix it so you can be there with us too... does you understand?"

Grace nodded again.

"Me and Sunny Blue gonna build us somethin' good, you see... and when we does, I gonna come back and fetch yo'."

He wrapped his arms around his wife and held her close; he felt that his heart would break at having to leave her again. He kissed her fondly, and turned to Sunny Blue. "Say goodbye to your Mammy we best git goin'." The boy clung to his mother sobbing, and she took his dear face between her hands and kissed it.

She couldn't bear to see them go. "Ain't you gonna take somethin' with you?" she asked her husband.

"We don' need nothing... I can find everythin' we be needin' as we goes. We can travel fast if we travels light... now come on Sunny Blue, we best git movin' so we far away by daybreak. Don' you git worryin' none Missy, we be jus' fine... and tell the Lady Lilybee I mighty sorry for havin' to run off like this, but there ain't no other way."

He pulled open the door and stepped out into the darkness, turning to his son, "Come now boy, you stay close by me; your old Pappy's gonna take you where you can be free."

'White Lakes' was a-buzz the next morning with what Mose had done to the overseer. The word had spread rapidly, and the workers were overjoyed that one of their own had at last dared to administer a small dose of his own medicine to Mr Ralph Clayton.

Grace had not slept at all during the night, fearing what form the humiliated overseer's reprisals might take. She went off to work earlier than normal, and she sought out her mistress as soon as she arrived at the house, for she was determined to tell her all the night's events herself, before the much elaborated stories reached her. She was nervous and upset, and Lilybee was anxious to know the reason why. She was still in her bedroom, not yet dressed, but she settled herself in one of her comfortable chairs and called Grace to join her.

"Now, do come and sit down, and I shall hear what is distressing you so Grace... upon my word, it cannot be so disastrous as your looks would have me believe. Now calm yourself, there's a good girl, and tell me what is troubling you."

Grace tried to compose herself as she recounted the whole sorry tale, and her mistress could hardly believe it. Had not Douglas conveyed her message to that abominable man, she wondered? She too became greatly distressed and angered at hearing that he had been the cause of Mose and Sunny Blue leaving. She commiserated with them and fully understood why they had left. She decided she must have a serious talk with her brother; something must be done about Ralph Clayton, for it was becoming impossible to go on ignoring his insufferable behaviour. She had risen from her chair and stood looking out of the window, trying to decide what to do. Her heart felt heavy; indeed it was at times like this that she missed her dear husband the most. She took a deep breath and turned from the window resolutely: "Help me to dress now, Grace," she said. "I shall speak to Master Douglas about this, without delay. Our situation here at 'White Lakes' will become untenable if our best workers are continually driven away, and I shall do my very utmost to keep this place alive, if only for the sake of my dear husband. I could never conceive of leaving, under any circumstances, for it holds far too many treasured memories."

Grace began to weep uncontrollably.

"Come, come, my dear… I know how you must feel about what has happened, but maybe things will improve somewhat in the future, and you might see your husband and son again one day. Try to remain optimistic."

"Sorry ma'am. I can't help it," Grace sobbed. "First I lost my young Minnie… she bin gone seventeen years now, and I ain't never seen her again. Now I'se lost my boy and Mose, ain't nothin' left for me... nothin' at all." She covered her face with her hands and shook her head back and forth slowly in despair.

"Oh, Grace... don't lose heart. Now that the war has ended things will get better... why, it might soon be possible for me to take a journey north to visit my family in New Jersey, and if I do, then I shall take you with me, you'd like that wouldn't you... you'd be able to see your daughter again, wouldn't that be wonderful? She'll be a grown woman by now, and you would have so much to talk about together. Now then, if we can find some way of improving Master Edmund's condition, he might even agree to accompany us on the trip, don't you think? Those crutches that Mose made for him have certainly helped him considerably... have you seen the way he has been walking around on them just lately?"

Grace brightened up a little and dried her tears. The thought of a visit to New Jersey after all these years, with the possibility of seeing her daughter again in the not too distant future, certainly cheered her heart; and she smiled at the recollection of Mose's gift to Master Edmund. He had spent weeks painstakingly fashioning the crutches for the boy, gradually improving them until they suited his requirements exactly. It had been a source of pleasure to everyone when they saw how well Master Edmund could get around with them. His mental wounds were presenting far more difficult problems, but it was hoped that time itself would prove a sufficient enough healer to bring about the poor boy's recovery.

When she was ready, Lilybee hurried down to breakfast, anxious to confront Douglas, but he was not to be found.

None of the servants had seen him, and apparently he had not returned to the house the night before, so Lilybee promptly sent one of the men to find him without delay, and bring him to the study. More than an hour later, Douglas appeared looking somewhat dishevelled and very bleary-eyed. Lilybee could not bear to look at him.

Sheepishly he began to explain what had happened to Ralph Clayton, and that he had had to stay and take care of him, but his sister broke in, she was not the least bit interested in what he had to say.

"I am aware of precisely what took place here last night," she said icily, "and despite my concern at losing so many of our best workers through Mr Clayton's insufferable treatment of them, we now have him to thank for driving away Mose and his son. That man has been at 'White Lakes' since before dear Percy and I ever came here, and I am deeply distressed that he has been driven away in this manner. We shall never be able to replace him, never, never."

"But he attacked Ralph," began Douglas.

Lilybee interrupted him again. "I am not in the least interested in hearing your account of what happened, for if it comes to choosing which account I should believe, then I have no hesitation in discounting yours dear brother... at best you have always been frugal with the truth."

Douglas slumped in his chair sulkily.

"And now, the time has come to take matters in hand do you hear? You must get rid of that man, for I will not tolerate his presence here. It is high time that you shouldered some responsibility for the running of 'White Lakes'; it is your home and has been for many years now, so you prove to me that you are capable of pulling your weight."

Lilybee's chin dropped to her chest; she placed the palm of her hand to her brow and sat for a while deep in thought. She felt completely despondent. Douglas fidgeted uncomfortably, he had had a disturbed night, trying to nurse his friend, and now he was tired, he needed to rest. Eventually Lilybee looked up at him, and with a deep sigh she went on, "Douglas, I want you to think carefully about what I am saying to you... this is an opportunity for you to make something of yourself, of your life here, but you have to get rid of that man, stand on your own two feet. I want to bring 'White Lakes' back to life again, make it flourish. I know that things can never be the same as they were, the glory days have gone, but we could gradually restore this place... you and I together... I can't do it alone, I need your help. Now what do you say?" She was looking at him steadily, disarmingly.

"Eh... well, yes... yes... I want to help you to restore 'White Lakes'. I have grown to love it too, but it's a tremendous undertaking Lilybee. I really think we shall need Ralph Clayton's expertise to bring about the restoration." He saw the look of consternation on his sister's face. He went on hastily, "But only for a short while, just until I feel that we could manage without him... until I feel that I could take over from him one hundred percent in the running of things. Then, dear sister, I promise you I'll get rid of him, now that's fair enough, isn't it?" he wheedled.

Lilybee had no alternative but to agree with his suggestion, but she too could be cunning; she resolved to keep him to his word and make sure that one day soon he would, indeed, get rid of his sinister friend, and learn to handle some of the responsibility, even if it meant having to formulate new plans for the future of her beloved home.

"You remember your promise Douglas... for I shall keep you to it," she said, as she rose to go. "And now I shall go in search of Edmund. You see, you are not the only one I have to nurse."

*

She came upon her nephew out on the verandah, in his favourite place, talking quietly with Grace. She smiled to herself, marvelling at how close he had become to her devoted maid. From the very start, he had been completely relaxed and at ease whenever she was with him, almost as though he had known her for all of his life. They would sit talking contentedly together for hour upon hour, but although she found it puzzling, Lilybee encouraged their association in the fond hope that it would hasten his mental recovery.

Only Grace knew the secret of their strong attachment to one another, and she guarded it jealously, never once divulging it to her mistress. It was, quite simply, that her own daughter had been this young boy's constant companion, and his sister's nursemaid, from babyhood, and when he had learned that Grace was Minnie' s mother, he was overjoyed. He welcomed the opportunity of talking about his childhood at 'Fortune's Hand', of telling this fascinated listener everything that had happened there for the past seventeen years. She never tired of hearing him talk, and he found it wonderful to recall all the happiness he had shared with his sister and the young nursemaid... her long lost child. The stories he had to tell were even more wonderful for Grace; she could not believe that she was hearing, at first hand, an account of the life her daughter had been living for all those years, so far away in the North, and now there appeared to be a distinct possibility that someday soon she might travel there herself, with her mistress, to experience the reunion that she had always dreamed of.